FATE OF RUIN

IRELAND LYDON

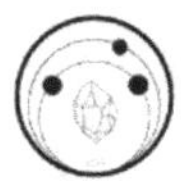

AN IMPRINT OF VEILORE PRESS

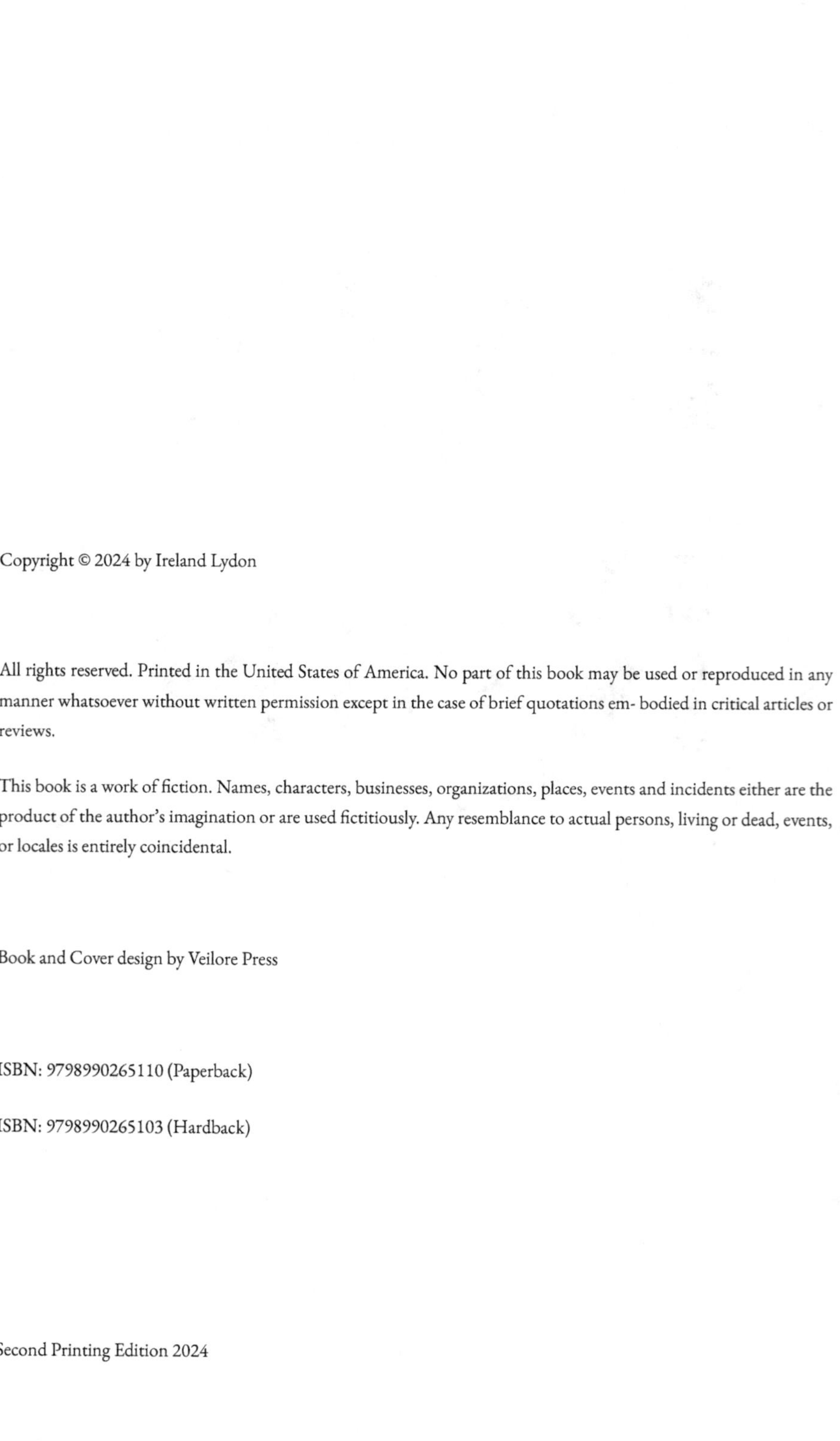

This book is a work of fiction. Names, characters, businesses, organizations, places, events and incidents either are the product of the author's imagination or are used fictitiously. Any resemblance to actual persons, living or dead, events, or locales is entirely coincidental.

Book and Cover design by Veilore Press

ISBN: 9798990265110 (Paperback)

ISBN: 9798990265103 (Hardback)

Second Printing Edition 2024

Faithless is he that says farewell when the road darkens.

J. R. R. Tolkien

For Kat.

In ancient ink and silvered thread,
This tale spun long from words unsaid.
Through realms of mist, past shadowed night,
You were the star, the whispered light.

When dreams grew dim and hope ran thin,
Your voice, like magick, called within—
Each line a spell, each page a door,
You led me forth, to skies once more.

So here's the book, as worlds unfold,
Bound by your heart, a gift of old.

JORN
PORT OF NORD
MONSELT
BRAC
HILVAER
JORN CITY
DENC
EIR
FOREST OF DERN
FOREST OF AAVIN
DERN
AUGUSTA
AAVIN
R'HUN
T'HOURNS
FIELD OF T'HOURNS
ALNWICK
SANCIA
LEJAL
FELOUR
SIGN
MVORS
DIVNA
WESTERN GAP

reacherous Seas
TAUF
ENTHEAS
THELGH
LEDENJOUR
PORT OF GHELFIN
TAASTRA
TAUDREN
CITY OF CORAD
CORAÐ
EHLMOR
NIHTAR ISLA
EHLMOR ISLES
VEILORE

FATE OF RUIN

Fate of Ruin is a fantasy romance novel that ultimately has a happy ending. However, all of the books within the series include elements that may not be suitable for all readers. Such as death, murder, blood, mentions of suicide and suicidal notions, rape, SA and descriptions of past SA, magical hallucinogenics, captivity, and sexual acts are all mentioned within the series. Readers who are sensitive to such elements please take note.

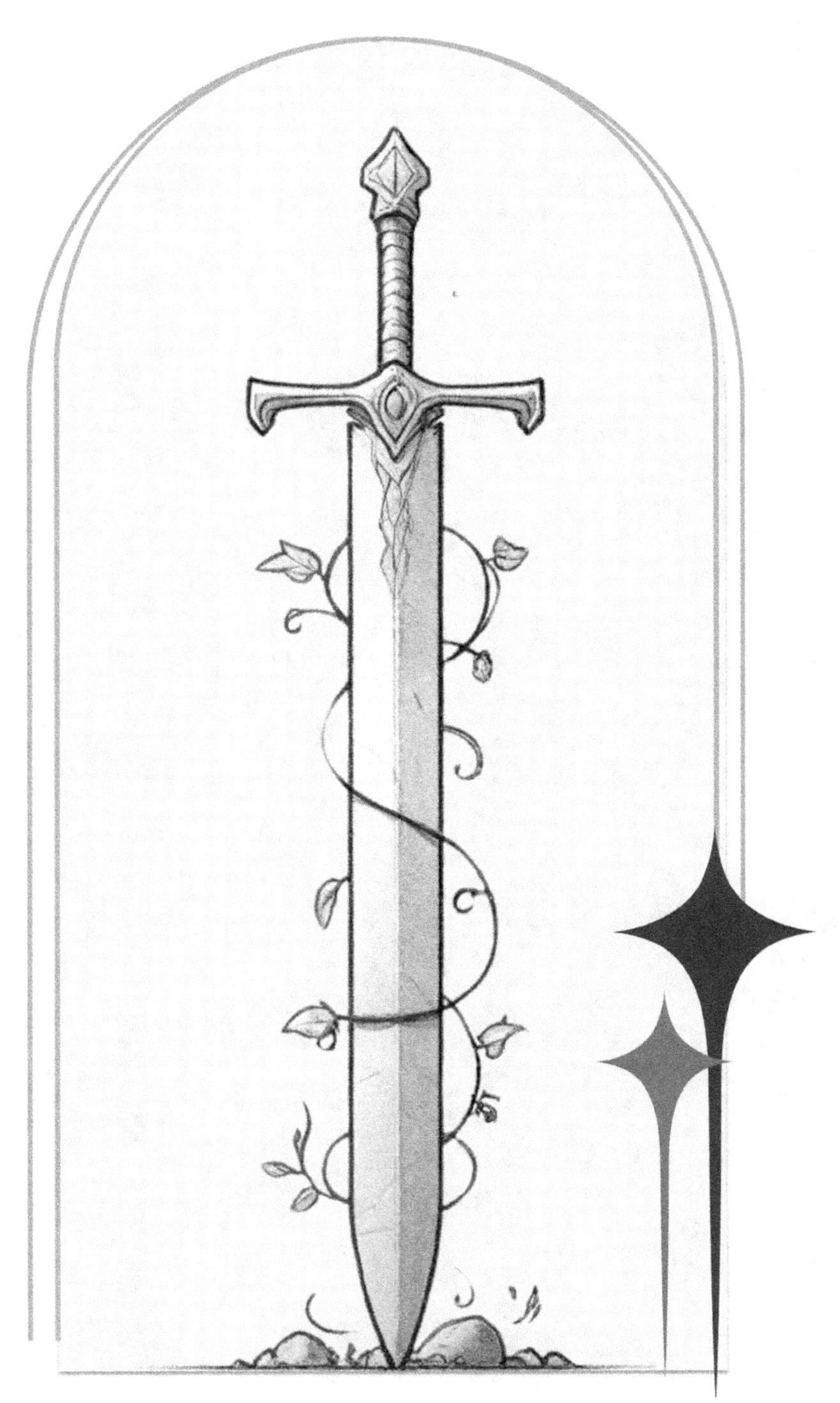

BEFORE

Ledenjour, Realm of Entheas. 1986.

R un Isaac…you must run…"

Isaac ran. On thin, young limbs, he pushed through the gloom of the blackened forest. Weaving a way through the maze of bent trees that twisted and gnarled in the darkness. Taking with him the last embrace of his mother, the last words she would ever speak to him.

Night-time had fallen. He was unable to see in the dark, scrambling over the protruding roots, slipping on the edge of a knoll. Fear drove him on as the shouts of the man followed after him, the sounds of thundering hooves threatened to overtake him. Isaac began to cry, gulping back tears as the pinch of exhaustion gripped his side.

Behind him came the thumping of hooves that matched the beat of his thundering heart.

"Stop running, boy!" a voice boomed in the darkness.

Thump. Thump. The sound of the horse's hooves were closing in

Isaac tripped. His foot caught on the root of a half downed tree, sending him sprawling down into the muddy gulch, landing in cold frigid water that stole his breath. Isaac lay there gasping, gazing up to the blanket of sky, a break in the great clouds that drenched the valley in rain. It was quiet. Apart from the whisper of wind, the world had fallen into complete silence

Pain was quick to follow, as the tumble had bruised and mangled his arm and leg. Isaac rolled over, grimacing through the sudden fire that burned through him. His broken bones mending as magick heightened his senses. Crying, he forced himself onto his knees.

"Isaac."

Sharp pain twisted in the pit of Isaac's chest, and his hands burned. He looked up at the man who approached from the darkness of the forest.

"Stay back!" Isaac's young voice shook.

"Give up, Isaac; you've been caught." The man's tone was threatening, his steely eyes caught Isaac's from under the depths of his hood. "Your mother is waiting for you."

Anger burned hot, as the magick in his blood heightened. He glared up at the hardened face of the man who stepped forward. Oiled boots made of glistening leather sloshed into the slow running stream. It was the same man from the village who watched while his guards held his mother down. Isaac remembered the smile that creased his sun tanned skin.

Isaac squeezed his hands into fists, feeling the same magick that had drained the life of one of those men, while also snapping the neck of the second man with just a turn of the wrist. In his palm, the cold metal of his mother's pendant began to grow hot under his touch.

"Liar," Isaac screamed, his shouts frightening the birds that nestled nearby.

Raising his foot, he tried to stand, but Isaac crumpled, glaring down at the ripped fabric of his trousers. Blood soaked the fabric from the deep gaping wound, remnants of his broken bone. Isaac pressed his hand against the wound, trying to stop the blood that seeped through his fingers.

"Your father wants you, Isaac. He sent me here to get you." The man's words were honeyed, reaching out a hand towards him, offering Isaac help, but Isaac knew the man was lying.

"I will never be his," Isaac hissed, hot tears spilling from his eyes. Gritting back the pain as his wound closed, standing on trembling legs to face the man that stood so near that Isaac saw the whites of the man's dark eyes shimmering in the moonlight.

Magick was easy to command; Isaac felt it to the tips of his fingers as markings began to form over his skin. Isaac watched the look of fear in the man's eyes, the awe in witnessing a kind of magick he had never seen before flickering to life in the boy standing before him.

"Foolish boy." His hardened words matched the calculating glare as the man drew a curved dagger from his belt, the blade shimmered in the moonlight. He was swift, skillfully plunging the point deep into Isaac's heart.

Isaac tightened his grip on the pendant now burning the palm of his hand. Gasping for the breath that would never come. He looked down at the protruding hilt of the dagger. His body grew hot around the blade, his world growing dark.

The laughter from the man faded into nothingness.

Isaac fell, embraced by the hands of death.

CHAPTER

1

London, England. 2000

The rain traced lazy paths down the window, blurring the lights of the city below into a shimmering haze. Isaac—no, *Pavan*—pressed his fingertips absently against his chest, where the ache from the dream still lingered. It was always the same—relentless, vivid, never allowing him to forget. Seventeen years, and yet he could still feel the phantom sensation of the dagger piercing his heart. The doctors had tried to explain it all away, saying his mind had fused trauma and fantasy to shield him from the truth. But the dreams felt *too real*.

Pavan exhaled slowly, his eyes drifting to the window, seeing his reflection staring back—a man now, not the terrified boy they'd pulled from the wreckage of his life. No one had believed him, not then. He was only nine when his family vanished, and everyone thought his father had lost it, spiriting them away to the North before the madness took over. The police, the psychologists, they all spun a story to make sense of it. They called his tale of the forest and the disappearance part of the delusions, a coping mechanism.

All except Neil, his father's twin brother, who never once doubted him. Neil had kept Isaac out of the papers, paid for his care, and held the crumbling pieces of his life together when no one else could. But Neil couldn't stop the nightmares. No one could.

Pavan blinked, grounding himself back into the room. His own distorted reflection glared back at him, dark hair unwashed, and eyes shadowed with the weight of exhaustion. He wasn't a fragile boy anymore, nor the frail addict tethered to machines in the hospital. He was here, in his uncle's office, standing tall, though hunched from the heavy weight of it all.

"Isaac—" Neil's voice cut through the oppressive quiet, pulling Pavan from his thoughts.

"I don't want to be called that anymore," Pavan blurted, heat rising in his face. His therapist had urged him to say it aloud, but each time the words had caught in his throat.

Neil paused, eyeing him carefully. "Has this anything to do with Penelope?"

The name hit him like a punch to the gut. Penelope—his wife. His thumb instinctively grazed the empty spot where his wedding ring once sat, now too loose to wear. Neil had kept it safe for him while he was in the hospital, offering it back when he was discharged, but Pavan couldn't bring himself to take it. The pain was still too raw.

"Among other reasons," Pavan muttered, avoiding his uncle's gaze, the shame heavy in his chest.

Neil sighed, his silence speaking volumes. "What would you like to be called?"

"Pavan," he said, the word soft but resolute. "Just Pavan."

Neil gave a slow nod, absorbing the change with a quiet acceptance. "Well, Pavan," he began again, "have you been paying attention to what I've said about the play?"

Pavan turned, his brow furrowing at the reminder. Neil stood near his desk, impeccably dressed in his usual tweed suit, sharp and composed as ever. Pavan's own ragged appearance—grungy flannel, ripped jeans, and his worn-out leather jacket—stood in stark contrast.

The mention of the theatre filled Pavan with a gnawing guilt. Returning to the stage had felt like the right thing at first, a way to immerse himself in a world that wasn't his own, to drown out the memories that haunted him. But every corner of that theatre whispered of Penelope. Her laughter, her presence—it clung to every seat, every line, every song.

"I understand," Pavan mumbled, though the weight of it felt unbearable.

Neil's gaze softened. "This wasn't an easy choice. But you've unsettled the younger actors again this week...with your temper."

Pavan's face flushed with heat. He bit his tongue, swallowing the surge of anger. His hands clenched into fists, shaking slightly in his pockets, and he forced himself to breathe, to not let it spill over.

Neil continued, watching him closely. "I know it's hard, this transition back to life here. But this—this isn't helping. You need time... your therapy—"

"I don't need more therapy!" Pavan's voice cracked, hating the vulnerability in it. He wanted to run, every muscle in his body screaming for him to flee, but he stayed frozen, trapped by his uncle's steady presence.

Neil sighed again, pinching the bridge of his nose. "Trent saw your bandages." His voice was gentle, not accusatory, but the words stung all the same.

Pavan flinched, his fingers brushing over the bandage beneath his sleeve, feeling the sharp pull of the wound underneath. He had been careful—*too* careful—but not careful enough.

"Pavan," Neil's voice softened even further.

The tears welled up before Pavan could stop them. He swiped at his face with his sleeve, hating the way his body betrayed him, shaking under the weight of it all. Neil stepped forward, pulling him into a hug, and Pavan stood there, trembling, as the wall he had tried so hard to hold up began to crumble.

"It's not forever," Neil whispered, his words warm, tender. "Just until the nightmares stop."

Pavan shook his head against Neil's shoulder, the words bitter and hollow in his mouth. "They're worse," he choked out. "They haven't stopped. Not even with the medication."

Neil held him tighter. "You need time."

"My wife is dead," Pavan hissed through clenched teeth, his voice thick with grief.

Neil's composure wavered, but he didn't let go. "Penelope didn't deserve what happened, but she's gone, Pavan. You can't let this destroy you too. Don't let the grief win."

Pavan wanted to scream, to push him away, but instead, he crumbled, hot tears spilling freely down his cheeks. Neil's voice, gentle but firm, was the only anchor he had left.

"It feels like that night," Pavan whispered, his voice breaking. "The night we disappeared."

Neil's face paled, his expression growing cold. He glanced over his shoulder, back to the door, before turning his focus back to Pavan with newfound urgency.

"We should leave," Neil said suddenly. "Go away for a while. America, maybe. Just the two of us."

"It won't stop," Pavan said, his voice barely a whisper. "It follows me...everywhere."

"Hang the theatre," Neil insisted, gripping Pavan's shoulders. "I won't lose you. Not again."

Pavan blinked, overwhelmed by the intensity of Neil's words, the terror gnawing at the edges of his mind. His hand instinctively brushed the cuff of his sleeve, feeling the bandage beneath.

"You won't tell them, will you?" he asked, his voice trembling. "I can't go back."

Neil squeezed his shoulders tighter, his voice a firm promise. "No, Pavan. You won't go back. I swear."

The icy bite of the cold frigid air welcomed Pavan; his feet carried him away from the large brown building. Pavan huffed hot breath into his clasped hands, numb from the cold. His fingers red from the bite. He stopped at the corner, waiting for the light to be safe to cross. As he waited, dread filled him, tightening hard in his chest, making it hard to breathe.

Lost in thought, Pavan walked until his feet felt frozen. Coming up to the white washed building in Camden Place, where he shared a flat with his best mate, Malcom.

They had lived together since they were twelve, after Neil became Malcom's guardian, keeping him from being sent to a juvenile home after his gran died. Since then, the two of them had shared a home, spending most of their time in each other's company. It was only natural after they left school that they would live together. They pooled their own funds to furnish the place with well used furniture.

The space was dim and heavy with the familiar weight of solitude.

Pavan dropped his keys into the small ceramic bowl on the counter, the one he had crafted in primary school with uneven edges and lopsided charm. The keys clattered against the bottom, the sound lingering in the silence. He sighed and glanced at the clock on the far wall—Malcom should have been home by now.

The thought stirred a pang of anxiety in his chest. It hadn't been that long since he was allowed to be on his own again, free from constant supervision or the endless rotations of people checking in on him. That knowledge unsettled him more than he liked to admit.

His movements were automatic as he crossed the front room, weaving through the clutter of their shared life. The furniture was an odd mishmash—pieces picked up from yard sales or handed down from relatives they hardly spoke to anymore. Side tables were buried beneath stacks of magazines and adverts, long since discarded and forgotten. The couch was draped with a black sheet, an attempt to cover the ghastly mustard yellow upholstery underneath. It hadn't been used for sitting in months.

On the far wall, the old piano sat untouched, blanketed in dust. It hadn't been played since Penelope. The thought made his throat tighten, a flash of memories swirling in his mind before he pushed them back down where they belonged.

In the corner, a tattered wingback chair was surrounded by an ever-growing mountain of empty pizza boxes, the remnants of countless nights spent in careless indulgence. The coffee table, once a rich mahogany, was now battered and worn, serving as little more than a dumping ground for takeaway containers and old receipts.

Pavan sighed again, shaking his head. Malcom had had the guys from the clinic over to watch rugby. Again. And, of course, they hadn't bothered to clean up after themselves. The mess, the clutter, the suffocating stillness of the flat—it all felt like a reflection of something deeper, something Pavan wasn't sure he could fix.

He stood there for a moment, caught between the frustration of the chaos around him and the empty ache inside his chest. Malcom would be back soon, probably laughing off the mess, but for now, it was just Pavan, alone again with his thoughts.

Pavan groaned as he sank into the couch, his long limbs sprawling out like a puppet with its strings cut. His fingertips brushed against something cold—his electric guitar. The head of the instrument peaked over the edge of the armrest like a forgotten memory. He grabbed it, his fingers naturally finding their place along the neck, though his heart wasn't in it.

His hand moved absently, strumming thick metal strings. Each note that hummed through the guitar felt muted, distant, as though the music itself was fading from him. He shifted his grip, trying to remember the chords of songs he hadn't played in what felt like lifetimes. The vibrations slowed, the air around him thickening with silence.

That silence. Always creeping in. He could hear it now, seeping into his mind between the ticks of the clock on the wall. His heart began to pound. Alone. The word echoed in his chest, carving out the hollowness he tried so hard to ignore. Alone...

Pavan squeezed his eyes shut, his jaw tightening. He fought to keep the thoughts away, to shove them back down into the deepest, darkest part of himself. Not now. He couldn't think about it now. Not the emptiness, not the pit growing in his heart like a wound that never healed.

But it was too late. A single tear escaped, then another, tracing down his cheeks, carrying the weight of his torment. His breath hitched as he gasped for air, overwhelmed by the rising tide of emotions he had been suppressing for too long. The guitar slipped from his hands, thudding softly onto the rug below, forgotten in the chaos of his breaking heart.

With a guttural cry, Pavan pressed the heels of his palms into his eyes, as if he could force the pain out, as if it would stop the tears. His voice cracked, shattering the fragile silence, but the room still felt suffocating. Still empty. Still cold.

He was alone.

And he hated it more than anything.

A sudden knock made Pavan jolt.

He sat up, looking toward the front door. Another knock. This one was louder but less jarring. Slowly, Pavan stood, crossing the room in a few strides to reach the front door. He threw it open. Standing on the front mat was their closest neighbor.

Mrs. Jennings was an older woman, possibly in her late 70's, with matte gray and brown hair, always worn in two tucked plaits over the top of her head. She was kind to them, always bringing them food or tending to their small garden.

"Oh, ye cryin' yerself somethin' fierce," she spoke in her thick Irish accent. She took a good look at Pavan. She had come to London from Northern Ireland nearly ten years back, for her husband's health, but stayed when she had lost him only three years ago. Mrs. Jennings was quick to visit them after Penelope...

"I'm fine," Pavan lied, stepping aside to let the small woman enter. She walked in gladly, taking one look at her surroundings and laughed in protest.

"Here's me wha? Look at this place…"

"I've been out all morning and haven't had a chance to clean up. It got a bit crazy watching the match." Pavan feigned cheerfulness, but he saw her raised eyebrow.

She put hands on her hips.

"Mal told me he would be out when ye showed back up here, asked me to watch out for ye. Here ye are and here I shall keep ye til he returns." She made her way to the kitchen without another word. Pavan followed her, knowing he would be beckoned there anyway.

"You really are generous, but I will be fine," Pavan tried to reason, watching the lady move about the small kitchen. First, she went for the kettle, then to the cupboards.

"Oh, tush ye head now, Isaac." Mrs. Jennings made tea, her busywork around the kitchen filling the space as she moved about.

Pavan sighed, sitting at the small table, knowing if he tried to help her, Mrs. Jennings would give him an earful. So, he sat and watched, listening to her warmth as she spoke about her cats and the conditions of her petunias. Soon the tea was served before him; he watched the steam rise from the welcoming cup. As Mrs. Jennings continued her chatter about one of their neighbors, she went to work cracking eggs into a sizzling pan.

CHAPTER 2

Malcom returned to the flat after his morning shift at the clinic. He worked as a nurse at the hospital and was called in earlier than he had been scheduled. Walking through the front door, he gave a sigh of relief, hearing the boisterous sounds of Mrs. Jennings from the kitchen, the space filled with the smell of toast and eggs.

"I'm home," he called out, as he usually did. He slipped his shoes off by the door and tossed his keys onto the counter, they clattered next to Pavan's familiar key set.

"Good seein' you home Mal...I was just tellin' Isaac here about how my little tabby Morris was gone up into the garden, the little devil. He set me out weeks to growin' my poor petunias." Mrs. Jennings always reminded Malcom of his nan. She was a soft-hearted old lady who was always quick to help.

"Thank you, Mrs. Jennings," he said. Looking around the kitchen, he saw a half full cup of tea, now cold. Beside the cup sat an empty plate, save for a few bits of burnt crust.

With the evidence of his friend having been fed and looked after, Malcom breathed easier. He looked at Pavan, who sat back in the thin kitchen chair, arms crossed over his chest. He was looking up at him with those strange green eyes.

"All fed and happy." Mrs. Jennings took the plate, returning it to the sink. Malcom noticed the clean counters, his eyes daring to peek around to the living room. It too had been cleaned and straightened out.

Malcom turned to catch Pavan's eye.

His friend was sulking.

"Such a good boy, he even challenged me with askin' about my poor Richard's time in Cardiff. There's a story I hadn't thought of in years. Bless him..." Mrs. Jennings reached out and squeezed Pavan's arm, giving him a warm smile.

Pavan's smile looked forced, but he returned the sentiment. They watched as Mrs. Jennings straightened, sighing confidently. Her hands untied the apron she had around her to hang it upon the hook near the icebox.

"Thank you for coming over." Malcom followed the small lady as she made her way to the front door.

"Oh, not at all, not at all. I would stay to take tea, but if I stay away I fear for my little Morris. He's such a devil and gets into mischief." Mrs. Jennings prattled on—she was always smiling.

She was gone with a flourish of farewells and the state of her petunias, leaving them both in sudden silence. Malcom turned; Pavan had not moved from his chair.

"She means well," Malcom began, knowing what was to come next. He pulled off his jacket, letting it fall over the empty chair. Pavan stood.

There was no grumbling, no snide remark about calling in a sitter. Malcom looked up at his friend. Pavan's eyes were tired. It was a surprise to not hear the gruff and puff of haughtiness.

"Mrs. Jennings is a kind woman," Pavan agreed, stepping around Malcom to head for the hallway.

"Did it go alright?"

Pavan stopped; his shoulders sagged as he turned to catch Malcom's eye. His mouth was set in a firm line. Malcom was not used to the unfamiliar gloom in his friend. He had always been quiet, but now the dejection made Pavan unreadable.

"My nightmares are back..."

This news was disheartening. Malcom could see it—the sleepless nights Pavan spent tossing and turning—in the dark circles under his eyes.

He didn't know what to say. Not anymore. There was a time when he could cheer Pavan up with a joke or a quick remark, but lately there was hardly anything between them. He could see the torment and strain of the last year; Malcom could see what it was doing to his brother. Pavan was just that—his brother. After losing his gran, there was no one left in his life to care.

Malcom remembered when Pavan had stood in the counselors offices between him and the two officials that had come to take Malcom away. Pavan shouted them back, resilient in determination until Neil appeared after the headmaster called him. There were months of legal notices, but in the end Neil had won, securing Malcom as his ward. From that point on they were inseparable. His new family fought so hard to keep him protected. Now it was Malcom's turn to keep Pavan safe.

Those long months in the hospital were difficult. It took everything to bring Pavan back; to be able to stand, to eat on his own without a feeding tube. There were still moments Malcom wondered if Pavan would fall backward. He was strong, he was stubborn, but Malcom knew it was easy for Pavan to fall back into his old habits. This was the crucial point: These next few weeks would be the hardest for him, Malcom had already put in his hours at the clinic, so he could be home now. He would not leave Pavan's side.

"I'm going to sleep," Pavan said, not waiting for Malcom to respond. He knew there was nothing to be done, or to be said. Malcom watched him disappear down the hall. The bedroom door clicked shut.

Gasping awake, Pavan sat up straight in bed.

He felt the cold sweat dripping from his damp hair, chest heaving with every breath. He tried to remain calm, pushing his shaking hands through his hair. His wakeful mind pushed back the remnants of the dream.

Bleary eyed, Pavan blinked back the shooting pain from looking up at the too bright digital clock upon his night stand. He grimaced, six thirty-nine, he had barely slept. Pavan's mind throbbed relentlessly behind his eyes. Pavan gulped back the sour taste before it could rise any further, his throat tightening as he fought the urge to retch. His stomach churned, twisting into painful knots.

In and out he breathed slowly, shaking with cold as his body began to calm.

He managed to swing his legs over the side of the bed; it groaned in protest. Pavan paused, reaching out to brace his weight against the wall when the room began to spin.

Walking blindly in the dark, Pavan stumbled into the hall, shutting himself away within the small washroom. He reached out, flicking on the bathroom light. It sizzled, before coming to life. Another groan and Pavan grabbed the sink for balance.

Pavan counted down from five to each inhale and exhale. In the hum of the bathroom light, his thoughts began to waver. Images flashed from the dream, the smell of rain and mud mixed with the stench of blood.

Drip. Drip.

Blood from his nose pooled in the stark white porcelain sink. Pavan glared at the bright streaks, rinsing them away. He grasped the tap so forcefully his knuckles turned white. Hearing his mother's screams haunted his nightmares. Pavan had tried for so long to forget, but the death of Penelope had brought back each renewed painful memory.

Pavan was powerless. He was unable to stop the despairing thoughts that consumed him. Unable to stop the pain that burdened his mind into dark reflections of his past.

A sudden knock startled Pavan. He stood up straight, wiping the blood from his nose in a hurry.

"Pavan, are you alright?" Malcom's voice sounded on the other side of the door.

He threw open the door. Malcom was still wearing the silk scarf, to protect his thin black dreads while he slept. He was half dressed in scrubs and one of their old band tee-shirts.

"Fine, I'm fine," Pavan managed. His stomach churned as he gulped down the lies and the pain.

Malcom's watch beeped, his alarm signaling it was time to get up. A frown turned down the corners of Malcolm's mouth as he rubbed the sleep from his eyes.

"I've got to go into the clinic today, but perhaps tonight we could go out for drinks at our usual place?"

Pavan scowled. "Fine."

"Right." Malcom nodded, scratching the soft layer of black hair upon his cheek and chin. "I'll make breakfast."

He slowly shut the door, leaving Pavan standing alone again in the bathroom. Pavan's stomach churned. He hesitated, for only a moment, before hurling into the toilet. Irritated, when he finished, he cleaned up before showering, washing away the grime.

Pavan emerged a while later, dressed in his usual jeans and flannel, along with the typical black shirt that had more holes than he could count. No longer dressing in the nice dress shirts and trousers his uncle had him wearing daily, he resorted to comfort. Even if it was the same thing he wore three days before.

Sitting with a hot cup of coffee in hand, Pavan watched from his usual chair as Malcom made a batch of toast, frying up some eggs, and a few slices of bacon. His stomach was still sour, but the undeniable grumble of hunger pangs welcomed the smell. They ate in silence as Malcom read the paper. Only the sounds of paper rustling and forks scraping plates filled the space between them.

He reached for the salt, extending his arm, the pain in his wrist was a reminder of the wound that lay hidden beneath his sleeve. Pavan drew back, shame making his face hot. His eyes flicked up to Malcolm, who remained busy with his paper. Quiet flooded the room—it was too quiet.

"Have you cleaned it yet?" Malcom's voice made Pavan jump.

He flushed, drawing his hand into his lap. "What?"

Lowering the paper, Malcom watched Pavan intently, those dark brown eyes unwavering, knowledge written on his face. "I'm not daft, let me see your wrist." Malcom extended his hand, resting it against the smooth table top.

Slowly, Pavan did as he was told. Giving up the arm, wincing as his friend rolled up the sleeve, seeing the dirty bandage that hid the damage underneath. Malcom stood quickly, hurrying to his canvas bag that hung near the door, returning to the table with a little case. Carefully, Malcom used sterile scissors to cut away the tape, pulling gently at the layers of gauze. His eyes assessed the cut.

"It might scar, but it doesn't look infected," Malcom said, rummaging through his bag, tearing off a cleaning towelette. He dabbed the cool little cloth over the red skin making Pavan hiss.

"That doesn't matter," Pavan mumbled.

There was a long silence as Malcom cleaned the skin, removing the crust of old blood, his hands expertly maneuvering with calm intent. Pavan saw the flicker of worry, knowing the look his friend expressed when there was something bothering him.

"Neil knows about it. He saw it yesterday."

Malcom glanced up. "So, you did see him then...that's good."

Pavan winced as the touch of ointment burned.

"Hardest part is over now." Malcom packed away the remainder of his supplies, pressing it under his arm as he got a good look at Pavan.

Pavan felt his chin quiver. "He...Neil thought it would be best if I don't continue with the show. That I don't return until...after I am better."

A long silence stretched out between them.

"You have been going to therapy, and you take your medicine," Malcom began, shaking his head as he sat in the chair opposite Pavan.

"It's not enough...the nightmares won't stop. I find myself drifting further and further, worse than before."

"Explain it to me, Pav.... Please, just tell me something," Malcom urged.

"You know I can't."

Malcom sighed. "Not can't...won't. I'm your best mate; we're brothers. Please, you can trust me with anything."

Pavan gulped, wetting his lips. "It's difficult...to be seen like this...you must understand how difficult it is to pretend."

"You don't have to pretend. Not with me." Malcom quieted, brow creased in unsettled concern.

"It's more than Penelope," Pavan began, forcing back the crash of emotions that plagued him, dragging his heart deeper into himself. "It is tearing me apart, knowing what the doctors are saying about me...it happened when I was a child, too..."

Malcom's gaze softened. "When you disappeared with your family?"

Pavan swallowed his anger.

"They told me it wasn't real, that I imagined going to another world...to a place full of magick. But it was real, the people I met were real after he left us and the men came to take my mother away...what else could I do but protect her?" Tears fell from Pavan's widening eyes. "To protect *them*?"

Malcom listened, unmoving.

"What happened, Pavan?" Malcom's voice felt far away, Pavan thought he had imagined he'd spoken, but those brown eyes watched him intently, encouraging him.

"My mother begged me to run...so I ran. I abandoned them to find my way home..."

"You were a child."

Pavan hissed, angrily wiping at his eyes and his nose with his sleeve. "I was a coward, Mal."

CHAPTER 3

He could not imagine an activity worse than returning to the low-lit curb beneath the fluorescents of the pub Malcom had taken them to, the place they had always gone to do vocal runs and warm ups. Pavan felt the buzz of irritation bubbling within him as the chalk sign near the front door read: Open Mic Night.

"Liar." Pavan followed Malcom through the thin glass doors that had been blocked out with heavy paper, stepping into the equally dim interior.

The space was filled with the clamor of glasses, and the rough sound checks from the small platform in the furthest corner. The small stage was engulfed by the glow of purple and blue hues under the stage lights.

"What would you have said if I had told you Thomas was in town and invited us out for drinks at open mic night?" Malcom's dark clothes blended in with the ambiance of the room. Pavan had to squint to see properly.

He hesitated, knowing that he would have rejected the invitation. He didn't approve of such avocations anymore—Malcom knew him far too well.

"Exactly." Malcom looked back at Pavan pointedly. "I said we had plans for dinner, and we do...there just happens to also be an added variable to the equation."

Pavan sighed. "But does it have to be with Thomas?"

Malcom rolled his eyes, taking a seat at one of the side tables, one near the front, but not directly in the stream of light that illuminated the stage.

"As far as I am aware, we are still friends with him; he went with his family on holiday, not across the world." Malcom looked tired, his eyes scanning the whole pub from his vantage point, his back always to the wall. His dark eyes darted from one end of the pub to the other, no doubt watching for their third party.

Pavan felt the pang in his gut knowing it wasn't really Thomas that worried him. He was unable to conduct himself rationally anymore. Not since...

"He hates me," Pavan stated. Malcom scoffed.

"Thomas doesn't hate you, he wants to be there for you, just like me. But you never talk to him, or come to the gatherings he organizes. You used to love it, but now you refuse—every invitation has been rewarded with denial. Why? " Malcom lowered his tone, as he noticed the room beginning to fill with more and more bodies.

"Thomas found me..." A lump began to form in Pavan's throat as his words slipped from his mouth. "You know what that did to him. I can't take away what he saw when he found me on the floor."

Malcom nodded. "You feel guilty."

Now, it was Pavan's turn to roll his eyes. But Malcom had no intention of backing down, not now that he had Pavan talking. Pavan felt flushed as the heat rose from his chest into his throat.

"You need to talk to him about it, Pav," Malcom instructed. They paused for a long moment as a waitress brought around three pints of golden frothy beer in classic steins.

Pavan pushed his glass away, leaning over the table to where Malcom sipped from his drink. "This is different."

"Maybe start with telling him your new name. That you would like to be called Pavan. He would be more than happy to—"

"I'm here now. Thomas will see that I'm not ignoring him, everything will be fine."

As if on cue, a familiar voice shouted of the din of the crowd that had gathered throughout the pub. Tossing a look over his shoulder, Pavan watched as Thomas's ginger hair bobbed and weaved through the masses—he was distinct, tall and wiry. Thomas Hidestone was nineteen years old and possessed an energy that Pavan thought inhumanly possible in one singular man, but here arrived the proof needed.

"Glad you made it," Thomas said, sitting in the spare chair between Malcom and Pavan, his eyes studying Pavan with a flicker of joy. "You're looking well, Isaac," he half panted as he spoke, as if he was slightly out of breath.

Pavan groaned inwardly, puffing out a hot breath. "Thomas." He nodded, ignoring the patronizing glare Malcom threw at him from across the table.

Malcom kicked him, making Pavan roll his eyes.

Beside them, Thomas was none the wiser, drinking from the nearest beer and jumping into a long chat about his recent holiday—he and his parents had been to Paris. He went on as he usually did, speaking with his hands and smiling brightly, looking from Pavan to Malcom, never once breaking until he was completely through with his story.

"But I am glad to be back, really," Thomas spoke again after taking a moment to drink from his beer.

"What will you be doing now? Have you gotten any more auditions?" Malcom asked, keeping the conversation casual.

Thomas sat back in the chair, nervously scratching his neck, a habit Pavan noticed had become a regular thing.

"No. No auditions, but I did get a call from Neil."

Silence fell between them, only the commotion of the pub around them as the first set of open mic night continued to fill throughout the room.

Malcom looked at Pavan but Pavan sat, staring blankly.

Thomas sighed. "If it's not alright that I take your place, Isaac...please let me know."

Pavan gripped his fingers tightly, under the shadow of the table, bearing down on his knuckles until they turned white. Every breath became thick as he swallowed his building resentment. It was not Thomas' fault, and Pavan knew why his uncle had called him in the first place. Thomas' skill with learning anything in record time was impressive, even to Pavan. Thomas was the logical choice but it hurt no less.

Finally, Pavan breathed out letting his body relax, looking up at Thomas with a well-rehearsed smile and said, "Don't be so modest, Thomas. You have nothing to apologize for."

Tap tap tap. A sound check on the stage caught their attention. A large man leaned into the mic, grumbling.

Pavan turned his chair away from the table, settling in with a clear view of the small platform stage in the corner of the room. One artist after another took their turn, some performing original compositions, others covering well-known classics. The variety was impressive, and after every set, the audience erupted into enthusiastic cheers. It brought Pavan back to his younger days, when he and his friends would play covers of Queen, Journey, and The Who. He could still picture it—himself on guitar, Malcom on drums, and Anthony, Penelope's younger brother, belting out lead vocals. Everything had been simpler then.

Performing had always been Anthony's dream. From a young age, he was drawn to the stage, and he joined the theatre as soon as he could. His enthusiasm was contagious, and it wasn't long before he convinced Pavan and Malcom to form a band. It was Anthony's vision, and they were all just along for the ride. That was how Pavan first met Penelope—Anthony's older sister. Anthony, with his wild black hair and bright blue eyes, had always been the life of the group, singing and dancing through school with Pavan by his side.

Thomas joined them later, much younger than the rest, but his talent was undeniable. He quickly earned his place in the band, adding a new layer to their sound. But this particular stage—the one Pavan was now staring at—held a bittersweet memory. It was the last one they had played on before Penelope got too sick to come watch them. Life had felt so full of possibilities back then, and now it was all just a memory.

Unable to keep up with band practice or the play, Pavan had spent the final months of Penelope's life at her bedside. Every waking hour was dedicated to her, her care becoming the center of his existence. He had clung to hope for as long as he could, but in the end, no amount of chemo or radiation could shrink the tumor. No matter how much money was poured into her treatment, nothing could save her.

Her illness consumed her, and it consumed him too.

From the stage, there was a pause as the bartender stepped under the lights, clipboard in hand, announcing the next three acts. Pavan barely listened, lost in his own thoughts, until the final name was read aloud—his own. A cold shock ran through him, tightening his chest. He shot a sharp glare at Thomas, his heart pounding. There was no way he was ready to get up there. Not now. Not again.

"Did you sign us up?" Malcom asked.

The russet haired man smiled. "Of course."

A knot formed in Pavan's chest. This wasn't new; they had performed many times before at other open mic nights, but that was when they were a group of four. There was once a time when Pavan loved open mic night, but now performing mediocre songs for personal ego felt repugnant.

"You didn't," Pavan growled.

"Oh please, just one song...they will love it!" Thomas' excitement was radiating, but his jovial exuberance was sickening and Pavan knew Thomas was already drunk.

He clenched his jaw.

Pavan stood, his entire body becoming hot as a fierce fire spread through him. Clenching his fists as tight as his jaw, the throbbing in his head made it difficult to think clearly.

"I have to go," he mumbled but there was a sharpness behind his eyes seeking out the path to the door.

Malcom stood, worry clouded his expression.

This was a mistake.

Cold air smacked Pavan in the face as he stepped into the night. Hot tears spilled from his eyes, scorching paths of spite along his cheeks as he walked down the stone path leading away from the pub. Stopping suddenly and turning on his heel, he began to walk back toward the pub, his heart beating madly. Grief gnawing through the pit of his stomach.

Hate. Grief. Spite.

Pavan stopped outside the door, pressing the heel of his hands into the sockets of his eyes, his body shaking. He tried to force back the intrusive thoughts that ravaged his mind.

"Pavan." Malcom's voice sounded so far from him but a warm hand on his back, told Pavan his friend was close.

"Isaac?"

Thomas' presence sent Pavan's thoughts scattering. Straightening, Pavan let his face cool, turning when the lanky friend approached them. There was a moment of silence before Pavan spoke.

"I'm fine...it's been a long time since I have drunk so much," Pavan lied, ignoring the look he got from Malcom.

A sobering look came over Thomas. "If it's about the play..."

Pavan shook his head. "You are the best actor around, Thomas. I am glad you will be the one to replace me."

"Can I help with anything?" Thomas asked, those wide blue eyes rounded in concern. Pavan felt the pangs of guilt in the half-hearted smile Thomas gave him. He was accepting the compliment, but Pavan knew there was something more; Thomas wanted more than Pavan could give him.

"It's late." Pavan took a step back, his heart thumping in his ear.

Thomas frowned. "Will you call me for coffee?"

Swallowing back his growing anger, Pavan shook his head. "I can't do that."

Malcom was eyeing Pavan coldly.

Thomas raked a hand nervously through his hair. "Right. Right."

Pavan hated himself. A hatred that simmered beneath the surface, eating away at his thoughts. He took another step away, desperate to escape the man, knowing his words stung, knowing that the wall Pavan was building between them was growing higher.

He tasted blood in his mouth and gulped.

"Coffee, next Tuesday. You can ask me whatever you like about Othello," Pavan forced between his clenched teeth. He could see the mend, hear the sigh of relief from Thomas.

"I have to go..." Pavan started suddenly, turning on his heel.

Pavan tore down the walk, shoving his hands deep into the pockets of his denim, in a last attempt to keep the cold from biting at his fingertips.

"Thomas isn't a child. Tell him the truth, he'd understand," Malcom was telling Pavan, following close beside his friend.

He shivered. "He has been through enough with me, Mal."

Malcom grasped Pavan's arm, holding him back. "Don't do that to yourself. Not with him. It was hard enough when Anthony..."

"Anthony left to grieve the death of his sister." Pavan pushed Malcom's hand away. "We couldn't have expected him to stick around here. They needed to move on. This matter is different, I will not bring Thomas down into my hell, he deserves to remain happy."

Malcom's glare was colder than the bitter chill around them.

"He will be unhappy one way or another in life...failed jobs, heartache...you can't protect him from it all, Pav." Of course, Malcom would be the thinker. He was logical, and his rationale was sobering but it did not hurt any less.

Tears threatened to spill from Pavan's eyes.

"This is different."

Malcom sighed. "There is no shame in what you have experienced, Pavan. I believe in you, so does Neil. Do you honestly believe that Thomas wouldn't *try* to understand?"

Pavan clenched his fist together so tight he could feel the nails digging into his palm, the pain making him wince. He had to face the truth, but the grief dug its claws in deeper, refusing to lessen its grip.

"If he hadn't been the one who found me the night I overdosed, maybe I could talk about it more with him. I have tried, Mal. I have wanted to let him in, but it's impossible." Pavan inhaled, his eyes burned as he tried to blink away the oncoming tears. "If I tell him the truth about all of it, he won't stay."

"He is no stranger to death. He was low for months after Penelope died, just like all of us were," Malcom spoke softly.

"But he doesn't know about my past." Pavan grimaced, his shaking hand wiping at the tears that dripped off his nose, shivering in the cold that eclipsed the night. "How could he accept me when I know he doesn't understand the cost of being my friend?"

"There is no cost to those that love you." Malcom took hold of Pavan's shoulders. "He will understand and accept you, Pavan, just as I have done."

His breathing was erratic, every breath a struggle, each intake sending a sharp pain into his chest—he was spiraling, Pavan could feel it now, stronger than ever. He pressed the flat of his palm to his chest, feeling lightheaded as he staggered.

Feeling faint, and suddenly so tired, Pavan's head began to throb. He could feel Malcom grabbing his arms, but it was useless, his head was swimming. He was falling away so quickly that Pavan could hardly catch his breath. Pain burned, slowly, through his entire body, until the last thunder of heat shot through his head, exploding into his mind like stars.

Pavan was cold, falling endlessly into the darkness that followed. There was no pain; there was nothing, Pavan felt nothing. Perhaps it was better this way—to be nothing. No more anguish to drag through his heart.

Ravaged with nausea, Pavan wretched.

Pavan blinked. Bringing himself up, he grasped the grass beneath him. Warm, lush grass. His head swam as he pushed himself to his knees, groaning against the second wave of nausea that flooded through him, stomach souring against the bitter taste in his mouth.

"Mal!" His voice carried, frightening a flock of birds nearby.

Pavan looked up, stretching his hand out to the stream of light peeking in through the canopy of trees, blocking the light that blinded his sensitive eyes. The birds now forgotten, Pavan watched as the light danced around his fingers. It was alive with vibrancy, buzzing, even the air was full of it, pulsing with his heartbeat. Magick. His chest heaved, a tidal wave of emotions erupting from deep within him.

He was back.

Pavan laughed. Deep. Hysterical. Unnerving, as his senses became overwhelmed with the sudden revelation.

There was a groan behind him and Pavan snapped his eyes to the source of the sound. Malcom.

His friend lay face down, shifting his body to roll over. Pavan began to crawl, closing the distance between them. As he helped Malcom to sit up, the darker man groaned.

"What the hell?!" Malcom snapped, pushing Pavan back, squinting through the hell of a headache he was sure to have. "Where are we?"

Pavan licked his lips. "I have no idea."

Malcom scowled. "No idea?"

Pavan looked at the trees, the grass. He took in the forest where they knelt, nothing within his line of sight was familiar to him but the magick that tingled the tips of his fingers was. This was not the place of his dreams, although it was similar. It held the same magick, but this was a different place—a place he had never been.

"I don't know where we are, but the air, can you feel it?" Pavan asked, his hand reaching out again for the stream of light, letting the hum of magick dance, lacing through his fingers.

"It is warm... Pavan, are you alright?"

Pavan felt alive with sudden renewed energy. Something was surging through his frame. Turning his gaze on Malcom, he looked his friend over from head to toe, like looking at him afresh. Dark shimmering locs, brown eyes twinkling with starlight, and the depth of Malcom's dark complexion, so warm and smooth.

Every moment danced around as he took in this new world, seeing with new eyes the shift and sway of the colors of the trees, the grass, hearing the buzzing of wings, the rustle of grass, and the babbling of a nearby brook. He could smell the dirt, the scent of the flowers, and the bark of the trees.

It terrified and delighted him.

"Pavan."

Suddenly, everything fell back to an earthy gray. Pavan's body felt heavy as a sense of cold filled him, his eyes locked with Malcom.

"Are you hurt?" Pavan's body and mind reverted back to the way it had been, tight, pained. He was faint, as his head began to swim.

"I knocked my chin, but otherwise unharmed...you don't look so good. Pavan, I think you need to lie down," Malcom instructed.

Pavan attempted to swat his friend away, but he was already falling back, his weight overbearing as he felt the ground collide with his temple. He lay there, shivering, aware of everything as his friend checked his pulse. A warm hand hovering over his mouth to register his breathing. Pavan tried to move, but his body was too heavy. His eyelids fluttered.

"Rest." Malcom's voice seemed so far, but Pavan could see him right there.

Pavan blinked, Malcom still loomed nearby, the warmth shattered by a growing chill. He tried to move, but was trapped by the unbearable weight of his body. He wanted to call out, but his throat was too tight. Pavan's eyelids began to close.

Flickers of images crashed within Pavan's mind—visions of a seascape drawing him in, warmth of the sun glittering over the bright blue sea. A voice drifted towards him, calling to him. Before Pavan could listen, or distinguish the voice above the sounds of the sea, Pavan was jolted awake.

He was laying immoveable upon a wagon.

CHAPTER 4

Malcom pressed his finger into the pulse point on Pavan's neck—it was strong. His eyes flickered to the watch on his wrist, but the hands had stopped moving. Malcom sighed in annoyance, moving on to evaluating the dilation of Pavan's eyes. His medical training taking over until he knew for certain that his friend was not in danger.

He sat back, leaning against the side of the wagon.

Looking up into the sky, a thick grove reached up and up into the blue sky above. It was unlike anything Malcom had ever seen before. This was unlike any place in England. Malcom rubbed his face, glancing towards the broad back of the man who sat before him with the reins in hand.

It was a jovial, laughing man who happened upon Malcom in the road. Malcom had waved him down, asking for help to bring Pavan to a doctor. The man had a look of wonder about him, but agreed, giving Malcom a helping hand to lift Pavan into the back of his wagon. He introduced himself as Iosef.

"Where was it you said you's both came down from?" Iosef called back over his shoulder.

"I didn't." Malcom grabbed the edge of the wagon, as the road began to dip, jostling him from side to side abruptly.

"Not many travel this way, unless they are headed to port."

"We are from the city. We got lost." Malcom felt uneasy, suddenly unsure of the man that drove the wagon onward, seemingly through deeper and closer settled trees.

"Lost? From Jorn City?! That is a full day's travel to get to the King's Road. Perhaps it is best if you and your companion settle in at the farm until we can wait for that *doctor*." Iosef spoke, but his accent was foreign to Malcom, his words conflicting with the surroundings.

"Thank you, sir."

"It's not often we get travelers through the east roads. Most trades take the King's Road further to the south. Iyda is a quick girl, she shall get a letter out to your healer if you can give her your direction."

Malcom's chest sank, dread flooding him, eyes scanning the road ahead. They turned down a narrowing of path, emerging into a long stretch that led toward a great building that stood amongst the tree line. To the left, further up the path was a large stable built of aged lumber.

"Iyda!" the driver's voice boomed.

A girl hurried from the front door, bounding down the steps towards them, dressed in a tattered gown of patchworked fabrics, her soft curled hair pulled back into a plait. Malcom kept close to the wagon, standing between Pavan and the man that hefted his great weight out of the wagon.

"Get those two in the house, I will see to the horses." Ioseph thumbed back towards the stables. "Send a messenger to his healer."

Iyda approached Malcom, her cheeks flushed.

"I can manage," Malcom began, but he stopped when he saw the quick look the girl gave to the man that began to unharness the two great horses. "He is heavy...but if you take his feet, I believe we can do this together."

Gripping Pavan beneath the arms, Malcom used his strength to hoist him up, nodding to the girl as she grabbed at the two limp legs. Heaving in unison, they took Pavan slowly across the short distance to the steps leading into the front door.

"Down this way, sir." Iyda was breathless, struggling beneath the exertion of Pavan's weight, but managing to take them down a long, darkened corridor.

It was a blur, with his focus narrowed in on not dropping his friend, Malcom did not have an opportunity to get a look around the interior of the entrance hall, nor the layout of the front room, before they were completely down a narrow corridor papered in dark green, illuminated by flickering lanterns that hung on the walls.

Entering a simply furnished room, Iyda hastened to deposit Pavan's legs upon the bed, gasping for breath, gripping at her side beneath the bodice of her gown. Malcom wished he was more graceful, but Pavan was extremely heavy, more so than Malcom had remembered.

"Thank you, Iyda." Malcom tried to smile as he knelt down beside his friend to push his dark hair out of his face, examining the pale clammy skin, pushing open the lids to search the dilation of a pupil.

"Are you a healer?" Iyda asked, watching Malcom work.

Malcom pressed his fingers into Pavan's neck, seeking his pulse point, counting methodically in his head as he felt each flicker of pulse. He was aware of Iyda's curious gaze, as she drew closer to the side of the bed, catching sight of her touching the material of Pavan's ripped black denim. Her curious fingers touched the old trainers that Pavan had worn for nearly a decade.

"I am a nurse, which is a kind of healer." Malcom dropped his hands, turning his attention directly upon her.

"His clothes are strange. Have you come from across the sea?" She looked up, her gaze wide. Iyda was young, with soft skin and faint freckles.

"We come from far away, yes. We are trying to get home. Your father believes that we can reach Jorn City, by the King's Road. There might be someone there who can help us get home."

Iyda's expression changed, her lips pulled down at the corners as tears pulled at the corners of her eyes. She quickly glanced to the door. Malcom's heart beat faster, seeing the point of her ears that jutted out from beneath her soft hair.

"He lied," Iyda stated.

Malcom felt the chill pass through him, as dread flooded his bones.

"My father is not a kind man by bringing you here." She turned back towards him, tears sliding down her cheeks. "I will send a letter, not to a healer...but to a good man, one you can trust."

There was a slam of a door, and Iyda jumped, fearful again and agitated. She quickly hurried forward to pull a quilt that was laying over the foot of the bed up over Pavan's legs, bringing the edge up to the curve of Pavan's shoulders. Iyda was close to Malcom now, as they listened to the heavy footfalls down the corridor.

"I can help you, but please, take me with you."

Malcom opened his mouth to respond, but Ioseph stood in the doorframe. Seeing him, Iyda forced a smile as she stood to face her father.

"Come on, girl, you got a letter to write," Ioseph growled, his thick hand gripping to the handle of the door.

Malcom wished Iyda would look at him, but she kept her eyes forward, slipping past the great hulking form in the doorway and out of sight. Crouched beside Pavan, Malcom watched the man smile at them. Then he slowly shut the door, saying, "Rest up now, I will call you for supper."

He could smell the sea while standing in a field of grass.

Pavan was at peace in his dream, lulled by a calm voice that sang on the breeze. An indistinct song that pulled him forward until his feet touched the sand. He stood, looking out to the miles of blue water. The pain in his mind made him wince. Reaching up, he touched the trickle from beneath his nose, tasting the bitter tang of blood.

Isaac.

He shivered. A cold damp cloth pressed to his head as he began to wake from the dreams of the sea. Again, the smell of blood, stronger than before, made his stomach dance with nausea. Pavan groaned, yanking himself over and retching the contents of his stomach into a bucket placed beside the bed.

"There now," a soft voice cooed.

Pavan fell back against the pillows, his nausea subsiding, he looked up to the face of a young woman. Feeling the damp cloth return to his forehead, he watched her with transfixed eyes. She had a pretty face, with blue eyes and soft brown hair that lay curled along her back. Keeping to her task, she turned away to dip the cloth into a waiting porcelain bowl. He could see the point of her ears—her elven ears. Pavan shuddered, remembering the events that led to this moment. Remembering the forest, the return to this world of the magick he wanted to forget.

A hot flurry that burned through his veins began to stir beneath his skin; it started in his fingertips, like a limb waking after falling asleep. Pavan winced. Unwanted magick was beginning to awaken.

"Malcom," he whimpered, searching the room where he lay, but his friend was nowhere in sight.

It was a modest sloped room with handcrafted furniture. A small space, brightened by the open window that let in a draft of warm air. Pavan grasped the bedding, a quilt of thin patched cloth.

Everything smelled of rose water, and blood.

"Your friend is down the hall, with my father," her voice returned. The elf was gentle, she spoke with a heavy accent, her words curved around her English with a familiar tone.

Pavan winced again, his brain on fire, trying to remember. All of the suppressed memories were buried too deeply; it was painful to remember.

"I am Iyda," she told him, as her hand lightly touched his own.

Pavan pulled back, panic building within him, the flutter of her magick making him flinch. He needed to get out. Hastening to push back the covers, he lumbered across the room, ignoring his trembling limbs and the fear in the girl.

"You must lay down..." Iyda entreated, her hands reaching out to touch his arm, but Pavan flinched away from the touch.

It felt as if his skin was set ablaze, a sickening roll of hesitation flitted through him. His own unease was rattled by the wide blue eyes, and the flushed cheeks of a frightened elf girl caring for a man more than twice her size.

"Mal-Malcom," Pavan stammered, pushing his frame as far into the wall as he could, maintaining a great distance from Iyda, her anxiety subsiding into curiosity. It was lessening the stifling nausea that clouded him.

"I shall get him." She stepped back, moving towards the door. Her eyes stayed on Pavan, not breaking eye contact as she slipped through.

At the click of the door, Pavan slumped back, pushing his head into the wood behind him, organizing the thoughts that were now a jumbled mess, he needed to be sure this was not a dream.

Pavan hastened to the side table, finding the basin of water, splashing it over his face, the cold water soothing his burning skin. It wasn't enough. Magick pulsed, thickening his blood, making his chest ache. He grimaced through the pain, stumbling to the bed.

"Pavan."

Hearing Malcom rush through the door was a relief. Pavan never dreamed of his friends in London, his episodes of elusiveness in reality were never of those he knew back home. Pavan was not dreaming, this was real.

"This place is real," Pavan began, more to himself than to Malcom, who began to guide Pavan to lay back, but there was too much life within Pavan to relax.

"Yes, it is real." Malcom nodded, forcing Pavan down when he began to sit up.

"Magick, Malcom, it is the magick…"

Malcom forced his hand over Pavan's mouth, halting the words that he spoke. Large brown eyes blinking back at him, fear spiked between them. Less than a handful of times had Pavan ever seen Malcom afraid, and even less had Pavan ever seen Malcom react the way he did in this moment.

"Do not speak of it, Pav…" Malcom whispered harshly, his gaze flickering to the partially open door. "Not here."

Pavan jerked his head away. "Iyda is an elf."

Malcom nodded. "Her father is human, Pavan. Her mother died…"

The door creaked on unoiled hinges and a man lumbered in, heavily booted, carrying a tray in thick calloused hands. Pavan felt his stomach grumble, his nose tickled at the stench of damp hay, sweat, and something else.

Pavan's eyes flickered up to Malcom, he could see the suspicion when others could not. Pavan recognized the placid smile and forceful grin as they watched the man approach with a tray of food.

"Stew is a bit thin…I had to add a bit more water and fat. This one is mighty hefty." The man's thick accent was abrasive. He was a short, fat older man with a balding head and a thick reddish beard to cover his double chin.

"Thank you, Iosef." Malcom reached for the bowl.

The man had not looked away from Pavan, with shifting gray eyes that lingered over his frame. That *something else* was rancid, Pavan understood it now—danger. With a noncommittal grunt, the man lumbered to the door where it shut with a bang, returning the room to stifled silence.

"Don't eat that." Malcom placed it back onto the tray. Standing up he went to bolt the large door, locking them inside.

Pavan sat up. "Mal."

Malcom returned, taking hold of Pavan's legs to swing them down onto the floor. "We need to leave."

"Who is that man...Mal, where are we?" Pavan winced, staggering to stand, even while being helped by Malcom.

"He found us, on his property. He gladly aided me in bringing you in his wagon to his home." They managed to shift to the window. Pavan could see out into the garden. It would be an uncomfortable fit, but they could manage.

"Malcom." Pavan gripped Malcom by the arm and looking at him pointedly. "Where are we?"

A sudden banging on the door made them both jump.

Malcom squeezed himself through first, jumping down to the garden in one swoop. Pavan bent uncomfortably, managing to maneuver himself through the narrow window, dropping himself down into the garden below where his bare feet sank into the mud.

"Come on, the stable is this way."

"Mal, you didn't answer me...where are we?" Pavan asked, following Malcom as they hurried across the garden hedge. Behind them, there was a great bang, and the splintering of wood.

"Somewhere bad...I never should have trusted that man." Malcom grabbed Pavan by the shirt, yanking him around the shelter of the hedgerow, out of sight from the bedroom window.

Pavan gasped, his heart rate beating faster. Glaring at Malcom, he asked, "What happened while I was unconscious, Mal?"

"Iosef is a farmer. He was kind at first. I don't know, Pavan...after we got here, I was ready to believe anything. Seeing this place, seeing Iyda...knowing what exists here, but this—"

Malcom was looking over his shoulder, before he hurried along the path that was adjacent to the hedgerow. He led them along a sloped path down and down, until Pavan could see the stable fast approaching. His heart was racing and his thoughts were running wildly.

"There are men coming today. Iosef told Iyda he will send for them when you awoke. He would send for them and they would come to collect you."

 "Collect me?" His limbs felt heavy as iron, unable to move.

Gripping Pavan by the arm, Malcom kept them moving, hastening to the stables. Slipping inside where it was warm, the sounds of horses covered their movements. Malcom led them along the line of stalls to the last one. When he opened it, Iyda was waiting.

"Iyda," Malcom greeted her. Releasing Pavan, he approached the young elf to take hold of the bag she held in her hand.

"They will be here before tomorrow." She was even more terrified than before. Pavan stepped back, his nose curling at the stench of her fear.

Malcom slung the bag over his shoulder. "Thank you, Iyda."

She smiled faintly, her eyes flickering towards Pavan. She straightened slightly, lowering her gaze when she could no longer contain her tears.

"How long was I unconscious, Malcom?"

There was silence. Pavan stepped around the young elf, ignoring her as he addressed his friend.

Malcom's nostrils flared, mouth set in a firm line.

"How long?" Pavan begged, his head throbbing behind his eyes.

"Three days...long enough for me to understand the danger you face. Pavan...they know of your magick. He has this device that measures it...you were feverish." Malcom's gaze flickered to Iyda.

Pavan sneered down at the elf.

"My father is desperate. Since my mother's death, he has not been himself," she spoke with a trembling voice.

"He has sold me, for your profit?" His throat tightened around the heaviness of the words.

Iyda began to shake her head as tears poured fervently down her paled cheeks. Terror returned to her frame, shaking her as she pushed herself away.

"It was not her fault, Pavan. She is an elf, she does not have the magick they seek." Malcom moved closer to his friend, stepping between Pavan and the girl.

Sliding his gaze to Malcom's, Pavan said softly, "You know nothing of what magick I hold, Mal. That farmer has no idea what I am capable of should they find me."

"You never told me any of this..."

Pavan scoffed. "I told enough to those doctors when I returned as a child. I told enough to realize never to speak of it again."

"Tell me, Pavan. Tell me everything."

Seeing the elven girl trembling behind Malcom's arm, Pavan stepped back, eyeing her warily.

"You should go, before your father sees you with us," Malcom told her. Iyda hesitated before quickly scurrying out of the stall. They listened as the stable door was opened.

It was the scream that followed, a scream loud enough to send shivers along their spines. A scream that was suddenly followed by silence. Pavan pressed against the stable door, hiding his frame within the shadow. Malcom joined him, pressed against his arm, gripping his wrist when Pavan went to grasp the latch.

"Wait, you cannot go out there."

They listened until the shouting started, a voice nearly hysterical was booming from the direction of the main house. Malcom's grip tightened on Pavan's wrist.

"Iosef," he whispered. They listened longer.

Again, the shouts continued, in a language neither of them could understand. They could hear the commotion just outside the stable. Metal crunched, chains moved against the ground, then there was a *thunk*, followed by more silence.

Waiting in the darkened corner of the stall, the horses within the neighboring stall began to dance about. Pavan felt a chill run along his spine.

"It is finished!" a bellowing shout from beyond the stable called to them. Malcom's grip tightened again, shaking his head. "Come out or my men shall slit the throat of your companion. She is pretty..."

Iyda screamed, a wretched sound that tangled in Pavan's stomach. Whomever these men were, had no intention of letting them all live.

Malcom reacted, releasing Pavan to yank open the latch. Now it was Pavan's turn to grip the wrist of his friend. There was a second silence, and the horses began to dance more feverishly, growing more afraid.

"They will kill her."

Malcom wrenched free. "They intend to collect...I shall not have it on my conscience I let her die when I could have prevented it."

There was nothing Pavan could say to stop him, not when there was a life on the line to be saved. Malcom dropped the bag containing the map and other necessities for a hastened retreat—there was no escaping the stable without detection. Pavan followed close behind Malcom, blinking into the sun as they emerged into the daylight.

"Stop," came the same voice from before.

Standing within fifteen feet of the stable doors stood a man in glinting bronze, his face a reddish tan and a shaved head. He wasn't very tall, but he made up for it in muscle. Pavan saw the others next, three other men in dark leather jerkins, each with a longsword upon his hip. There was one who held a slack Iyda, who was whimpering against the boorish man's hand over her mouth, a thin blade pressed up to the curve of her slender throat. Pavan could see the blood trickling from the superficial cut beneath.

Lying in a bloodied heap on the floor was Iosef, where a short-handled ax had been embedded into the back of the large man. Pavan felt the nausea roll through him.

"Old Iosef won't be engaged in this deal after all," the shaved man laughed, his hand resting on the hilt of his long sword.

Malcom was the first of them to speak.

"Let Iyda free. She is innocent."

Dark eyes shot in their direction as the brutish man frowned. "Iyda, yes...poor little Iyda."

Around them, all the men began to laugh.

Pavan sneered. "Take your prize. Let her go." Offering his arms out, Pavan saw the men watch him closely, their hands tightening on their swords. The brutish man motioned them calm.

"You are the one they whisper about. All of Hilvaer is abuzz with the pure blood magicks old Iosef managed to catch poaching upon his fields."

"He was mistaken. I have no magick," Pavan growled.

Slowly the man approached, stopping a few feet from where Pavan stood, looking him up and down. Then he smiled, a wicked smile exposing brown teeth. His reddish tanned skin creased around his mouth.

"Lord Credieu shall see for himself. You don't look faie to me, but again, it has been many years since the last of the Athrun have been in Jorn."

Malcom shifted, catching the eye of the man. "We are human. We have no magick in either of us. Iosef lied. His watch that measures magick was wrong."

Anger flooded the man's face, making his face redder in color. Stomping towards Malcom hotly, he snarled, "The Aoculsk is never wrong. They have been made with precision by the craftsman that Lord Bannon has handpicked himself. Each eye is made of the purest concentration of dragon glass. They can never be wrong."

"There must have been a forgery. I have no magick."

Pavan held firm, breathing deeper, concentrating to quiet the magick that rushed hot in his veins. Slowly, the magick began to cool.

Not once did Pavan blink.

"The truth shall be known. No one is capable of deceiving Credieu. He is a High One of the council." This man was smiling smugly, so near to Pavan now there was a strong smell of camphor, a strong tang that burned inside Pavan's nose.

"You have me, let her go," Pavan stated flatly. "Take us to your High One, and let this girl grieve her father's murder."

Skin stretched over the man's face as he grinned. "Bring the chain, kill the other," he ordered, turning away.

Pavan had only a moment to collect what the leader of the bronzed men said. He turned his head as the man closest to them lunged towards Malcom. For a man dressed in stiff leather, he moved agilely, but Pavan was faster, grasping Malcom by the shirt to throw him back behind him. Turning his attention to the man with the lethal glare and the brandished dagger, Pavan blocked the blade as the man swung. Seizing the man by the throat, Pavan felt the burning of magick at his fingertips, forcing the man down onto his back.

Thick gurgling sounds emerged from the man's lips, Pavan's hand was restricting all the air from escaping. Leaning onto the man's chest, it was easy to ignore the thrashing of the thick arms but Pavan was immoveable.

"Enough!"

The loud voice snapped Pavan's attention. He looked up to the leader who now held Iyda by the hair. Pavan forced his thumb deeper into the throat of the man, who began to grow purple in the face. He glared at the leader who held the whimpering elf.

"Release him," the reddened faced man demanded, pressing his blade closer to Iyda's throat. "Or I shall paint the ground with her blood."

Pavan felt the heartbeat beneath his hand beginning to lessen. He glared at the elf girl, her frightened eyes pleading. At once, he released the guard, who gasped and coughed, clawing his way back away from where Pavan remained knelt.

In exchange, Iyda was tossed to the ground. Sheathing his blade, the captain frowned deeply, glaring at the pair of them, then snapping at his men, "Bring them."

A sharp solid thud to the back of the head, and Pavan was swimming in darkness.

CHAPTER 5

P avan jolted awake.

His eyes opened wide as he began to shiver, trying to focus on the bird that woke him. It was perched high above him, a large raven sitting on a swaying branch. He could see it clearly, with its unnatural white eyes unblinking down at him. There was nothing around but the raven.

Swaying branches danced above the patch of ground where he lay, unmoving. Pavan's body felt weightless, his mind aloft and dancing amongst the leaves fluttering in the cool breeze. He did not know how long he lay there, but he knew he was bound, a sharp pain settled where metal restricted around his wrists. Memories emerged of shouts and metal, the smell of blood. The pain came second.

Pavan shouted, the sound echoing on the wind. High above his head the raven opened its large wings, taking flight without a sound.

Sunlight danced through the branches above him, dazzling sunbeams that kissed his face. Lying beneath the low hanging canopy, he could see the men who captured him begin to set blaze to the stables. Horses neighed as they were rounded up by those second guards that wore leather jerkins. They tried to keep the beasts contained, but they danced about with fright. The sound mixed eerily with the wails of the elven girl, Iyda.

Pain erupted in Pavan's head as a large set of hands grasped him under the arms, a second pair grasping his bound legs. They hefted with great effort, heaving Pavan along the narrow road, giving distance between them and the blaze of the fire. He felt for the elf girl, a glimpse of her sunken form and the dead body of her father would be forever branded in Pavan's mind as he was carried away.

Nausea swallowing the pain, Pavan succumbed to the clutches of unconsciousness once more. "Mal..." he whimpered, drifting back again into the darkness.

Cold stone pressed against Pavan's cheek, his body was heavy with exhaustion. He blinked to regain himself but found the darkness of a deep, wet chamber that smelled of seawater and urine. Pavan grimaced. Trying to pull himself up, he strained his muscles against the grasp of the shackles that rubbed against his wrists.

"Malcom." Water trickled around him, dripping over stone to leave tiny droplets over Pavan's skin.

"Quiet you," a deep voice grumbled.

Tidal waves of sound shocked through Pavan's mind. He searched in the darkness for the source of the voice. Pavan licked his dried lips, trying to wet his mouth.

"Where is Malcom?"

"You will be silent," a thick oily voice burred in Pavan's ear.

There was a sudden movement to Pavan's right, a large shadow in the dim hold of moistened rock. Pavan searched the man out, but dizziness clouded his vision. Thick fingers yanked a fist full of Pavan's hair, dragging him from the stone slab that was his bed. Pavan clawed at the hands that held him, his feet slipping on the wet stone underfoot. Scrambling to keep himself upright, his weight yanked the hair uncomfortably from the root.

Pavan was half dragged through shadowy corridors, his eyes dripping tears as he grimaced through the pain.

All at once Pavan was falling, being dropped.

Jolts of hot agonizing pain erupted in his shoulder where he landed. He choked on the mouthful of dirt kicked in his face by the man's muddy boot, who shouted in the strange dialect before turning on his heel. Pavan watched the boots thud away, each step thundering in his mind. It was not silent for long. Soon, he could hear a grating sound, like metal on stone. Pavan trembled to think of what made that sound.

He didn't move, focusing each breath to maintain control. Pavan felt the stirrings of magick begin to creep along his spine. His shoulder throbbed with pain, desperate to mend the wound that prevented him from sitting up.

Thick fingers weaved through Pavan's hair, blunt nails dragging against the curve of his scalp before grasping tight, yanking his head back. He was shouting through his teeth. Metal was pressed against the curve of his jaw, driving him cold with fear.

"You shall not bleed, the High One has a buyer for you, but..." The warmth of the man's breath tickled Pavan's cheek. "I cannot promise a quick slip of the blade as I make you presentable for the Lord Credieu."

A sharp yank, and Pavan was brought to his knees against the sharp stony dirt.

Fear grew as the silence made Pavan tremble, shutting his eyes. He gasped at the first swift slice of the blade to the bend of his hairline, shaving a strip free. It was an unexpected feeling—the first of the clumps beginning to trickle over his exposed arms. Inch by inch the man yanked, shaving uncomfortably close with precision and speed.

Each sweep was more careless, until the sharp sting.

Pavan hissed back the pain, biting hard on his teeth to keep from crying out, tears sprouting into his eyes. Blood began to trickle along his ear, and down the line of his neck.

Finally, it was finished.

Gripping the fabric of Pavan's shirt, the man used the sharp knife to cut the fabric away, yanking at the cut cloth until Pavan sat bare-chested. A thick, muddy boot raised to Pavan's shoulder, knocking him back. Falling with an audible gasp, Pavan glared at the man in the dim light, watching his large hands, skilled with the knife he held, shredding the length of his trousers. He yanked the scraps free, and then stood back to admire his work.

Pavan shifted in an attempt to hide his nakedness from the man, but it proved useless. There was a low chuckle, and the large hand was taking hold of Pavan's wrist, hoisting him to his feet and dragging him to the far wall to stand.

It was too dark to see, making Pavan blink hard, the man's actions lost on him until a shocking wave of ice-cold water drenched his naked body. Pavan gasped a shout, swearing loudly as a second shock of water chilled him through. A third took the last of his breath, before he remained a chattering mess. He held his hands awkwardly at his groin, shielding his manhood as a fourth and final bucket was tossed over him.

Pavan hissed, his skin starting to prickle with unfavorable heat.

"Enough."

A second voice halted the actions of the man who had prepared him. Pavan blinked through the dripping water, but there was nothing he could see but the haze of darkness.

"He is being prepared—"

The second voice was slick. "Sir Eske requires him."

Beyond the door, it was colder. The draft was unsettling and shifting, letting a chill creep into Pavan's bones. He winced with every step, as the rough hand guided him down and down, before stopping in front of a large oaken door, a light flickering from behind it.

It was opened to a well-fitted room; a roaring fire, and tapestries hung over the dark stone walls. It was a chamber used as an office. He could see a desk, large ornamental things littered the surface. But as Pavan was thrust forward, he stumbled, seeing a shadow shift. A frame was rising from one of the large winged backed chairs.

Sir Eske was as tall as Pavan, with a confident stance. Pavan blinked past the pain to get a good look upon him—he had a square jaw, lined with a dark beard. He watched Pavan with a harsh gaze, one gray eye and the other a milky white, Pavan gulped. Seeing the old skin, that had once been burned, over the brow line of his milky eye, the new skin stretched over in waves, red and angry, reaching up into his hairline. No hair grew over the temple down to his ear. The rest of his peppered hair was slicked back into a low ponytail.

He spoke, his accent heavy and dark.

"A little thin, to be sure, but very promising."

Pavan's gaze shot up, locking eyes with him again. Sir Eske nodded dismissal to the man who had brought him. Pavan dared not turn his gaze away. Behind them, the door shut. Hair standing up on end, Pavan realized he was alone with this man.

"New to this realm, I hear. Unmarked by another. Shall I be the one to carve into your flesh?" A rueful smile parted the man's lips, creasing the scar above his eye.

Pavan gulped, but words could not find him. Pavan let his gaze flicker over the dimpled and distorted scar over Sir Eske's milky eye, before returning to look into the cold gray one.

"Courtesy of one not yet broken. He was young, so full of life." Sir Eske gestured to his face, undisturbed by Pavan's gaze. "Would you like to know what I did to him in return?"

He smelled of spices, and a heavy scent of cologne, Pavan's nose twitched as the man stepped closer. He eyed Pavan thoroughly as he neared.

Pavan gulped again, but remained silent.

A smile creased Sir Eske's haggard face. Raising a hand, his large fingers trailed delicately along the line of Pavan's shoulder.

Pavan's stomach shifted, forming knots.

"Shame I am not to mutilate you, as I had done to many of the others. Our time here is short." His voice was soft.

Those large fingers trailed along Pavan's collar, sending unwanted shivers over his skin. Nausea began curling in the pits of Pavan's gut. He clenched his fist, jerking his body away reflexively when the caress smoothed lower over his chest.

Pavan's head snapped back as the man's ring jeweled fist hurled up with precision. Blood began pouring from Pavan's nose. That thick hand was gripping him by the throat to keep him from moving back, forcing him to look into the eyes of Sir Eske. Sir Eske was wrought with fury.

"Now, now...*behave*..." the other man said, squeezing tighter.

Anger pooled in Pavan's veins.

A cruel smile formed on the man's lips. "Descent muscle tone. Tall for a human. Yes, I do believe you shall be worth more than most we see through here. All half-butchered, bloodied, and tainted. But does your body pulse with magick? Lord Credieu shall put a test to that."

Pavan shut his eyes, breathing harder as the fingers touched his exposed chest, his arms, his stomach. But the man did not stop touching him, his large fingers, rough and calloused, eased over his hips, rounding the swell of his backside. Pavan's stomach rolled with nausea with every grope.

"Pity there is already a buyer for your flesh, I would enjoy taking my time with you. It brings me to mind of the one who gave me this scar." Sir Eske's voice was quieter as he raised Pavan's bound hands, his rough calloused fingers trailing down below Pavan's navel. "He was full of spirit, and vigor. Barely old enough to grow hair upon his freckled skin...but you are grown."

Anger coiled deeper through Pavan's veins.

"Pity," Sir Eske reiterated, finally releasing Pavan, whose hands fell like dead weights. "I would have enjoyed teaching you the same lesson."

Dread flooded through Pavan, watching the man unlatch his belt.

Pavan stepped back.

Sir Eske sneered, gripping the back of Pavan's neck. Throwing his head forwards, Pavan struck the front of the man's face. Sir Eske shouted, gripping at his nose as blood pooled down his face.

"Fuck you," Pavan spat.

Enraged, the man swung a fist into Pavan's gut, taking his breath away. Pavan crumpled, falling to his knees. Gasping for breath while his diaphragm spasmed, the taste of blood was on his tongue, the sting of tears in his eyes.

"Buyer be damned, you shall feel my mark upon your skin after this night." Sir Eske kicked Pavan.

Pavan crashed hard onto the stone floor, the rough edge scraping painfully across his cheek. He winced, hissing through clenched teeth as Sir Eske's knee dug into his back, the weight crushing him against the unforgiving ground. A large, calloused hand forced his head down even further, his face pressed uncomfortably against the coarse carpet beneath him. The pressure on his neck grew unbearable, cutting off his air supply.

Pavan's body trembled as he fought to breathe, his chest heaving in desperation. The hand around his throat tightened, leaving him helpless, his limbs immovable. His vision blurred, black spots forming in the corners of his sight as his head grew light. His mind screamed for air, but his body was paralyzed under Eske's brutal grip. Just when he felt he might lose consciousness, the pressure suddenly vanished.

He gasped, lungs burning as they filled with air. Each breath came in ragged, desperate gulps, his head spinning as he fought to steady himself. The taste of blood lingered in his mouth, his pulse thundering in his ears.

"Submit to me," Sir Eske huffed, breathing heavily as he turned Pavan's head to face him. Pavan could see the cold glint, the shift of a smile—Sir Eske's scar dimpled horridly.

"Fuck. You." Pavan's voice was hoarse.

Chuckling, Sir Eske shoved Pavan down hard again.

Pavan almost expected Sir Eske to return to the brutal punishment of suffocating him, but the man did not press his knee into Pavan's back. Instead, there was a groan from the man as he stood, his boots thudding about the room as he maneuvered to the fire pit.

Pavan could see the silhouette upon the wall and ceiling, Sir Eske's boots stood inches from the large hearth. He was soon returned, glaring down at Pavan.

"You will not submit, but you will always remember." The man's voice grated in Pavan's skull as the hard press of a boot settled onto Pavan's neck.

He could see it in the corner of his eye, the man held something in his hand—a long tool of dark metal, the end red hot. Pavan struggled, but the man pressed his boot down hard. Pavan's shouts became garbled. It was sharp and sudden, Pavan's body seizing as the hot branding tool contacted his skin. Seated just over his shoulder blade, the man held it firm and unyielding as it seared Pavan's skin. It was smoldering hot. Soon, the room smelled of burning flesh.

CHAPTER 6

Pavan was carried in by two guards, who laid him out on the stone floor. It was a dark cold room in another part of the fortress of stone. Pain swimming through Pavan, he grimaced as the dirt ground into the fresh wound upon his shoulder.

"Pav—"

Hearing Malcom tipped the composure Pavan held firmly in place. He was weeping openly as his friend was beside him, grasping his ankles first, guiding his way in the dark to touch Pavan's face.

"You're alive," Pavan breathed, swallowing his tears. Awkwardly, he raised his bound hands to touch the hand that was warm against his cheek—they were familiar, gentle.

"I thought the bastards were going to kill us. Are you harmed?" Malcom asked, resting a hand over the flat of Pavan's chest.

Fighting with the coming tears, he was grateful they lay in the dark, not wanting Malcom to see him this way, knowing he was coated in blood, hair, and mud. Pavan swallowed thickly around the lump in his throat.

"It doesn't matter, you're *alive*." Pavan shook his head. "I am so tired..."

Shifting himself, Malcom pressed his fingers into the pulse point on Pavan's neck, then rested the flat of his palm over Pavan's forehead. Each movement felt like an eternity; Pavan was swimming in the drowsiness of pain and weakness.

"Rest," Malcom said at last. Keeping a warm hand on the dip of Pavan's elbow; it was a reassuring hold to let Pavan know he was there.

Unconsciousness lulled Pavan back, his mind drifting to the safety of sleep, but fear whittled its way in—Pavan was afraid of the nightmares that would plague him.

There was no nightmare though. Pavan stood on the beach of a great vast sea, he let the warm breeze wash over him as the smell of the salty air bathed him. Luscious smells of flowers and oils soothed him, as the voice of a woman singing returned to his mind.

He jumped as the large wooden doors clanked open, grating hard against the floor, before opening wide. Standing in the doorframe was a large man dressed in heavy woolen clothes, his jacket and breeches were embroidered with jewels and floral brocade and a cavalier hat was pressed over his head. This opulent man's hair was pressed in thick curls, powdered with yellow dye.

He shouted in a dialect that Pavan had never heard before then blinked at him. The large man huffed, shouting again, mimicking the motion of standing.

Pavan and Malcom stood up slowly, each of them covering themselves in ways that hid their nakedness from the man before them. His booming voice was demanding. This time, the man motioned for them to follow.

They entered into the corridor just outside of the room where they were held, and as they were walking the long, narrow corridor, Pavan could see seven opened doors. Four were on one wall, void of much light, and did not have more than a sliver of a window. The other four, on the same wall as the room they had come from, faced the ocean. The windows were taking in the light but the rooms were all empty—Pavan and Malcom were the two only people there.

They neared a staircase. The man went down gracefully, but every step Pavan made sent a shooting pain up his legs. His feet pinched against the descent, his every muscle was sore, a brutal reminder of the man who had branded him.

Reaching the floor beneath them, Pavan squinted into the dim light. A large open space greeted them, tapestries lined the walls, depicting two great cities. On the right, the city of tall spires were reaching up into the sky. People danced in the streets, and poles with colorful banners fluttered in the sky—it was a scene of great prosperity. But on the other tapestry, it raged with darkness and malice. Fire rained down on the tall spires of the city, as large monstrous beasts breathed fire and ice, destruction and death."

Pavan shivered at the scenes illustrated so vividly before them.

They stood now, at the center of the room. Large chandeliers hung high above them. At the farthest end of the room, a desk was placed near a large roaring hearth, though the great blaze did not stave off the cold that seeped into Pavan.

"Step forward," a great voice boomed from behind the desk.

Squinting hard against the glare, Pavan saw the man sitting in the large wingback chair, hidden behind a stack of books. A thick hand pushed Pavan roughly forward, he stumbled, trying to regain the dignity of shielding himself while standing before the great desk.

"You speak the Common Tongue, do you not?" Narrow beady eyes glanced over the tops of darkened half-moon glasses.

He was old with very wiry grey hair, his mouth was set in a firm frown on his long face. He dressed in a similar brocade as the larger man, but his dress was more decorative and billowing, drowning an old frail body with layers of fabric. He leaned over a leather-bound book, a quill in his hand as he wrote on the blank pages with a foreign script.

His beady eyes watched Pavan, expectantly.

"Yes." Pavan's throat was tight.

"Step forward," Lord Credieu motioned to Malcom. Malcom stepped up beside Pavan so they stood shoulder to shoulder.

Standing from his great chair, Lord Credieu walked towards them, adjusting his glasses as he inspected them both with an impenetrable scrutiny. Pavan felt hot under the dark eyes of the man. Lord Credieu retrieved a pocket watch to inspect it, but Pavan realized it was not a watch. Narrow metal rings clicking around in alternating directions, at the center shimmered a translucent stone that seemed to glow brighter as the rings spun around.

This was an Aoculsk, a device that measured magick.

All at once the stone stopped glowing, the rings slowing to a quiet tick. Facing Malcom, the rings within the Aoculsk began to whir, spinning around as the stone began to glow before going dim. Snapping the Aoculsk shut, Lord Credieu returned to his desk. Scratching on the page, muttering under his breath,

"Non-magicked humans, both unmarked. Worth two hundred uile gold."

Behind Malcom the yellow haired man guffawed, his cheeks turning red as he shouted at Lord Credieu, however, seemed undisturbed by the larger man's outburst. He began speaking calmly in the unknown dialect. As the soft tone from Lord Credieu came forth, the larger man became more compliant.

"Two hundred gold, to be paid in full before receipt of transport. Your papers shall be prepared in prompt time before your departure." Lord Credieu reached into a small box, retrieving a worn down wax nub.

"Are we being sold?" Malcom snapped, his eyes looking from the yellow haired man to the lord.

Dark eyes glared scornfully over half-moon glasses. Pavan clenched his jaw together.

"You are property of Sir Adrian. Under the royal declaration of the Realm of Jorn, you shall be taken from this stronghold of Hilvaer to Denorn in one week hence. Upon such a day, your licensure is signed and ownership is forfeit in documentation to your new master, you will remain in sole property under his name. Should you die in transport, or grow ill, your ownership is not forfeit. Should you run from your master, your ownership is not forfeit and punishment is hereafter at the discretion of your new master," Lord Credieu stated.

Pavan felt his blood run hot, anger boiling under his skin, burning the skin of his shoulder where the brand ached relentlessly. Sir Adrian, the yellow haired man, bellowed in laughter.

Lord Credieu waved them away, turning his attention to the paperwork. "Tehrn, take them to be washed. Feed them gruel and dress them in something suitable."

They were escorted out of the chamber by a servant who stood out of view, leaving Lord Credieu with Sir Adrian. Down and away, they followed a maze of corridors and into a descending set of stone steps. They enter into a cold cellar room, with two wooden tubs at the center. Tehrn guided them forward.

Pavan had no choice but to step into the basin of water. His breath came in sharp gasps as he was met with ice cold water, his feet plunged into the cold depths, memories of the buckets of water that had doused him made him shiver harder.

Tehrn did not speak, but Pavan felt the unwavering eyes of the thin man who led them here as he brought forward a bucket. Pavan watched him as he dove his hands into the bucket, retrieving a large bar of soap. Pavan clenched his jaw, trying not to move as he was scrubbed. The clear water now tinted red, flecks of hair muddled with the grime that swam around him.

Pavan trembled as shock settled in him, hissing back the pain as Tehrn worked the soap into the wound.

Pavan shivered as he lay flat on his back with his hands cupped in front of him, the iron around his wrists was chafing and rubbing his skin raw. A loose wool compress was pressed against the seeping wound on his shoulder blade. He and Macom had been scrubbed from head to toe, the cold water chilling them through, taking in sharp breaths with each dump of ice water over their heads. Pavan and Malcom had emerged from the bathhouse only to be dried with rough wool.

As instructed, they were given a thick, tasteless porridge but Pavan ate the contents of his bowl without complaint. The tight clench in his stomach prevented him from a second thought about what he was eating.

Returning again to the room where they had first arrived, they remained there, shackled, and locked away. Pavan shivered, his teeth clacking together. Beside him, Pavan could hear Malcom shifting around on one of the other beds. The sky had grown dark, and the room was without light, save for the sliver of the moon peeking in through the high-up window.

"Denorn."

Pavan looked over as Malcom's voice sliced through the silence.

"It may be best not to dwell on it, Mal." Pavan was tired, his eyelids heavy.

"I think of her...Iyda. If she survived."

Pavan remembered the vision of the elf girl who stood watching her father's stables burn, he quickly shook the thought away. "She was left in ruin, but otherwise alive."

"How much do you remember of this place as a child?"

Pavan took a breath. "I remember everything, Mal."

With a shift and a creak of the metal frame, Malcom sat up. He broke the distance between them by sitting on the edge of Pavan's cot.

"This happened before, when you were a child? Is this why you never told me? Why you never spoke of what happened?"

Pavan remembered the first time he awoke in this world, all those years ago, but the memory pained him, quickly shaking it off.

"It was different." He licked his cracked lips, trying to calm his nervous words. "We were found by a man with long, dark matted locks that chimes like bells. He was the kindest man, soft-spoken...he took us to a village. We were safe there."

Malcom rested his warm hand on Pavan's arm.

"This place is not the same. There is darkness here, Mal. Forgive me, I have doomed us here. We can never return home. *Forgive me*." Tears spilled freely now, tracing sorrowful paths along Pavan's skin.

"You think I am without hope?" Malcom asked, his soft tone a comfort in the dark. "We have been to some of the more dangerous cities in the world."

Pavan chuckled. "This is more than petty theft, Mal."

"We spent that summer in Venice. I nearly passed out from the heat."

"You refused to take the advice of our guide and decided to wear a full track suit on our tour." They laughed together at the memory. Pavan's laugh fell into a frown. "There won't be any more holidays, Mal. I can't...we can't go back."

"We will figure this out. Together."

There was a long pause. Pavan felt a shift in the air, Malcom's hesitation was apparent to him. "Will you tell me what that man did to you? Did he *touch* you? I can see the bruises...the brand—"

"I can't." Pavan shook his head, unable to bring himself to speak of it, not yet.

"Alright. For now, please sleep."

Malcom stood, Pavan's bed shifted as the weight lifted. He closed his eyes, shutting out the remainder of light that spilled through the room—he was desperate to stand at the seaside again, but he was disappointed. There was nothing but a large fire and a sickly laugh as Pavan smelled the burning of his skin and the heat of the brand.

CHAPTER

7

Denorn, Realm of Jorn.

Simeon Bannon sits in the large carriage being pulled along the graveled street of Denorn, seated upon the brushed velvet seat and looking out through the drape of curtain covering the thin glass pane of the window, separating him from the smell of the foul stench of fish and manure.

"Was this port a once vibrant city of wealthy tradesmen? This certainly is not what one envisions..."

Simeon looked up at the man who sat across from him upon the bench seat. Leuthere was ruthless, but a well-trained man. He was narrow-faced with a stoney gaze. If there was one man Simeon trusted, it was Leuthere. But only because the man feared him.

"King Beaumont's name is sung from every corner of Jorn, he has brought our realm out of fear. Now, with the trade routes open since the fall of Augusta, we have seen an abundance of trade."

Leuthere scoffed, his sun kissed skin creasing around his mouth. "Tradesman. Fisherman. Now that the king owns Entheas, it seems fruitless to join in treaty with the south."

"Fruitless, yes. I believe it shall waste precious time. But King Beaumont needs a distraction; he has been so distraught these last few years of unrest, now it is time to come to a fulfilling conclusion with the elves at our flank."

"Unrest? The marauders that attack villages along the coasts and the shipping vessels? Are they not your own men?"

Simeon smiled, his teeth bared, hissing in mirth. "But a small group of bandits who have brought the great knees of the elves at our heels, with their tails between their legs, like a whipped dog. Burned crops, stolen goods, all in my warehouses. Now, we shall let the council and the southern king burden our king with treaties."

Simeon pulled upon a cord connected to the carriage driver that rang a small bell, at once the carriage rolled to a stop.

"It is unwise." Leuthere placed a hand upon the latch, but Simeon slapped it away, unlatching the door himself to step out into the foul sea air and the sounds of the streets.

"This is my city, Leuthere. These are my subjects, and these are my streets." Then, watching as the guard stepped out, Simeon gave him a cruel grin. "And should there be such a threat, then that sword of yours shall get some use after all."

Leuthere nodded, following dutifully behind Simeon, who walked the wet cobbled path from the road to the merchant setting up his small cages of prized birds. Golden feathers sat upon the crest of their heads—it was a prized song bird from the north—the little creatures no doubt had their wings broken, Simeon thought, as he watched them hop about pathetically.

"Good morrow." Simeon was firm speaking to the merchant, now seeing them approach. At once the merchant bowed, his bald head cracked and blistered beneath the thin starched hair combed over atop his head.

"Lord Simeon. You are early, my lord." Nervously the merchant dabbed at his brow, with a stained handkerchief.

Shuffling around as he beckoned them to follow through the stall, stepping around cages of whicker, housing small creatures that scratched and snorted. Yelps of small foxes, the yawls of small beasts that had nowhere to burrow, echoed.

At the back of the stall, out of view, stood two large cages made of iron, locked with enchanted chains. Simeon smiled, leaning down to inspect the dirtied face of a faie. He saw matted hair of moss colored green, and large vibrant eyes the color of fire. He inspected the ears seeing the jagged edges of scars that ran along the outer edge.

"Cut their own ears," the merchant wheezed, leaning his fat girth down to shove his large hand through the bars, turning the heads of the faie to give Simeon a clearer view of the creature's ear. Indeed, the point of the ear had been cut in a crude attempt to look more human. Simeon stood, sneering.

"What magick have they?" he asked, now eyeing the merchant who also stood.

Pulling at his jacket, the merchant fumbled in his pockets. A once lavish fabric, it was now soiled and starched, stitched and worked on to keep the appearance of finery, but Simeon saw the bulging man's girth trying to break through the ill fitted garment. He saw the years of use, the merchant's feigned riches he presented to the world. Anyone who saw him would assume him a rich man, but Simeon's eyes were not deceived.

At last, the merchant pulled from his pocket a brass pocket watch, but instead of a watch face was an oculus of rings, each turning in different directions, with a small purple stone at the center. It thrummed with magick, Simeon could smell the lilacs and taste the licorice on his tongue as the merchant watched the little rings click around, and the center stone began to glow. A secondary Aoculsk obviously worn down. Now, slipping it shut with a loud audible click, he smiled warily up at Simeon, who watched in silence.

"Fair amount of magick in the blood. Not much to use, but simple labor should do." The merchant sounded surer of his words than he looked. Simeon saw the look of terror in the squint of the man's bagged eyes, he saw the slither of sweat on his heavily powdered face.

Simeon smiled, more teeth than partiality, watching the man stiffen. He was sweating more, his nerves making the man heave a breath, he began licking his lips, looking around them for the source of the sweltering heat, never to fully understand the heat Simeon raised within the man's blood with his own magick.

"You will take fifty." Simeon smiled more cheerfully, motioning for Leuthere.

At once, the guard took a velvet pouch from his belt, tossing it to the man, but the merchant was lethargic, dazed. He fumbled to catch it, the pouch falling to the straw and dirt beneath their feet with a clatter, the coins rolling out.

"Magick...my lord is strong with magick."

Simeon's gaze slithered to the second cage, where an older faie crouched, his large cyan eyes looking up at him in awe.

"Silence," Simeon hissed, the sharp tang of magick whipping around him, satisfied when the faie shrunk back.

"Come, Lord Bannon. I shall see to their transport, you must return to the king."

Leuthere was calm, turning Simeon's gaze from the cage, sneering down momentarily at the merchant who gathered his coin from the dirt. He watched the lumbering man bent low.

"Have you any more magick shipments?" Simeon demanded.

Flinching, greedily plucking the gold from the dirt, the merchant chuckled. "Human...not a magick in them, my lord."

Simeon sneered, turned on his heel, and trudged away. Leuthere was quick at his heels following Simeon out of the stall back to the noisy street where his carriage waited.

"Less and less, we see far less magick in these parts," Simeon muttered.

Leuthere kept his voice low. "We lost many of our the magick users to the war, and during the fall of Augusta. But perhaps there is another way, do not lower your standard to this welp, my lord. They will service you well in Jorn City."

"No, no, they will go to my estate here in Denorn, and no further. I cannot risk bringing them to the castle. Beaumont has his guards on high alert, with the King of Corad entering these realms it has made him more cautious. Now, I shall have them waiting for me in Denorn, when I next have a chance to get away. Do this, Leuthere, they remain in your charge."

A smile came over the guard.

Simeon raised himself to enter the carriage, but stopped, turning to Leuthere with a knowing look. "They are not to be from death's door...whatever else may please you, have your way with them. But leave them whole so I may break them myself."

Signe, Realm of Corad.

A warm sea breeze came up from the southeast, bringing with it the conditions deemed favorable for the boatmen all along the docks of Signe Harbor. The grandest ship was in port, ready for sail to the north, a ship with large green sails and the insignia of the royal house of Moreau—a large blackbird, flanked by olive branches. Awaiting on board, as the boatmen crew and captain were ready to make way, King Sabian stood at the ship's bow looking out over the waters ahead, shimmering under the sun.

A breeze carried over the harbor, bringing with it the shifting smell of the sea and the salty air, making the long grass of the lanes beyond the boathouse shift and sway. Nearby was a small, tiny patch of ground where the elf Sir Lahrs, Knight of Corad, found his ward, the youngest daughter of King Sabian. She was kneeling in the grass, singing a lullaby and plucking small purple flowers nestled within the grass.

Sir Lahrs sighed, lifting his hand to shield the sun from his stony gray eyes as he watched the young princess stand. Her gown, the shade of ground mustard seed, made her easy to spot against the shifting grass. He watched her retrieve another bloom, before she turned to see him standing upon the walk. He was reminded of the young girl's mother, a faie mistress with the same dark onyx curls and olive skin.

Brendolyn approached, a girl of barely fourteen, her smile vibrant and cheeks flushed with youth. He could not help but smile down at her affectionately.

"Some purple perennials for my queen mother." She spoke with a delighted tone, admiring her conquest, Sir Lahrs smiled.

"Queen Natalia will appreciate such a fine bouquet, but we must make for the ship; we shall be setting off soon," Lahrs advised, gesturing up the walk.

They took the boardwalk, leading to the docks just beyond the grassy pitch. It was early evening, so many of the villagers of Signe still took indoors for rest, as the sun was growing hotter overhead.

Approaching the largest ship in the harbor, Sir Lahrs followed the princess up the gangplank, swaying on his feet uneasily as he reached the deck. He was approached by the king, a strong build man, with thick gruff facial hair and dark curls that lay about his neck, laying just over the stiff lining of his collar.

King Sabian did not look upon them approvingly. "You are late, Sir Lahrs. Punctuality is the pinnacle to catch the wind just right."

"It was my fault, Father. I wanted to pick flowers for my queen mother." Brendolyn showed the king her small bouquet.

King Sabian frowned. "They are lovely, *amore*. But promptness is the vitality of honor."

"Come, Brendolyn. We must go below, your chambers have been made ready for your journey."

"Return to me at once, there is much we must speak on for the remainder of our journey, Sir Lahrs."

Sir Lahrs nodded.

He took Brendolyn's arm gently, guiding her to the directions of the steps that lead below. Out of earshot, Lahrs could see the pained look upon Brendolyn's face as she cast a forlorn glance around his shoulder, catching one last look at the king before they disappeared below.

"Your father is nervous about the treaty, Bren. Do not take to heart his coldness. When this is all over, he shall be himself again," Lahrs said at last as they descended the stairs.

Brendolyn sighed. "He is always the same Lahrs...this will be no different. I would like to visit my queen mother before I am shut away for the duration of our travels."

"One quick visit, then you must go to your rooms."

She nodded. "You will go to my father?"

"I must, but I will return to you soon." He leaned in to place a kiss upon her hair. "Keep out of trouble."

He turned, bounding onto the top deck in search of his king. He found the king at the stern, his brow deeply furrowed in thought. Upon his approach, King Sabian jumped.

"Forgive me, Lahrs. I did not hear you approach," Sabian said, looking out again over the water.

"You have need of me, my lord?" Lahrs asked.

"Yes. As you know, Queen Natalia is heavy with child," Sabian began. This was true. The Queen and King Sabian had been blessed after so many years of stillbirth and miscarriage with a child. All the midwives and wise women predicted a boy—an heir—if this was to be true, it would change the outcome of this treaty drastically.

"She is stubborn not to remain in Corad while we travel to Jorn." Lahrs smirked, knowing the argument had lasted a loud afternoon of elevated blood pressure and heated threats that Sabian would leave Natalia in her state and potentially risk missing the birth of their next child.

"Her Felourian blood is hot, all the women are, but Lahrs, we must be cautious. Her midwives are to attend her, but should the need arise..." Sabian's dark eyes glazed over, his tanned complexion paled as the king shivered. "Your mother was the best healer, she trained you..."

Lahrs nodded, grasping his kings' upper arm.

"Natalia is the very image of health, Your Majesty. But I give you my word that should you need me, I shall be there to aid her." He was cautious. Untrained as only an apprentice healer, Lahrs knew only what his mother had taught him before her death.

"Good. Good." This appeased the king, he softened slightly and looked out over the shimmering waves of the sea.

"Is there something else?"

"She must not sing. Not in Jorn." Sabian turned to look into Lahrs' waiting gaze, his mouth a firm line. "Keep her silent. There must not be even a whisper or melody. It is too much of a risk if her faie voice should emerge while in another realm. Has she had any more signs? You are an elf, Lahrs, you have the eye for this sort of thing."

"Brendolyn has not received the gift of a faie voice. There is always a chance she did not inherit her mother's magick."

King Sabian gave a stern nod.

"Tell me as soon as it does. We cannot risk such a development."

"On my honor."

Sir Lahrs could only lie for so long. For the sake of Brendolyn, he would not tell the king that she had always possessed the voice of the faie, a voice that could shake mountains, that could move men to forget who they are entirely. He could not tell his king that his daughter possessed all the power that her mother held. If Sabian knew, it would send Brendolyn into exile. Or worse.

Brendolyn hummed, stepping lightly up to her queen mother's door, knocking lightly. She was smiling to herself, the smell of the perennials light in her senses. At once the door was swung open and Brendolyn's smile fell.

Standing before her was Lisetta, her tall and gorgeous sister. Born four years before Brendolyn, Lisetta was the natural born daughter of Queen Natalia and King Sabian. The look upon Lisetta's face was as it always remained whenever the elder princess looked upon her sister—distain—Lisetta never let Brendolyn forget her birth.

"What is it?" Lisetta hissed.

Hesitating, Brendolyn lifted her hands that held the flower bouquet. Lisetta sneered and rolled her eyes but she stepped aside to let her sister pass. Brendolyn hurried inside before the door slammed in her face.

"Oh, *amore*." Queen Natalia's accent was thick as she greeted Brendolyn in their mother tongue.

Queen Natalia lounged in the lush apartment of the well-fitted cabin, adorned with all the luxury and style that Queen Natalia herself had hand-picked. Velvet curtains tied back with thick rope braided with gold adorned the round port window and covered the narrow bed. The bed was dressed with a feather pillow top and furs, where the queen sat, upon the lounge chaise. Queen Natalia sat in her dressing gown and chemise, the swell of her belly before her. Her long expensively oiled hair curled about her shoulders, tumbling over the arm of the chaise, grazing the floor beneath, a floor that had been recently draped with furs.

Queen Natalia loathed the cold, and although her brow was already dewy with sweat, she would not see an inch of fur or down removed. They were to travel to Jorn, the coldest climate in all the realms.

Brendolyn sat upon the edge of the chaise, kissing her queen mothers' cheeks. She presented the flowers that were now slightly wilted in her grasp.

Natalia gasped. "So beautiful. And my favorite color." She smelled the blooms and touched Brendolyn's cheek.

"Mother, she cannot be in here," Lisetta said as she walked the distance of the room to stand beside her mother.

Brendolyn snapped her gaze in her sister's direction. "I am not forbidden to speak with her, Lisetta. I have not caused her any distress."

Lisetta scoffed.

"*Amore, amore*, girls please, no fighting on this trip. We shall be in Jorn and we shall be right again." Natalia smoothed a thin hand over Lisetta's crossed arms, touching her eldest daughters' hair with affection.

"She was humming at the door."

Brendolyn's cheeks grew hot with anger, looking hard at her sister. Natalia tsked, clicking her tongue as she smelled the small bouquet in hand.

"You know it is forbidden, *amore*." Natalia was stern. Finally setting her flowers aside, she took both of Brendolyn's hands in hers.

Unable to look away, Brendolyn was face to face with her queen mothers' dark brown eyes, she had looked at her this way only a few times.

"I won't sing, I promise. Will you ask Father to not keep me bound to my rooms?" Brendolyn asked, ignoring the laugh she heard from Lisetta. She kept her eyes locked on Natalia's.

The queen sighed, twirling a long lock of Brendolyn's onyx hair in her fingers. "We shall see. He is very anxious about this meeting, *amore*. It has been so long since he has seen the King of Jorn."

"They used to be friends, a long time ago?"

Natalia smiled, kissing both of Brendolyn's hands. Her warmth radiated between them, let Brendolyn feel her queen mother's love.

"Things shall be right again."

A soft knock came to the door—it was the lady's maid who brought a tray of tea. Brendolyn was pulled by the arm Lisetta hurriedly pushed her out into the corridor of the ship's belly.

"Farwell, Mother," Brendolyn called, getting one last glimpse of her queen mother, before the door was shut firm in her face.

Brendolyn stumbled back. She could hear the muffled voices beyond, the quiet and dimly lit corridor behind her, her feet unsteady as the ship moved, swaying on the waves beneath the hull. The walk to her chamber was a way down the corridor, making her way there, Brendolyn turned to the left, and stopped.

"Princess." His voice made her stiffen.

Sir Varick, a knight of Corad, was bound as escort and protector of Princess Lisetta, as Sir Lahrs had been placed over her own protection. But there was something shifty in the pale brown eyes of the knight who now loomed in the corridor, blocking her from reaching her chambers. Brendolyn disliked the man, from his well-groomed hair of chestnut brown, to his clean-shaven face. He performed an air of chivalry and honor, but beneath his façade, Brendolyn has seen the slithering, putrid vile things he had done.

"Excuse me," she said, trying to keep her eyes down. Pressing her back to the wall of the corridor, her breathing caught as the knight gripped her upper arm.

Stilling under the firm grasp, Brendolyn stared at his hand, his rough fingers wrinkling the fabric of her sleeve. His breath was sweet, like candied fruit. He leaned in to be closer to her height.

"Little pigeon, you have flown so far from your gilded cage," he smiled, his teeth bared. "Lahrs has left you to venture out alone. What a delight. Perhaps I can escort you the remaining distance."

The pit of her stomach rolled. She used her free hand to pry the knight's hand free of her arm. Stumbling out of his grasp, she shot him a sharp look.

"I can return on my own, Varick. Do not linger in the corridor, Lahrs will be along shortly," Brendolyn stated, her mouth formed around the words on her tongue, they tasted bitter and sharp.

Sir Varick straightened, hearing from along the neighboring corridor the aloft voices of crewmembers hurrying along to the deck. He eyed the direction she had ventured from, before plastering a fictitious smile upon his thin mouth.

"Alas, we shall meet again, pigeon." He bowed, his hair flopping into his eyes. As he straightened, he ran a hand through the weight of his hair, pushing it back into place. His eyes lingered on Brendolyn's frame.

She held her breath and waited until he disappeared along the corridor before she quickly ran to the room that would be her prison for the next three days of sailing. Now with the door shut behind her, Brendolyn let a shaken breath escape her. Her heart was hammering against the confines of her ribs.

Brendolyn took a look around the simple room. It was half the size of her queen mother's chamber, but held all the necessities. A bed, wash basin, wardrobe, and a small desk was pushed up against the farthest wall, and high overhead was a small round window—a gilded prison—it was much like all the other rooms she had been before, and placed at the farthest reaches away from her family.

She crawled upon the small bed, hugging herself as the silent tears fell from her eyes. Listening to the waves crashing against the ship, each sway unsettled her stomach. Brendolyn wished for Lahrs to return, she wanted his soothing presence to comfort her.

A gentle knock roused her. Brendolyn had not realized she had fallen asleep until the door slowly opened to the dimly lit room. She watched a young maid enter with a tray in hand and a small lamp that illuminated a faint yellow glow.

"Pardon my intrusion, miss. Sir Lahrs has been kept above deck, he instructed me to bring you some food." She was a timid little elf, with round violet eyes and long silvery blonde hair plaited away from her long thin face.

"Thank you." Brendolyn stood, watching from afar as the maid rested the tray atop the desk against the wall. There was a plate of cheeses, fruits, bread, and jams and her stomach grumbled.

The maid stepped back, bowing slightly, watching Brendolyn with curiosity. Feeling the unfamiliar eyes upon her, Brendolyn slowly turned. She let an awkward silence grow between them, to give the maid a chance to speak or to leave.

These moments the servants played became a game to Brendolyn, because without fail, the gardener to the kitchen cook would stand and watch her, like a prized horse for show. They all wanted the same thing, but they were all disappointed.

"I'm not going to sing," she said dully, suddenly irritated at the violet eyes that watched her. Brendolyn turned away, examining the food placed perfectly upon the plate.

"Lahrs instructed the cooks to not serve you meats, and to give you extra servings of pie."

Brendolyn smiled. "That is very kind of Lahrs."

"Do you believe that the Prince of Jorn is really very handsome?"

"I have seen a miniature that was sent to Father in his study; he said that Prince Barrow was just like his father. But I have not seen King Beaumont any more than the portrait that hangs in the library. They said he is very tall." Brendolyn smiled, seeing the maid light up, her violet eyes were glistening.

"You shall see both king and heir. Then when you return to Corad, you shall know for certain."

Brendolyn frowned. "Perhaps the prince is not handsome and the king is not tall."

"King Beaumont is the tallest man I have ever seen." Sir Varick's voice chilled the air.

He stood in the open doorway, leaning upon the frame as he looked in on the pair of them talking. He smiled at the maid, and Brendolyn could see the girl blush. A knot coiled in her stomach, but she steeled herself, standing straighter.

"You may go," she told the maid. She watched the young elf bow and scurry from the room.

Sir Varick sighed. "Spoil sport. She had very nice eyes."

Varick remained a solid force at the door. Brendolyn realized quickly; he could not enter. As her eyes quickly got a glimpse of the rune scratched at the base of the doorframe, carved into the wood, she realized it was a ward to keep unwanted guests from entering.

Lahrs had been there already.

"What do you want?" Brendolyn demanded.

She stared at the man who loomed in the doorway. He was no longer wearing his knighted tunic, but a plain linen shirt and a brushed leather doublet. His hair was falling around his eyes. In another world, he would be considered handsome.

But Brendolyn knew him in this one.

"You did not appear for dinner in the dining room, naturally I grew worried for you." He lifted his arm up to brace himself on the frame, keeping his footing as the ship swayed.

"I do not dine with them, you know that." She narrowed her eyes, holding herself firmly in place.

"True. You are locked away and guarded with wards and spells and enchantments. He keeps you sealed away, never to be touched." Varick squeezed the frame, his eyes scanning the wood, before falling back upon Brendolyn.

She grew nauseated at the sight of his look.

"You have no true business here. I must ask you to leave."

Varick sneered, his grip tightening on the frame of the door. "Foolish tricks meant to keep me out, little pigeon. One day he will forget to lock your cage, and that day you will be mine."

Brendolyn watched the veins in Varick's hand coil. He hissed, throwing back his hand, gripping it tightly.

"Try as you may, your simple cheap spells bought in the market cannot break his magick, Varick. He is an elf of pure blood, or had you forgotten?" Brendolyn asked, watching the knight cradling his injured hand.

Varick growled, wincing again as he turned away to leave.

Brendolyn began to breathe easier, her nails loosened from the palms of her hands, as deep crescents began seeping blood. Brendolyn quickly washed them away in the basin of water provided, splashing her face to cool her nerves.

CHAPTER

8

Sir Lahrs saw the man who cradled his hand as he returned to the dining hall. The small compartment where the royal family took their meals was alive with the scrape of knife and fork to plate and the distinct voices of each. Lahrs was seated near King Sabian and one of the men on his council, as they discussed formal papers sent to them weeks previous. He tried to pay attention, but the brown-haired knight who emerged from the door to take his seat beside Princess Lisetta set his teeth on edge.

"Oh, you are injured," Queen Natalia cooed from her place at the far end of the table. The sight of Varick's hand made his blood boil, he saw the knight smiling at the queen.

"It's nothing, just a small—" he began, to dissuade the queen of her worry, but as he spoke, his hand curled in on itself.

Lahrs stood abruptly, his chair scraping against wood, every eye at the table turned to him, but his eyes were locked on Varick.

"Sir, you are injured." Lahrs knew how to keep his tone calm. "Allow me to see to it."

Natalia clapped, thanking Lahrs in Felourian tongue as Lahrs walked around the table, watching Varick closely. They exited the dining hall in cordial manner, Lahrs stepped around the other knight as he led them into a spare room along the hall.

With the door suddenly shut, Varick did not have a chance to open his mouth before Lahrs had a grip on the front of his doublet.

"Touchy, touchy," Varick chuckled, trying to seem coy, but the pain in his hand made him wince.

"I have warned you, Varick..." Lahrs gritted his teeth.

Now Varick laughed heartily. "Warnings, spells, enchantments. You mock me with your stupid curses to protect her."

"It is my duty, Varick. Just as it is yours, or have you forgotten your vow?" Lahrs hissed.

Varick pushed Lahrs' hands away viciously, cradling his injury as the action sent jolts through his body. "Vow...I only vowed to Lisetta, she is the true heiress of Corad. She has the blood of the kings. Your welp, she is nothing. Just as her mother was nothing. What other value could she hold but a place to stuff your cock?"

Lahrs struck him hard across the face, his fist burned in agony from the blow, but he relished the pain. He welcomed the suffering that it caused Varick, who stumbled over. His wounded hand crippled against his chest, his other hand bracing the swelling flesh of his cheek where Lahrs had struck him.

"Speak ill of my lady again, or her mother, and I shall end your life in suffering," Lahrs said in a calm voice as he gripped the other knight's doublet tightly.

Varick chuckled, spitting blood from his mouth onto the floor at their feet, he stood straight to look the elf in the eyes.

"There he is, the always dutiful, always pious Lahrs. I see who you truly are. I have seen the darkness in you." Varick winced as he pushed away from him. "Perhaps you do not wish to share. Save her purity for yourself."

Lahrs gripped the crippled hand, ignoring Varick's shriek of pain. Clenching his jaw tight, he held the coiled, shriveling thing in his grip. "Do not look upon her. Do not speak her name. Provoke fear or unease in her, and I shall end your life. Remember that I am good to my word, that I take my vow to my death."

"I do not fear you."

Taking hold of the knight's nape, Lahrs gripped Varick hard, the crippled hand still held firmly in his grasp.

"Do not test my patience, Varick."

He felt the hot magick burn from his fingertips, as the hand he held straightened, returning to the way it belonged. It was agonizing; choosing the quicker healing was always more painful. Varick crumpled, gritting his teeth as the crippled hand straightened.

Varick stumbled, catching himself on the wall.

"Do we have an agreement?" Lahrs straightened his tunic, his voice was level and calm as it once was.

Varick ran a hand through his now moistened hair. "Yes."

It was the following morning when Lahrs found King Sabian standing at the wheel, watching the captain steer the ship through the channel between the realm of Entheas to the east, and the realm of Jorn to the west. Upon his approach, the king turned with a broad smile.

"Lahrs! The winds are on our side, we shall arrive before high noon tomorrow," Sabian exclaimed.

"Excellent." Lahrs nodded, following the king as he walked the length of the deck to the stern. Here, where there were no more crewmen to overhear them, Lahrs spoke freely. "Your Majesty, there is a matter I wish to discuss."

Sabian's eyes seemed to darken but forced a smile. "Yes, what is it, Lahrs?"

"Sir Varick has been overstepping his bounds," Lahrs began, watching over his shoulder for any interruptions. "As I have mentioned before, he has begun to give Princess Brendolyn improper attachment."

Sabian rubbed his beard. "Varick is my highest-ranking knight. Not only has he provided necessary guidance in the war room for dealing with thieves and traitors, he is vital in preparations to negotiate relations of war within this treaty."

"I am not saying he should step down from your war room, Your Majesty. But please…" Lahrs stepped a little closer to the king. "He makes Brendolyn uncomfortable. He enters her rooms unannounced and does not adhere to the vows of—"

"Lahrs, your own duty is her protection."

Lahrs stopped, astounded by the words he was hearing. "As her sworn knight, it is my duty to protect. I have seen first-hand the deficiency of Sir Varick's intentions and merit as a Knight of the Rose, I do not believe he is fit for protection of Princess Brendolyn or Princess Lisetta. To be given the liberty of rank, to take advantage of his position of power—"

Lahrs was treading very dangerous waters, he could sense the shift and change in the king's mood, but he held firm.

"Lisetta has not spoken to me on this."

"It is not towards Lisetta that he has made advances. Young maids have spoken of his liberties with them, and the flirtations."

"Allegations of such an alarming nature would surely have been brought forward," Sabian said thinly.

"But it is to Brendolyn that Varick has focused his designs. I cannot sit by and allow such a man the opportunity of ruining her."

"I will look more into the matter. Speak nothing of this until we return to Corad. I must focus on the treaty, this treaty must not fall through." Sabian patted Lahrs on the arm, leaving him to stand on the deck alone.

They arrived in Denorn the next morning. Stepping out onto the docks, King Sabian was aghast as they looked out at the few fishermen just in from their morning run for fish—not a welcome party in sight.

It was half an hour later that a gilded carriage arrived. Stepping out from the rig, a man dressed in furs approached where the King of Corad waited.

"What is the meaning of this?" Sabian demanded, looking around at the lack of proficiency.

The man huffed, out of breath, and straightened to bow and address the king before him. He wore a livery of opulence, the wealth of his master apparent.

"Lord Dean regrets that he is not here to welcome you…"

"We were expected," Sabian nearly shouts. Standing beside him is Sir Lahrs, and on the other side, Sir Varick.

"You are a day early, Your Majesty. They did not expect…" The man turned red and bowed again. "A carriage from my lord, to bring you to Hedgerig Estate."

Sabian looked at the carriage, his mouth parting in a sneer. "We are a party of eight, sir, that carriage only takes six."

Again, the man blushed.

"And my wife is great with child, she has attendants and servants. They shall be apart from her for how long while we wait in a house not prepared?" Sabian was growing impatient.

"We can call a wagon from the village to bring the servants along behind. Who are the others in your party?" the man asked then, looking from Sir Varick to Sir Lahrs.

"They may stay behind and wait for a second carriage, I shall go with my wife. This man here is knight for my daughter Lisetta." Sabian motioned for Sir Varick, who quickly left to see to his ward.

Lahrs did not move. After the man nodded, to relay the message to the carriage that waited, King Sabian turned to Lahrs.

"Keep her below decks, the ship will be docked until they restock supplies. The second carriage shall return for you shortly."

Lahrs nodded.

Brendolyn peaked over the edge of her book, she was meant to be reading to practice learning the Common Tongue, but the confusing words began to give her a headache. Now she looked at the man who was seated in the chaise chair opposite of where she sat lounging on her bed—Lahrs had fallen asleep.

At once, Brendolyn closed the book, swinging her legs over the edge of her bed and carefully stepping down, her eyes were watching the sleeping elf where he dosed, his nearly white blonde hair was falling along his collar.

She tiptoed across the floor, her gown gently scraping across as she hurried from the room before Lahrs noticed. Brendolyn was tired of waiting for the carriage, she was always waiting. Now it was nearly impossible when she could see and smell and hear the excitement of the town of Denorn right outside her little window.

Safely upon the docks, Brendolyn hurried down the steps, stumbling as the solid ground greeted her. She smiled, regaining her balance before following the small road that led into the town built on the edge of the sea.

Shops lined the road, carriages pulled by horses rocked side to side as they passed, she could see women in wool and furs and men in large hats. Brendolyn had never seen so many faces. Smells mingled together, the bakery to the fish market, the tannery—where they stretch the hide—and the stench that made her hold her nose from the sewer.

Brendolyn marveled at the beautiful hats in the shop window, decorated with colorful ribbons and feathers. As she got a glimpse of herself in the reflection, she turned away, turning to face another road. Her frivolity stopped, her heart sank as she saw across the lane a stall set up at the end of the row of merchants. There were cages of frightened birds, foxes, and other small animals that cowered away.

Her feet moved, drawing her closer to the merchant's stall. The merchant was nowhere in sight, but a voice was loud from within a large canvas tent. Her palms began to sweat, fear making her step away. But something caught her eye.

She gasped. Quickly stepping around the front of the stall at a larger cage just out of sight, her heart ached. She crouched down to see a man seated within.

Brendolyn looked at the man who was crouched in the cage. His body was bent uncomfortably in the small space, his body was covered by a patchwork of garments and covered in filth. Her heart climbed into her throat as she blinked away her tears.

A man caged like an animal.

She placed a hand on the bars, looking in at a pair of wide, bright green eyes. He grabbed the bar, just below where her hand held. He spoke, but she could not understand. She cursed herself for not taking her studies seriously and for not knowing any Common Tongue.

She shook her head, and she saw him shrink back, drawing his dirty hand away, but she grasped it. He held it there as she reached into her hair, pulling free the ribbon that held it partially back. She smiled, trying to remember, her mouth forming the blessing Lahrs had taught her. It was the one thing she could remember in Common Tongue.

"At first of the sun, favor find you," she said timidly, his eyes grew wider as she put her hands through the bars, wrapping the ribbon around his wrist. "As the day is done, favor find you." She wrapped the ribbon around once more. "In triumph, in sorrow, favor find you." Her eyes stung, tears threatened to fall from her eyes as she tied off the ribbon. She looked up to find his green eyes, *such green eyes*, watching her.

"Favor find you," she whispered.

"Brendolyn!" Lahrs' voice made her flinch. She wiped away her tears as she turned, seeing her elf knight running up the lane, his eyes wide as he reached her. He gripped her arms tightly. "Don't you ever run off like that again, do you understand?" he demanded.

Brendolyn took one last look at the man with green eyes, he held his hand on the bar, Brendolyn saw the ribbon there, her heart was beating madly.

Lahrs' voice softened as he pressed her to his side. "It's alright, but we must get back."

She let him guide her, falling farther and farther away from the cage as they walked, turning back once more before they turned along the lane. Brendolyn faced forward, keeping her eyes down to her feet. She let Lahrs guide her from the town, along the docks and to return to her rooms upon the waiting ship.

Lahrs shut the door, sighing heavily

"What were you thinking? This isn't Corad, Bren, you can't go wandering off in a foreign—"

Brendolyn looked up, her eyes now filled with tears. Lahrs had silenced, seeing her face. She broke into a sob when he wrapped his arms around her, his embrace was warm, welcoming and she clung to him tightly.

"There are many things wrong in the world, Bren...I am sorry I could not shield you from this forever," he whispered, placing a kiss on her head.

CHAPTER

9

Pavan watched the girl with dark hair and golden eyes being whisked away by the elf with silver-blonde hair—her eyes were so vivid—Pavan could never forget her expression.

Since leaving the stronghold in Hilvaer, he and Malcom had been treated as nothing more than the bags of goods that the merchant had also carted away. They were fed the scraps of the meals that the man Adnoran and his servants ate over the week-long journey. They were starved and cramped in the small cages, only brought out to relieve themselves by the road's edge. It was never long enough for their muscles to ease before being pressed back into the cold bars.

Denorn was a lively town, full of sights and colors. From his place within the bars, Pavan could see the townsfolk walk by, not one of them stopping to glance at the cages within. Pavan had seen only a few children stop and point, their guardian pulling them back with a sharp word of scolding—always in a dialect that Pavan couldn't quite translate.

It was much the same as the dark-haired girl approached him with her golden eyes. But Pavan had never seen her style of dress in the town, nor heard the dialect she used—it was entirely new—she was whisked away as all the other young people had. But the elf who came for her did not out of fear of him, but for fear of the place.

"What did she give you?" Malcom's voice whispered. Pavan winced as he turned his body to see Malcom in the cage behind him, his friend was leaning with his back to him, but it was the easiest way to talk without the merchant noticing.

"A ribbon. She took it from her hair and tied it around my wrist," Pavan told him, his eyes scanning the merchant's tent a few yards away.

"What was it that she said to you?" Malcom asked.

Pavan thought of her words, the struggle as she had formed the phrases she uttered under her breath. He was drawn to them as she spoke, Pavan was drawn to her voice that hinted at magick and the pained look upon her face as she looked at him.

"Just a prayer..." Pavan shrugged, tracing his thumb over the soft line of ribbon. The weave was fine and delicate, with golden flecks made into an intricate design.

"Oi, none of your chatter now," Sir Adrian shouted, his sharp tone causing Pavan to flinch.

Pavan shrunk, his large frame sinking deeper into the cage, he could feel the cold bars pressing into his bare skin, pressing into the healthy reminder of the man's brand. Seeing Sir Adrian approach the cage Pavan held his breath, clenching his hands tight as the burn rose within him, pushing it down deep. Sir Adrian's sharp glare looked at him through the bars between them and a sickening feeling settled hard in Pavan's gut.

"I've had you for long enough, perhaps I can find other uses for your body if these swine have no need for you." He began to reach his hand through the gaps of the metal when Pavan shrunk away.

A cough came from behind Sir Adrian. Pavan could see a gentleman over his shoulder. Sir Adrian retracted his hand, standing to turn to the newcomer.

The man was well built. Peering through the bars, Pavan watched the exchange between the two—they spoke in words he could not understand. His cheeks grew hot as the man looked over at him. He had bright orange eyes, dark copper hair that was pulled back out of his face, and a fair complexion of milky white in a galaxy of faint freckles. Pavan could see the difference in the way he dressed; it was not in the same woolen tunics, or the dark mangled boots from years of use that he saw everywhere, but dressed in fine silk, and his tunic was embroidered with colorful threads. He stood tall and assured, as he spoke with Sir Adrian. But Pavan's breath hitched, as the feeling of magick rolled off of him.

"I will clean them and have them prepared for you," Sir Adrian said, this time in Common Tongue, his open hand now hefting the weight of a small purse.

To this there was a firm shake of the head as the man frowned. He looked at Pavan directly as he spoke.

"I will take them both now."

His tone was deliberate, enchanting. At once Sir Adrian bowed, shouting behind him to the servants he kept. "Draw up the papers for the gentleman, Fiern. Lord Brous will be leaving directly."

A thin servant scurried into the tent.

"May I have the key?" Lord Brous' tone made the merchant stop dead, he turned a shade of scarlet.

"It is unwise to allow them such liberties until your servant can come collect them, Lord Brous." Sir Adrian shook his hair tussling it about, flakes falling to the shoulder of his tunic.

"My new property shall learn obedience at once, unless you swindle me by selling me maimed properties." Lord Brous spoke with a firm voice, making the merchant stutter.

"They are of peak health for such a quality of human found in the northern shores, sir. I would not insult you, upon my honor." Sir Adrian drew the long chain from around his neck, offering it to the man in silk's waiting palm.

"We shall see then, won't we." Lord Brous dismissed him, his grip firm on the key.

Sir Adrian disappeared into the tent nearby.

"My name is Thad," Lord Brous said as he knelt to unlock the thick iron bars, it swung open with a groan and Pavan shrunk further back.

On closer inspection, Thad Brous was not human—Pavan could see slanted back points of his ears. Magick buzzed around Lord Brous as he leaned down, offering a hand to Pavan.

"Please, take my hand. I assure you there is peace."

It tasted like honey in his mouth, hearing the words that the faie spoke. He used words laced with magick, but the magick had no effect on Pavan.

"I do not need your peace," Pavan hissed as he gripped the bars, pulling himself forward, quieting the loud thump of his heart as he emerged from the constriction of the cage, his knees wobbled as he stood. A hand quickly gripped under his arm, keeping him upright. Thad quickly drew away as soon as Pavan was steadied. In the quick moment, Pavan felt the strength of the faie in the unmovable stance.

"I must retrieve your friend, will you be alright to stay there?" he spoke low.

Pavan watched him move on swift limbs, rounding the large cage he had been held in, to the one where Malcom crouched. A sigh of relief left Pavan as Malcom was helped out to stand beside where Pavan stood. Pavan's legs began to cramp, but he stood, holding the bars of the cage behind him for support.

"Here is the cart. It shall fit you both, I believe." Thad tucked a hand under Malcom's arm.

A horse pulling a wagon was waiting just along the lane. It was being led by a man who was dressed in similar fashion, but not as opulent, with his long dark hair braided back away from his face. Malcom winced. Pavan could see the discomfort on his friend's features as he was eased up into the cart.

Sir Adrian emerged but he was not alone, he was joined by a man not as large but red in the face, angrily stomping over to them.

"Not so fast..." the other merchant stated gruffly.

"I have made my purchase, sir. Your partner has taken my coin," Thad stated.

With his great bulk, the merchant placed a hand on the hilt of a dagger. Thad stepping between Pavan and the merchants.

"I will not sell my properties to a filthy half breed faie. Get off my stall."

Thad's voice was calm. "I have made my purchase."

Thad turned, showing his back to the merchant.

Anger made Sir Adrian's face go nearly purple, Pavan flinched as a large hand gripped Thad's shoulder. The faie turned, eyeing the merchant as the profanities grew louder and more vulgar. Cursing of being swindled in an unfair trade.

Remembering the death of Iosef, and the man in bronze that held such power over them, Pavan reacted. Gripping the wrist of the large merchant and prying the large hand from Thad's clean garments, Pavan wanted to break the thick meaty wrist under his grip, knowing it would easily break under the right pressure.

Magick tasted bitter on Pavan's tongue, churning darker, deeper.

"Leave," Thad's voice cut through, it was hurried and laced with magick.

In a moment, the merchants were gone without a word. Pavan was left to stand in the center of the stall, with Thad close beside him and Malcom leaning on the closest table for support.

Pavan was hot and overwhelmed as panic rose in him as he watched Sir Adrian step back. Pavan breathed, trying to silence the raging fire within him but it was bubbling up, ready to boil over. A firm grip held his arm—it was the same strong hand that held him before. Thad's grip was uncannily strong.

"Pavan, you must breathe."

He could hear Malcom's voice, but the thoughts began to enter into his mind, dark unwanted thoughts after he grasped the merchant's thick wrist.

"Ease your thoughts...*breathe.*"

Like a cold washing over him, Pavan breathed sharply, his eyes came to lock on Thad, who stood before him. His vibrant orange eyes were welcoming, calming the dangerous fire within Pavan.

"There now," Thad spoke calmly, smiling to one side of his face in a crooked grin. "We should return to my camp, it is not far from here."

"Where are you taking us?"

"In good time, Pavan. I shall answer all of your questions. For now, if you please..." Thad motioned for the wagon.

Pavan felt faint, his heart rate slowing as exhaustion ached in his bones. He crawled into the cart, collapsing beside his friend, who at once checked his pulse.

Pavan's muscles flexed, every inch of his body was rolling in fiery heat and pain seared his brain. Pavan closed his eyes, as the rocking of the cart sent his stomach in a tumble, he gulped back the urge to vomit, breathing to calm his nerves.

"Rest." A gentle timber of voice drifted to meet him. Pavan blinked hard, bringing Thad into focus.

Stomach settled, his eyes became heavy against the shift and sway of the cart. Nestled back against the sacks of goods and with a cape now draped around him, warmth wrapped around Pavan as sleep found him. But in his sleep, there was only the smell of the sea.

Malcom watched Pavan closely.

They arrived at the shoreline, not long after departing from the merchant's stall. Out of the noise and smells of the city, there was nothing but the crash of waves upon the shoreline. They could hear the seagulls call from high above them in the sails of a great ship—the ship was smaller than the great galleons that docked in harbor.

After giving a heavy purse to the man with the wagon, Thad disappeared beyond a great tent, leaving Malcom to sit with Pavan near a large growing fire. It was just after midday, but the cool breeze of the sea against their partially naked bodies made the warmth of the fire a relief.

Malcom watched Pavan stare blankly over the water. His gaunt skin grew more and more pale as the hour progressed. He wanted to look at the wound upon his friend's shoulder, but his mouth felt dry, and he was unable to bring himself to ask. He saw the withdrawn look, the one that he had seen years ago, after Pavan had returned from Paris. It was the summer he saw the greatest change in his friend, it was the summer that Malcom knew what had happened to Pavan while at school there.

"Pavan," Malcom breathed, catching a glimpse of those green eyes his words caught in his throat.

Pavan's gaze slid away, back over the great sea.

From the fold of the tent, Thad emerged again with a bundle of linens in his hands. He was dressed in darker clothes, made of wool, and wearing a dark green quilted doublet that made the orange of his hair brighter. He stopped nearest to Malcom, offering him the bundle.

"Here are some garments. They are little more than under things, but they shall keep out the chill enough until we can return to my home."

Malcom took the clothes, but said nothing.

"I know you do not trust me," Thad said softly.

He sat nearby, watching Malcom rummage through the pile, pulling a rumbled tunic over his head before finding one that would fit Pavan. He tossed the found garment to Pavan, who clutched the linen in his hands, but did not move to put it on.

Thad watched Pavan particularly. It was clear that there was something in the look akin to perturbation, as if he was waiting for Pavan to fall, so that he could catch him again. Malcom remembered the quickness of Thad when Pavan was first helped out of the cage that held them.

"Our last few weeks have not been kind," Malcom admitted, catching the orange eyes flicker again towards Pavan.

"No. I know they have not been kind to you, Malcom." There was sadness with Thad's words. "That is why you shall be given the choice."

"Choice?" Malcom's voice astonished even himself.

"I offer you freedom." Between them the fireplace crackled as a log fell into the embers. Thad sighed, finding the words as he gazed into the fire. "You may walk free of this camp and my company with gold and your papers."

Malcom looked to Pavan, but his friend would not look away from the water, leaving Malcom the only one to engage with the faie in conversation.

"What is our other choice?"

"Sail across the great sea, into Entheas. I shall take you into the realm of the elven kingdom." Thad reached into the front pocket of his doublet. "I believe this belongs to you."

Taking the folded parchment, Malcom felt his chin shake, looking down at the familiar writing that he had seen Iyda write in her father's study. Malcom had watched her do it, had seen the scrawl of her hand as she begged for help.

"Iyda," Malcom whispered. "She wrote to Meilyr, imploring him for aid."

Thad nodded. "Here I have come in his name, Malcom."

"Where were you, when the soldiers slaughtered her father?" Pavan's voice cut the air, drawing their eyes towards him. Pavan glared hard at the faie. "Where were you, when they shaved our hair and starved us? Where were *you* when that man—"

Malcom felt like he was hit in the gut, watching the anger written on his friend melt into anguish, and seeing the swell of tears fall from Pavan's wide green eyes as he gripped the tunic in his hand until his knuckles were white. All at once, Pavan stood, storming towards the tent where he ducked inside. Malcom wanted to follow, but a strong hand gripped his wrist.

"Leave him," Thad cautioned.

"I can't let him suffer alone." Malcom felt tears burst forth, anxiously eyeing the tent where Pavan had retreated.

Thad lessened his grip, but did not pull away. "He must rest. That is the safest place for him right now, Malcom. Let him rest. The time will come and he will speak."

"You want me to trust you, Thad, but I cannot trust you until *he* does."

"You must rest too, Malcom." Thad released him, giving him the ability to retreat, but Malcom hesitated.

Putting his face into his hands, Malcom found himself shaking—he was trembling to his core. After everything that had happened since the night of the open mic night at the pub, he had been running on adrenaline. He forced himself back to what had happened with Iyda, her father, and then in Hilvaer. He had been alone in a dark room, after being shaved and washed in ice cold water. Malcom had feared the worst for Pavan, believing that they had killed him.

Wiping his face, Malcom bit on his fist while he wept.

"Hilvaer is unrelenting. I know what it is you have faced, Malcom," Thad spoke softly. "In Entheas, I promise peace. In Entheas, there is rest."

"I cannot lose him," Malcom's words were a breath. "After all of this, I cannot lose him now."

CHAPTER

10

Denorn, Jorn.

Brendolyn could hear the loud music that came up over the balcony from below. They had arrived at the great estate of Hedgerig a few hours before the dinner was to be served. They slipped in unnoticed, and now having been dressed in clean garments, her hair brushed and her tears dried, Brendolyn wondered at the party happening below. Sitting in the chaise beside the opened door to the balcony, a soft melancholy washed over her.

"Brendolyn," Sir Lahrs voice drifted through, causing her to turn her attention from the open window to the elf who sat in the high-backed chair near the low burning fire. He held one of the many books he had brought with them on this trip, he had been reading aloud from it, but Brendolyn had lost interest.

"Sorry, um..." she thought hard, standing to pace as her mind fought to form the words from her lips. She was terrible at Common Tongue. "Why do you keep alone? Of sorted fancies your company makes. Things without remedy should be without regard. What is done is done." She fumbled around the feeling of the words in her mouth, then when she turned back to face Sir Lahrs, she groaned.

"Your diction is perfect but your memory is horrid." Lahrs smiled.

Brendolyn sat down hard, her long onyx hair falling around her as she hid her face in her palms.

"I shall never be able to speak fluently. This is hopeless," Brendolyn groaned, her tone now familiar with the mother tongue of Corad. She refused to look up again as her heart wrenched. Tears sprang to her eyes.

"You are very eager now, what is your change of tone, Bren?" Lahrs asked, forgetting the book at his side. "Before, I could barely enter the room with your lessons in hand, and now it was nearly insisted upon as soon as we had arrived."

Brendolyn sat straighter, trying to ignore the loud laughter from below, the noise making her head hurt. But being vexed by the constant parties and dances and feasts she had never once attended now felt like nothing compared to the world she had seen beyond these walls. Her thoughts raced back to the man in the cage and his emerald eyes.

She blushed hot, looking over to Lahrs who awaited her answer.

"It is time I grew from my childish tone and respected my studies. There is much that could be gained from knowing all the languages of the realms." Brendolyn picked at the fine stitching of her gown, she was trying to keep composed and willing the tears to remain at bay.

She had cried enough that day.

"Bren..." Lahrs knelt before her, taking her trembling hands in his.

Brendolyn had refused to talk during the carriage ride from the harbor to the estate. She was eager to stay hidden in her rooms, and there was no defiance when she was not permitted to join the festivities below, she acted as they expected her to—this is what worried Lahrs most.

"I shall go in the morning and inquire after him. Would that set your mind at ease?" Lahrs asked, his voice gentle.

Her eyes widened, taking in the elf before her. She saw his gentle gaze of soft gray eyes and fine lines around his warm smile. She said nothing, but embraced him. She held him close, allowing the tears to slip from her lashes.

"Buy him, if you can. Set him free of that prison, Lahrs," she said at once, pulling away from him.

"I shall, if he is still there, but if he is not..." He hesitated, looking down at her vibrant face now full of hope. "Brendolyn, if he is already sold, there is nothing in my power to free him."

She understood. Brendolyn knew that was possible, but she wanted to linger, to hold tightly to the grasp of her hope. Silently saying a prayer for the man with emerald eyes, he nodded, knowing the chance was small.

Lahrs stood. "Now, I must go see to your dinner."

"And some wine?" Brendolyn asked, catching the elf smirk before he slipped through the door of her apartment.

She dozed, leaning back against the chaise. Brendolyn felt the chill of the cool breeze reach her through the open window. Her eyelids grew heavier, waiting for the return of the knight with her meal.

Hearing the door click shut, Brendolyn started. She sat up at once, her heart hammered as she looked about the empty room—there was no one in sight.

"Hello?" she called out, but there was no response.

Brendolyn went to the window, hearing the loud voices and drunken laughter over the din of the music from below and her head began to pound. At once she shut the balcony door, closing out the chill and the noise. Her rooms were silent about her. She felt a sense of eyes watching her, her ears twitching as she turned to a fraction of sound—a door shutting from down the hall.

Heart hammering, Brendolyn went to her door, placing her ear to the wood. Feet shuffled about on the other side, thick boots on the stone floor. They stopped just outside and her breath caught as she stepped back.

Every hair on her arms raised, reaching up to the base of her neck she felt the chill again—it was like a million eyes were upon her at once. Brendolyn stepped back again and again, her gown catching on the hook of a table, ripping the fabric and sending her to stumble back, her footing was lost and she found herself on the floor.

Just as the door to her apartments opened, Lahrs stepped through with a tray in hand. Seeing her on the floor, he rushed forward, placing the tray on the chaise to help Brendolyn to her feet. She was shaking, looking around wildly, but the feeling was now gone.

"There is so much," she gasped, looking around her. Lahrs placed his hands on her cheeks, bracing her head, keeping her from thrashing her neck this way and that.

"Breathe," he instructed, guiding her through deep calming breaths, his hands remaining on her cheeks.

Brendolyn followed his guidance, slowly letting air in, then out through her mouth. This was helping calm her nerves and quiet the senses that overwhelmed her.

"I heard someone enter, or so I thought. Then there were voices. There were so many voices, Lahrs."

"A new place will have new sounds," Lahrs nodded, now guiding her to sit beside him on the chaise chair. "Sing, it will calm you."

She hesitated. Brendolyn looked nervously to the door but Lahrs held her hand.

"No one is nearby, they cannot hear you, Bren," he whispered.

She sang, her voice soft and lilting, and as she sang her body relaxed. Leaning into Lahrs, Brendolyn welcomed the warmth and comfort that he provided. At last, her nerves were gone, her eyelids now heavy.

"There now." Lahrs brought her food tray towards her. "Eat, then we can talk if you would like."

Brendolyn took a bite of the bread. It was dry on her tongue, but she swallowed it down.

"Is King Beaumont aware of the things that happen in Jorn?" she asked, looking up to Lahrs' gray eyes.

The elf sighed heavily. "I believe there are many things that have gone unchecked. Jorn rules under the guidance of a council. Unlike Corad, there are many who stand between the crown of the king and his governing cities."

"How could he be so blind..."

A knock at the door, made them both pause. Lahrs stood at once, opening the door. Brendolyn watched as a leering smile greeted them both on the other side. It was Sir Varick.

"Brendolyn is requested," he said, his voice amused, his brown eyes scanning over the princess where she stood.

"She is not dressed for a party. For what purpose is she needed?" Lahrs asked, crossing his arms over his chest, standing between his ward and the man at the door.

Varick scoffed. "It was requested that she be formally introduced to his lord and lady of the house. She was summoned, I have come to fetch her."

Brendolyn stepped further behind Sir Lahrs, letting her gaze fall to the floor.

"We shall be down," Lahrs affirmed. When Sir Varick did not make to move, Lahrs was more assertive. "Leave us, sir. I have every capability to bring her down myself."

Varick frowned and turned on his heel.

When he was safely away, Lahrs turned to Brendolyn, she was hot, she had never been requested like this before. At once, Lahrs looked her over before they made their way from the apartments. Brendolyn followed the elf closely as they made their way through the corridors, descending the steps until they reached the parlor—loud, boisterous laughter greeted them.

Brendolyn felt a flutter in her stomach as she emerged into the room, following closely behind Lahrs. He walked with confidence towards the party that had congregated around, drinks in hand. She first saw her queen mother, perched on a sofa, a fan cooling her, held in a gloved hand. Then her father came into view, his eyes watching her warily as they approached. There was the lady of the house, Lady Elhain, she stood beside her husband, each of them had golden hair, were tall, and dressed in fine silk brocades.

Her heart was aflutter as Brendolyn was guided forward by the gentle hand of Lahrs. She bent in a delicate curtsy, as she practiced many times before.

Lady Elhain smiled, looking down her thin nose at Brendolyn. "What a charming child...how old are you, my dear?" She spoke with a thick accent, her mouth forming words that Brendolyn did not quite understand.

Brendolyn felt her cheeks grow hot, looking quickly up at Lahrs, who leaned forward slightly to address the lord and lady.

"She does not understand Common Tongue well enough to converse, but she is proficient in Jornedian tongue." He smiled briefly.

Lady Elhain began again. "You are very young." She was speaking her native tongue, and Brendolyn sighed.

She nodded to the lady with another slight bow. The lady chuckled.

"Speak up girl, we cannot hear you if you look at the floor," Lord Dean boasted, his drink in hand sloshing around in the slender glass he held. Brendolyn grasped her fingers behind her back.

"Forgive me, sir," she said in her light tone.

Lady Elhain smiled. "She is charming. How old are you, girl?"

"Fourteen," Brendolyn replied, her legs were starting to shake.

"Bless the goddess, a young woman indeed!" Lady Elhain was all in shock, her slender hand placed firmly to her heavily layered bodice. "And you wear your hair down so freely, how extraordinary. Are you not out yet, my dear?"

Sabian stepped forward. "She is at an age where the formal fashions are desired, but with Princess Lisetta unmarried, it is not customary for the youngest daughter to be presented in company—"

Lady Elhain tried to follow, forcing her smile as she looked the young princess up and down. "Your customs are elusive in these matters, King Sabian, I believe your own lords and ladies do not follow the old ways as closely as yourself."

Sabian flustered. "Certain circumstances of her heritage make it more ideal to screen her birth with concealment of those certain attributes that would cause gossip…"

Lady Elhain opened her fan. "Certainly while in Jorn you can make an exception. Perhaps use of one of my maids should suffice in making your stay more beneficial in presenting her to our king."

Here Brendolyn saw the shift in her father's features. His calmness fractured, as the woman continued with talk of dress making and costs of silks.

"It is out of the question," Sabian snapped.

Lady Elhain was nearly horror stricken. Extending her fan to cool her face as she eyed the King of Corad sharply.

"We appreciate your generosity," began Queen Natalia, coming to her husband's aid. "But it is impossible for Brendolyn to dress at the height of fashion as her sister does. Our way is not common, but it is how we have designed it, my lady."

Annoyance fluttered in the Lady Elhain, she kept at her fan while she eyed Brendolyn more closely. "She is a very pretty girl, perhaps you shall change your mind when she is in Jorn. There is where the height of society influences all."

Prolonged silence crashed around them.

"She is of faie birth," Lahrs gritted through his teeth, bringing the eyes of the room onto him. He let the gasps subside before he went on in a hastened tone, "Respectfully, your guests ask that you do not impute on them any longer with talk of alterations of our customs. With respect to your home and your king, it is for the better of our kingdom's protection and privacy that you not sour the beginnings of peace with your impudence."

Every look in the room remained on Lahrs.

Lady Elhain was flushed. "Well, you are outspoken for a servant."

"He is a Knight of the Rose, Elhain," her husband whispered. Her expression did not change from one of disregard, but she examined Lahrs coolly.

"To be sure, she is quite thin, don't you believe so," Lady Elhain then said, looking Brendolyn over more closely before whispering to her husband like she was no longer in the room.

Lord Dean nodded, grumbling something into his glass as he tried to look away.

From her seat at the sofa, Queen Natalia became quite roused by the sudden shift of temperament in their hosts. She fanned herself quicker, looking from Brendolyn to the lord and lady that watched her.

"She is such a darling girl. I have never seen a more well-tempered and easy child, aside from our Lisetta, but I am always partial to my children."

Lord Hedgerig swallowed his drink, while Lady Elhain smiled.

"Does she eat? I cannot but sense there is a strange gauntness to her complexion, was she an ill child?" Lady Elhain addressed Queen Natalia, suddenly unable to look at Brendolyn at all.

Brendolyn's cheeks grew hot, standing attentive as she should while the lady of the house ignored her completely.

Queen Natalia's fan stopped. She shifted on the sofa as she looked the lady over with a curt smile. "She is in the peak of health, Lady Elhain. Not a complaint or ill-natured a day of her life." She reached dutifully over, Brendolyn looked at her queen mothers' hand as she felt a hand at her lower back.

Again, Lahrs spoke freely. "Forgive me. I should really return Princess Brendolyn to her rooms, she has not finished her dinner and we have lingered here long enough."

Brendolyn breathed a sigh of relief. She squeezed her queen mothers' hand in return as she turned when Lahrs instructed. But her attention was stilled when the Lady Elhain chuckled softly, leaning to her husband to whisper in not a very concealed tone at all.

"To bring such a child out…to think of what King Beaumont should say upon hearing of this slight of propriety…"

"Hush my dear, we shall speak no more of this."

And with that, Brendolyn was out of the room. She was hurried along the hall, Lahrs' firm grasp on her elbow was nearly painful, but she was glad of it. Her cheeks were growing hot, her throat burned and her eyes began to fill with tears as they reached the upper landing.

"Insufferable…" Lahrs muttered, his tone seething as they reached the floor leading to the apartments where they slept. He made it into the door and slammed shut, raking a hand through his silvery-gold hair.

Brendolyn sat down hard on the edge of the nearest chair, her chest was heaving as she fought for control, every breath burned as her eyes stung with tears.

"She is like all the others, Lahrs," she muttered. She smoothed the skirts of her gown, but the wrinkles remained where her hands had gripped so tightly as to crease the fine silk.

The elf had turned on his heel, he was pacing the space before the shut window, his hands placed firmly behind his back.

"She is a gilded hog not worthy to claim the title of duchess," Lahrs seethed. "Such disregard, such outright vanity to presume she could insult you in such a way."

Brendolyn felt a warmth for the knight who always sought to defend her, but the princess knew of the effect her birth mother's breeding had shined ill on her own presentation to others. It was an ill-conceived notion about the faie. She knew how much the heritage of the faie were thought of only as thieves, con artists, beggars, and all things contrite.

"But Lady Elhain only speaks her own truth."

Lahrs turned to Brendolyn. "Do not excuse her behavior, no matter where her beliefs made birth. There is no right in belittling any of Ehnarea's creatures. We all live and we all die. We laugh and cry just the same as any who walk the realms."

"Do you believe King Beaumont to be of such prejudice to the faie?" Brendolyn asked then, after a long moment of silence.

Lahrs sighed, pinching the bridge of his nose. "I have not met with him in many years, and the rare moments of conversation were in formal chatter. I do not know, Bren."

Brendolyn stood tall, looking now to the forgotten tray of food, her stomach was uneasy. She was no longer hungry, but she grew tired.

Lahrs drew up his horse to a slow trot, dismounting as he neared the merchant's stall. It was early, and he could see the canopies of canvas being dismantled. His heart sank in his chest.

"Hello there." He nodded, looking at the young elf who stood rolling up the rope used to tether the canvas down.

"Good morrow, sir. We are all sold out, come back in a month and we should have more birds for the ladies of those great houses," the elf spoke in a timid voice. Lahrs approached, his eyes scanning the nearly empty stall, taking in the large cages, seeing them vacant.

Lahrs waved him off. "Of course, but I have an inquiry about two in particular. They were sold yesterday."

With a flush, the young elf hung up the rope, shifting his attention now to the hooks that were used to line the canvas front, holding it in place.

"Please, I just need to know if they were sold. Particularly the pale one at the front," Lahrs lowered his tone, his eyes scanning the stall, looking for the merchant. It was never spoken of, or questioned so openly. Lahrs knew the customs of these people. He understood the unmentionable affairs that happened on this street.

Nervously, the young elf looked back, towards the large tent, where the master no doubt remained counting his gold. Those eyes swiftly turned again to his.

"A faie, he came late yesterday. He bought them both with the purest of shielk glass, my master was honorable in the transaction, but his business partner was... less than pleased."

Lahrs frowned. Shielk glass was rare in these parts—it was a rare stone coming from the mines of Entheas, and highly valued on the market. "I see..."

A whisper, "He took them in his wagon. Took them to the shores of the harbor, I saw his ship. He comes from across the sea."

"Thank you."

Lahrs walked away, giving a last glance back to the elf who hurried about his tasks, keeping his attention away from Lahrs as he followed the lane down towards the sea front. He walked along the path that the fisherman used to reach the smaller docks.

He found the familiar sails, and the crew that readied the ship to make the journey across the sea. He approached the tent that had been set up nearest the shore, just as a familiar form emerged from within, leaning over to take up one of the many large bundles. He had dark copper hair messy from sleep and shoulders wrapped in a woolen cowl over the dark jacket. Bringing a sack up over his shoulder, he stood to face where Lahrs approached.

"Well, aren't you far from home." The faie smirked, the morning breeze rustling through his hair.

Lahrs looked at the ship. "You are on an errand from Meilyr?"

"He received a letter from Iyda, it was urgent." Thad's orange eyes shifted, glancing up to the sails. "But they have been secured. Two men shall be far from these shores by midday."

"It is dangerous to enter the port without papers, Thad."

"This was important, Meilyr accepted the risk. I accepted this risk." Stepping closer to Lahrs, the faie kept his voice low.

Lahrs shook his head. "A risk too great for you to come alone, Thaddeus, not on this errand. Svein would not accompany you, nor would Lilja?"

Thad scoffed. "They are busy preparing for the great hunt. I was free to make the crossing, no other has the skill to sail the ships through the summer winds."

"You must leave at once, before you are detected. Do not wait for the tides. Sail out now," Lahrs told him.

"Why are you here, Lahrs? Why are you in Jorn and not locked away in Corad with your princess?" Thad stood so near, Lahrs could see the flecks of gold in those orange eyes. Magick was vibrating through him, it was an aura that drew those closest to the faie inward.

"Not here, I cannot tell you here." Lahrs shook his head. "When I return to Ledenjour, then I shall explain all."

"When shall you return to us, then, one month? One year? We have seen you far less and less as the princess gets older."

Lahrs clenched his jaw. "You know I cannot be away from her for long; she is my charge. It is my duty—"

"*Duty*," Thad hissed, his voice was cutting with the cold sea air. "You pledged your duty to Meilyr long before this girl was born. It is your duty to Meilyr that should come first."

"That is not fair, Thad."

Thad rolled his eyes. "Then leave, return to that princess. I shall manage alone. As I have done."

Before the faie could get two steps away, Lahrs reached out, gripping Thad's upper arm. His bright orange eyes were sharp, piercing through Lahrs, filling him with regrets.

"Do not blame the girl. She needs my protection."

Thad smirked, his mouth pulling sideways. "Perhaps you are right, after all. But would your duty survive should the princess fall into the hands of those that would strip her of her innocence..."

Lahrs yanked his hand away, glaring at Thad.

"She will not stir again."

Thad closed the distance between them, his face now only inches from Lahrs'. Flecks of gold flared brighter in Thad's orange eyes, his lip twitched into a frown.

"A faie girl, Lahrs," he whispered harshly. "Your king is a fool to bring her into this realm, with those here that would not hesitate to snatch her from her bed."

"She will be safest with me."

"Not until she is in Entheas. But even then...How long before the king of this realm has greed enough to take from our shores?"

Lahrs frowned. "I must return to my duty, Thad. I expect to see your two companions singing your songs by the next great hunt."

A wide grin split the faie's lips, a grin of mischief and mirth. Thad reached out, clasping a hand to Lahrs' shoulder.

"Favor find you, Lahrs."

"Favor find you."

CHAPTER

11

It was cold with the bitter wind of winter.

Isaac was huddled against the warmth of his mother. As the wagon jostled over the stone and ice, Isaac felt afraid. Clasping tighter to the firm body beside him, he looked up to see the kind green eyes looking down at him.

"Do not be afraid, my loves," she whispered, her long brown hair curling around her face. His mother was beautiful.

Isaac nodded firmly, but the fear lingered.

Beside him, a smaller frame was clinging to him. Isaac turned to see a mirrored face, a young boy with dark hair and emerald eyes—Eyes that were terrified—Isaac at once grasped his brothers' hand, holding tight. He looked out beyond the bitter wind and fall of snow to the large gate that loomed before them, its white stone jutting out from the darkness of the trees, and a large wooden door.

His body trembled as the gate lowered.

Pavan was not sure he wanted to remember. He did not want to think of the day he left, nor the people who had been abandoned as he found anger. Pavan could feel the simmering heat as it tingled in his fingertips, he could taste the cold copper on his tongue, so much anger was seeping through the tiny cracks of his memories. It was anger fueled by fear, the fear of a little boy running in the woods.

Startled by the sudden clang of metal, he was aware that he had lost himself in thought, he was trapped in the spiraling loop before now being reanimated in the world.

Pavan threw himself back, catching himself on stone. He blinked hard, pushing back the wave of tears that spilled from his eyes, his hands grasping at the mossy rock beneath him—he was no longer in the wagon.

A coolness flooded the woodsy air. Here the trees were dense and the clouds that loomed overhead spoke of rain. Rock formations jutted out from the thickest of the trees, Pavan could just make out the peaks of a mountain that jutted up into the low drifting clouds. It felt like a dream.

Pavan's breathing slowed, as he felt the air caress his cheek. Magick hung around them, mingling with the wetness in the air. Pavan could taste the tang of it on his tongue, making his teeth hurt.

He was kneeling in the rubble. It was the ruin of a statue, a long-forgotten deity in the walled-in-shrine, overrun with weeds and vines. Pavan heaved in a breath, seeing the fallen statue's face—he had been here before.

Ledenjour.

It was a blur for Pavan when he slept on the shores of Jorn, feverish and in a stupor as he watched the waves crash against the sand. He thought he dreamt of the singing, the voice that always found him when he closed his eyes.

It was only the wind.

He remembered stumbling onto the deck of the ship, a small vessel that shifted beneath his feet. Uneasiness and nausea kept Pavan from watching the progression of the days they spent bobbing up and down and swaying from side to side against the waves.

Pavan hated the water, and the unpredictable winds that tossed them. But now, he was safe on land. Brought in a daze to the land once more, Pavan slept again. He slept away the cruel ache of his mind in the back of the wagon along with the dried bags of goods, leaning up against the barrels that creaked against the restraints of the ropes that tied them together.

Dreams plagued him, fusing the realities of this world with the old. Pavan raised a hand, running his fingertips against the shaved curve of his skull.

"Pav!" Malcom's voice shouted.

Malcom stood behind Thad at the crumbling archway, they were watching Pavan closely. Thad stopped Malcom from crossing the threshold.

"Move aside," a female voice carried over them.

She was fierce, with long braided hair of a silvery blonde, angular features, and a strong violet gaze. She was looking down her nose at Pavan. Pavan saw her pointed ears, adorned with little metal rings on her face, her eyes. He would have thought he dreamed her, but now she stood before him, very much real. She was a phantom of his past.

"Lilja." He spoke her name, as the vision of a young elf girl emerged into his mind. Now, the woman stood before him, hand on her sword.

She paused, scanning him with her violet eyes. Pavan stepped up, nearing the entrance of the shrine. Without hesitation, Lilja drew the blade from the sheath, the point of the sharp edge pressed into the curse of Pavan's throat.

"Lilja, this is not necessary," Thad said firmly, placing a hand on the elf woman's leather braced forearm.

"Bring them," she ordered, her glare lethal.

Pavan stumbled as he stepped across the threshold of the shrine, his limbs going stiff with every step. Malcom was beside him then, with a cloak wrapped around him.

"Are you alright?" Malcom asked, in a hushed tone.

Trembling, Pavan shook his head. "I don't know. It's all jumbled."

Malcom stood closer, warily. "You began to panic in the wagon. At first I thought you were dreaming, but then your eyes were open, and you were shouting in a strange language, before you jumped from the wagon to run to that place."

Pavan gulped. "I wasn't dreaming...I was remembering."

Ahead of them, the elf looked back at them. "Come on, Meilyr is waiting!"

They walked through the small thicket of trees, emerging into the beginnings of the small village, safely concealed within the walls of Ledenjour. It stood the same in Pavan's memories, exactly as he left it all those years ago.

Stepping onto the street, he was looking up at the image of his past.

Stone was the first used source in the village, each brick beneath their feet chiseled down by hand, worn smooth by the hand carts, horses hooves, and centuries of villagers walking over them. It was difficult to decipher the old and the new, each added home and shop built into the joints of the original buildings. Stone bases curved as the road did, joining the wooden slats of the walls, and the carved doors, beneath the thatched roofs.

Everywhere they turned, Pavan saw many faces emerge to look at them from windows and shop doors. The children that played in the street all stopped to stare as they walked, following behind the tall elf.

Coming now to the center of the town, they entered into the large keep, through the tall doors, and into the great room where fire roared in three separate hearths. Ornately carved pillars stood holding up the large roof above. Tables lay out down the long hall, all with platters of food. A minstrel strummed a lively tune as many who mingled about enjoyed the lavations of a fine meal.

At the top of the hall, on a large pile of furs upon the steps to a platform, sat a man with dark eyes and a kind young face. But a closer look into his eyes would reveal his age and wisdom. He sat watching them approach, his hair chiming as he moved from the small beads and loops of metal worked into the many thick and thin plaits that fell the length of his body. This man, Pavan presumed, must be Meilyr.

Pavan and Malcom stopped, just behind Thad, watching as Lilja approached the man seated before them. She leant down to whisper in his ear, as she did, the man's eyes locked on Pavan, growing wide as the she-elf spoke.

The man stood, his hair and clothes like chimes as he approached Pavan immediately. Grabbing hold of his face, turning him this way and that.

"These long years have not been kind to you."

Pavan blinks back the coming of tears, recognizing the voice that speaks to him now. Meilyr was one of the men that had cared for them all those years ago. A young hunter then, now he stood as a leader before him.

Pavan pushed back the memory, unwilling to let it surface.

"It was a blessing that Iyda sent me her letter. Now, you are returned to us again, son of Eleanor."

A low hush fell over the great hall. Pavan's breath caught, as many eyes now fell upon him in the dim lit room. He grew hot from embarrassment, not taking his eyes away from Meilyr.

"He is not that boy, Meilyr. He died that day in the forest," Lilja interrupted. Pavan could see the strain in her jaw, the sharpness of her eyes.

Meilyr was unrelenting. "I see the boy in these eyes."

Pavan swallowed, his chest aching as he could no longer meet the gaze of either the elf or the man who examined him.

"Isaac." Meilyr's whisper was like ice along his spine.

Catching the smirk from the dark-eyed man, Pavan's gaze found a pair of familiar violet eyes. Lilja turned on her heel, trudging through an open doorway beyond a wall of tapestries and disappeared out of sight.

"I am called Pavan." He found his voice again.

"Then we shall sing your new songs. Be welcome here, Pavan, rest and find your strength."

"We travelled long hours" Thad told the man, standing so near that Pavan could see the freckles scattered over the pale cheeks.

"Tomorrow is a new day," Meilyr said, linking his arm with Pavan's as he guided Pavan towards a set of stairs through a low arch. "Thad will take you to your rooms. You will be able to eat, bathe, and rest."

Meilyr returned to the festivities throughout the great hall, calling for more drink and asking for more music. As the hall came alive once more, Pavan took a shaky step along the first stair before him. A hand came firm under his arm, Pavan did not jump, but grasped the railing along the wall. Thad stepped up to stand close at his side.

"A room has been prepared for you." Thad was nervous, taking Pavan under the arm. He was emboldened when Pavan did not object.

"I *am* Isaac," Pavan said after a long silence as they ascended the stairs. "Meilyr was right when he recognized me."

"You have a wish to hide who you were?"

"It was so long ago..." Pavan stopped, his grip tightening on the banister.

Malcom was close behind him, a second hand grasping his other arm to steady him. Pavan was unable to look at either of them, shame flushed his cheeks, pain boiled and twisted in his blood.

"Pavan...Pavan you need to breathe." Malcom's voice was far away.

Growing hot, Pavan's eyes began to burn, his throat became thick as the heavy weight of guilt and grief weighed on him, pulling him down. Around them the corridor became cold, full of cracks and splinters of ice as their breath became puffs of vapors.

Someone shakes his arm and Pavan's eyes snapped open.

No longer in ice, the heaviness was lifted but the bitterness remained as an awful taste in his mouth. He took the remainder of the steps in silence.

"You must want sleep…this is your room." Thad opened the first wooden door along the long corridor.

It was a pleasant little space, with a large bed, a sitting area, and a bathing tub placed behind a changing screen. On the wall above the bed was a tapestry, and a small desk was set just below a small window with a carved chair. Candlelight flickered shadows against the wall, but it was warm and inviting.

Thad hurried forward to a low table at the center of the room, uncovering a tray of dried meats, cheeses, and fruit. He reached for a silver decanter and pouring clear water into two cups made of the same metal. His movements were quick, but elegant.

"There are tunics in the wardrobe, and a few trousers." Thad walked around to a box on the nearest shelf. "We shall call for the tailor in the morning to have you properly fitted. Hot water has been brought up, and there is a bath ready to wash."

"Thank you," Malcom said for both of them.

Unable to speak, Pavan watched the man with orange eyes turn, carrying a small leather bag. Timid was not the word Pavan would use to describe how Thad watched him, but observant. He was quiet, but not unsure of himself.

There was confidence in Thad's walk, a purpose only he knew about. Those eyes were observing him closely, Pavan saw the orange eyes sparkle.

"Would you allow me to dress your wound?"

Taking a seat on a stool that was presented, Pavan sat, unmoved, as Thad approached him. He took a small box from the bag, quietly opening the lid to extract a small vial, its contents dark and inklike and extended it out for Pavan to take.

"Drink this. It is a potion I made myself; it will remove any infection."

It was unlabeled and unknown to him making Pavan hesitate.

"Trust me, Pavan. I am a healer and there is nothing I would give you that would not help you."

Pavan hastened to take the vial, tipping his head back as the thick liquid slithered down his throat. He gagged, but said nothing, setting the vial down upon the table.

There was movement, as Malcom shifted to inspect the contents of the box, speaking to Thad of medical treatments as the faie carefully inspected Pavan's back. The delicate touch gave Pavan chills.

He hissed, blinking back the tears as Thad removed the old unchanged bandage, the crusted cloth pulling at the scabbing wound. Discarding the old scrap, his fingertips returned, but suddenly stopped.

"Is everything alright?" Malcom asked.

"Yes." Thad looked distracted, if only for a moment, before resuming his cleaning of the wound. "Apologies, Pavan. I cannot heal this wound with magick. A wound of this particular nature can only be healed naturally."

Pavan gulped, heat creeping to the tops of his ears.

"What does it mean, Thad, this symbol?" Malcom asked under his breath. Pavan breathed deep, his heart racing.

Thad hesitated. "Possession."

There was a long silence. Pavan felt the pounding of his heart in his ears, unable to look up to meet Malcom's eyes, tears prickling in his eyes as those soft hands fell away.

"Pavan," Thad began to speak, keeping his tone even. "Did the one who gave you this...that man..."

Pavan pulled away sharply, embarrassment thickened his throat, making it difficult to swallow. He stood swiftly to his feet. "I cannot speak of it."

He hated the pitiful wavering in his voice, but the memories of that night, nearly suffocating under the man's weight, the touch, the brand; it was almost too much for Pavan and his body began to shake.

"Pavan, please." Thad approached him, he kept his distance, but was unable to let this pass. "I must know if he did more than brand you."

"It doesn't matter." Pavan shook, wiping his nose on the back of his hand—he was trying not to cry.

"It happened in Hilvaer...there was a man they call Eske—"

"There was nothing," Pavan stated flatly.

His skin was hot, desperately wanting to escape. Instead he simply trudged the length of the room, disrobing of his tattered garments, stepping into the water with determination. He sat, water splashing over the edge from Pavan's size.

Thad was there, leaning before him, those shimmering orange eyes begging. "That marking is magick, Pavan, a certain dark magick that can make your life unbearable. There is not any shame in it, but I must understand the gravity of the situation, to better help you. I must know if Eske has taken you."

Pavan looked down, tears falling from his eyes. Memories of the man's hands upon him, the hot breath on his ear as the breath was forced from his lungs.

"Pavan, do you understand what I am asking you?" Thad's soft voice was asking.

"He didn't fuck me, if that's what you meant. But he touched my body. I spat in his face; he pushed me to the ground and stepped on my neck until I couldn't breathe. He commanded I submit to him, but I refused. Do not torment me with your soothing sentiments, Thad. I have known his like, and the drowning words of those who attempt to comfort my pain, but I don't want them."

Thad nodded, standing.

"Leave, please," Pavan said firmly.

Silence shimmered, a moment of thought, to react, but there was nothing more than the quiet tinkering of vials returning to the little bag.

 "Do not feel restricted to these chambers," Thad began calmly. "If you should need anything more, do not be afraid to ask."

Pavan was tense as the door was shut.

He pushed his long frame further into the narrow bath, the water was rising to touch his cramped limbs. Pavan snatched the waiting wool cloth. Grasping the wool hard, he wanted to rub away the feeling crawling over his skin. He scrubbed until his skin was reddened and the water was cloudy from dirt. But no matter how much he scrubbed, he felt the touch of the brutal man, felt his whispering breath on his skin.

"Have some of this." The voice of his friend stopped the spiral of thoughts that began to swallow Pavan down.

Malcom came around the corner, a small plate in his hands. He moved a stool from a far corner to prop it near the edge of the tub, where Pavan sat washing his neck.

Seeing the small morsels of food made his stomach twist in ways he thought he would never feel again. He reached a clean wet hand to take a bite of the portions presented to him, each bite after the next filled the void in his stomach.

Pavan sighed as the sharp hunger pangs began to drift away. His body cleaned of dirt, his eyelids began to grow heavy. Even now, the smell of the sea lingered in his nose. He was just barely able to hear the voice that sung within him.

The door shut, jostling Pavan awake.

He became alert. Removing himself from the bath was difficult in his lethargic state. He dried himself with a linen draped over a panel of the dressing screen. He pulled the warm clean trousers, left for him, over his hips heaving a sigh.

"The water is tepid, Malcom," he admitted, glancing down at the muddy water. Guilt etching at his heart; there was no more warmth left in the dirty bath.

"I will manage." Malcom disappeared behind the screen. "Remember the week we spent backpacking with Neil in Prague? We shared a bath with three other men in that hostel."

Pavan sat on the edge of the bed, listening to the hasty sounds of water splashing.

He smirked. "Isn't that the same trip where you left your backpack in Letna Park?"

"It was stolen, Pavan."

He could hear the laughter in Malcom's voice as they talked about the old times, how many adventures they had taken. Pavan knew it had been Neil's plans to travel every summer, to keep them occupied. In those days, when it was easier to forget and the nightmares did not frequent him so often.

"You're quiet again," Malcom said, emerging from around the screen, dressed in dark trousers and a tan tunic.

"I was thinking." Pavan felt small. "Neil will be looking for us."

Malcom sat beside Pavan on the bed, watching him with ferocity.

"Neil knows about this place. I know he does, Pavan," Malcom stated calmly. "He protected you all those years."

Pavan felt the shame wash over him.

"This time is different, Malcom. I cannot return as I once did." Burning tears glistened in his eyes.

"Don't think of that." Malcom gripped tightly to Pavan's hand.

Pavan examined the paleness of his friend's dark skin—the last few weeks had been draining him of vitality. He thought about how long it would take the richness of his skin to return, he thought about the agitation Malcom must be under to be in a place like this.

"You need to sleep."

"I have slept enough." Heaviness crept into his bones.

Malcom placed a vile in Pavan's palm. "Thad left it here for you."

"I cannot take more medicine."

Malcom gripped him hard, forcing the vile into Pavan's palm.

"As your nurse, Pavan, I demand you take this to help you sleep. You cannot heal unless you have rest."

The thick liquid slithered down his throat, leaving a bitter taste on his tongue. This one was different than the other vile, it hit him immediately, lightening the ache in his head. Pavan's vision became sluggish.

Pavan collapsed on the soft pillow down of the mattress. His whole frame groaned, welcoming the soft comfort, pulling the soft cotton blanket under his arm. Enveloped in the warmth of the bed, he did not want to sleep, but he was unable to fight the exhaustion.

He slept, dreaming of golden eyes.

CHAPTER 12

Denorn, Jorn.

Lahrs steps into the apartment suite where King Sabian is roomed within the Lord of Denorn's home. He is dressing for the morning, after ordering the attendant he was given to leave. Lahrs was briskly asked to attend him.

"What use is a servant if he cannot perform a simple task?" Sabian grumbled, tying up his own cravat in the full-length mirror. Lahrs approached the subject carefully.

"Not every household accepts a neighboring kingdom as an attendant. I was told for certain that the man who was to attend you was right for the job." He smiled, watching the king tuck and pry at the silk around his neck.

"He was an idiot. Presumptuous and deliberate in denying he could not tie a silk cravat, for it is not the style." Sabian at last undid the knot, tossing the rumpled thing aside in frustration.

Lahrs could tell there was something bothering him that had nothing to do with the silk scarf, or the attendant.

"Are you alright, Your Majesty?"

"I haven't seen him in so many years. We were friends once, did you know that?"

Lahrs looks down briefly. "Yes. You have shared with me of your close kinship with our neighboring king."

"He was such a high-spirited youth, I wonder if he is much changed." Sabian turned then, handing his jacket to Lahrs.

Lahrs assisted the king, pulling the stiff silk garment up to rest on broad shoulders, and untucking the king's dark curls from the collar.

"I believe he will be just as he ever was. He is a good man, or so I am constantly told."

Sabian smiled and Lahrs could catch the small hint of humor in the edge of his mouth. Then, suddenly, Sabian turned, looking into Lahrs eyes with a serious look.

"Do be clear with Brendolyn, she is to remain even more vigilant, Lahrs. Not a word is to be spoken while in the castle. Servants talk, if she was to speak out of turn, if a whisper was to emerge..."

"Do you believe King Beaumont to be intolerant of her heritage, my king? I understand the people are uneasy after the fall of Augusta, but would their king be also?" Lahrs asked.

"It is uncertain what King Beaumont can tolerate, but it is best to remain on the side of caution."

Sabian took one last look at his reflection.

"If it pleases you, you may ask for Sir Varick's assistance. He is honorable and will gladly take the time to split the duties of keeping Brendolyn out of trouble. Natalia always has Lisetta by her side, so he is hardly in need of escorting her."

Lahrs felt the hairs on his neck raise as anger twinged in his jaw.

"Varick is not needed, I assure you."

Sabian almost looked offended as he took up his cravat again, draping it over his neck.

"What makes you believe this?"

Lahrs eyed the king sternly. "Brendolyn has voiced her discomfort with a multitude of incidents with the knight. He does not respect her boundaries."

Sabian turned. "Sir Varick is a very renowned and decorated soldier who helped tremendously in the crisis during the war. He is honorable and I cannot see him ever approaching a woman in such a way. Besides, Lisetta has always spoken of him respectively. I cannot understand what you are on about."

Lahrs blinks, taken aback. "He has deliberately gone against the oath he was sworn, entering her chambers unbidden. He refuses to leave when asked and on multiple occasions has been seen watching the female maids in their quarters."

Lahrs could sense the irritation blooming in the king.

Sabian tied his cravat viciously.

"I respect your authority in my realm, Sir Lahrs, but the matter does not give him credit where credit is due. I am aware of these incidents with the maids; he simply took a wrong turn in the castle. And as for Brendolyn, the more eyes watching that girl the better. I will not have her running wild and causing a scene. She is far too prone to wander and stir up trouble. The faie in her is far too mischievous."

"She has shown no magick, Your Majesty. And I am sufficient enough to watch over the girl."

Sabian sighed heavily. "Perhaps, but you give her leisure that will cause her embarrassment." The two looked to one another, a silence ringing between them. Sabian began on the closures of his jacket.

"She is but a child," Lahrs said at last.

Sabian stopped his work on the buttons. "Yes. She is my child, Lahrs. As my servant and most trusted of men, it was to you that I entrusted her with. Not many would have risked damaging their honor to be guardian to a bastard girl born of a faie woman."

Lahrs cooled his colors, keeping his face void of the raging emotions stored within him as he listened as Sabian continued to speak.

"I trusted you above many to keep her from trouble. Even still news reaches me of her walking the streets of Denorn. You know more than anyone this city is no place of gentile breeding to witness the world. Now, my advice to you..." Sabian looked Lahrs over, clapping the man on the shoulder. "Be sure she is seen in cleanliness or not at all. I do not want to give King Beaumont the impression I have a deficiency."

Lahrs was stunned into silence, but nodded. He watched as the king retired from his rooms, now dressed and ready for the day of travel—they were leaving Denorn today.

Finished seeing to the luggage of himself and Princess Brendolyn, Lahrs removed himself from the great estate to walk the gardens, in search of the very person he needed to see. He knew she would be here, hidden among the hedges or up in the trees. Coming around a bend in the path he stopped as a flail of branch toppled unceremoniously to his feet, clattering amongst the pebbles that made up the path.

Lahrs sighed, picking up the branch; the blooms hacked and the bark marred. He turned as a second chunk of tree came sailing through the air, he stepped aside to let it fall.

"What will the great lady make of you ruining her favorite grove?" he called out, a familiar yelp and a clatter of a sword made him smirk.

He walked into the small clearing, where he found Brendolyn amongst the trees, hack marks marring the bark of the tree she had been taking a sword to. He spotted the small thing on the ground, near her feet. Slowly picking it up, he looked down at his charge with an approving gaze.

"As much as I approve of your practice of the sword, perhaps a more willing partner is appreciated." He handed her the hilt, and she took it.

She was breathless, clearly exerting her energy into it more than she should, he knew it was for frustration.

"I will be glad to be free of this place," she huffed, pushing sweaty curls from her face.

"You have behaved admirably. I am proud of your attendance to Lady Elhain this morning." He visibly saw the look of disdain upon her pleasant features.

"She disapproved of my dress 'it was ill fitted for a girl my age,' yet Lisetta wore the same cut of gown. If it was not for my queen mother who specifically requested I have tea with them, I never should have accepted," Brendolyn said flatly.

Lahrs walked with Brendolyn as she returned the short sword to its casing, a weathered old leather that has seen better days.

"Where did you manage to find that?" he asked, indicating the sword.

Brendolyn held the thing weighted evenly between her two hands, looking up at Lahrs. "There was a crate of them in the kitchens, next to the back door."

"Let us return it."

They walked for some time in silence. Lahrs kept his hands behind his back, and his brow was furrowed. He had something particular to tell her, but it was something he could not bring himself to say.

"You have that look, what's wrong?" Her voice broke his thoughts. "Please, tell me, or I shall imagine the worst."

"I went into town this morning."

Brendolyn stopped. Her face was exactly as he expected, her eyes told him everything. It pained him to tell her the truth.

"He was sold not long after, Bren..."

"I see." She held her head up. Lahrs could tell she was trying to remain calm but Lahrs also knew there was a harsh war raging within her. He wished to ease her distress, but there was nothing to be done.

"We have to hope that his new owners are kind and treat him better than life within a cage."

Her gold eyes shifted to him. "Do you believe they would?"

Lahrs sighed, taking her arm under his, leading them along the stone path to the estate.

"I always think there is some good left in the realms. That man shall take your blessing and one day be free of his chains."

Jorn was a beautiful countryside full of green and fields of deep colored flowers, which was a marvel to be seen as the three carriages traveled in tandem followed by the wagons of baggage, the footman on horseback, and the soldiers on guard at the front and back. Security was taken into full effect as they exited the boundaries of the cities, winding around and up to meet each new hill, all the while the seaside fell further and further behind.

In the first carriage rode King Sabian and Queen Natalia. Inside, they smiled at each other and Sabian listened as the queen talked of nurseries and fitted gowns for when the baby came. The second carriage held Princess Lisetta, her lady in waiting, and Sir Varick, who sat in agony listening to the two women gossip together. And in the third and last carriage sat Sir Lahrs and his charge.

Princess Brendolyn sat on the cushioned bench, swaying from side-to-side as the carriage rolled along the road, following the path behind the two heavily adorned carriages in front of them. Brendolyn felt at ease, being alone to speak as freely as she chooses.

"I'm bored," Brendolyn sighed, for the second time since the beginning of their journey, looking across from her at the knight who proceeded to ignore her, face hidden within the soft leather book he held.

Sighing again, Brendolyn pulled at the silk brocade of her gown, tracing the patterned thread that made up the intricate design some poor woman spent days, weeks, months to complete, just for this journey. She admired the beauty of it, but found it maddeningly useless to own such frivolities.

"If you keep doing that, it will pull apart," came the dutiful voice of Sir Lahrs, just peaking over the top of his book.

"Give it time, it rains often in Jorn, as soon as I step out of the carriage it will be ruined." Brendolyn rolled her eyes, folding her hands together instead.

"When I was last in Jorn, it did not rain for three full nights." Lahrs smirked, watching the princess become restless.

"But that was ages ago, you do remember that you're old? I'm sure the city is flooded and is now underwater, perhaps we must swim to the front gate."

She was smiling now, playfully, waiting for Lahrs to join in her fun. At last, he set aside his book, looking very cross and at once, her smile fell.

"Thirty-three is hardly old, Bren." There was that smile.

"Ha! You do jest, perhaps you have not grown into a tiresome old man after all."

"Yes, now, it is a very long journey. I suggest that you utilize it to your advantage." Lahrs pulled from the folds of a pouch beside him a treacherously dull book wrapped in chartreuse stained leather. He handed it to Brendolyn, who groaned immediately.

"You expect me to read? The whole way?"

"Not the whole way. I have also brought the maps of the kingdoms as well as the lines of kings to memorize, should you like that instead?"

Brendolyn opened her book, lifting it to her face the way Lahrs preferred to read, mimicking his expressions when in deep thought. Looking up, over the edge of the book once, she saw that Lahrs did the same, and in that moment, they smiled.

Jorn City neared and the full city was all abuzz with the arrival of the king of the south. Many people lined the streets waving small flags of Corad, welcoming the new kingdom to their city streets. They pulled into the long drive of the Castle, taking in the long line of trees to lead their path and pulled around the large fountain at the center of where the lane curved around the entrance to the castle.

The courtyard held a large tree at the center. It had white bark, with unchanging leaves the color of garnets.

Jorn Castle appeared before them. After hours in the rattling carriage, Queen Natalia was all complaints. Every movement brought her nausea, and with her complaints came the overwhelming stress to Sabian as they were exiting the carriages. His queen shunned the cold, insisting she be escorted to her rooms. Not long after the ordeal was over, Natalia was settled in her apartments with Lisetta at her side and all her attendants to see to her, Sabian arrived out to meet the third carriage as it arrived.

Lahrs stepped out, handing Brendolyn out of the carriage.

"Oh Brendolyn, my dear. Do not be uneasy," Sabian began, looking at his youngest daughter. She was pretty enough. Her cheeks flushed a soft shade, her long dark hair fell down her back. Her pleasant lilac gown reflected well enough the vibrancy of his house. He was a wreck, this should not be the way of things but the royal family was to present to the throne room.

"Is everything alright, Your Majesty?" Lahrs asked, no doubt witnessing Sabian's distress.

Sabian took Brendolyn's arm. "Natalia is unwell from travel, she has taken to her rooms. Lisetta is to attend her."

Beside him, he watched as Brendolyn's eyes grew wide. He patted her hand gently. "You are well enough. Just walk beside me and keep your eyes ahead."

Her body was fighting to run away as she walked in step beside her father through the grand hall, taking in the large walls of stone, every tapestry and painting. But her mind was reminded of her goal as they were announced. They approached the end of the large hall, walking to a platform. Standing before his throne was King Beaumont, her breath caught, he was the tallest man she had ever seen.

Brendolyn thought her father was a tall man, reaching nearly six feet tall, but the king who stood before them, coming down from the steps of the platform, was nearly a full foot taller than her father. He had broad shoulders, with bronzed skin glowing in the light of the room.

King Beaumont smiled down at her, then he looked to Sabian.

"Welcome to Jorn," he said in a full voice, his tone filled the room, but he was calm and gentle.

Brendolyn curtsied, just as Lahrs had instructed.

Beside her, she saw her father bow. Sabian went into a full welcome, speaking in clear Common Tongue—the words were lost on Brendolyn. But as her gaze dared to leave the presence of the tall king before her, someone else caught her gaze.

Brendolyn's face burned hot.

Standing on the platform his father had abandoned stood Prince Barrow. She recognized him from his portrait, which was incredibly accurate. He was tall and had golden hair, with stunning blue eyes and a warm smile, he was more than handsome, he was like the portraits of the deities of the first Elven Kingdom in Eir.

She thought of the many hours she poured into the tomes and books that Lahrs brought back from his travels to Entheas.

Prince Barrow was introduced and he stepped forward. He was already taller than King Sabian, but did not come close to the height of his father. The three men talked, and Brendolyn felt silly, unable to keep up with their Common Tongue.

Her embarrassment grew when she was then addressed by the prince, but his words went unheard—Brendolyn could not understand him at all.

"Forgive her, Prince Barrow," Sabian then spoke in the native language of Jorn, casting a side look at Brendolyn. "She does not understand Common as of yet."

"Not at all," Barrow spoke beautifully in the tongue of Jorn, his elegance surpassed hers as he gave a gentle bow.

She curtsied again, her cheeks flushed.

"You must be tired from your journey, it is not an easy one from Denorn. Please, feel welcome here in Jorn City." King Beaumont smiled, looking down at Brendolyn, his eyes were more grey than blue, but they were kind and set beneath two dark eyebrows.

It was a moment, and then her elbow was being firmly grasped. Brendolyn was guided away by Lahrs, who had been behind them the entire way through the great hall. Behind her, she could hear her father talk vivaciously with the northern king and the prince who stood between them.

They were safely within the stairway leading to the upper rooms when Brendolyn felt she could breathe again. Stopping to catch her breath, she pressed a hand into her side to stop the aching there.

"I never want to do that again," she huffed, regaining her composure to catch a smile on the knight's mouth.

"You did excellent, I am very impressed."

Brendolyn rolled her eyes. "You are not the one paraded in there like a horse for auction."

They ascended the steps, leading them to the upper landing.

"It was a formal meeting. As tradition, between the royal houses they present to the hosting nobility as a sign of respect and a way of agreement between the realms to show civility." Lahrs smiled as he looked down at her.

"Tradition or not, I did not like having all those eyes looking at me. Did you see them staring?" She remembered the looks of the older women watching her as she passed through the outer foyer before the great hall, of the men watching her as she tried to keep in step beside her father.

"New scenery is always a cause for an audience." Lahrs unlatched the door to the apartment, allowing Brendolyn to enter.

She stepped through the doors and froze. Her eyes grew large at the size of the room before her. It was twice as big as the rooms she had slept in in Denorn, and far more elegant than her own bed chamber in Corad. Ahead of her stood an open door frame, leading out onto a small balcony. The thick drapes were pulled aside, letting in the bright sunshine and the cool air. The room she stood in was a small sitting room, with two chaise lounges that had a table between them. There was a hearth to the far left, and a small door flanked either side of the roaring hearth. She entered the door on the left, it led to a small closet, where her gowns hung neatly up on the thin dress forms around the room. Her shoes were placed precisely on the shelves beside a full-length mirror.

"Is this really my room?" Brendolyn asked, passing Lahrs on her way out of the closet, hurrying to the door on the other side of the hearth.

She gaped at the basin seated just below a window shaded with gossamer. A cushioned sofa adjacent to a vanity. She didn't even own any face powders, lip creams, or blushes and there they sat, untouched, in glass containers across the vanity's surface, along with golden combs, pins, and brushes.

"It is the smallest suite on this wing, I specifically requested this particular room." Lahrs smiled when she returned to the seating area. Brendolyn looked him over.

"Why this particular room?"

Lahrs smirked, pulling open the two joined doors, opening her world to a whole new room—the bedchamber—she gasped. Of course, the bed was enormous with velvet curtains hanging from golden rings from the bedposts and mountains of pillows littered the down pillowtop. But her eyes did not linger on the size of the bed, but to the equally open doors beyond, open and looking out over the massive gardens below. The most impressive garden Brendolyn had ever seen.

Brendolyn stepped out onto the balcony, letting the chill take her as she looked out over the green swirls, tapered hedges, swaying trees, and fountains. She counted eight fountains, all laid out in the most elegant pattern with the hedges and gravel paths.

"Satisfactory?" Lahrs asked, coming to stand beside her.

"It's beautiful." She smiled, unable to take her eyes from the sight of it, her toes curled in her boots. Her hands tapped delicately on the railing, she wanted more than anything to be in that garden.

CHAPTER 13

You must be tired from your journey, it is not an easy one from Denorn. Please, feel welcome here in Jorn City." King Beaumont smiled, looking down at the young dark-haired princess. Her features were so similar, so strikingly exact to the woman he knew was her mother, it took him back when she had walked towards him.

Now he watched as the elf knight Lahrs escorted his young charge from the room, leaving King Sabian to stand before him, his breath caught. There was so much he wished to say, so many years between the last they met and the moment he stood before him now. Beaumont took a good look at his childhood friend, the young dark king who was once the pinnacle of his admiration and praise.

"Father, forgive me, but Sir Eero is expecting my return to the training yard." Barrow's voice cut through Beaumont's revere, he smiled, nodding to his only son.

"Of course, we shall not detain you." Beaumont nodded.

"Favor find you," Sabian spoke then. He bowed to the prince, then they were alone. A quiet fell over them.

"You look well," Beaumont said at last.

Sabian's mouth creased beneath the fullness of his beard as he smiled. "As do you."

There was a cough and Beaumont stiffened, he had forgotten the man who had been present whilst the southern kingdom arrived. He turned to see the thin frame of Lord Bannon approach him from his hidden perch behind the throne. He was an older man, with thin gray hair slicked back along his narrow head, his crepe skin was sallow and devoid of color. Beaumont did not know how old the man truly was, but the dark unnaturally black eyes look young and lively.

"Yes, let me introduce Lord Simeon Bannon. He is an advisor, and has been a prime ruling on bringing this treaty to the days we have entered." Beaumont gave a curt nod to the elder man who stood beside them, who was now directing a smile upon Sabian.

"Your Majesty is highly spoken of in the best regard. May this kingdom and your own become fruitful allies. We shall regain what was always lost."

"Well, aren't you a fine well-spoken man." Sabian bowed briefly.

Lord Bannon bowed. "My education is vast, I have spent many years in the households of the finest scholars of my time."

"Magick is his specialty," Beaumont spoke again. "With the ever-growing populations of magick users and the expansion of my rule in gaining Entheas, he is highly valued to navigate the mysteries of the unknown magicks.

Simeon chuckled. "You are too generous."

Simeon swept away from the throne room, his steps hard on the stone as he made his way through the castle. For years, he had been preparing for the moment these men would meet again, now as kings. Though the moment was brief, the impact was present; their allegiance would ruin all he had worked to become.

Within the locked rooms of his study, in the less accessible areas of the castle, he closed his door with a bolt. His heart was hammering as the call nagged within his chest, a pull of magick deep in his blood.

Simeon extinguished the candles with a flick of his wrist, in the darkness he muttered the arcane words he memorized long ago, taking hold of the small dagger from his belt. As he drew blood from his palm, the words became slurred on his lips. Flickering candles whispered to life, illuminating a glow of red. His eyes ink black as the voice of his mistress of magicks echoed within the fortress of his mind.

"Your heart is uneasy, Simeon." The voice was silky, a mixture of seduction and malice.

"Here I have come as instructed when the kings should finally meet. Meet they have, but they are smitten as they once were. Ready as ever to become a united realm of fortitude and fortune." There is a shift in the room as a cold chill enveloped Simeon, his breath coming in clouds before his lips.

"Stop them. At all costs, you must stop their joining. At all cost-ost-ost..." the voice echoed as the magick shifted around him and cold began to burn his limbs.

Simeon clutched the wound that throbbed against his palm. He could feel that the voice that echoed within his mind was becoming agitated, shifting with such vibrancy he began to shake against it.

He asked, "Give me the strength. All I need is your blessing, and their houses shall fall."

There was a pause, a stillness in the air that brought panic to his entire being, believing the force of the voice and the magick to have left. He was greedy, eagerly wanting his fix of darkness to pool within his veins again from the magick linked between them.

He sighed as the voice echoed again within his mind.

Soothing him.

"You know what must be done." The lights flared before extinguishing.

Simeon gasped as the cold and magick rushed away from him all at once, the lights of the candles flickering to life, illuminating the room in a familiar gold hue. Opening his eyes, he dared to look at his bloodied palm, there, coated in the clotted blood over the healing wound was a thin vial, within it was a shimmering liquid that moved on its own. His heart was all a flutter, the substance was known to only a few. Simeon turned on his heel, emerging from his private rooms in a flourish and intent.

Walking the halls with dutiful purpose, his eyes scanned each servant and each courtier he passed. Bowing to few, his eyes always watching, trying to catch a fault in any heart. Then...there...he stopped short. He saw a man who trudged across the courtyard below the walkway Simeon stood, looking over the small courtyard near the western walls of the castle.

This was too rich, Simeon smiled deeply, he had found his catch amongst the men of the realm of Corad. Magick pulsed within his heart as he descended on the man, who frowned deeply.

"Eager for penance, sir?"

The man stopped and looked at Simeon, surprised. He shuffled uncomfortably. "Only lost in thought."

Simeon smiled, a deep-set grin. "You are a lord, worried about your estate in these dark times."

The man flushed slightly. "I am but a knight sir, a Knight of the Rose." Recognition flashed in Simeon's eyes as the man spoke clearly. Honestly.

"My apologies. Tell me, which rose is befallen to you for guardianship?"

"Princess Lisetta," he seethed through clenched teeth.

"You do not approve of your position? I hear it is an honor among the leagues of Corad."

The man stood taller. "An honor for mere common knights, but my father was a lord of great refinement until the day he was killed in the battle of Thourns. It was me who should have been given the honor of taking up his place, but King Michel did not see me as fit for that honor."

There was fire in Simeon's chest as he listened to the man, so full of seething torment that fueled his design.

"Your grief is shared, sir. What do they call you?" There was a long pause as hope raised in the man's eyes.

"Sir Varick. You are Lord Bannon, the Hand of King Beaumont."

Simeon's smile is thin, his eyes so keen to the life essence that grew within the weak, hungers. "You seem to know me, but I am at a loss on your history. Come, let us find a drink and you can tell me about your resolve, Sir Varick. You have such a strong will about you that makes me wish to know you better."

Varick was surprised. Honored, he stiffened and bowed to the man. Walking beside him, they made their way to the deepest parts of the castle.

Chapter 14

Ledenjour, Entheas.

Pavan opened his eyes slowly, his mind was groggy from long hours of sleep. Memories flooded him and he groaned, sitting up abruptly.

His body was heavy. Heaving in deep breaths as his lungs burned with every intake. Now he was blinking against the light coming in through the windows to his right.

Beside the bed, placed upon a nearby chair, was a pile of neatly folded garments. He stood, examining the fine linen pieces—undergarments—he looked again at the folded pile. Black trousers and something an ash-colored gray. He dressed, wincing as he lifted his sore legs but he managed.

There was a mirror, but he avoided it, not caring how he looked. He didn't want to see the shaved head, or the gauntness of his features. Pavan already knew he was thinner than he once was. His clothes fit, they were warm and beside the door was a pair of boots.

Emerging from the room into the long corridor beyond, he walked the length of it to the stairs, his muscles throbbed as he descended below. It was quiet.

Meilyr was seated at a low table which was plated with food, next to him was Malcom, and nearer was Thad. As Pavan arrived, Malcom stood, greeting his friend with an embrace, bringing him over to the table to sit beside him.

"Welcome to my table," Meilyr spoke out, looking at Pavan from his place of seat.

Pavan nodded.

Beside him Malcom spoke up, popping grapes into his mouth. "They have smoked meats and fruit trees and even a vineyard. Here, Pavan drink some of this—" Malcom handed Pavan a mug, its contents frothing and bubbling over the side.

Pavan sipped the mead that was sweet and tasted like honey whilst he listened to Meilyr talk to the men that came to greet him.

"We are grateful to you and your generosity." Pavan's voice felt foreign, his hands cradling the cup on the tabletop, as he looked over the food at Meilyr.

"Please eat, this table is made in honor of your arrival."

Pavan did eat, slowly. His belly, which had once been restricted, cramped at the sudden intake of richer foods. As he chewed, his eyes glanced over to Malcom, who was watching Pavan with a close eye. It was a familiar look from the days after Pavan left the hospital. A sinking feeling made the food in Pavan's mouth taste of ash.

"How did you sleep?" Thad asked, there was a warmth in the faie's glance, making the pit in Pavan's stomach flutter.

"It was a much needed rest. It has been a long time since we have slept in such comfort." Pavan reached for the mug, swallowing large mouthfuls of mead.

"After you have eaten, allow me to dress your wound, keeping it clean shall minimize the chance of infection," Thad spoke with a lingering accent.

Pavan smiled, but his skin prickled, the scab itched where the burn had now crusted. It was difficult to shift his arm around completely, each movement, each pull of the scab reminded him of the man who had seared it into his flesh. Pavan unwillingly thought of Eske, his voice, his hands.

"Thad is a healer, among many talents he processes," Meilyr said, drawing Pavan's attention back to the large vast hall.

In the flutter of a heartbeat, magick shifted and danced, pulling Pavan's eyes from Meilyr to Thad, who looked away hastily. It was a strange magick, like none Pavan had felt before. After so many years, this was new. He could not look away from the man, staring openly at the freckled skin, eager to have him look up.

"A noble talent. Thad, it would please me to have you care for my wound. Forgive my harshness before." Pavan watched Thad look up quickly, glancing at him with those orange eyes. He smiled slightly as the taste of warm honey tickled his tongue, followed by the bitterness of oranges. Magick.

There was a loud clamor as Lilja sat at the table, her sword was awkwardly angled as she knelt. Meilyr gave her a frown, packing dried leaves into a long slender pipe.

"No swords at the table, Lilja. You know the rules of my house."

Lilja rolled her eyes, but did as she was told. Unlatching the buckle of her belt, she placed the sword strategically behind her so it remained within arm's reach.

"I have sworn an oath to protect you, but do not blame me if you shall encounter dangers here." Lilja's tone was sharp, her edges cold.

Meilyr laughed. "Nonsense, Lilja, there is no danger here."

Pavan could feel those violet eyes slither towards him, unblinking. Guilt rattled in his bones, fear prickled at the edges. He glanced her way, looking in each violet eye, then to her ears. Each hoop and earing chimed as she moved, hurriedly glancing away, serving herself from the food provided.

"You spoke before...of knowing Pavan's mother?"

Malcom had asked it, the question now hung in the air. Pavan's breath stilled, his heart beginning to hammer in his chest, he could not look up from the food in his hand.

Meilyr spoke. "She was a dear woman to many within the village. It was a sad day when she left us."

Pavan's eyes shot up. "*Left*?"

Meilyr swirled the mug in his hand. "It was not an easy choice, but for her losses, it was for the best. She took her leave of us in the spring all those years ago. She went with the boy."

"Hal..." His pulse quickened, and his stomach churned, his mind racing as his body began to sweat.

"You claim to be Isaac," Lilja spoke, harsh and coarse from her perch beside Meilyr.

"*I am Isaac*," he growled.

Lilja scoffed. "Isaac died in the forest; he could not have survived the men who hunted him. They were trained men who sported on bringing criminals of higher magick to their knees. You would have me believe that you are the boy, the quiet boy who helped feed the elderly, who entertained the younger children with juggling? No, you are not that boy."

"Lilja, enough of this," Thad hissed, anger dancing around them.

Pavan gulped, pain digging further in his chest. "They did hunt me, and I ran. Fear and anger drove me for what they accused my mother of being, who she was accused to have aided."

"No one blamed you, Isaac," Meilyr's voice was gentle, but Pavan felt the anger slowly returning.

"My father was a murderer. They came looking for him here, demanding she give him up, but they found resistance. She was afraid of them and I would not let them touch a hair on her head. It was not an accident that they hunted me. I know that is why you fear me, Lilja." He felt the door to his grief and his past unlock. Unable to stop the hate from entering his heart, he glared at the elf with contempt.

"Pavan," Malcom warned. There was a warm hand on Pavan's arm, but it was too late. Pavan's wounded heart was ripped open and angry tears welled in his eyes.

"I killed one of their men with magick. It boiled hot in my blood as I snapped the man's neck. He was twice my size, but I hated him for threatening my mother. For laying a hand upon her, frightening her the way they did..."

Silence followed.

Pavan scoffed, hot tears cascading down his cheek. "I see it in your glances, Lilja, that you are afraid. You can feel the danger of my presence here, yet you do not submit to the truth that I am no longer the little boy who clung to your tunics. I am no longer the innocent boy, but the monster..."

Lilja was pale, stone still, no longer glaring at him as she had been. Pavan stood at once, his limbs shaking. Desperate to escape the pounding in his heart, he hurried from the stifling room that threatened to suffocate him with heat and despair.

Malcom followed, catching him in the corridor.

Anger made his hands shake. "I cannot stay here."

Pavan shook it away. He tried to relax, but the anger began to burn. Heaving in painful breaths, Pavan tightened his hands into fists.

His control was slowly slipping away.

"One big breath, come on, Pav..." Malcom mimicked the deep intake of breath, slowly letting it in and out.

Pavan shook his head.

A strong grip tightening on each of his biceps, loosening, then tightening again. Malcom breathed in slow through his nose, letting it out through his mouth. Pavan's mind was flayed open, his body trembled but followed the pattern, breathing in tightly through his nose. He let it out in one shaken breath.

"That's it, breathe," Malcom encouraged.

Again, they breathed, and again, until Pavan was cooled. His limbs ached, slumping back against the cold wall, keeping his breathing even and well-paced. Remaining quiet, Malcom watched him progress in calming himself, all the while keeping a hand tight on Pavan's arm.

"Come on, you should lay down."

Meilyr set his goblet aside, looking at Lilja who remained stone still and paled. They watched after the man who stormed out, followed closely by his friend.

"This is exactly as I have warned, Lilja…" he began, his voice was calm but the undertone made the elf flinch. "When I spoke on this matter last night, I heard your doubts. We agreed to enter into this with him slowly."

"He holds magick like none have seen for centuries, it was but a small sliver when he was a child. Now he has reached the age when it manifests at full strength. He is damaged, Meilyr. You cannot deny that seeing his control with his emotions is dangerous." Lilja's voice was low, keeping her tone so as not be heard, but Meilyr frowned.

"Yet you dig in the knife to further aggravate the wound." Thad glared at her.

Meilyr felt for the faie, seeing the irritation in him.

Lilja scoffed. "I hold the knife, but it was I who have been trained to wield it against him. Should he unlock the magick that lay dormant for all these years, not even your strength or basic spells could stop him from tearing you apart, Thad. And no manner of flattery would stop his magick from slithering into the deepest parts of your soul to rip it from you."

"Enough," Meilyr raised his voice. It was not often he needed to, but the result was immediate; the pair of them fell silent.

"Forgive me." Lilja bowed her head, resigning herself to silence.

"Do not quarrel, Lilja. You were once lost in the forest of Taudren, a child bride to an old religion, a sacrifice to those deities they worshiped. But you forget your promise."

She looked affronted. "I have not forgotten my promise."

Meilyr sighed. "Yet, my fearless one, you abandon the protection of Isaac to your hardened heart. He is lost, as you were all those years ago."

"He is Ehlfern, Meilyr." Lilja was trembling, unable to look up.

"Yes, he is of a powerful magick but now is not the time to divide ourselves. Walk with him and guide him, as only you are able to resist that natural magick."

Thad was silent until then. "He will not ease into his magick when he is weakened by his hurting heart. Where Lilja has seen his danger, I have seen the pain. He guards his heart with so much anger it would be impossible for him to wield magick, and it would be his undoing to unlock a dangerous magick without first healing what his past has damaged."

"It would take years to unravel all his past, Thad. He has already unlocked the magick. If he is not guarded now, he will unleash his magick upon us all," Lilja spat.

Meilyr sat, thinking for a long moment. "For now, we must be mindful and wait, and allow him time to find rest, to ease the tension of being captive."

Pavan searched for Thad, after sitting in the small room.

It was Malcom who advised him to seek out the faie, as the wound upon his shoulder began to seep through the bandage.

Wandering the narrow little roads of the square, Pavan followed the direction given to him on where to find the little hut out of reach of the villagers, where Thad lived alone. But Pavan did not follow the path, as he neared the large stone wall that bordered the eastern side. He could hear the distinct sounds of swords grating stone, and the familiar sounds of men play fighting.

Pavan stopped at the gate, looking in at the training yard.

So many days had he spent sitting on the great pile of sandbags at the furthest end of the yard, where he would watch Meilyr train with the young. Pavan remembered watching Lilja in her youngest years, she was only an elf girl then, with a sword nearly as tall as she was. Now there was a new group of faces, a new era of men and women that trained on the field. Pavan kept close to the inner wall, nearest to the door.

A young-faced elf approached him.

"Come to train?" he asked, hopeful. "My name's Trisk, I am joining my first hunt this season."

"I am looking for Thad." Pavan saw the tilt of the ears, the young elf was willowy, barely old enough to hold a sword. "I seem to have gotten lost in search of his hut."

A smile brightened the young face.

"You wouldn't have found him there, my lord. Thad is there!" Trisk turned, pointing across the yard to the sunken ground layered with sand, fenced in a long circle.

There were many trainees who wore padded tunics and bracers to protect themselves that stood around, watching a fight that went on within the ring. Pavan felt the same flip within his chest as he followed Trisk across the yard, drawing closer and closer. Pavan was amazed, standing at the fence line along with the others.

"That is Svein." Trisk stood at Pavan's elbow, pointing out the large behemoth of a man with a long ginger beard and dark auburn hair pulled back out of the way. "He is a half giant."

"It seems an unfair fight," Pavan stated.

Thad stood nearly his whole height shorter than the half-giant Svein. They were in the midst of a match of hand-to-hand combat. Pavan anticipated the larger hulking man would take Thad down, which gave him great unease.

"Not a chance!"

Trisk shouted in Elvish to the two, egging them on—Pavan recognized the dialect—it was stirring his memories of the past, when the tall bronzed body of the man who knew his mother, was once in the ring. Pavan remembered it clearly, while he watched from atop his piles of sandbags, but the memory did not last. His attention was drawn again to the men in the ring.

Svein gave a great shout, as Thad's arms were wrapped around his thick middle, being hoisted in the air as if he weighed nothing. Pavan held his breath, shocked and amazed, watching Thad heft the bulking man up and over his head. Svein landed hard, displacing so much sand around him, it left a crater.

"Thad!" Trisk shouted.

Helping the half giant to his feet and setting him off with a clap on the back, Thad made his way across the ring, sweat was glistening on his face and neck. As he neared, Pavan saw the tint of pink upon the faie's cheeks. Pushing his loose copper hair out of his eyes. He was wearing dark brown wool trousers and a thin linen tunic that was damp from sweat. Pavan could see the distinct lines of muscle beneath.

"Good morrow, Trisk. I see you have abandoned your training."

"I was on my way to the blacksmith's, when I saw Lord Pavan and asked if I could be of service. He was looking for you!" Trisk spoke loudly, and animated. His eyes brightened as he looked admiringly at Thad.

They locked eyes. Pavan saw the shimmering smirk at the edge of Thad's lips as he took a cloth offered by a man that walked by, wiping at his sweaty face and neck.

"Thank you, Trisk. I can manage from here."

Trisk could hardly contain himself and began in earnest to praise Thad for his fine skills. As the young elf spoke, Pavan saw the hesitation growing in the faie, and the uncomfortable stance that straightened Thad as the elf spoke of past conquests.

"Trisk," Thad hissed. At once the elf fell into silence. "To the blacksmith's. I must speak with Pavan, alone."

He was gone quickly.

Thad turned suddenly, trudging across the ring to the farthest curve, where the gate swung open. Pavan walked towards him, keeping his eyes upon Thad as he pulled a doublet over the damp tunic that he wore, tossing the cloth aside.

"Shall we?" Thad motioned towards the gate that led out of the training yard. Pavan followed, ignoring the looks he received from the hunters as they pushed past.

"Meilyr was right; you do have many talents," Pavan said when they were safely out of the city and taking a path further down the lane, away from the main square.

"I am a healer," Thad corrected.

Pavan laughed. "That was not healing. I have never seen a man of that size be upended by a man of--"

There was a frown, and Pavan stopped.

"You are the strongest man I have ever seen," Pavan corrected.

"Clever." Smirking up at him, Thad slowed to stand before a fountain carved into a large stone basin. Water trickled over the carved alcove beneath the yawning gap above the stone. Dipping his hand to splash his face and neck.

"Trisk admires you," Pavan stated plainly.

Thad sighed. "He is young. He has much to learn."

"You think that over time, he shall lose interest in his admiration?"

"I think he should focus on his training, not foolish pining over an old healer that lives alone in the ancient crest of the village."

Pavan chuckled, leaning back to sit upon the fountain's edge.

"Are you an old man, Thad?" He asked. "You do not look more than twenty."

Those orange eyes blazed as magick tickled in Pavan's throat. He felt heat spread over his face under the gaze.

"I have reached my thirty fourth year this spring."

Pavan smiled. "You're practically ancient, Thad."

Leaning back, he winced as the pain in his shoulder broke what thoughtless joy he had begun. It was something Pavan could not hide away from. He leaned forward instinctively, trying to straighten the burn that felt like fire up his arm. He blinked back the tears that pooled from his eyes.

"Do you trust me?" Thad extended his hand.

Pavan hesitated before he took hold of the offered hand. He was standing straight, so close to Thad that he could see the flecks of gold in the orange blaze of his eyes.

"Come with me."

They walked in silence towards a small stone building, nestled between the overgrowth of two large trees. Hidden within was an uneven path. He stepped inside after Thad, finding himself in a well-fitted chamber full of shelves that housed bottles, gems, trinkets of simple magick. The stone floor was covered in well worn rugs.

"Sit here." Thad placed a stool near the hearth. With a wave of his hand a low fire was set ablaze, radiating warmth. Magick crackled in the air that tickled Pavan's nose.

Pavan watched Thad retrieve a little canvas bag from a cabinet at the farthest wall. Pavan unlaced his tunic, letting the warm material fall from his shoulders. He looked back up to see Thad watching him. At once the faie flushed, hurrying to Pavan's side with the canvas bag.

"Drink this."

Thad held out a vial, similar to the one Pavan had downed the night they had arrived. Taking it, his fingers touching the warm hand that held it out. Magick fizzled. He could feel the current zip between them like a shock of electricity.

Pavan winced, pulling back.

"Keep your feet on the rug." Thad swallowed hard, his gaze flickering down to the booted feet on the stone. Pavan shifted, his boots now firmly planted on the tattered rug that was laid out between the door and the other wall.

"Like this?" Pavan asked, his long legs bent with ease, his knees positioned to either side of Thad. Pavan looked up into orange eyes. The color flickered and danced with magick.

Thad did not speak, but extended the vial to him. This time there was no spark, only the warmth of thin hands. Pavan uncorked the vial, his head falling back to let the bitter contents slither down his throat. It was unpleasant, but he swallowed it. Then he returned the vial to Thad's open hand.

Quietness lingered between them, as Thad turned away to deposit the empty vial in a basket to be reused. Then he turned to a basin of water, bringing a dampened cloth to stand behind Pavan, removing dried blood and cleaning up the oozing pus that seeped from the thick scab. Pavan hissed, inhaling sharply. Warmth pressed against the base of Pavan's neck, where Thad's hand held firm. Magick seeped under the surface, easing the tightness in his muscles. Pavan sighed suddenly. Leaning back into the welcomed touch. It was soothing and delightful; the magick was bright and new.

Pavan licked his dried lips, smelling honeysuckles, tasting nutmeg and clove. It was a peppery spice that soon turned sour in his mouth. Pavan scowled, his muscles clenching as he tightened his fists. Anger caught fire within his blood.

"Easy," Thad sighed, resting a warm palm over Pavan's neck.

"Be careful," Pavan cautioned, feeling the tightened growing darker, the magick threatening under his skin.

"I have healed men with the worst of tempers; you do not frighten me." Thad's voice was smiling. Pavan felt the electricity of excitement and amusement at the touch of those long fingers.

"I could—" emotion restricted Pavan's throat, he swallowed thickly around it. He pushes back the angry tears.

"You are *not* a monster." Thad's voice was soft.

"That is because you do not know me, Thad. If you knew the things I have done; The things I could do."

Those long fingers tightened on Pavan's neck, hugging the contour of his shoulder. Thad ceased his cleaning of the burn.

"Monsters do not grieve for their prey; they mourn not the actions that leave scars upon the flesh and soul. The man that did this to you, he felt no shame in branding you his property." As he spoke, Thad's hand trailed down the length of Pavan's spine, giving him shivers. "I have seen monsters; I have known their wrath. You are no monster, Pavan."

Magick shivered through him. Pavan felt hot.

"Who am I now, Thad, if not the monster? I have been lost for so long...I know not what I have left." Pavan gulped; his body was tired. Those warm hands left him, and he felt a sudden chill.

"Here is where you shall find purpose again. You are welcome here, Pavan. Do not be hurried away."

Pavan smiled.

Despite his aching heart, he could not resist the swell of delight he felt. Once again, those warm hands began to work, dabbing ointment into the wound, a cooling herb that relieved the pain immediately.

"Perhaps you shall teach me your skill of healing, or perhaps how to fight." Pavan closed his eyes, following Thad's movements by the feel of the faie's hands. Now there was a clean, dry cloth being applied to the wound, being held in place by a wrap. Thad reached around Pavan's middle to secure the bandage in place.

"When you are healed, you may join the hunters if you wish. For now, there is much you must learn about the village."

Thad offered up the tunic left discarded.

"Afraid to train me, Thad?"

"I have upended Svein; you are no greater feat, Pavan." Thad gave a mischievous gaze, one that Pavan wished him to make again, but Pavan's words failed him. Thad turned away, righting the room to what it had been.

Pavan slipped the tunic over his shoulders, tying the front loosely. It was easy, in the silence, to watch the faie work. Listening to the tinkling of little bottles, the sounds of water cascading into the basin as Thad cleaned the ointment from the linens, hanging them to dry before a little window looking out over a garden beyond.

"How do you know about the mark?" He asked. Standing to approach the faie.

"I am a healer." His voice was a whisper.

Pavan stood so close, he could smell the clove and eucalyptus oil that perfumed the faie from his medicines. Thad stood, resting his hands on the edge of the basin.

"Dark magick, it is not known to many healers, Thad. I felt your restraint, I felt your fear of it. What would you have done if I said he had taken me?"

Thad gasped, a breath falling from his lips as if he had been holding it, and his hands began to tremble. Magick danced upon Pavan's tongue, tasting citrus. Leaning closer, he was looking to the point of Thad's ears, glancing at his neck. Here, Pavan could see the pulse of his vein; the edge of his tunic was undone, the lines of a thin scar was just visible. Pavan knew there were more, hidden beneath the loose garment.

"Thad. You are more than a healer. You traveled across the great sea to foreign soil, risking your own life on the word of a young elf that we were in danger." Pavan lowered his voice, slowly pressing himself into Thad's space.

"Iyda is an old friend." Thad shook his head.

"You know much of the world, Thad. Too much, by your fierce desire to protect those you don't even know." Pavan dared to lift his hand, resting his fingers delicately upon the faie's shoulder.

Thad lowered his head, his dark copper hair falling over his eyes. Pavan fought every urge to lift his chin, to push the fallen hair back into place.

"What would you have done if Eske had taken me? Stormed Hilvaer to slaughter those who dared to give me pain?" Pavan knew the answer. He could practically hear the force of Thad's heart pounding against the restraints of his ribs.

"I am a healer, Pavan," he breathed, trembling.

Magick stifled beneath the tunic he wore, Pavan inched closer to Thad, desperate to be nearer to him. He trailed his hand further down his shoulder, along the clothed path of his arm, before holding the tender flesh of Thad's wrist.

"I have seen these hands do remarkable things."

Thad blushed, his fair cheeks splotched. Turning away, he said, "Return in the morning, so I may clean the wound again."

"Perhaps I bleed through this cloth..." Pavan kept his voice low.

Thad pushed Pavan the short distance, stopping just in the doorway of his little hut.

"See the blacksmith; he could use someone to chop wood to keep the fires hot. Or you may see Agarha; she is in need of a pair of strong hands to carry her grain from the store rooms to her shops." Thad pointed.

Pavan did not track it, he kept his eyes lingering upon the pale freckles that scattered over the faie's skin, whose dark copper hair fell waywardly over his forehead. Pavan could feel each prickle of anticipation shiver over his skin.

"Can I not see you before morning? Must I keep my distance from you, Thad?"

Thad smiled. "It is commonplace for many who meet me to not yet distinguish the unnatural yearnings my distinct heritage provokes. For those of higher magicks, sometimes that yearning is greater."

It was true, Pavan could practically smell the magick rolling from Thad like a heavy cologne, it tingled his nose and made his stomach churn in hunger, but there was a different yearning that Pavan felt for the faie, one that came from his own heart.

"You assume that I am not in earnest?" Pavan lowered his voice.

"I am faie, Pavan. It is the nature of my kin to attract those in search of something more. There is nothing natural about that," Thad breathed.

"Human. Faie. Elf. It should not matter." Raising a hand, Pavan desired to touch the slim fingers of the man, but he stopped.

"Pavan!" Malcom's voice called from behind them.

Reluctantly, Pavan sighed, raising a hand to Malcom.

"Your friend has been of great assistance within the village; perhaps there is much the two of you can accomplish together." Thad smiled, squeezing Pavan's arm reassuringly, before turning into his little home, leaving Pavan no choice but to walk the length of the yard to Malcom.

A warm smile waited for him.

"What?" Pavan asked, eyeing that well-known look Malcom gave when he was aware of something glaringly obvious that took Pavan longer to deduce.

"Have you anything to tell me?"

Pavan blinked, bemused. "Is this an interrogation?"

Malcom chuckled, taking Pavan by the shoulder as he steered them towards the great house. "Not at all, Pavan. In all honesty I am shocked; I had not imagined Thad to be the one to crack that hardened shell of yours."

Now, it was clear. Pavan frowned. "He's a healer, Mal. Of course, I can relax with him."

"In all these years I have known you, do you think I can't tell the difference when you fancy someone?" Malcom was smiling, his teeth flashing, brightening his whole face. Pavan admired the optimism in his friend and the cheery disposition, so long as it didn't involve Pavan. Now, he was unable to run away from the soft brown eyes that shimmered with hope.

Pavan's frown deepened, he drew back slightly. "It's not like that. It won't be like that, Mal. I can't open myself up to that again."

His words instantly deflated Malcom's humour. Pavan watched the brightened look in his face dampen. Guilt flushed over Pavan, hating himself a little more that he could not be more optimistic. He couldn't pretend to not be wounded, or to not have reservation for the wound left in his heart.

"Pavan, I didn't mean—"

He shrugged, scratching his neck. His fingertips found the short hairs that itched at the base of his neck. Their identically shaved heads, reminded Pavan of their journey to this place, of that voice in his mind whispering to him of the fool he had been.

"Let's find some food. I'm starving." Pavan hooked an arm around Malcom's shoulder, keeping them on the path towards town.

Chapter

15

Malcom gazed into the flickering flames, feeling the steady warmth seep into his skin, a welcome contrast to the crisp evening air. His fingers lightly traced the edges of the book Meilyr had gifted him—a simple thing, bound in dark leather, its pages unmarked, waiting. It felt precious, not because of the book itself, but because of the gesture. Meilyr had seen him amid the crowded tailor's shop where Malcom would sketch on whatever scraps of parchment he could find. That quiet moment of recognition lingered in Malcom's thoughts, filling the silence as he contemplated what to create on these blank pages, the firelight casting long shadows on the ground around him.

"You drew these?"

Malcom looked up from his sketches, startled by the soft voice. A familiar figure approached.

"Farren," he smiled warmly. "Yes, just something to keep my hands busy when my body can't find rest."

She sat across from him, the firelight casting a warm glow over her features, making her skin seem to shimmer. Her long lashes framed large, luminous eyes that held his gaze, and for a moment, Malcom couldn't deny it—she was the most beautiful woman he had ever seen.

"I'm glad to see you outside," he said, her voice soft but cheerful. "How's your arm?"

Farren's smile widened as she flexed her left hand—the one Malcom had treated three days earlier with a potion at Thad's request. The deep gash she'd sustained during her horseback training was healing well. It had been her first attempt at something so daring, and though it left her with a nasty injury, her determination had earned Malcom's quiet admiration.

"It's much better, thanks to you," she added, still flexing her hand, her expression grateful.

"Thad has approved my return to training."

Farren's large brown eyes glittered with excitement as she reached up, fingers brushing the cascade of dark hair that fell freely about her shoulders. She had abandoned her usual braids, letting her thick tresses flow down her back. Tall and striking, like many of her kin, she carried the grace of an elf, her dark skin gleaming in the firelight. Her unmatched skill with the longbow was well known.

"They will welcome your return," Malcom said, his voice steady.

"The Great Hunt is upon us," she continued, her tone more serious now. "As many have given themselves to honor the village, it would be a disgrace to dishonor Ehnarea if I did not attend." The Hunt was on everyone's lips as the season approached, a time of tradition and reverence.

Malcom hesitated, feeling the weight of her words. "I shall not attend."

Farren's hand crossed the table, grasping his with surprising warmth. "But you are touched by the goddess of light, Malcom," she said, her voice gentle yet insistent. "You, the healer of my people, and the one who tends to the highest magick."

"You mean Pavan?" Malcom withdrew his hand, his expression darkening at the mention.

"He is a gift. Sent to us by Ehnarea to protect us from the great evils of the realms. It is spoken by the wisest among us. To have the Ehlfern walk among us is to be blessed by the goddess herself."

"Are there more Ehlfern in Entheas?" A frown pulled at the corners of his mouth.

"In all of Veilore, there are none that remain. There are stories of the very last Ehlfern in Taudren, that he took the Oath of Silence that blanketed the realms in his power. That because of his last dying wish, the Ehlfern walked amongst us as phantoms, trapped between the living and the Veil. Those that follow the Last One's Oath believe that when an Ehlfern walks among us once more, showing his true power, those blessed shall ascend to live with Ehnarea herself on the throne of her father, T'hall."

Listening to her talk, Malcom watched the fire flicker to life. Her words wove the tale with magick that danced against the flames, Malcom blinked away the trance, rubbing away the tiredness from his eyes. Farren sat quietly, looking through the many sketches that began the first of the book given to him by Meilyr.

"But they are just stories," she sighed, glancing up at Malcom.

"Are there still those that believe in the Last One's Oath?"

Farren's eyes flickered up, glancing across the hall. She watched as Lilja crossed from the open door towards the large staircase, just out of view. Farren lowered her gaze, her long eyelashes fluttered against her cheeks.

"Lilja comes from Taudren. She was raised in that ancient religion. Her village waited for the return of the Ehlfern, marrying their maidens to their brotherhood, and preparing for the return."

Malcom swallowed hard.

"But she did not remain with her people in Taudren?"

"She ran away from the altar, refusing to be married to the brotherhood. It was Meilyr who found her wandering the forests."

Malcom asked, "How old was she?"

"She had reached her thirteenth year."

Pavan stood near the blacksmith's, chopping wood to fuel the fires of the hearths, a familiar white-haired elf stood at a distance watching him. Lilja remained there without a word. Her arms were crossed over her leather tunic while she examined him with interest. He cared little of what she thought as her keen eyes followed his movements, but the elf stood too close to the chopping block.

"There have been many grateful men and women talking about you, Isaac."

Pavan wiped his forehead on his arm. His lack of hair caused the pour of sweat to slide along his skin. He made no effort to speak to her, but eyed her warily as she walked closer towards him.

She continued, "You are strong, I have seen for myself you carry double of what is carried from down in the mines. And in the village, you can work for hours without tiring. Malcom has been to cook countless times to retrieve more portions of food to keep you sated."

Pavan said nothing, placing a large log upon the block.

He readied himself and in one large swoop. *Thunk*! The log split in half with ease. In only a few weeks, he was stronger and more fit than he had ever felt in England. Potions showed up at his door, which he took whenever Thad or Malcom handed him a vial. He ate and worked for Agarha, bringing her sacks of grain, flour, or whatever other goods she needed for her shop.

Lilja's violet eyes scoured the length of his body.

"It is impressive. You are remarkably strong for someone who has been chained, who had been starved—"

Thunk!

The sound of the axe drowned out her words. Pavan grew irritated listening to her speak, eyeing him with a look he could not quite read.

Pavan frowned.

"Determined. Yes, you are so determined to keep your head down, not to draw attention to yourself. But everyone can see your change, they can see what your magick is providing you with, Isaac."

"Please, don't call me that," he mumbled as the head of the axe thumped to the ground, slipping through his fingers gracefully.

Lilja strode forward, coming dangerously close to Pavan. "You wish to hide yourself away, but I know who you are, Isaac."

His jaw clenched. "You're trying to push me. I will not yield."

"I can help you, if only you will let me." Her words shaved at the edges of Pavan's composure. His chest heaved with desperation for air, clinging to the last remnants of control.

His eyes flashed. "You have helped plenty."

Trudging past her, Pavan was held back by a hand upon his chest.

"Holding what is inside of you will kill you." Her voice was smooth, gently coaxing into his mind with every honeyed word.

Pavan grimaced. Grabbing her wrist, his fingers prickling with a familiar heat. Angry magick bubbling beneath the surface.

"If it kills me, so be it. You think I'm ignorant of what magick I possess, but there is no one who understands better. I would rather die than watch the world burn under my own doing. There is no glory, or purpose, for the darkness in my blood."

Lilja pulled away from him, gasping.

Clinging to the wrist he had held, angry, raw blisters began to form in the shape of a hand. Magick fire.

CHAPTER

16

It was warm in the little workshop as Lilja weaved her way through the hanging herbs dried in bunches, and the little baskets of gems that were neatly organized along the narrow passage of shelves. It was an old storage room Thad had long ago transformed into a place where he made potions—his tinctures of healing. Lilja rarely came here, unless it was absolutely necessary. Now, the pain in her arm reminded her of the necessity of needing to be here.

"Stop."

She froze, her foot raised to step into the little den, but there was an acidic smell that made the inside of her nose tickle. Her hair stood up on end along her arms and neck. She glanced up to the faie who sat at his workbench in the far-left corner, his back to her.

"You are busy." Her mouth was dry from the magick that hung in the air.

"You have a wound; come here. Just avoid the stone."

There was no retreating now. Lilja entered the den, mindfully stepping only on the tattered rug that was stretched out from where Thad sat, to the door. Once near him, she plopped herself on the stool, jostling the little empty bottles that sat neatly in rows.

Thad glared, his wildly vivid orange eyes going brighter as magick fizzled, permeating the air with an abundance of different smells. Each one filled her senses until her eyes began to water and her throat tickled. Lilja stifled a cough.

"Was it Svein, again? I told him not to practice his magick shield until he got the movements..." Thad's voice trailed off, looking down at the burn upon Lilja's forearm. His eyes lingered far too long over the finger and palm marks, then looked up at her suspiciously.

"It was not Svein," Lilja said, magick continued to bleed deeper into the burn.

Hastily, Thad stood. Striding across the room to the cabinets at the far wall, he returned with a vial of violet liquid and a canvas bag. He leaned in to examine the wound.

"How long ago?"

Lilja flinched at his touch.

"Maybe twenty minutes. However long it takes to walk from the blacksmiths to here." She hissed through her teeth, trying to ignore the roll of nausea as Thad scraped skin with the back of a glass knife, dipping the thin blade into the vial. They watched the violet liquid turn black and thick, smelling of death and decay.

He did not say anything for a long minute, but set aside the vial, hovering a hand over the wound. Lilja braced herself, at once the warmth became excruciating. Tears filled her eyes as the heat radiated up her arm. Unable to look as blisters bubbled and ruptured, taking the burn through the stages of healing. Lilja had seen Thad heal burns before, but she never imagined they could be this painful.

"Nearly there." Thad's voice was stolid.

Now, the burn grew colder as her skin tightened.

Lilja sighed, letting out the breath she had been holding. Looking down at her arm where the burned handprint was now sat new skin, stretched but slowly healing. Lilja stood, pulling her sleeve down to cover the fading scar.

"Thad, this was—"

But the faie was turned away, cleaning up the workspace. "Leave. You don't need to explain yourself to me." His voice was mechanical, unable to look at her.

She hesitated, noting his behavior. He was always reserved, even with her, but this was something new. This was a Thad she had not seen since...

"I know what you must be feeling."

"Lilja, do not patronize me; I am not a child," he stated, his voice bitter. There was a harshness to it that Lilja did not expect.

"It is clear to me that your desires to protect him comes from a place you once were in, Thad, but believe me this is best for his safety." She chose her words carefully.

Thad glared, his cleaning forgotten. "Safety. You cannot force him to do it, Lilja. This"— he gestures to her arm. —"this is not safety, Lilja. Your persistent attempts to get him to submit are putrid," he all but sneered.

"I only wish him to agree upon his own word. Could you believe me so cruel to force him beyond his will? Thad, you mistake me for your master. If he willingly accepted my guidance, it would be all his own choice."

She watched Thad's eyes darken, his frown deepening. "I know your magick, Lilja. Do not think I am ignorant of the religion you were raised in. He would choose that path, believing what he did would help shield those he loved, but it would not be right, not at the cost."

Lilja smirked. "The cost would only be mine, giving away my own soul, willingly sacrificing my years to protect this village, to protect you?"

"I do not need your protection, Lilja. He does not need to be quieted, made to obey at your command. He would be little more than a dog; it would eat at his heart. You cannot ask him to satisfy your yearning."

Seeing the flicker of fire in Thad, Lilja felt the wringing tug of jealousy igniting in her chest, laying down the hidden feelings she wished to set aside. Desire for Pavan, for his power, made Lilja tremble. But the same flame burned in Thad. She knew him well enough to know when Thad was pining.

"My yearning, it is not so different from your own, Thad, but can you honestly believe it would work?"

"Would what work?" He looked affronted.

Lilja smirked. "I know that look of yours. I saw it so often when you first came to Ledenjour all those years ago. You followed Aron Dourn around like a lost puppy."

Thad's fine features darkened.

She was digging into the wound she knew belonged to Thad. It was hardened jealousy; after years of trying to get Aron Dourn's attention, working hard to heighten her status in the ranks, earning the approval of Aron, only to be stifled. He was lost to her forever because of a faie who walked into the training yard and gave Aron Dourn one sultry look.

Lilja was not ignorant to Thad's beginning.

Sold into servitude in Denorn by a cruel master, freed by Meilyr and brought to Ledenjour to be placed under his wing. A new protege for the old wise elf to mold into a version of himself, like he had done for Lilja and before her, Lahrs. Thad stepped into that role quickly. But it was not only Meilyr who had changed because of Thad. Lilja saw the faie time and time again seduce Aron Dourn. Now, Thad was her superior. Thad was Captain of the Guard, as well as a renowned healer, while Lilja remained in her station of huntress.

"This has nothing to do with him," Thad stated flatly.

Lilja was not so convinced. "Does it not? He has been gone for three years. You shared our late Lord Dourn's bed for so many winters, now you wish to belong to another. Isaac is powerful, but the power he holds would kill you, Thad."

"You claim him as yours, Lilja? Yet, you disrespect his simple requests. He wishes to be called Pavan, yet you insist upon calling him Isaac. He detests to speak of his past, yet you plague him with cruel words from his childhood." Rage flickered to life in the heat of those orange eyes. "He may not choose me, Lilja, but you certainly do not deserve his heart."

Meilyr blew a puff of smoke from between his lips, watching Lilja from across the table. She had entered his offices in a fit of agitation, but had not yet spoken a word.

"Perhaps I might ask—"

Lilja sighed heavily. "Thad is unbearable."

Meilyr smiled, he knew the quarreling they had offered to each other since Meilyr had brought Thad to Ledenjour all those years ago. It had not changed, the two quarreled and pestered each other as every sibling should, but now there was something in the glint of Lilja's eye that told him it ran deeper than normal.

"Thad is doing as he believes is best, just as you. But perhaps there is a chance you are more eager to appease that urge within you that has been engraved upon your soul since birth," Meilyr pushed, seeing the elf change color, her violet eyes flickering to look away, unable to look at him.

"This is different." Her voice was a whisper.

Meilyr nodded. Returning to his pipe, another long silence stretched out between them. He watched Lilja closely, admiring her passion but wary of her determination.

"He cannot contain his magick, Meilyr. Not at his age. Not at the strength he has." Her face was pained but she did not relent. "Yes, I desire to fulfill my designed purpose, but is it not right that it should be my own choice in this? Pavan cannot hold it for long; he cannot rely upon his own will to keep the Ehlfern magick from manifesting. If we wait, there will be only danger. At what cost then? Any number of our own people."

Warm smoke slipped from Meilyr's lips, curling into his mustache, as he looked up to Lilja's violet eyes.

"He will not concede."

His words did not please her. She huffed haughtily, crossing her arms. Lilja was proud and passionate, but her temper was the worst of his children. He smiled patiently, setting aside his pipe.

"If you speak to him, surely you could help Pavan see the advantages of surrendering his magick in such a way that could lessen his burden—"

Meilyr raised a hand, and Lilja was quieted, angrily wiping at her silent tears.

"I will speak with Pavan, but not in a guarantee that he shall be pressured into this." Meilyr could see her muscles relax, but he went on. "But perhaps this shall be the end of your disagreement with Thad."

Lilja scoffed. "He is boorish and spoiled. He cannot have everything he wants, simply because he wants them."

"You know as well as many the disadvantages of a disjointed home. If you cannot make amends or end your harboring resentment towards Thad...As my family, you should—"

Lilja stood suddenly. "This was a mistake. I should not have taken so much of your time."

She was angry, more than Meilyr had ever seen her before. He stood to comfort her but she looked at him sharply, her eyes glittering with tears.

"We are not a family, Meilyr. You are not my father, no matter how much you wish it." She took a sharp intake of breath, calming her nerves. "He is dear to you. I know how much you love him, but Thad is not your son. Perhaps it was foolish to save him from Denorn. He would have risen to great heights there; instead he has plagued our village, enchanted the heart of our lord. I fear he has enchanted your own heart."

Meilyr prickled, withdrawing a hand from the comfort he bestowed upon the elf. She did not need it, she was not a child, but a grown woman.

"Thad wishes only to find his place amongst the world, for the life he was driven to by that horrible man before he came to us here. What happened with Aron Dourn was not his doing. You understand as most the dangers of the forests. When the Vohlgrum attacked the encampment of hunters, they were overpowered..."

Lilja shifted back, casting her eyes away. "Thad survived."

"Thaddeus endured agonizing torment for three days and nights in the forests, with a wound full of venom; even his own strength was diminished. He carried Aron Dourn home to us, to bury our lord properly. That is not the act of a man who wishes for power or for greatness. He wishes for what any soul of Ehnarea's blessings wishes for. Love." Meilyr saw the shame wash through the elf as he spoke, recounting the momentous last moments of their late lord, Aron Dourn.

"Love." Lilja scowled. "He is faie...they do not love. They make you believe what you feel is love, but it is only a guise before they have entrapped you in their web of lies and deceit. He hasn't the heart to love another."

Meilyr sighed. "Go, you should rest, Lilja. We begin the great hunt upon the morrow. You will need all your strength."

She was gone in a moment, leaving Meilyr to his offices, alone with his thoughts and reflections.

CHAPTER

17

Jorn City, Realm of Jorn.

Brendolyn frowned, looking at herself in the long mirror, wearing a far more elegant silk gown. It was one that was given to her by her sister that was worn three seasons ago. Three maids had set to work on Brendolyn's hair, all attempting to pin her errant curls up into an elegant design to hide the point of her faie ears, but many curls spilled out, falling down her back and shoulders.

Lahrs stood watch as the maids did their work, his smile becoming more apparent as the princess became more distressed. Brendolyn hated being painted like a doll. Now she was also set in the lavender silk gown that was pulled too snugly about her middle, in an attempt to give her a figure that she clearly did not have. Her hair was pinned too high and made her head feel heavy, drawing out a headache that pounded behind her eyes.

She looked at Lahrs through the reflection of the looking glass.

"I am to dance?" She was horrified.

Lahrs nodded, taking the necklace from the box that the maid held in hand. He stood behind the princess and secured it in place. "You are to stand up with King Beaumont in place of your queen mother, who is still very unwell from her travels."

Brendolyn sighed, her hand touching the shimmering jewels of their country around her neck. They were glittering gems taken from the dunes of Nihtar Isla, where it was said

140

the scales of the dragon shed off when the great beast emerged from the mountain that once dwelt there. Nihtar's scales shimmered like sea crystals, raining down over Corad as she took to the great sky. But that was before the great expanse of the realms, when the Ehlfern crafted the creatures both big and small, helping T'hall shape all that they now walked upon. Brendolyn had only ever seen the great sands of Nihtar from the ships of her father while on tour of the eastern coasts, but she had been younger then.

Brendolyn could barely remember the reason for the journey, but she could never forget the gems that had glittered up at her. Wearing the well-crafted jewelry as a gift from Lahrs was her only token of ever leaving Corad City.

"She should not have come, but she would not miss this...it's not the baby, is it?"

Lahrs shook his head, taking up the gloves from the side table.

"It is early for her to deliver, Bren. It is simply nerves from her time on the boat, nothing more."

She nodded, her gloves snug and her heart beating fast. Together, they finally made their way to the banquet.

Barrow stood atop the stoop of the stairs, he waited astride his father for King Sabian and the party of Corad, who walked from the set of steps to the other wing, so they could ascend the stairs into the banquet hall together. It was an occasion to begin the celebrations of their treaty.

He fidgeted, the collar on his tunic pinned tighter by the family crest, a wolf. His jacket was embroidered with the flowers of his country and made of dark silk and thread of silver that made him shine under the candle light.

"You must be calm," his father's deep voice whispered beside him.

King Beaumont stood tall, broad and bronzed beneath the chandelier. He was dressed in a nearly identical tunic to his son, but pinned to his left shoulder was the crest of kinghood, two wolves flanking a crown that had been encrusted with diamonds. It was an old heirloom passed from father to son. King to heir. Beside the crest were his ribbons of honor, one for the Battle of Thourns. The other was The Valour of Augusta, a tribute given to those that fought to rebuild the fallen city. Finally, to heighten him further, there was a crown upon his father's head. It sat upon his brow snuggly, made of polished white gold that would never tarnish. It was a recent gift crafted by the elves as a token of gratitude in the alliance between their realms.

"You say the queen is still ill, father?" Barrow whispered back, as the few servants and footmen of the southern kingdom began to emerge from the opposite side of the staircase, a two-sided sweep down to join on a singular landing before they would all descend down the staircase to the lower level.

"Not ill enough to warrant alarm, but she is unwell to dance the evening. Her eldest daughter is with her, so you shall not be needed to join in the beginning dance."

Nodding, Barrow sighed. "She is more a nurse to her queen than a princess. Who is it you shall dance with, in her stead?"

"That delight shall befall the youngest of King Sabian's daughters. Princess Brendolyn, I believe."

Barrow laughed. "She looked too young to be presented—impish and small. Are you certain she is Sabian's kin? I could hardly see any resemblance but the dark hair."

His father gave him a disapproving look. Barrow felt its sting; it was unfair to insult the princess. She was pretty, but pretty was all that the women of title and rank could offer. She would no doubt be just like the rest of them. He had met with so many young ladies that paraded around him, batting their eyelashes and showing their bare necks, all in the hopes of earning flattery.

"Do not make yourself uneasy," Beaumont instructed again. Smiling over at his son. "There are worse jobs a prince could cope with than entertaining a pretty girl. Soon the meetings shall begin and so too shall the treaty be finalized. "

That was what worried him. For years, there had been whispers of Barrow's name being written into the treaty. As the next heir of Jorn, it fell to him to keep the treaty going should his father die. And as the Realm of Corad had no heirs as of yet, it was every intent of the council to finalize the alliance by marrying Barrow to the Princess Lisetta of Corad.

He had no intention of marrying her, or any princess.

Barrow's eyes darted to the entrance of the Corad Royal Family, flanked by their guards in Corad colors. There, walking beside the Southern King, was the youngest princess. She was dressed in Corad silks and wearing a necklace made of shimmering jewels known only to the southern region. Her hair, while there had been an attempt to pull it into an intricate pinning atop her head, spilled curls down her back. Barrow chuckled.

"Remarkable," Beaumont kept his voice low, regarding the family across from them. "I thought I had imagined it when I saw her this morning, but I cannot deny there is so much of her mother in the look of the princess."

Barrow glanced at his father. "I have only seen portraits of Queen Natalia, there is little resemblance."

King Beaumont smiled, keeping his eyes on the king of Corad. "Brendolyn is faie. She was born to the lady in waiting for Queen Natalia, who died not long after her birth. It is not often remarked upon; they pride themselves upon their private affairs remaining in secret. Queen Natalia dotes upon both her daughters equally."

Barrow was surprised. "But she is faie. Lord Bannon tells me stories about the faie, and their uprising. Was it not the reason for the fall of Augusta?"

"There is more to this world than those of gossip and whisperings of uprisings, Barrow. She was raised in Corad, to one of the highest families of Veilore. Do not forget who her father is, and why we are here today, Barrow. They shall not forget you, after today. The fate of our two kingdoms depends upon the kinship between us, to set the example of the years to come."

"Yes, Father."

After the entrance into the great hall, now filled with fine dressed courtiers and ladies and gentlemen, Brendolyn sat along a vast table, with Lahrs at her left and her father at her right. She watched as a whirlwind of colors danced before her eyes. Music and laughter fill the air around them. She wished to lean in and talk to Lahrs freely, but with her father so near, she didn't dare.

"You have never attended a banquet, Princess Brendolyn?" a deep voice from before her said, she looked up to see the King of Jorn standing before them.

She gaped up at him, unable to speak.

King Beaumont smiled, offering out a hand.

"It is customary that the king begins the dance with the lady of his choosing."

Brendolyn froze, her heart hammering, but Lahrs nudged her, standing to help her from her seat and escort her around the table to stand next to King Beaumont.

In this moment, Brendolyn was thankful for her gloved hands, for her palms felt cold and sweaty as she placed her right hand over his left. He led her down to the center of the floor, where the crowd of people parted. All eyes were on her. She hated the stares, but steeled herself to the poise that Lahrs had taught her.

Together the king and Brendolyn waited, listening as the beginning tune of the first dance began, a dance that she had practiced many times, but never imagined she would actually ever dance it without the laughs and giggles that she and her tutor shared.

King Beaumont was an elegant dancer. He was beyond elegant; he even surpassed Lahrs in his skill, and Lahrs was best at everything.

Brendolyn turned. Her arm was much shorter than the king's, so she stepped closer to him, causing her to step lightly on his foot. She looked up at him as they faced towards each other now. He was much taller up close, causing her neck to lean back in an awkward angle to look up at him. Her cheeks became hot as she searched his face for any sign of her mistake.

He only smiled, and continued like nothing happened.

"You are very gifted in your dancing. I have not seen many young ladies of your age so unchallenged by a dance not of their own realm." The King of Jorn smiled, looking down at her as he guided her up the room.

Brendolyn's cheeks burned, but she felt no shame in his words. "I have been in lessons since I was four years old, dancing is one of my strengths."

Beaumont smiled genuinely. "Then you shall find many wonderful evenings to entreat us with your charm and grace."

Now Brendolyn did not smile. "Are you mocking me, Your Highness?"

There was a serious look that came over the king, but he did not frown. He kept his features pleasant as his courtiers watched them take a choreographed turn. When they were side by side again, he finally spoke.

"It is not in my way to mock, Brendolyn. Forgive me if I have said anything untoward. If I say you are charming, it is because you are."

Brendolyn watched him for a long moment, studying his expression as best she could as the dance moved them down the hall. When they returned to face each other, she gazed up into his expressive eyes, a flicker of magick fluttered in her chest.

"Thank you, Your Highness. You honor me with your compliment." She knew how she must address him, his smile confirmed he was pleased.

He took her waist, guiding her as the others that danced beside them had already begun to do. She giggled, feeling herself being hoisted briefly by large hands, then righted again so they may continue in the way the other dancers progressed. It was exhilarating, dancing in a room full of couples instead of the little hall she had practiced with Lahrs since childhood. Brendolyn had never seen a dance of this nature up close, nor had the thrill of enjoying the benefits of dancing with another skilled partner.

"Are you fond of dancing?" Brendolyn asked, lifting her hand to Beaumont's shoulder, her eyes catching the amusement he expressed.

"Perhaps I did once, but it has been many years since I have been fond of dancing. Tonight, I am extremely fond of it, which must be because of how remarkably well my partner is. Many clomp around or make terrible conversation, but you are a delight." Beaumont was charming, like so many of the ladies of the court in Corad openly expressed, whether by hinting at a previous interaction themselves, or of a relative who had met the King of Jorn. Brendolyn understood him perfectly.

He went on, "I am not as well as my tutor could have hoped. Being so tall, it was always so awkward to dance with elegance."

"You dance so gracefully, your tutor must have been ill informed."

Now, it was the king's turn to laugh, an amiable sound that made Brendolyn blush. Her eyes flickered around, seeing the lords and ladies of the court watching her. Her heart fluttered again, feeling the sensations that were not her own. Magick pulsed around her in an aroma of feelings—jealousy, indignance, disdain. Her eyes searched again, seeing more eyes watching her, hearing the whispers behind opened fans, the laughs.

"Brendolyn." She looked up, King Beaumont was watching her closely, his steps seemed to slow. "Are you alright?"

Brendolyn took a breath, nodding. Her cheeks grew hot.

"Shall you retire to your chair? You must be in need of refreshment." Beaumont turned them, stepping them in the direction of her chair. But Brendolyn did not want to retreat.

"No." She was flustered, speaking now in Coradian. "I shall be alright, there was just a moment I felt...I cannot really say how I felt."

"It is difficult to discern the emotions of others when there are so many looks and whispers." Beaumont kept his tone low, concerning, but his expression was meant to appease the onlookers. "How long has your faie magick been blossoming?"

"I have always had it...at least, Lahrs has taught me how to conceal that part of me. But lately, it has become difficult." Brendolyn glanced towards her father, who watched them from across the room. They turned, and he was out of sight again.

"Your father is a cautious man." King Beaumont caught on quickly.

As they turned, the music slowed, ending, as did the dance. Suddenly, their time to speak openly was over. Brendolyn lowered herself into a curtsy, one she had practiced so often. King Beaumont, bowed, his face unreadable, but Brendolyn sensed the conflict in the king. They turned, Brendolyn taking his arm, as he led her through the hall and returned her to her seat.

"Thank you, Your Majesty." Brendolyn curtsied again, earning another bow as Beaumont left her at her chair. "I shall never forget your kindness."

It was dark in the cold and drafty estate. Simeon had not cared to keep on the servants it takes to run a full house, leaving many of the rooms unfurnished and blanketed in dust from years of neglect. This place serves one purpose; there was no room for unwanted eyes to see and listen. Following the path of lit candles that dripped old wax along the curling wallpaper beneath the sconces, Simeon ascended the narrow steps to the second floor, following the pull of magick.

Simeon could hear the voice in his head, his body overcome with longing for the magick that called to him.

Entering at last into one of the upper rooms, the key on the chain he wore around his neck went smoothly into the lock. He entered to see the older of the faie looking up at him from the window. The faie had been bathed and dressed in wool to keep out the cold.

Simeon smiled, shutting the door behind him.

"My lord, it has been days." The faie bowed. Simeon could hear the shallow breaths and knew the faie had a parched mouth from lack of nutrition.

"Five days, to be exact. Leuthere was last here the day before yesterday." Simeon nodded, circling the faie that stood trembling in his presence. A smell of fear hit his nose.

"He...he is not to return?" There was terror in the faie as Simeon stepped closer, cooing as he brushed back the matted curls that frizzed along the sides of his face. He knew the things Leuthere pleasured in, behind closed doors, with no one watching.

"No," Simeon hushed softly, caressing the faie's cheek tenderly. "He shall not return here again. I know what it is that you fear."

Beneath his fingertips, Simeon felt the flicker of magick bend as his heart fluttered, the excitement made him smile. The faie eased in his fear, but there was still hesitation, a resistance to give. Simeon needed to be careful what he did next.

"What I offer you is not captivity, not pain. You were broken, depraved of your dignity..." Simeon breathed in deeply, catching the warmth of magick. His blood quickened, hungry, ready to take everything from this creature. "I offer you reprieve. Let me ease your burden. I can release your fear."

Instinctually, the faie stepped closer, licking his parched lips, hanging onto the words that Simeon spoke. The air danced with magick, cradling them in a cocoon of unbreakable warmth.

"Do not fear," Simeon whispered. The faie shuddered, tilting his head back as Simeon curved his hand along the faie's jaw. His other hand wrapped around the faie's middle, trapping him there. "Do not feel," Simeon whispered, his heart racing in his chest. Magick stifled his senses, clouding his eyes in a sheen of white.

It was quick. Simeon flicked his nail along the curve of the faie's neck where the large vein pulsed. Blood began to flow heavily and the faie sighed—it was a sound of ecstasy. Simeon smiled, his teeth bared, and leaned down to latch himself to the small wound. His mouth was at once hot with blood—it was rich and coppery on his tongue as he gulped hungrily until his stomach ached. He pulled back with a gasp.

As the faie bled out, Simeon watched the color drain from those vibrant eyes, his body slumped in Simeon's grasp. Taking hold of his neck, the magick was quick to emerge. A sudden vibrancy ignited in Simeon's blood; he felt the vigor of it yield to him. At last, the faie slumped to the floor, dead.

Simeon stepped over it, his boot smearing in the spilled blood, as he draped himself in the nearest chair. Magick flushed his cheeks, his body newly invigorated. Life surged anew in Simeon's bones. It was nearly an hour before Simeon stirred again. He stood from his chair, leaving the dead body upon the floor. He entered the chamber along the corridor, smiling at the youth with bright shining eyes.

Fear was thick in his nostrils. Wiping his blood-stained mouth, he stepped further into the room, closing the door behind him.

CHAPTER 18

"Should you not be resting?" Pavan asked Malcom, stepping up to stand beside his friend, who was drinking from a tankard.

They were watching the crowd of villagers who danced languidly to music. It was played by a group who were placed at the far end of the room, where the sound would carry all around them. The fire pit was roaring, illuminating the room in a glorious glow and light as the sun began to set. Light was streaming in through the glass-paned windows.

Malcom smirked. "I am resting. Besides, I won't join them on their hunt."

Pavan frowned. "You will be safe; they are all skilled warriors, and you have shown great skill."

"It's not that..." Malcom looked over. Pavan followed his line of sight, seeing the woman who danced with other women. Her skin was beautifully tanned, her long dark hair shimmered in the glow of the light. Trinkets of metal were braided in the curls.

It was the blacksmith's daughter, Farren.

There was little said between Pavan and the blacksmith's daughter, but she was always kind to him when he went to see her father to chop the wood for their fires. Farren gave him water whenever he had need of it, and showed him how to work the grindstone to sharpen his axe. It had been Farren who taught Pavan how to utilize every aspect of the smithery, to use the bellows to heat the fires, or to draw out the iron for her father's needs. He had noticed over time that whenever they met, she would ask him about Malcom. Or to deliver some paper she had collected on her errands around the village to Malcom.

"Does she know?" Pavan smiled, seeing his friend hiding behind his drink.

"Don't be daft, Pavan. We have attraction, but it has not gone to more than flirting," Malcom told him, swallowing mouthfuls of ale.

At once, Pavan took hold of the cup, setting it aside. He hooked his hand beneath Malcom's arm and guided him forward but Malcom dug his heels in.

"What are you doing?" Malcom whispered harshly under his breath.

"You are going to dance with her."

"I cannot dance with her. This is ridiculous." Malcom pulled back, unable to shake his larger friend off. He eyed the room cautiously as they began to draw attention.

"The only thing ridiculous is your shyness, Malcom. Dance with her, and see for yourself how much she fancies you."

Farren saw them approach and her smile brightened.

"Malcom would love to dance with you," Pavan said loudly, releasing Malcom to the throng of dancers; the pair of them were now at the center.

Happily leaving his friend with the dance, Pavan walked the edge of the room. He kept his distance from them, but caught Malcom's eye when his friend chanced to look up. Overcoming his natural shyness, Malcom became bolder, drawing closer to the dark-haired Farren.

"You do not dance?" Meilyr's voice drew Pavan's gaze back. He looked up at the man who watched the celebrations commence. Meilyr made room on his furs for Pavan to sit.

"I have not danced in a long time," Pavan admitted, scanning the room of celebrators, the cascade of limbs and bodies languid with the beat of the music.

He admittedly admired the dancing of these people; they found almost every occasion to celebrate. How different it was to when he was younger, when his mother had sent himself and Hal to bed, and he could hear the music from his room. Pavan always wondered how they celebrated after they sent the young to bed. Now he understood, as he watched the throng of limbs and bodies begin to draw closer. Everything was alive with the beat of the music and the dance of magick that seemed to spiral around the room.

This was like the other dances, but Pavan was lost on the reason why.

"You wish to dance with one not here?"

Heat crept into Pavan's face, his first thought was of an orange-eyed faie, as the man suggested, but the guilt flushed through him. He was unable to admit to himself the longing of companionship with the fiery captain. Meilyr was observant, the little trinkets of gold shimmered in his hair beneath the glow of the chandeliers that hung from the banisters high above their heads in the rafters of the great building.

"Thad is not here," he pointed out.

Meilyr smiled. "Thad is not often at these celebrations. Tonight, it is for the people to send up their prayers to the Ehnarea for the health of our hunters."

"I had not realized it was so soon."

Meilyr nodded, his dark eyes scanning the room, before leaning closer to where Pavan sat so near to the lord of these lands. Sitting so near, Pavan could smell the ash and clove, the spices that lingered over the leader of Ledenjour. Meilyr was the same as he remembered him, from when he was a child. Pavan remembered listening to the stories he told of adventures in the forests of Entheas, of the dangers that crept in the dark. Now, the stories brought with them the hint of danger. No longer mystified by the tales woven to him as a child, Pavan feared what lay in wait for the hunters.

"They shall return to us within two weeks' time; they go deep into the forests, at the base of the great mountains where it is densest. There, the hunters shall teach the youngest of the hunt the ways of the forest."

Pavan nodded. "To take only what is needed, nothing more."

"You have been listening." Meilyr smiled, his whole face glowing with youth, but the shift of his dark eyes showed their age. It was fascinating to Pavan, to see the man not altered in looks, not aged by the years like so many others.

"I remember your tales, as a child. You would give us such descriptions it nearly kept us up at night, but you would return to the village when the hunt was over. You might be covered in blood, but there was never a time you did not smile..." Pavan trailed off, suddenly overcome with the thoughts that began to blossom in his mind.

Memories of this man began afresh in his mind. The night it had begun, when his mother was frightened, it was Meilyr who had been there to comfort her children, while she spoke with the other man, the tall one. Pavan's eyes glossed over at the memory.

"It is never easy to remember," Meilyr told him as he nodded. He reached a hand to rest upon Pavan's arm.

Quietly, Pavan wiped at his nose. Looking about the room, trying to forget the bitterness that blossomed on his tongue, he tried to regain the tranquility of watching the dancers. Pavan opened his mouth but his gaze turned as a flourish of color drew his attention. He caught sight of a young woman who was dressed in patchwork garments.

She was pretty, with long reddish hair pulled back in two long plaits; her ears were pointed, sloped down slightly. He recognized her now to be the pie maker, with a little shop down the main road. She attended to the kitchens most days, bringing with her delicately crafted pies and little pastries.

She approached Meilyr, with her tray of food.

"Thank you." Meilyr smiled, removing his hand from Pavan to accept the offering of a small pastry. He spoke in a low hushed tone to the elf, she listened intently, smiling as she replied.

Pavan couldn't hear; his heartbeat began to pound relentlessly in his ears, drowning out their words.

His mouth became dry as he looked at her. Those rose hued eyes glanced his way, only briefly. It was enough to recognize the desire he felt. Not his own, although he believed her beautiful; she was thrumming with magick. Longing tasted sweet on Pavan's tongue, like honey. Pavan felt her desire for him, awakened like a fresh fallen snow that blanketed him with magick.

"She is a timid girl," Meilyr was now saying, nibbling at the pastry in his palm.

She had not offered him pie, Pavan realized, watching her weave her way along the outer edge of the dancers, stopping when a villager needed replenishment. Occasionally, she would glance up to catch his eye. A smile, and a quick blush, before she turned away again. Pavan's body was uncontrollable as the magick pounded through every vein, making him drowsy and languorous with want.

Pavan began to stand.

Meilyr held his arm. "Stay. There is much we need to discuss."

He shook him off, ignoring Meilyr's sudden urge for Pavan to stay. He felt the music hum around him, following the path along the edge of the dancers until she came into view. Pavan felt her longing as he drew nearer to where she stood.

"Dance with me?" he whispered, leaning in close to her ear.

She jumped, but smiled up at him. Pavan's stomach churned, she was beautiful. Large pink hued eyes blinked up at him, flushed cheeks sprinkled with freckles.

"You wish to dance?" she asked, her voice timid.

"So long as you desire it, but you cannot dance with a tray of food," he encouraged. He took the tray from her, placing it on the nearest table. He then took her hands in his, walking her towards the dancing.

At once she paused, nervous. Pavan felt the flutter of her heartbeat, it was like a hummingbird, quick and fervent. He smiled.

"It is easy," he began, letting the music sway his hips, guided by the rhythm.

Her eyes flicked about; he knew that look of reserve.

"Look at me," he whispered, drawing himself closer. He placed his hand upon her lower back; her eyes were mesmerizing, but she did as he asked, as he guided her through the steps. They moved slower at first, then quickened with each step.

She laughed, finding her confidence as he led her through steps, her eyes did not look away from him. Pavan's smile brightened as they danced on their own. They were apart from the other dancers, but just as earnest. He was losing himself in the moment. The song ended, but quickly blurred into the next. Pavan sighed, seeing the generous flush move over her cheeks. He took her hand, guiding her away from the heat of the dancers, to a darker, quieter corner.

"Sit here, allow me to get you a drink." Pavan smiled, leaving her in a small chair to search for a cool drink.

When the large barrels of ale were found, he downed a full tankard, filling another he turned, returning to his companion. She sat up straighter, her smile returning as he approached her.

"You are a lively dancer," she told him. She spoke lightly, looking Pavan up and down. Under her gaze, he felt hot.

He was admiring her fine pink hued eyes.

"Oh, you are charming." Pavan smirked, sitting upon the seat nearest to her. He let the darkened corner cool his flushed skin. The sun had long since set, leaving the great hall in a sultry glow flickering from the large fire at the center.

"My name is Sophie." Her hand slid across the small table between them, resting on the curve of his wrist.

"Hello, Sophie." His eyes slid from her hand, up again. "I am Pavan."

She giggled. "Yes. I know who you are, Pavan."

The way her mouth fell around his name made him shiver.

She leaned closer, pressing into the table and looking at him earnestly. Shivers of magick burst from her touch into his. Pavan smiled; it was sweet, like early springtime blooms. Pavan leaned in, his hand now warmly pressed to hers. Each thrum of her heart he felt through the touch of his fingertips.

"You are flawless," he sighed, his words igniting a dazzling warmth. His senses were invigorated by the shimmering taste of vanilla. Pavan began to feel his blood rapidly heat, at once reaching up to touch her chin with the flat of his thumb.

Sophie crashed her warm mouth to his, sealing them together with a kiss. He welcomed it, relaxing into the growing need that her mouth provided. She was the only thing that consumed his thoughts, from the taste of her mouth to the feel of her hair. Pavan did not remember her moving, but suddenly she was seated in his lap. Her hands wrenched apart the top of his tunic, exploring the curve of his neck and shoulder.

Pavan's arm wrapped around her slender waist, his other hand gripping her thigh relentlessly through the layers of her skirts. Accepting the kiss in the darkened corner of the room, the sights and sounds of the celebration fizzled away, leaving only the beating of their hearts. Pavan's mind was fuzzy, drunk on the ecstasy of the magick Sophie provided. It was an intoxicating aura that slackened the pain in his heart. Her beating heart was rhythmic against his own chest.

It was the smell of the ocean that caught his attention first, drawing his thoughts away from the elf in his lap. It returned him to the crash of waves, as though he was standing in the sand as the tides rushed in over his feet. Pavan sighed, bringing Sophie closer to him, slowing his hands to press against her while their mouths melded together.

Shifting waves began to sing, humming in his ear. Pavan pulled back, the waves crashed again. Now he could see dark hair fluttering in the breeze, a vision he had seen before. He was standing upon the beach looking at the flowing curls that danced in the breeze. Instinctively, Pavan reached out to take her hand.

Her fingers were smooth, but cold. His heart sank as she began to slip away, walking toward the crashing waves. Pavan called out, but the figure did not stop.

A copper tang soured his mouth. He sneered, the magick made him nauseous. His grip slackened on Sophie's frame. She wiggled, her hands roaming the curve of his neck, touching his skin. Pavan winced. His skin prickled, like a million needles were piercing his skin.

"Stop." His voice sounded foreign to his ears.

Sophie sat back, blinking down at him with large innocent eyes. He touched her cheek, breathing heavily to slow his racing heart.

"Are you alright?" she asked.

Pavan stood abruptly, letting Sophie slide from his lap. He made no excuse, but left her standing there in the darkened corner. He hurried from sight, maneuvering through the side door, out into the cool night. His blood was still hot. Magick coiled in the pit of his stomach. He was trudging up the path away from the promise behind him.

"Pavan?"

That voice made Pavan clench his jaw. It sharpened the edges of his gnashing torment. He swallowed, not turning to look at Lilja, as he was making his way towards the woods. He needed to escape, to run until his legs gave out. Behind him, he heard footsteps upon the gravel drawing closer.

"Are you leaving?" Lilja asked. Her approach only made Pavan want to run more.

"I...I need some air." He shook, his blood hot and his stomach churning violently.

Her hand was on his arm, sending a shock of pain through him. He winced, stumbled aside, and lost his footing. Pavan found himself hunched near the side of a shop, desperately looking up to the elf who loomed over him, her violet eyes gleamed in the moonlight.

"You look ill." She reached up to touch his sweaty brow, but Pavan gripped her arm.

"Leave me alone," he whispered harshly.

Lilja pulled out of his grasp. "Your magick is trying to break free. If you keep it dampened, it will consume you."

Pavan scoffed. "I'm fine."

"Liar."

He stumbled to stand upright. Anger pitted in Pavan's gut, hardening his heart even more. He glared down at the elf who grew wide-eyed as he leaned in towards her, looking deep into her violet eyes.

"Let me help you." She placed her hand flat on Pavan's chest.

Pavan scowled. Towering over her as fear rippled between them, Pavan could feel the elf trembling. He was close to her, he could smell the oils in her hair, the perfume lingering in his nose. He didn't need her; he didn't want her.

"I don't need your help," he growled, gripping the slender curve of her throat where the pulse quickened beneath his touch, her fear sharp on his tongue.

"Then you must sleep," she stated, resolute. Magick rolled from her tongue.

Pavan scoffed, opening his mouth to speak, but his eyelids grew heavy. His limbs were like iron, dragging him down. Collapsing to his knees before her, Pavan looked up, her eyes were brighter, glowing. Her skin was shimmering. Magick cooled his blood, but it did not belong to him.

Lilja touched the curve of his brow, leaning down to see closer into his face. "You will feel better in the morning, Pavan. I'm sorry."

She kissed him hard.

Warm magick washed through him. He was unable to stop the ground from colliding with his face, before he was swimming in sudden unconsciousness.

Rising early, Pavan dressed to accompany Malcom down to the blue morning haze. Watching the hunters begin to prepare their horses for departure, Pavan saw the horses dancing with excitement as the hunters latched their saddlebags and swords to the harnesses.

They walked between the rows of the somber youth that tried to look fearless in the perturbation of the coming weeks. Pavan was silent, while Malcom gave each of them a satchel of tonics and small provisions of food. He gave them a quick prayer before they went on to the next group of hunters. Pavan followed Malcom until the last satchel was given to young Trisk, the vibrant youth was quiet with reserve.

"Thank you, Lord Malcom." Trisk nodded, tucking the satchel into place.

Pavan blinked back the headache forming behind his eyes. Turning away from them, his eyes scanned the length of the grounds. He scanned the familiar faces until he saw the familiar white hair at the edge of the field. Lilja stood by the other guides who were going to lead the hunt. She did not look their way, but Pavan could feel the chill run up his spine.

His lips tingled, remembering the kiss she forced on him to make him sleep. Feeling her power seep into him with such force; it was unsettling. It had given him an unwanted desire that he could not shake. Quickly, he looked back to Malcom.

"I will meet you later," he muttered, trudging back up the path, stopping a good distance away.

He could see Malcom in close conversation with Farren as she prepared her horse. It was delightful to see Malcom smile, and caring for the blacksmith's daughter. Finally, he turned away when he saw Malcom kiss Farren, believing no one was watching them.

Walking along the bending path leading up to the training yard, Pavan was surprised to see Thad lingering there, watching him approach. He was dressed in simple wool, and a thick cloak was hanging over his shoulders to stave off the early morning chill. Thad looked pale and somber as he watched the hunters prepare for their journey.

"You do not hunt with them?" Pavan asked.

"I have not for many years. I remain here, for their return." Thad tried to smile, Pavan felt a shift in the faie. It was a sadness that made his head spin.

Thad began to walk back towards the training yard, following the path along the stone wall. He was moving back in the direction of the great house.

"I am sorry for your loss."

It was quiet in the early morning, casting an eerie loneliness over the usual clamor of busy hunters at work to condition their bodies. They were undertaking preparations for this hunt, which would bring in the food supply to last the winter in Ledenjour. Pavan remembered how bitter and harsh the village would become, even under the protection of Meilyr's magick. He knew of the ice and storms that would freeze the roads, making it impossible to go further north, or return to the sea-bearing south.

Thad chuckled. "I see your magick has begun to emerge."

"It is not magick that tells me of your pain. I have been told of the recent loss of Aron Dourn. He was a young man when I was here in my childhood, a companion to Meilyr. It was he who told me of Aron Dourn's death."

Beside him, the faie stopped; his usual calm expression was grave and pained.

"He is grieved by many."

Pavan felt the sting of it, gulping back the force that climbed into his throat and threatened to overflow. Magick was tightening its grip.

"But to have loved him must have been a burden."

"*Love* is a strange word," Thad muttered, his cheeks turning a healthy shade of pink. "I did not love him. Not in that regard, at least. I was devoted to him in a way that I have rarely felt for any man."

His sadness was stifling, drawing Pavan in with a sharp intake of breath. He found it difficult to contain such a deepening desire to rid the faie of his sorrow.

"Devotion is in its own regard a form of love. Is it not?"

Thad looked up with a strange, guilty look. "Devotion can be given without regard. It is devotion to Meilyr for taking me from Denorn when I was unable to part from my master. My devotion to him, over time, became a great esteem. For Aron Dourn, it was a new kind of devotion. I wanted to please him, in any way I could."

"That devotion sounds an awful lot like love to me." Pavan stopped, glancing down at Thad with earnest entreaty. "Your master? Were you not a tradesman?"

Thad frowned. "That is the lie given to those who questioned my loyalties. Meilyr has always tried to protect me since I was first brought to Ledenjour. He regards me as his own son in that way."

They stood nearest to the low built wall, where the practice targets hung. In the chill of the morning, there was frost on the metal casings. Now alone, shutting out the noise of the world, Pavan could see the hesitation in Thad. Watching him closely in the span of a single breath, many things became apparent to Pavan as he watched the faie closely. He heard his words and understood the notes of sadness.

"How do you know of the mark given to me by Eske?"

Thad's lip pulled down at the corners, betraying the stern indifference in the faie's demeanor. Pavan could feel the shift of magick. Pavan reached up, drawing nearer, he placed a hand on Thad's shoulder. Warmth radiated from within.

"I saw his face, before he held me down." Pavan shivered. "I heard him speak of a young faie, with a fiery spirit. One that gave him a hideous scar."

"He has taken many of my people. He has mutilated them and sold them for decades." Thad's voice was a hiss. A growing hatred festered inside him that Pavan felt burning beneath his palm.

"Such pain," Pavan whispered.

His heartbeat quickened, Pavan could not distinguish if it was the magick that burned between them, or the fire of yearning in Thad's being. It was beautiful, twisting within Pavan like vines.

"He sold you. Just like he did to me and Malcom. But there was no 'Thad' to save you from a new master." Tears slipped free, dazzling the curve of Pavan's cold cheek. Magick shimmered with urgency. Pavan could see the twisted features of the freshly burned Eske while the man bent down to accost Thad. Pavan could see the harsh grip of the man with a new face, bright eyes, and brown hair that was neatly styled.

Thad gulped. "Pavan. Stop."

Cold rushed through Pavan. He stepped back, hardening himself to the pain and numbing his magick to feel nothing. Shame made his cheeks flush, as he glanced away from Thad, who watched him intently.

"Forgive me, Thad. I did not mean...my magick is unpredictable..."

Thad took his hand.

"It is alright. I have no shame in what is past, Pavan. I was sold by Eske to a man who kept me in a gilded cage where I remained for most of my young life. I was used as a pawn, as a sport in his business in Denorn. But I was saved by Meilyr."

"I feel your anguish," Pavan breathed. He could hear the words, but his body was suffocating in the rich pain that burned through him.

"Forget how I felt then, Pavan. How do I feel now?" Raising his hand, Thad pressed Pavan's palm to the flat of his chest. Pavan could feel the slow rhythmic thump of the faie's heart. It was not like when he had felt the connection of his past—it was delightfully warm, Thad's magick tasted like honey on his tongue, with a hint of citrus warmed with clove.

Pavan's desire clawed further up into his throat, souring his stomach.

"I do not want this magick," Pavan spoke, his voice strained. "Since I was a child, I have run from what happened. But it always returns. I can see everything, I remember everything. Even then, I could feel their looks. Their fear..."

Edges of cold thawed away when Thad gripped his hand painfully hard.

"I do not fear you." A hand moved to touch the curve of Pavan's neck, magick danced from Thad's warm fingers. "Do you sense my fear?"

Pavan smirked, shaking his head and sighing into the touch.

"You lost someone dear to you. It must be painful, to carry that grief in your heart," Thad said, his hand remaining on Pavan's neck.

Pavan gulped. "Using your magick, Thad?"

Keeping his fingers at the bend of his neck, Thad shook his head. "My magick is complex. I can look into another's mind. Sometimes it is unwelcomed, while other times, it can connect me to those in need of comfort."

"Can you read my thoughts?" Pavan felt his insides flip.

"I have seen the fade of your hurt; it is more than what this world has done to you, or what Eske has done to you. It is something deeper, a pain that has broken your soul. She remains in your memory, the girl with dark hair."

"I have told you about Penelope."

Thad shook his head. "You speak her name, but you do not speak of your loss. If she was your lover, if she was your wife…"

"She died, Thad." Pavan trembled against the force of speaking.

Pavan pulled back, drawing himself away from the comfort that was being given. He was unable to look into those beautiful orange eyes. They tormented him the most, guilting him for the way he felt for the faie.

"Unlike my devotion to Aron Dourn. I grieved his loss for a time, but your devotion to Penelope is the truth of devotion to another. Yours is the truth of love in its purest form." Thad's orange eyes shimmered.

"Thad, it is best if you stay out of my mind."

"I do not fear you, Pavan. There is nothing in your past or present that would turn me away. But I shall do as you ask."

"We begin training, do we not?" Pavan asked, suddenly.

Thad sighed heavily.

"It is what Meilyr wishes. We shall begin and keep training until they return from the Hunt. Then, you shall be tested with them."

"You do not think I am ready to train?" Pavan looked up to see Thad was calm.

"It is not what I think, Pavan, but what is right. Should there be a time you need to defend yourself, it is important that you know the proper techniques. With your magick, it will be more challenging."

Pavan nodded. "I understand."

CHAPTER 19

Jorn City, Realm of Jorn.

Barrow walked the gardens beside Princess Lisetta, who strode in lavish pink silks and a parasol held by her maid. Her lady-in-waiting, Clara, walked behind her as did her knight Sir Varick, all at a small distance to give them space to talk but close enough to chaperone.

They had been walking for nearly half an hour, at the urging of King Beaumont.

Barrow smiled. "We have thirteen gardeners responsible for the care of our grounds. Do you like the roses we planted last summer?"

"They are very fine. But Corad has wild roses that bloom in the spring, in bright colors. Nothing beautiful ever grows in a cold climate," Lisetta said at last, looking to the prince from beneath the shade of her parasol.

"Yes, I hear your gardens in Corad are exquisite."

Lisetta sighed. "Only the best was ever planted for my mother. She has excellent taste. Felour is known for its many blooms. My gown was handspun and dyed with the rare pink blossoms of the flower from my mother's homeland."

A servant approached them, carrying a tray of fruits. Barrow offered the princess a sample of the fruits from their orchard.

"I never eat out of doors," she said and she curtsied slightly.

Barrow offered a new route, saying, "We could walk the grove. The trees have bloomed for the season."

The princess stopped suddenly.

"My gown is made of hand spun silk. Am I to ruin it by walking through the mud? It rained only this morning and I can still see a glisten of dew on the leaves." She was looking at the ground beyond the cobbled path with disgust.

Barrow opened his mouth to speak, but Lisetta smiled, taking his hand in hers.

"Thank you for joining me in a walk, Your Highness, but I should return to my queen mother. It is nearly time for tea and she will be expecting me."

Barrow nodded, kissing her hand before watching her and the party that followed her leave. When she was gone, Barrow sighed heavily. Trudging to the stables, he found his close companion and knight Sir Eero.

The knight was nearly fourteen years older than Barrow, with short cropped hair that was so blond it was nearly white. They stood about the same height, with Sir Eero having a slight advantage of build. Barrow could not remember a moment in his life that he was without the company of Eero. Since they lived in Brac when he was a child, only coming to Jorn City when his father was crowned king, Sir Eero was always with him.

"How was the princess?" Eero asked.

Barrow rolled his eyes. Stripping himself of his fine jacket, he tossed it over the stall door. "She is insufferable. Nothing appeases her."

Sir Eero nodded, returning his brush to the mare before him. The dark brown coat flickered as the horse twitched beneath the rhythmic care.

"She is a princess, Barrow, and a princess of Felourian blood."

Barrow groaned as he leaned his back against the stall.

"We were not five minutes from the castle when she complained of the sun in her eyes. But then there was not a path she wished to take without complaint of the cold breeze. I cannot understand why my father insists I entertain her. There is nothing she enjoys but sitting in her mother's chambers, or walking the galleries."

"Then I suggest you walk the galleries. Would it be so terrible to look at old portraits beside a pretty girl?" Eero was laughing, Barrow could see the man's shoulders shaking with it.

"Have your laugh now, but I cannot see that woman again today. Pretty or not."

Eero turned. "Then let's ride the grounds. It has been a long while since your horse has had decent exercise."

"Very well."

Simeon was pruning the odd-looking plants in his offices, when Sir Varick entered. Simeon commenced with his work, he offered no words and no welcome, letting the knight come and sit in his chair, waiting. Until at last, the last of the dead leaves and buds upon the plant were placed in a small bowl.

"You are late," Simeon said at last. The knight shifted uncomfortably in his chair.

"Forgive me, I was with the princess."

Simeon scowled, placing the bowl on one of the tables tucked back away in a corner, retrieving a small vial from a little black box made of velvet. He returned to face the knight.

"No excuses; your duty is to me. You pledged your life to it, Varick. You made a blood pact." Simeon smiled, a cruel, cold thing, as he watched the knight turn a shade of green. Varick touched the skin of his neck, where a small wound was now healed.

"You told me you have a particular job for me, my lord," Varick stammered, watching Simeon approach. There was hunger in the knight's eyes.

"Yes, a particular job." Simeon sat on the chair opposite where Varick waited. He watched the knight closely before showing him the vial, its contents shifted to a shimmering pale liquid.

Varick eyed the vial. "Potion?"

Simeon smiled, his lips parting back over his teeth. Varick gulped, terror flooding through him. It was welcoming.

"Poison."

The words brought terror to Varick as he stood. "My lord, please, I beg of you..."

Simeon hissed, vengeful. "Beg? Beg? Only a slave begs, Varick. You are a knight, it is your duty to do as you are told."

Varick wrung his hands. "But poison, my lord." He quieted. Simeon could taste the discontentment, could taste the very tremors that shook the knight's body. "You cannot wish me to poison a courtier."

Simeon laughed. "This is a poison meant only for kings."

"I cannot…" Varick shook, sweat beading on the man's brow. His face went pale, revulsion seeped from his pores.

Simeon leaned forward, inching closer to the taste of Varick's magick, so repulsed by the task set to him. He would do it, there was no doubt of it. Simeon felt the coil of the tether in the knight. It was a connection that bound Varick completely to himself, and an entanglement that could not be undone.

He smiled. Varick whimpered.

"You will kill your king, Varick," Simeon hissed, pressing the vial into the knight's sweating palm.

The knight gulped, his pale face now green.

Simeon brushed back a fall of limp hair from the knight's face. Wary brown eyes looked up to meet him as Simeon shifted himself to sit beside the knight, who trembled violently. Simeon wrapped an arm around the broad shoulders of the once brash man who was devoted and eager. Now, he was reduced to what he truly was–a frightening man.

"Do not fear," Simeon fussed, comforting the man with an embrace.

Magick flared; the taste of despair was rich. Simeon hummed, trailing a long finger along Varick's hair, curving down the knight's jaw to the scar on his neck.

It was there the magick pulsed beneath his touch, begging to be taken. Simeon smiled, tightening his grip, his fingers flexed against the neck readily exposed to him. Beside him, the tremors stopped, as pliancy exuded from Varick. It was resignation against Simeon's magick pull.

"You will do as I order, Varick and your reward shall be great," Simeon whispered, lips brushing the stubble on the man's cheek. Now the man trembled again, but a different sort of trembling—it was desire, flickering in the heart of the man.

"She will be mine?" Varick's voice was lofty, drunk upon the stupor of magick. Simeon's hand tightened, so close to the coursing blood well beneath the surface.

"You will have that faie bitch, but not until the royal line is vanquished." Simeon closed Varick's fingers tight over the vial in his palm, securing it there, with assurance.

Brendolyn walked with Lahrs through the castle to each of the portrait halls and eventually came to the libraries where many of the other lords and ladies of court seemed to be walking about as well. Lahrs stood speaking with a courtier who was asking about the history of a castle in one of the paintings.

She found her way through a second side hall, with a quiet space where no one stood. She had looked up at the first painting to catch her eye, when someone came to stand beside her. But it was not Lahrs. She turned to see it was the Prince of Jorn.

Prince Barrow looked flushed, his hair was disheveled as he pulled his jacket sleeves down over the dirty cuffs of his tunic. She smiled, catching his eye.

Brendolyn curtsied but said nothing.

She walked to another portrait. A moment passed and he was standing there beside her again. Behind them, a few more lords and ladies shuffle past. The prince acknowledged them before returning to look at the painting.

"Is this a location within Jorn?" Brendolyn asked, her eyes never leaving the painted landscape before them.

"It is the coast to the north. A gift from a painter who resides in Nord. I am told he captured the sunset perfectly," Barrow spoke, his voice a soft timber.

She nodded to the prince before moving on to the next painting along the wall.

"Do you frequent the gallery often, Your Highness?"

He frowned. "I was looking for someone."

Brendolyn felt a pang, eyeing the other courtiers that roamed the quiet gallery. They were whispering and gossiping behind their fans of the latest fashions, and scandals, of the city. She did not see anyone from Corad.

"My sister is not here. She remains in my queen mother's chambers."

"Perhaps I was looking for you." The prince was standing so near to her, she could see the brightness of his blue eyes in the light of the windows.

Brendolyn curtsied. "Then I would respectfully call you a liar."

Turning away, she found herself in the alcove of another portrait, where there was less visibility to those that whispered. Barrow followed her, reaching out to touch the curve of her elbow.

He was smiling. "That is not how an ordinary princess talks, but you are not ordinary."

Brendolyn frowned.

"I was looking for your sister, as you said, but I have found someone much more pleasant. Forgive my forward nature, but I cannot imagine spending an evening in any other company than your own."

She blushed, searching those blue eyes for the truth. He was brightened with delight, his lively expression hopeful. Brendolyn could not discern any falsehood. Prince Barrow was genuinely impressed.

"I have my studies, and cannot stay long."

"Then perhaps tomorrow, we can walk the gardens. We can sample the harvest in the grove." He lowered his hand from her elbow, to take her hand.

Brendolyn's heart beat faster. "I would like that, Prince Barrow."

He smiled. "Until tomorrow, princess."

Leaning in, he bent to kiss her fingers, a smirk playing on his lips.

"Brendolyn," Sir Lahrs' voice cut in, breaking their seclusion.

Lahrs watched them, his face still and unreadable. Brendolyn was aware of the prince who no longer bent to kiss her hand, but still held her bare fingers in his own. Her face grew hot and she drew her hand out of his.

"Thank you, Prince Barrow. These paintings are remarkable and I am grateful for your kindness in telling me about your realm." She turned away, following Lahrs and taking a quick glance over her shoulder as they reached the doorway.

Out in the corridor, Lahrs stopped.

"Be careful how you are seen with him, Bren," he cautioned, looping her arm with his as he steered them towards the staircase. "The courtiers love to talk. We do not want them to whisper about any untoward connection."

"He was telling me about the paintings."

Lahrs gives her a sharp look. "Don't play the fool, Bren. You understand how things stand between him and Lisetta."

She flushed hot. "Yes."

"Come, your lessons are waiting."

CHAPTER 20

Barrow was brought before his father to be informed of the council's decision for his future. He was to be married to Princess Lisetta, heiress of Corad. To say that he was stunned would be an understatement.

Barrow was furious and perplexed.

"They can make that decision so decisively?" he inquired, his knees threatening to buckle from under him where he stood before his father, who sat with a creased frown on his face.

"It was a notion placed into the lines of the treaty when you were very small, after the war was over, when there was finally peace. Had I known it would have been moved into action so suddenly, I would never have signed off to this heinous—" King Beaumont thumped his fist upon his chair, aggravated.

"It was necessary, to ensure the throne of Corad would be graciously handed to us without quarrel," the sleek sound of Lord Bannon's voice slid between them.

Beaumont sat straighter, eying his advisor with annoyance as the man came into view.

"Handed the throne?" Barrow scoffed, looking at the older man who smiled down at the king where he sat.

Lord Bannon looked back at Barrow, narrowing his eyes.

"Your father is a powerful king; he is known throughout our kingdoms as the man who brought peace and strength to the realm. We have secured the Realm of Entheas. Soon it will be under Jorn rule, now we shall have Corad. With the Three Realms under one banner, the rest of the world will not question us and our king."

"You speak of the lands to the east, where you slaughtered down villages before their ruler waved a white flag? Peace and security have no place on your lips."

"Where would your station be, young prince, in the war room? There is no mistaking your ignorance of the world. You have not been alive long enough to see the destruction one uprising could cost a great kingdom." Lord Bannon shifted his stance, leering at Barrow.

"Lord Bannon, I suggest you hold your tongue." King Beaumont had stood to his feet as the lord rounded on his son, eyes ablaze. "You may command my armies as you choose, but you forget to whom you speak. He is my son and heir to my throne."

Lord Bannon bowed his head. "Of course."

"Leave us. I have matters I must speak to my son about. Alone."

Lord Bannon bowed. Once the man was gone, King Beaumont's eyes softened, as he placed a hand on Barrow's shoulder.

"She is an ill-hearted woman, Father. I have tried everything to entertain her, but she is vain and cares little of anything but finery and needlepoint and having new gowns made. She is nothing like—" Barrow stopped, blushing. He coughed on his words.

"Brendolyn is a charming girl, but she is very young, Barrow and not of noble blood."

Barrow rolled his eyes, pulling away from his father. "Noble birth, her father is King Sabian. You cannot tell me that a man of his blood would diminish the merit of her birth because she was born of a faie woman."

"You do not know the gravity of the situation."

"Her mother was a lady, faie or not, you cannot deny her birthright is any less than that of her sisters."

There was a long silent pause.

"She is not of child-bearing age and cannot hold sanction in our court. There are laws in place that make it impossible."

"Father, please."

"You cannot marry Brendolyn Moreau."

Barrow grit his teeth, clenching his jaw. "Yet you make me marry a woman who is both fertile and who I would never look upon with love and admiration. I would be king, she would no doubt have me, but I would be a fuel to her desire of possession and finery. She would want for nothing and I would be a miserable king in the company of none who desire me for who I am, but for what I can give them. I would have no soul to share my passions."

His words stung like a knife in Beaumont's side.

"Could you be so certain Brendolyn does not share her sisters' eye for finery and needlepoint?" Beaumont snapped.

Barrow faltered, uneasily shaking his hands at his sides.

"You know nothing of women, Barrow. Or the realms. Lisetta is all finery and reserve, as she should be as a lady of nineteen. She has entered womanhood and would wear a crown with a dignity that will reflect upon her king. But Brendolyn is a child who will run and laugh as she pleases because duty has not formed within her. She will marry a lord or duke, if it pleases her father, or he will send her to the ladies of the south who dress in white gowns and commit their lives to the prayers of Ehnarea."

"She is kind and spirited. If you knew her better, Father..." Barrow argued.

"Brendolyn is a charming girl, I have known her spirit well before she was born. But even if you met her years from now and her manners had tamed, her laughter had quieted and she walked and talked of finery and needlepoint, her heart would not fetter to the simple dealings of becoming a queen. A pretty face shall not persuade the lords that she is worthy of a throne."

"You are the king, you married a commoner from Entheas."

Beaumont looked hard at his son. "She was not *faie*, Barrow. Eleanore was not born of those that our people have proclaimed as traitors and murderers that have caused a plight in our country."

"You told me the fall of Augusta was unwarranted. That it was wrong to have killed the faie for defending the honor of their people."

"I am but one man, Barrow. My crown and duty are not enough to change the hearts of those that have lost in the fall of that great city. But it is within my power to rebuild what remains. To be the hand that strengthens what was once lost."

"You cannot make me marry Lisetta. "

Beaumont sighed heavily. "It is out of my hands, Barrow. I am sorry."

Anger flushed through Barrow as he stormed from the room, leaving his father with his maps and treaties. He had no need of them.

In his frustration, Barrow walked through the castle in agitation, returning to the orchard where he could walk alone without the prying eyes of the courtiers or the lords and ladies who frequented the castle. There were only the gardeners and tenders to the orchard who smiled as he walked by.

It was here he had ventured since he was a young child. He could escape the firm clutches of finery and duty and just breathe. Slowly he unlaced his tunic, letting it fall open to reveal the under shirt. It was a cool evening and he enjoyed its freshness.

At the farthest trees near the edge of the orchard he stopped, a voice finding his ears from beyond the tall hedges of the forgotten gardens beyond. It was overgrown now from years of neglect. These gardens that were once his mother's had been long forgotten.

Now he heard a voice from beyond the gate. He entered it slowly as he followed the voice through the labyrinth of hedges, it became louder and louder as he neared its center. The voice was singing, and it was soothing. He could feel the anger he had being etched away and leaving a warmth within his chest.

Barrow stopped.

Before him was something he was not expecting to see. Brendolyn, in a silk gown kneeling over a hedge, her hands deep in soil. She was singing. To her right was a blonde elf, who Barrow knew to be Sir Lahrs, he was seated upon a carved stone bench.

Sir Lahrs saw him first, his eyes growing wide as he spoke to the princess in a quick Coradian dialect. She immediately stopped singing, turning in a flash to face Barrow, her face was smudged with dirt.

"Prince Barrow," her voice was rushed as she stood, giving a small curtsy. Her cheeks grew red as Barrow tried to find his own words.

Lahrs took pity on them both.

"You are well, Prince Barrow?"

Barrow breathed deep, smiling. "Remarkably, though I will admit I had come to escape the duties of being a prince. It appears I have been beaten to my favorite sanctuary. I am surprised to see you here so soon."

He looked then to Brendolyn, who smiled sweetly. She hid her dirty hands behind her back.

"I have not forgotten our engagement, but I happened upon this place while searching for worms. It is a remarkable garden with very rich soil."

Barrow could not have heard her correctly. He repeated, "Worms?"

She smiled, nodding, pulling her hands to her front to reveal she was holding a handful of worms in one hand. Barrow looked from the princess to Lahrs, who didn't look surprised at all. Brendolyn placed the worms in a small bucket she had nearby, wiping her hands on a cloth.

Brendolyn curtsied, attempting not to touch her silk gown with her hands.

"We need no formality out here; there are no prying eyes of courtiers to be gossiping about. Please, call me Barrow," he offered, reading her discomfort as she flitted about.

She smiled. "Only my closest companions call me Bren."

She stepped in time with him as they started a turn of the aging gardens, Lahrs following some paces behind.

"I hope we can be companions." Barrow smiled.

"Do you often find yourself outdoors? Personally, I think there is nothing better; the trees and flowers have no care for silks or lessons on needlework." There was a shine in her eyes as he looked down at her, small specks of light glittered in her golden eyes.

As they walked, the latticework of branches above them the sunlight caught on her skin and hair with a glow. He caught himself staring, but she didn't seem to care. She walked beside him in silence for a time, a pleasant look about her.

"Your voice is beautiful." His lips betrayed him, and he found himself biting them hard at the betrayal.

They stopped. He looked down at her with regret.

But she simply smiled. "I sing when I am alone...well, when I am with Lahrs." She acknowledged the elf who walked behind them.

"It is a voice I could listen to every day."

She paused. "My father had forbidden me to sing to anyone but Lahrs. He fears I would enchant someone."

Realization strikes Barrow in an instant by her meaning, not failing to recognize why Lahrs was so sudden to silence the princess. Her voice, as a Faie, could enchant any man who listened to a number of extraordinary things.

"Forgive me, I had not realized." He looked also to Lahrs, who nodded his acceptance.

"It is no certainty that my Faie voice is used every time I sing, but we must remain cautious. But if I do not sing, I become quite sad."

"It would be a shame to see you sad," he said in a low voice.

Brendolyn smiled, but her eyes caught the sight of their path. Ahead of them was a small pond, filled with dark water that rippled and glinted under the sun. She picked up her skirts and ran towards it. Barrow watched as the young princess peered inside, before stepping into the water.

Barrow realized she wasn't wearing any shoes and her feet and ankles were bare, he turned away quickly as she splashed about. Lahrs stood next to him, watching his ward.

"I hear you have the best horsemen in the country?" Lahrs offered, shifting a look to the prince, who looked at him confused. Then the gentle nudge of Lahrs' chin in the direction of Brendolyn made Barrow aware of what he meant.

"Do you ride horseback?" Barrow called out in the direction of where the splashes came from.

There was a pause, and the princess peaked around his side.

"You want to take me horseback riding?" She was smiling wide, her face clean of the dirt and the hairs around her face wet. Bren looked from him to Lahrs and then back to Barrow.

"Only around the open pasture. No farther." Lahrs nodded.

Brendolyn took Barrow's offered arm and together they walked through the gardens towards the stables. Barrow talked of the grounds and what every building housed. Upon stepping into the stables, the sounds of the horses and calls of stable hands and masters greeted them. Barrow walked the princess along a long line of stalls and boxes until he reached a familiar box with a door painted yellow. Inside was a familiar man attending to the horse inside.

"This is Sir Eero, he attends to the royal horses and when out of the castle attends as my guard."

To this man the princess curtsied, smiling up at him.

Sir Eero nodded. "It is a pleasure to meet you, princess."

After a few introductions they finally acquired a horse in gear and Barrow helped the princess onto the horse, explaining the reins and commands. She smiled at the prince before knowingly kicking the horse into movement, cantering from the stable out into the pastures beyond the doors.

Barrow was shocked. Lahrs smiled. "You better mount your mare sir, if you ever want to have a chance to catch up."

Barrow smiled, doing just that.

Out on the fields, Barrow smiled as he watched the princess handle the horse she was saddled on. He caught up to her with some effort, but when they were finally in stride, he patted his horse for the valiant efforts.

"You are very skilled." He smiled at Brendolyn as she turned the horse to come side by side with the prince.

"Skill has little place near the quality of enjoyment. When I enjoy something, I cannot keep away for long. Horseback, archery, and long walks."

Barrow smiled knowingly at the princess. "We cannot forget digging in the royal gardens."

Princess Brendolyn laughed. "Are you flirting with me?" she asked, making the prince's cheeks glow red.

He looked away quickly, a smile curling the edge of his lips.

"I am sorry," Brendolyn said to him.

He looked up, her eyes shining.

She spoke on, "I really like you. You make me laugh. You never smiled when I saw you with Lisetta; she is very proper and will make a lovely queen. Oh! Do not misunderstand. I enjoy every chance meeting we share, you are always so very kind. I only ask because I cannot discern if it is your nature to flirt or are particularly fond of my company."

Her words were so eloquent, and she was so poised atop her horse.

Barrow had never heard someone of her age speak in such a decided way, he was so used to all the young daughters of court and every woman who fancied him to be rather stupid, simpering and blushing, displaying their fans and batting their eyelashes. He liked the direct and decided manner of the princess.

"I admit it, selfishly, every chance I am in your company, it is the happiest I have been in a long while." They walk their horses around the farthest point of the pastures. Brendolyn smiled back at him.

CHAPTER 21

Ledenjour, Realm of Entheas.

His muscles ached as the clang of a metal sword to shield vibrated through him. Pavan hissed, stepping back from Thad, who had advanced with shield ready. Gripping tighter to the handle, Pavan stepped forward, then again, swinging the blade with practiced skill. Years of play-fighting in the theatre had come in handy when training the last few days with Thad. Standing against the faie, after so many weeks of watching him spar against so many others, Pavan understood the anguish it was to go against him.

It wasn't only the strength that Thad possessed, nor his quickness of footing. It was the raw unyielding power behind his movements, the determination to complete every strike, then following through with each sweep and blow. Pavan grew tired, wiping the sweat from his brow with the edge of his tunic. He glanced up at Thad, who stood watching him with careful eyes.

"Follow through with your sweep, do not clench down on the blow. That sword is an extension of your arm." Thad returned to his stance, but Pavan did not pick up the sword. "Come now, Pavan, your skill improves."

"It has been hours, Thad. I cannot continue. There is no chance I can fight without my magick manifesting."

Thad approached Pavan, pulling his arm free of his shield.

"You reserve yourself, do not be afraid of the magick you carry. In battle, it will benefit you. Come, let us restart hand to hand, it will be useful if you should lose your weapon."

Pavan rolled his eyes, finally leaning down to retrieve his sword from the ground. He was happy to be able to wield it without any recurring panic attacks, as he had done before while practicing in the theatre. Here, there was only the pain of holding the weapon, instead of the harsh memory of the blade that struck him down.

He remembered the first training he had with Thad. It had resulted in him being knocked back on his ass multiple times because he was afraid to let his magick through. Thad always instructed to not pull his punches, but every time, it landed Pavan on the ground. As they continued, he could feel the magick begin to build, resulting in a few splintered shields that Pavan shattered with ice, or the broken blade that had occurred when Pavan struck the ground in rage.

"No hand to hand. I cannot risk my magick to manifest, not while I can strike you with it," Pavan stated flatly.

"Do I look to be one who cannot handle your magick?"

Thad was disheveled, his copper hair darkened with sweat, his fair skin flushed from exertion but there was little exhaustion in the faie's look. Thad did not tire easily, Pavan noticed. He could train for hours, not tiring before there is no one left to train against. Pavan could see there was a heightened spirit in the orange eyes, a beat of heightened delight that thrummed between them.

"Your strength is no match for the magick I wield, Thad. You know that perfectly well." Pavan raised his sword to ready position.

A look of worry came over Thad. "We must have complete trust in each other."

"I trust you, Thad."

Thad raised his fists. "Then fight me, hand to hand."

Pavan hesitated. His grip tightening on the handle of the sword, he could feel the flutter of his own heart beating in his chest. "I don't trust myself."

"Your battles cannot be won with a sword."

"I cannot use magick, Thad. I will hurt people."

Thad did not move. "You are afraid. It's only natural. But you cannot run from your past forever."

"I cannot control that part of me, Thad!" Pavan shouted, throwing the sword to the ground, glaring at the faie. "I have willed myself to control the magick, but it burns across my skin, it is hot like fire that wishes to consume every living thing that comes close enough."

A stillness blankets the training yard.

"You're not a monster."

Pavan chuckles, bitterly. "You say that now, Thad. But what should happen when I cannot contain the fire? What would you do when I cannot stop the hunger that consumes me whenever I feel the pain of those nearest to me?"

Drawing closer, Thad touches the damp tunic that hangs limp over Pavan's trembling arm. As he touched the tense muscle, Pavan flinched reflexively.

"Your guilt for killing that man when you were a child is just," Thad said. He spoke quietly, his wandering eyes taking in Pavan's wild expressions. "There is a darkness that lingers in the soul, when you kill. Pavan, I understand your sorrow."

"I do not feel guilty for killing that man," Pavan seethed, tears burning his eyes.

Thad nodded, smiling bitterly. "No? Then why are you so heavy with guilt?" He reached up to gently swipe away the falling tears across Pavan's cheek.

It was painful as his emotions emerged, years of agonizing torment flooding up, he was unable to stop the memories that were buried so deeply come to the surface. Anger flickered in Pavan, as he pushed Thad away.

"He deserved to die," Pavan hissed. "They all deserved to die for touching my mother." His fists were clenched, holding around the fire within him.

"Your guilt, Pavan."

Thad was moving, his hands languidly shifting as magick blurred around them. Pavan could feel the cool shift begin to sway as the anger burned hot. He stepped back, unsettled, glaring hard at the faie who watched him with unblinking eyes. The orange eyes glowed bright.

"What did it matter in the end? Killing that man did not stop them from taking her. It did not stop my father from killing as he pleased." Ice crystalized over the sand of the training yard, covering the place in a sheen of cold. Pavan felt his breath in puffs, seeing Thad's lips go blue, but the magick he held was firm. It was a counter to whatever Pavan had begun; it did not extend further than the training yard.

"You were powerless." Thad nodded, sliding his feet to step closer.

Pavan struck hard, as he was instructed before in training. His movement was solid, feeling the magick flow fluidly with every strike. Lunging into the fighting dance with

Thad, the magick he held at bay now moved languidly through his limbs as he struck a second blow to the side of Thad, who grimaced briefly and slid back in the icy sand. Pavan felt the rush of energy as he made a connection, but Thad's arm came down in a force-grip that was unrelenting. Pavan swung his leg, taking the man down. He pinned Thad to the ground after knocking him back. Suddenly Pavan paused, drawing back.

"You have been holding back," Thad chuckles, his mouth pulling into a wide smile.

Pavan pulled himself to stand, hoisting Thad to his feet with an offered hand.

"You are a fool." Pavan kept his hand upon Thad's arm, making sure there was no sign of concussion in the faie but Thad was smiling like a mad man. His orange eyes were vibrant, the corners of his mouth curved up, flashing his teeth.

"I felt your magick begin, but you stopped as you struck me down."

"That is not the point. I could have killed you."

Thad radiated warmth. "But I remain unharmed, as I predicted."

"You are far too excited for this." Pavan smirked, he felt the buzz of calm hang in the air as the frost began to lessen. Thad's magick receded to bring with it the sounds of the wind rustling the trees and the songs of the birds within the trees.

"There are not many who can catch Thad off guard," Meilyr said.

Thad pulled away suddenly, creating distance between them.

"I should attend to my duties. Meilyr." Thad nodded to the man who approached, offering his excuses before he hurried away. Pavan wanted to follow, to avoid the look that Meilyr gave, to avoid the words this wise man would speak to him.

Reluctantly, Pavan remained, smiling to Meilyr. The man motioned with an open arm, guiding them now to a path leading away from the training yard. They took it, and for a long while they remained in silence.

"Thad is an excellent teacher." Pavan spoke freely, his heart pumping wildly and adrenaline surging through him still.

"Your skill with the sword has improved. And your magick?"

Pavan faltered in his steps. "There are moments I remain in control, but that is the most challenging—to regulate my emotions to prevent any further harm."

"It will come with time."

Silence fell between them as they walked the path along the edge of the village. A gentle breeze was catching just right, sending the smells of fern wafting towards them, with a hint of blossoms.

"You have become quite fond of each other," Meilyr stated.

Pavan blushed. "You mean Thad?"

Meilyr made an affirming noise, smiling up at Pavan. "Yes. Thaddeus is reserved, I have not seen him get close to many since the death of our late lord."

Uneasiness flickered through Pavan. "I know his death was a great devastation."

Meilyr stopped. "Aron Dourn was killed on a hunt, by a beast that roams these woods. It is twice the size of a bear, with poison in its blood and fangs. A hunt of six went out for our rations of meat to last the winter; Aron was among them. This time of year is always a stressful one for Thad."

Pavan shivered, glancing back at the village. It was quieter since the hunters left, quieter since the training yard was not in use.

"He was there, wasn't he?"

Meilyr gave a great sigh, nodding. "Thaddeus was the only survivor. He was changed by that hunt."

There was something amiss. Pavan sensed a shift in the woods—it was dangerous magick, something sharp and foul. He looked at the sway of the trees, waiting, listening. It was a long moment before Pavan realized that Meilyr was watching him closely.

"I feel something out there." Pavan kept his voice low.

"Your magick is attuned to the very heart of the realms, to the Veil itself," Meilyr spoke in hushed tones. "Ehnarea's light blesses you."

Pavan didn't believe him, but the magick crept up along his spine, making him tremble. He was clear of mind, unlike before he trained with Thad. Using the magick lessened the buildup that plagued his heart and mind. Now, the magick was clear and crisp like the autumn breeze that made the trees dance. He was drawn to the woods, wanting to follow the tug upon his soul. A hand grasped his arm and Pavan looked back, seeing Meilyr watching him again with a cautious stance, and a prickle of apprehension.

"Beware the pull, Pavan. Do not follow blindly," he whispered.

Pavan gulped. "Did my father follow the pull, the one that took him away from here, away from my mother?"

"Your father chose the unforgiven path, but you have that same choice. Only you have the ability to resist the darkest turn of your gift."

Pavan frowned bitterly. "Gift? This is no gift, Meilyr, but a curse. I refuse to be like my father. I know Lilja wishes to control it, to tame the magick within my blood, but I do not believe it would work."

"You are Ehlfern, Pavan, an ancient magick born of the Veil."

"I know what I am," Pavan hissed.

"Yours is a magick worshipped by an old religion practiced in the deepest parts of Taudren. That is where Lilja was taught the way of resistance to the deepest magicks," Meilyr spoke hopefully. Pavan could see the trepidation in the man, whose own magick was softened; it was not of elven birth but of human fathering.

Pavan sneered. "I will not leech Lilja of her magick. I have read of her religion, Meilyr. Let Thad continue to teach me, it shall be enough to control the magick."

"Should that not be enough? Should you fall too far?"

Pavan clenched his jaw, tightening his fists as his sides. Anger flickered within him, but it was dampened as he remembered to even his breathing, to take his breaths in slow, just as Thad had taught him. But the man beside him was insistent, Pavan knew that look.

"If I should fall too far, then I shall end my life." He felt nauseous, tasting the bitter revulsion on his tongue.

Meilyr sighed. "It is not possible."

"The pendant that I wore, given to me by my mother, was made of dragon glass." Pavan kept his voice low.

"That is an unpredictable magick, Pavan. One I wish you to think of clearly."

He sneered. "I have thought of it clearly, Meilyr. It was the reason that my body survived, sending me to the world beyond this one. I cannot explain it, but it worked. If I wear that pendant again—"

Meilyr gripped Pavan hard. "It would take deeper magick to pierce the heart of an Ehlfern, Pavan. You were but a child when the men struck you down. But your magick has hardened to shield you from harm. Do not speak of this again; it is forbidden."

"Fine." Pavan looked away, downcast at the disapproval.

Meilyr softened, sighing slowly. "You have trained hard. Go and rest, you have exerted much magick, for tomorrow shall begin a new path."

Pavan was alone, when he managed to walk back to his room, emerging into the main house to ascend the steps, deep in concentration. Tired, he only wished to crawl into the comfort of his bed, and fall asleep.

Opening the door, he stopped, hearing noise from within. The door swung open and he glanced about him; these were not his things. He frowned, looking to the corridor—this was not right, this was not his chamber.

"Pavan."

He shivered, glancing back towards the chamber. This was Thad's room, where he slept in the main hall during the winter months. And there Thad stood, linen wrapped about his middle. He was dripping with water, his skin flushed from the heat of his bath. Pavan scanned the well-toned muscles, the pale skin painted with pale freckles. His heart quickened, his desire coiling tight within his chest, lingering in his bones.

"Sorry," He turned, averting his gaze. "I thought...I must have taken the wrong corridor." Face hot, Pavan began walking the length of the corridor in the direction he had intended to go.

"Wait," Thad called.

His feet took him away down the corridor, then another, retreating even further from the comfort of his bed. Pavan was down the first two stairs when a strong hand gripped his arm. Pavan turned sharply, forced back and coming nearly face to face with the faie. Thad had hastened to dress in his trousers and tunic, but his feet were bare. His skin was still damp, his orange eyes had brightened, and his cheeks were glowing pink.

"Pavan, you are always welcome in my chambers." Thad's voice was soft as he slowly touched the front of Pavan's jacket.

Pavan gulped. "It's not that..."

Thad smiled. He was gorgeous and Pavan felt his stomach flip. Magick began to burn, making his chest hurt. He recoiled back, afraid of hurting the faie.

"You cannot hurt me," Thad implored, leaning closer. They were close now, at the right height. It would be too easy.

Pavan glanced at the faie's lips, wanting to kiss him.

An echo of a horn drew their attention. Pavan looked around, unsure of the source. Thad went pale, at once his magick hardened and became fearful. He pressed at Pavan to urge him down the steps.

"Go to Meilyr's offices, Pavan. You must stay there..."

Pavan shook his head, confused. "What is the matter?"

But Thad was insistent, pressing Pavan further along the corridor, impatiently.

"Please, go to his room and stay there Pavan..."

In the distance, he could hear the horns again. Thad's body became taught and he gripped his hand roughly. Pavan winced under the faie's strength, but pulled back.

"Not until you tell me what is wrong. Something is happening. Tell me, Thad," Pavan demanded, raising his voice.

Thad trembled, his eyes longing for the large front door. "Vohlgrum...it is the horn of the hunters, there is a Vohlgrum nearby, hunting them...Pavan, I must go to them."

Pavan blinked. "I will go with you."

Panic seized Thad, he pressed Pavan hard, who stumbled back. There was a harshness to Thad that Pavan had never seen before. Worry fluttered around them.

"No, please stay. Where it's safe."

"Wait." Thad's voice was soft, crouching beneath the shield of a large felled tree, his orange eyes flicking about, taking in their surroundings.

Pavan crouched close behind him, his body pressed to the warmth of his shoulder. They wasted no time, after Pavan refused to be left behind. Thad had grabbed only his boots, quickly slung his great sword over his back, and kept a small satchel of potions at his side. Meilyr was reluctant to let them leave.

Now the quiet of the forest enveloped them. Pavan's skin shivered with magick, his senses were heightened the deeper they ventured. He placed his hand warily on the hilt of the sword at his belt—it was cool to the touch.

"How far out are they?" Pavan spoke quietly, leaning close to whisper in Thad's ear.

"A three day hike to the northeast, we must make that in under an hour." Thad was always watching, his eyes trained on the trees that blended in one single mass. It was a blend of unfamiliar terrain to Pavan and his mind began to spin.

"Thad, that is impossible."

Those orange eyes glanced back at Pavan, smirking. "We are unencumbered by the gear of the hunt, and I know these woods better than anyone. How fast can you run?"

Pavan felt the flicker of magick, the racing hearts, the heightened sense of worry coming from the forests. He nodded.

"Then we must be quick."

Thad began, and Pavan followed. They hurried over uneven terrain, circling thick gnarled trees, splashing through trickles of streams, keeping their breaths even as they hurried. Each step taking them closer to the danger, each step making Pavan more uneasy.

Rage was a sharpened blade in Pavan's head. He winced. Stumbling along the path, he fought through it as he pushed on, seeing Thad ahead of him along the path, his vision shifted. Pavan felt nauseous as magick thickened the air, along with the sharp coppery stench of blood.

Isaac.

He faltered. Pavan stepped hard, his food sinking deep into the soil beneath his feet. Looking down, his chest heaved as panic flooded him. Blood flowed, reaching up to his ankles. Pavan dragged his feet, trying to reach higher footing, but each step plunged him further down. Magick flared, his skin burned. He dragged himself forward again and again until he was waist-deep. He grasped the nearest root at last. His blood was hot. With fire burning in his gut, Pavan grasped it to pull himself free.

Pavan gasped, his eyes snapped open. He was standing alone in the forest, as snowflakes fell. Frost coated the green leaves, the healthy thriving moss and every flowered bloom glittered in the sheen of ice. Pavan blinked, numbed against the cold, his magick rushed hot under his flesh.

He was alone.

"Thad!" he shouted, his voice drifting. A staggering silence responded. Pavan called again. And again.

There was a snap of branches behind him. Pavan turned swiftly, his eyes searching the shimmering forest. He could just make out a pair of large eyes that reflected the light.

Pavan swallowed hard, stepping back as a large beast the size of a small black bear emerged into his line of sight. But it was not a bear, nor was it large—it was a Vohlgrum. It was young, he could see the soft layer of fur that crossed its neck, the long nose held high as it sniffed the air.

The young Vohlgrum cub was smelling Pavan, drawing closer and closer with every swagger. Pavan took another step back, but slid down the loose ground, stumbling back to splash into the slow running stream.

Shouts echoed aloft in the distance, and a horn blazed.

The young Vohlgrum clacked its jaw, making a grunt. Pavan's eyes snapped towards it, realizing there was another beast within the woods somewhere off in the distance. A much larger beast, one that was far more dangerous. An adult Vohlgrum, searching for its young. Now again there was a guttural sound, more like a moan. Pavan eyed the young Vohlgrum that sniffed the air. Drawing close to the edge of the stream, those large dark eyes were watching Pavan, unblinking.

"Go." Pavan pointed, but the young Vohlgrum watched him.

There were more shouts, the sounds drawing closer. Pavan looked in that direction and he wondered if they found this young cub, if they would kill it.

Again, there was a sound the Vohlgrum young made—it was more strained. Pavan stepped to the side, his feet sliding over the slick rocks within the stream, he kept his eyes locked upon the large cub. Then a flicker of sunlight shone over its dark coat and Pavan saw a ring of metal, tightly held against the beast's neck.

A shackle. Those large dark eyes watched him closely.

"Alright..." Pavan said slowly, cautiously stepping forward, there was no sign of protest. Pavan continued moving slowly, until he was within a few feet of the young cub.

Kneeling, Pavan extended his hand out towards it, his heart beating wildly, he was amazed when the beast stepped closer, watching him with those large dark eyes. Until the soft fur upon its head was flush with Pavan's outstretched hand.

Pavan smiled, magick tingled through his fingertips.

Guiding his hand slowly around the large head, he saw that up close the beast was larger than he expected, with a long snout and sharp pointed teeth. Pavan was cautious as he felt the shackle; the outer surface was smooth, but the inner ring was lined with sharpened spikes. His finger grazed one, piercing his skin.

He winced, but kept feeling around until he located the latch. It was a rusted portion that did not give. Pavan grimaced, trying to use the force of both hands to pry the metal open. It was no use.

The Vohlgrum's jaws snapped impatiently. Pavan drew back.

"I'm trying..." He grimaced. The large head of the beast hung low, its body collapsing down, resigning itself to a fate it could not defeat.

Pavan sat back on his heels, looking up to the sky that peaked through the canopy of trees. He slowed his breathing as he calmed himself, each breath strengthened his resolve.

He would free this creature.

Looking down, where the body heaved, Pavan let a hand run over the soft fur. Magick wavered, hesitant, but it was there. Slowly, the beast eased, and relaxed. Pavan returned to the shackle, fingers clasping the lock; it would not give, but Pavan grunted, gripping the metal firmly. Gritty rust slipped. Pavan focused, breathing through it as magick shifted beneath his touch. As he changed the metal beneath his grasp to the aged weathered material, it began to crumble.

All at once, the metal snapped.

Breaking it under his grip, Pavan yanked it free just as the large beast yelped. Falling to its large paws, in a tremendous bound it tore away, leaving Pavan where he knelt, looking down at the shackle. It was thick metal lined with bloodied spikes.

Pavan sighed, head lolling back with tears falling from his eyes. Magick flickered to life as his body ignited with fire.

"Pavan."

He could hear the voice deep in the distance; it was Thad's voice. Tightness coiled in Pavan's chest. Gritting through the pain, Pavan stood, uncertain before he took a step, then another. As he followed, he could hear it again.

The smell of rotting flesh hit Pavan's nose, he recoiled. Nauseated, he hunched over, gripping a tree. Hoarse voices echoed off the trees, surrounding him. Pavan glanced up, squinting into the tree line. Blood splattered the ground, Pavan saw the corpse of a dead welk, with flesh ripped from the once thick neck.

A beastly roar echoed through the forest, frightening a flock of birds. Pavan shivered and hurried forward towards the noise.

He was close. Magick hung thick in the air.

Pavan heard the shouts of the men next, the precise calls of the familiar voices. Pavan's head was on fire, blinking to bring them into focus, but the colors of the forest began to swim.

"Get back!"

It was Svein. Pavan could see the large half giant ahead of him, waving his large bulking arms. Pavan shook his head, unable to hear him, unable to understand what the man was saying. Svein turned, rushing towards the left, away from Pavan, heading in the directions of the men's shouts.

Pavan could feel the beast's magick before he saw it. He hunched down as he followed the sound, peaking around the large boulder sheathed in moss, taking in the sight of the large lumbering creature—it was nearly seven feet in height on all fours. Pavan shuddered. The large beast would stand nearly fourteen feet tall on its back legs. Tears stung his eyes as pain hammered behind them.

Glaring at the beast that lumbered towards a small clearing, he could see Trisk standing in the clearing. Then Pavan spotted others, flanking about the outer rim.

Pavan moved rapidly forward, that plan would never work, this beast was large and powerful. Pavan could feel the magick radiating from its large body, hot and enraged. It would not stop, it would overpower the men.

Thad entered the clearing behind Trisk. Pavan's stomach lurched, bile rising in his throat. That fool, how could he think he could face such a creature and live a second time?

Pavan stepped into the clearing, nearing the back end of the beast, moving soundlessly. Pavan's eyes flickered forward, seeing Thad's eyes round wide, his skin going sickly pale.

"*Beast of the forest.*" Pavan did not know if the creature would hear his thoughts, but he reached out with his tentative magick.

All at once the lumbering beast stopped, hairs raising on the back of its neck as it turned its large head towards him. Pavan shivered, but remained calm, staring directly into the large black eyes, seeing the blood dripping from the long snout, the thick sharp teeth that protruded down from that pointed maw.

He needed to act, but he could not think what to do.

Pavan raised a hand, searching with his magick, slowly stepping to the side without breaking eye contact. Now the beast's large nose was sniffing the air, pawing towards where Pavan maneuvered to stand closer to where Thad was.

Thad moved, Pavan saw his movement in the corner of his eye. The beast snarled, his head whipping towards Thad and Trisk. Now Pavan could feel the magick prickling his skin.

"Hey!" Pavan shouted, quickly stepping on agile feet, maneuvering himself between the hunter, and the beast.

Rearing back, the Vohlgrum stood on hind legs, showing the large mass of belly dripping in blood. Shouts echoed around them as hunters readied their weapons.

Pavan held out his arms outstretched wide.

"Wait, do not attack!" he shouted, his eyes never once leaving the dark pools of the beast.

"Pavan..." Thad's voice was a warning. Pavan could hear the trembling from the faie, the fear.

He gulped, shaking his head, without looking away. He kept his eyes fixed upon the beast as he raised his hands up. Reaching his thoughts, magick blossomed, unfurling in tidal waves. It crashed into the confines of Pavan's chest, making him gasp. Forcing himself to blink through the pain, he concentrated his whole power upon the beast. Pavan found the magick and connected with it. He gripped it tight, tethering himself by an invisible bond that linked them together.

Pavan hissed. Ahead of him, the Vohlgrum roared, clomping down onto all fours. It snarled, showing its teeth as it bounded forward, swiping at Pavan. He stumbled back, collapsing to one knee.

Where the large claws struck, Pavan felt the burn. His flesh began to writhe and his tunic tore as blood seeped from the wound. It was not deep, but the poison within the beast's claws was lethal. Pavan blinked against the drowsiness, banishing it away, he could not let the wound consume him.

Heat burned Pavan. His raised hand shaking, feeling the beast's magick begin to hunker back. Holding it firm in a vice of magick, he willed it to stop. Anger flashed in its eyes.

Pavan continued to hold firm, bearing down on the magick he could command, without breaking eye contact with the beast. Drops of blood and drool fell from its gaping maw, the sharp teeth excreted venom that sizzled as the drips pooled beneath its feet. It was resisting him and snapping madly. Pavan grimaced, every inch of his skin prickled.

Tingling and numb, Pavan flexed his fingers. A low snarl came deep from within the Vohlgrum's throat.

Pavan snarled too, clawing deeper into his magick.

It lowered, head bowed. Pavan stepped up, his strength growing in a rush of adrenaline, magick pulsed hot in his palms. He fixed his eyes wholly upon the Vohlgrum that had begun to convulse, heaving its great body.

He hardly noticed the markings that began to etch upon his skin, he could not see the lines that began to glow beneath the surface of his outstretched hands. Pavan stepped forward as the Vohlgrum collapsed, laying its large body heavily upon the forest floor. It was breathing, but only in deep, heaving, breaths.

Pavan knelt, resting his hands on the thick fur, matted with slick blood. Magick coursed under Pavan's touch. He could not resist the flow of magick that entered him, filling him up completely, mixing with his own blood. It pulled as the Vohlgrum conceded to Pavan's magick, gave one last heave of breath, and then the beast moved no more.

Tears came next. Pavan could not stop the agony in his bones; the beast was dead. He mourned for it, his weeping echoing in the now quieted forest. Blood stained his hands, desperately he wiped them on the tattered remnants of his tunic.

Strong hands grasped him. Pavan flinched, scrambling away as he looked up into the bright orange eyes of Thad.

"You are alright," the clear voice whispered. Thad knelt, holding out his hands.

It was difficult for Pavan to breathe.

"Pavan."

He flinched away from the faie, who moved closer. Thad's hands grasped Pavan's arms gently, keeping him from moving further back.

Magick tasted foul, like decay and rotting.

There was a flash of white and Pavan felt the presence of another, blinking again to focus. Lilja was approaching them, her mouth moving but dizziness washed through Pavan. His blood was rushing, his heartbeat thumped loudly in his ears.

Thad stood, approaching Lilja with haste, but Pavan could see she was determined, shaking the faie from her arm. Pavan blinked again and she was kneeling. Terror was written on her face, her mouth moving with words Pavan could not hear.

Pavan was falling, heavy beneath the warm touch of Lilja's hand upon his cheek. Falling back against the hard ground, darkness embraced him warmly.

"Lilja, I really must protest..." Thad clenched his teeth hard, glaring at the elf who was crouched over Pavan's hunched frame. The tension and strain in the large helpless man was gone.

Rounding on him, Lilja frowned.

"Protest all you must, Thad. I did what I needed to, for our people," she growled. Swiftly stepping around Pavan's frame, she shouted for the hunters to gather their supplies.

Thad shook, clenching his fists. "He just saved their lives."

Lilja did not meet Thad's eye, glancing down at the unconscious body lying next to the massive dead Vohlgrum.

"Take him to Meilyr and administer your medicines, Thad. We shall bring the Vohlgrum to Ledenjour."

Thad did not move.

Finally, Lilja glanced back. Their eyes held each other for longer than they should. She tightened her stance, holding her shoulders back. "Do it, now."

Thad watched the elf shout directions. He could see the hunters set to work, they gathered their supplies with somber faces. They were scratched and bruised, but otherwise alive. He could see their eyes glancing his way, wary of the charge he was set to.

Thad bent, gripping Pavan's upper arm. He pulled the man to sit upright, but Pavan slumped forward. Tightening his jaw, Thad bent, shouldering Pavan so his chest was over the broadest part of his back, hoisting him without difficulty.

Pavan awoke with a start, gasping and clutching his side that was now searing in pain. At once a woman in long cotton and wool tunics sat beside him, dabbing at his brow with a wet cloth, easing him back to lay down. Pavan searched her kind old face, and he began to breathe easier.

"What happened?" His voice was heavy.

The fine lines of the woman's mouth creased as she smiled down at him. "You have been asleep for five days."

Pavan looked confused, blinking around his room, but it wasn't his room. There was gossamer draping around the bed, hanging from loops from the stone ceiling. Candles burned on every flat surface and from notches cut into the stone walls.

"This place..." He blinked, trying to process all of his thoughts.

"Leave us." A familiar voice.

The old woman nodded, standing from beside Pavan and taking her leave.

Pavan slowly sat, finally looking at Lilja.

"Don't get up," Lilja instructed. She neared the side of the bed, where Pavan visibly struggled against the bed linens. His middle was bandaged, but his shoulders were otherwise bare.

Pavan flinched at the throbbing in his head, splitting open behind his eyes. The pain became unbearable, as nausea rolled over him.

Lilja was at his side, a small bowl at the ready as he vomited stomach acid, dry heaving. Lilja offered him the wet cloth, which he used to wiped his mouth.

"What happened?" He groaned, falling back against the soft pillows, he could sleep for ages here. He wanted to, as he let his eyes drift shut.

Lilja sat beside him on the bed, her hand upon his shoulder to shake him awake. He sighed heavily, looking up into her violet eyes.

"You must listen, Pavan." Her words were forced calmness. "You must remain here, in my room. I shall care for you, until you are well again."

Pavan scrunched his eyes shut. "I don't need you...not to care." He fumbled with his words, trying to keep his eyes open, but he blinked heavily.

"Pavan." Lilja shook Pavan again.

"There is poison in his blood." A second voice could be heard. Pavan blinked hard, searching for the source.

Lilja scoffed, her hands still shaking Pavan firmly.

"Not enough to kill him," she corrected, glancing back down to look deeper into Pavan's widening eyes. He felt cold, breathing heavier.

"I killed it..." Pavan breathed, seeing flashes of what happened in the forest. Pavan shook his head, fighting back the urge to vomit again, pulling himself back from Lilja's tender touch.

"Lay still." Lilja touched his cheek.

Pavan shook his head, ignoring the grips of pain as he sat up, struggling to get up from the confines of the bed. "I took the creature's magick. I found the connection it held and I severed it."

Thad was shifting quickly around the bed to where Pavan tried to stand. Pavan could see the faie clearly now, dressed in clean wool. His features were subdued and his color was dampened, like he had been awake for days.

"Stay," Thad encouraged, a hand pressing Pavan's shoulder.

Pavan sighed, relenting, and leaned back. He impatiently raked a hand through his hair. He paused, looking at his hand, then pushing his fingers again into the fall of dark waves. His hair had grown significantly fast.

Thad sat gently beside him, taking both of his hands in his own.

"The poison will linger in your blood, we cannot know for certain how your body will dispel the toxin. It has not lessened in these last five days with the potions I have administered, but perhaps, you can dispel it yourself." Thad was hopeful, speaking clearly and allowing Pavan to understand what he was telling him.

"He cannot use his magick again, not so soon," Lilja interjected.

"If his body does not burn the toxin, it will begin to eat him from within. It will make him crazed and confused. If he does not, there is more danger there, Lilja," Thad rationalized. Pavan watched his mouth as he spoke, seeing the galaxy of freckles that lightly spotted his skin, and the fiery orange stubble that graced his jaw and chin.

"He can remain in slumber while the toxins dissipate." Lilja's voice was hard, her hand on Pavan's upper arm.

Thad growled, forcibly removing Lilja's hand from Pavan's arm. Pavan glanced from the faie, then to the elf, while they watched each other with a firm stare.

A chuckle rolled from Pavan, sharp and unwarranted. At once he clamped a hand over his mouth. Shaking, he tried to contain his sudden fit of horrendous laughter.

"Pavan, breathe." Thad looked into each of Pavan's eyes. Now they rapidly filled with tears, his body rolling as the fit of laughter commenced.

He shook his head.

Wincing, the laughter died away as pain shot through him. His stomach clenched, writhing back in the comfort of the pillows, his blood began to burn. Cold touched the contours of his cheeks and his forehead. He peaked through his blurry vision to see Thad pressing a dampened cloth to his feverish skin.

Irritation flashed through Pavan, pushing Thad away.

"Don't coddle me," Pavan hissed, fighting for breath as the pain worsened, doubling him over. Pavan grasped at the bandages, where the beast had sliced through his skin. Poison seeped deeper into his bloodstream.

"Leave them." Thad fussed over Pavan's groping hands, keeping him from removing them to expose the wound.

Pavan growled, tossing his head back.

"This is madness, Thaddeus," Lilja warned, looming at the corner of the room and watching the scene unfold. "He should be asleep. His magick is heightened; can you not feel it?"

With a scoff, the faie rolled his eyes. "Of course, I can feel it, Lilja, but you mistake his magick of distress as a threat. He is wounded."

Pavan winced, the poison was sharp, burning his veins.

There was a knock at the door, breaking the tension between Thad and Lilja.

Rolling away from them, Pavan groaned.

"You should go," Thad advised Lilja, the faie standing to his feet as he approached the door. "This shall be Mal with my supplies."

Lilja stood, coming around the bed as Thad approached the door. Opening it wide as the dark man entered, carrying a canvas bag. He looked warily at Pavan, who squirmed upon the bed in pain.

"I shall stay," Lilja told him. "In case I need to—"

Thad closed the door heavily and it clanged shut with a loud bang. Thad stood glaring at Lilja, crossing his arms.

"You will not interfere. Stay if you must, but do not get in the way of my duty as his healer." Thad pressed past her.

Standing beside Malcom, he watched as the man began to check the pulse at Pavan's neck, looking in each of his eyes before clambering upon the bed to kneel beside him.

"I believe he is septic, Thad. His wound must be infected, and not just with the poison of the Vohlgrum claws. His heart rate is far too fast, and he is feverish. Do you have any remedies?" Malcom glanced up to the faie.

Thad went to his bag, retrieving a vial of thick potion.

"This shall stave off infection, but he must expel the poison. If he does not...it will travel to his heart and kill him." Thad hurried around the bed, ignoring Lilja who glowered at him as he retrieved the water basin.

Pavan shivered, his limbs numb and cold. He could feel Malcom lift his head to tilt his head back as he emptied the contents into his parted lips. Thick liquid slithered down Pavan's throat; he choked, but drank it obediently.

"Pavan." Thad leant over him, turning his face to look into those brilliant orange eyes. "Pavan you need to focus. I know you are tired, but you need to extinguish the poison in your blood."

Sitting on the edge of the bed, Thad pressed his palms to the sides of Pavan's cheeks and his neck. He grasped his shoulders, and then ran his hands along his heaving chest. It was unusual, as the faie felt around, but soon Pavan understood. Warmth was invigorated within his skin, but the faint shimmer of magick with each press made Pavan sigh deeply.

The warmth grew to a sharp pain as Thad pressed to Pavan's left side. He hissed sharply, nausea plaguing him.

"There." Pavan licked his lips, mouth done dry. "It's there...I can feel it..."

"Good, that's good. Now, you must draw the poison to one point. Just one singular location, so you can push it from your system." Thad's voice felt so far. Pavan blinked hard; he was so tired.

"Pavan!" Malcom's voice was distant, persistent.

"Don't fall asleep, not now. Come on Pavan. You must concentrate." Thad's touch was cold, pressing against Pavan's cheek.

"This is useless." Lilja's voice was hard.

"We must give him the chance to do it, Lilja. He is strong," Thad spat back.

Pavan could hear the voices, but he could no longer focus on any of them. His breathing slowed; he felt cold. Was he on the brink of death? It felt too peaceful. Pain had long since ebbed away, now he wanted to sleep.

His skin itched. Pavan whined, touching his arm. There was something touching him on the wrist. Bringing his hand up to his face, he blinked, focusing at last upon the source of the irritation. A ribbon was tied securely there, unmoving from its spot where the girl had tied it. Pavan's hand fell down with a thump against the bed.

Agony ignited within his chest, winding tight about his heart—it was poison. He remembered the Vohlgrum, and the wound it had inflicted. Pavan groaned.

Shouting, Pavan felt the poison flow within his veins, mixing with his blood, agonizing as he recoiled against the touch. He was burning so hot he believed his skin would melt away. Then all at once, it was gone. His blood cooled and the poison settled, stagnant.

"Pavan." There was a voice, drifting him towards consciousness.

Pavan sighed, blinking awake. He looked up to see Thad smiling at him. A damp cloth was pressed to the contour of his jaw and against his forehead.

"You have done well," Thad encouraged.

Slowly Pavan sat up, slumping back as nausea crashed through him. It was now only the faie who sat with Pavan—the danger was over. Malcom and Lilja had left the room.

"I feel terrible." His mouth was dry, making it difficult to speak. Thad offered him a glass of water, helping him drink. Now Pavan rolled to the side.

"Your magick is resilient."

Pavan scoffed. "Was anyone injured?"

There was a long silence. Thad began to stand, but Pavan gripped the faie's wrist reflexively.

"Was anyone killed?" His voice was strained, seeing the hesitation of the man.

"Pavan." Thad shook his head, looking more tired than he should. Guilt made Pavan's chest hurt. How long had the faie sat up with him? How long had Pavan been unconscious? These were the questions he wished to ask, but his throat was tight. It was difficult to swallow.

Finally, Thad sat, grasping Pavan's hand in his own.

"Two men...another three were injured."

Trembling, Pavan tried to stop his tears, but they came anyway, hot and vengeful against his cheeks. His throat ached with torment and each breath was strained. He wiped them away angrily.

"You should sleep," Thad whispered.

Pavan brought the faie's hand up to kiss it, shaking his head. "I have had enough sleep. I cannot rest."

Thad sighed, sitting on the edge of the bed. "You saved more lives than were lost, Pavan. Do not be wary of what cannot be changed. But I advise you to sleep, you are not fully recovered. I can go fetch you some broth, but you must remain in bed."

Pulling on his hand, Pavan yanked him down with what little strength he had. Thad fell forward, leaning over Pavan with a grin—he was gorgeous. Pavan felt the thump of his heartbeat, the magick that was warm.

"I do not need anything but your comfort in my bed. Stay with me, please," he breathed, seeing that his words made the faie blush.

Thad sat up, smirking. He leaned down to yank off the boots from his feet, they clunked upon the floor loudly. He crawled over the frame of Pavan to ease himself on the outer layer of blankets. His head resting on his arm, watching Pavan, who smiled wider.

"Now sleep," Thad told him.

Pavan felt silly, smiling as he did, but his eyes soon drifted closed, eased by the humming from Thad. It was a voice weaved in magick, coiling around Pavan to coax him into a dreamless slumber.

CHAPTER

22

Closing the door to the chambers while the man asleep within, Thad breathed heavily as he leaned against the surface of the door. Malcom watched the faie for a long moment before deciding to approach him. He did not start, but glanced over to Malcom with those unusual orange eyes.

"He is regaining himself well, Mal. For now, he must sleep."

This news was a relief, as he knew the toll of sepsis upon the body. But now, Malcom's astute vision took in a new patient. Thad was a strong healer, but there was no one to care for him when he needed it.

Malcom motioned towards the great hall. "You should come sit and have respite, Thad. These last five days you have done nothing but aid others. Now, you must let me see to your health."

Thad sighed, rubbing his face. "I will endure, but I should like a drink."

They walked quietly through the darkened corridors, night was upon them, with a chill creeping into the air. Malcom took glances now and again toward the faie.

"You have questions?" Thad smirked, catching Malcom's eye as they rounded towards the steps leading down.

"It's nothing." Malcom felt his cheeks go hot, glad that his darkened complexion hid his embarrassment well.

They descended in silence, walking the length of the corridor to the great hall. In the time he and Pavan had made their home here in Ledenjour, there was hardly ever a time Malcom spoke more than a few words to the faie, but now there was plenty of chance.

"Come, I see the concern in your eyes, and you have never been this melancholy before." Thad kept his tone low. They walked through the hall and sat at a large oaken table, it was alight with candles that glowed and flickered in the darkened chamber.

Around them milled about others who spoke in hushed tones. Thad reached for the chalice that sat in the center of the table, remnants from the large dinner just hours before. Malcom, likewise, reached for two mugs.

Thad poured them a drink, silence returning between them.

"Have you encountered an Ehlfern before?" Malcom asked after taking a long drink, it was a hearty wine and sweet to taste. Malcom took another large gulp.

Thad sighed. "No. They were once coveted for their power and extorted. But there was a time a few centuries ago when the Ehlfern were slaughtered."

Malcom blinked. "What can kill an Ehlfern?"

Thad drank, looking beyond him to one of the large hearths that flickered and danced with a roaring fire.

"There are few who know, I am not one of them, but it was said to be one of their own. An Ehlfern of such power none had ever seen."

Coldness crept onto Malcom's skin as he cast a glance around them. But the fire still roared, bringing them warmth. Malcom returned his gaze to Thad, the faie gave a somber smile.

"Forgive me, Mal. I am not in the cheeriest of moods."

Malcom nodded. Drinking again, he began to feel the warmth of the wine warm his belly and soften his brain. It was not something he did back in London, but here, he felt safe amongst these people.

"You are well acquainted with Pavan's past. Has he always exhibited a reluctance to convalesce?"

Malcom chuckled, tilting his head back slightly. "I have known Pavan since before, when he was still called Isaac. He has always been of a destructive nature." A long thought, to the moment of meeting his friend all those years ago. Such melancholy, such pain.

Malcom always had a fondness for the brooding man, but he never understood from what. "He was troubled even then. Did he tell you of his past?"

Thad looked down. "He mentioned the wife he lost. It is difficult to talk about much of anything with him."

Malcom observed the faie, as he had over the last few weeks whenever he was near his friend. It became apparent to Malcom relatively fast that Thad was deeply dedicated to Pavan.

"He isn't an easy man to love." His words made the faie look up, orange eyes went wide and Thad's face paled. He quickly drank a hefty mouthful of wine and Malcom chuckled uncomfortably. "Forgive me. It really is none of my business, but I only caution you when it comes to it...Pavan is challenging, he does not love by halves. If there should be a chance it will not endure, the result would be shattering."

Thad looked away. "I understand."

"He seems to really enjoy your company, for what it's worth. When he is with you, it is the happiest I have seen him since he lost Penelope."

Thad scoffed. "Happy? He seems barely content."

Malcom smiled. "Yes, that is his way of things. He is not as expressive as you or I, nor Lilja for that fact."

Now the faie frowned deeply and Malcom observed something more. "You do not agree with Lilja?"

Thad rolled his jaw, clenching his teeth, working around his thoughts before he spoke again. "We do not see eye to eye when it comes to Pavan's magick. Lilja wishes to extort her own prowess with an old enchantment and power to subdue his magick, to utilize it in her own way. I wish to help Pavan understand his magick in order for him to have complete control and access to what he processes."

Malcom thought about this. "What does Meilyr suggest?"

"Meilyr is currently leaning on the side of Lilja's objective. With Pavan's expedition in the woods, he is more inclined to keep our people safe. His interests with them have always been honorable."

"But you believe Pavan could learn to control his magick, on his own?" Malcom leaned closer to the table, watching the faie closely.

Thad downed the remainder of his cup. He reached to refill it again, but Malcom stopped his hand.

"Thad, be honest with me now. Is Pavan a danger to this place, to your people?" Malcom felt his heart beating faster.

Thad pulled his hand free, pouring his glass, and drinking a hefty gulp. Malcom waited, seeing the contrition in the faie as his features began to change. Perhaps it was a realization he did not wish to openly admit, or perhaps a truth he was ignoring.

"I fear for my people, I always will. But I fear for what Pavan would do to himself should his magick not be controlled."

Pavan awoke with a start, outstretching a hand to find the space beside him cold and vacant. Thad was not there, making Pavan frown. Shifting himself to sit, his body ached but he was no longer in pain. Now, all that remained was a grumble of his stomach.

Driven by his hunger, Pavan dressed, finding his garments placed upon a nearby chair. He emerged from the room where he recovered, it was a familiar corridor. Pavan walked to the end, where Thad's door remained shut; there was no light from within.

Descending the early morning hours in the quiet darkness, Pavan found himself wandering the halls before stepping out into the cool morning air. Hunger tightened his stomach, the smells of something in the air drawing Pavan forward.

It took no time at all to find himself standing on the threshold of the little pie shop, where Pavan had delivered bags of flour to Sophie, the young baker, the elf he had danced with. He smiled. Clearly she was awake in these early morning hours to prepare for the day's fares.

Above his head, the little bells chimed when Pavan opened the door to step inside.

The shop front was a small room with chairs that stood along one wall. There was a bare counter where pies would be displayed, but the lamps were not lit, save for the lantern towards the back. Pavan could see it through a low hanging drape of brightly woven threads that separated the kitchen from the shopfront.

"Oh, it is you, Pavan."

He turned to see Sophie standing with her usual bright smile. His stomach churned again, seeing her carry a tray of pies to the counter and positioning them in the far corner.

"Forgive my intrusion," he stammered, smiling bashfully.

"Not at all." Sophie tucked the now empty tray under her arm. "I did not realize we had a delivery scheduled."

Pavan smirked. "No, I am not on an errand, I have come of my own desire." He watched the pie maker's expression change. Her smile softened, and her eyes lingered over his mouth.

Those demure pink hued eyes quickly looked up again.

"Hungry?"

Pavan stepped closer, looking down at her. "Starved."

"This way, Pavan," she said, her voice sending a shiver up Pavan's spine. Desire crept in, settling beside the hunger.

He followed where she led him, into the back of the shop where her little kitchen sat. It was warm, heavily saturated with the smells of crusts and fruits freshly baked. All at once, his mouth began to water.

"Sit here." She smiled, pulling out a chair at one side of the table.

Pavan sat dutifully. He saw the flour that scattered the tabletop, the eggs shells, and the remnants of a pie recently baked. His eyes rested on Sophie, her soft hair reflecting the light as she walked around the kitchen, reaching in tall cabinets, returning to place a cracked plate before him, and a wooden spoon.

She was light on her bare feet as she pulled open the large cabinet on the far wall, and there Pavan saw the cooling pies, each one just as perfect as the last. Reaching in with a tablecloth, she brought over a crosshatch pie, placing it before him.

"Careful, it's hot," she cooed softly, looking into his eyes. At last breaking eye contact to cut him a slice; it looked as heavenly as it smelled.

Pavan took a spoonful, ignoring the burn in his mouth as he consumed the slice in six hurried bites. His stomach groaned, so he turned to the pie itself, ignoring the serving spoon and eating it directly. Beside him, Sophie watched in silence, until he swallowed the last mouthful.

"My, what an appetite." She took the pie plate and placed it aside.

Pavan stood, walking towards the cabinet. Sophie saw him, and quickly shut it, blocking his path to her baked goods. The smell lingered, but he could also smell the sweetness of the fruits and sugars on her skin. His eyes roamed her flushed skin, seeing the beads of sweat from the heat of the room.

"I still hunger," he growled, placing his hand on the cabinet behind her. A rich taste began to blossom between them. Pavan could taste her tender magick, her excitement as he loomed over her.

"The pies are for the celebration today. Meilyr has planned a feast in honor of the last hunt. They are not for you, Pavan." She tilted her neck, glancing up at Pavan with a flutter of eyelids.

Pavan sighed, smiling briefly as Sophie pressed her shoulders back, making her hips shift forward, her skirts grazing him. "Perhaps not, but there must be something else to satisfy my growing appetite."

"I have seen you every day." Her hand touched the front of his tunic. "You work with such passion."

He sighed, his hunger changing in his stomach as she caressed his neck. Her skilled hands, thin but strong, curving around his throat. Pavan pressed into those hands, gazing into her eyes. Her heartbeat fluttered, beating rapidly in her chest.

"I have wanted none but you since we danced that night."

Sophie licked her lips, pulling Pavan down to crash her lips onto his. He would not protest. Sighing into her mouth, his hands grasping the curve of her waist as Sophie deepened the kiss. She was eager, fingers tangling in the fall of his dark hair, bringing them as close as she could, but he was taller, broader.

Pavan growled, his want pressing at the confines of his trousers. She was supple, yielding beneath his hands. Each deepening moment of her mouth to his drew him deeper and deeper into it. At last, Pavan hoisted her up, hands gripping her rear, and slamming her into the cabinet with a loud *thunk*. Sophie gasped, clutching his shoulders at the sudden shift.

"Shall I stop?" he breathed, noting the redness of her lips, the blush of her face, and the desire in her eyes.

"Don't stop." Sophie leaned in again to kiss him.

Her mouth was hot and tasted of fruits. Clutching her desperately to him, he pressed her against the cabinet, making it rock. Sophie tsked, breaking the kiss to yank Pavan's hair back.

"Do not ruin those pies," she breathed, raspily.

Pavan smiled. Keeping her upright, he carried her to the table, a plume of flour puffed around them as he set her down amongst the rubbish. He eagerly kissed her, pulling her legs around his middle. Sophie sighed, giggling when Pavan's warm hands caressed her bare thigh, her layers of skirt pushed up around her waist.

Leaning up, Sophie gripped the ties of his trousers, loosening them with speed as she sought her prize. Pavan kissed her neck, tilting her chin back slightly to let his lips trail along the thumping of her pulse point. She smelled amazing, like excitement and sweetness.

Pavan moaned, her hand grasping his lengthened member, biting into her pulse point as he entered her. Sophie moaned, welcoming him, as she grasped his tunic, holding his neck, anything she could hold as he shifted. Each thrust was efficient, scraping the table legs against the stone floor. Pavan grasped Sophie's hips with one hand, the other holding her upright as his mouth latched onto her neck.

"You are charming," Pavan groaned, breathing into her ear. She was lost in pleasure. Pavan smiled as the taste of vanilla greeted him. His blood began to burn, desire and want magnifying with every powerful thrust.

Sophie leaned back, her face exposed in the low lantern light, her hair sticking to her forehead and neck where perspiration began to pool upon her skin. Her head fell back.

Her magick was building. Pavan felt it under his grasp, each thrust, sending her closer and closer to bliss. Pavan sighed, longing for it, the sweetness of vanilla now stronger. Each sound falling from Sophie's lips brought him closer to the end. His hand curled up, slowing his thrusts, bringing her neck to his mouth. As he kissed her there, her body began to tremble until she reached her peak.

Magick clawed its way from Pavan, gripping her hard, his teeth sinking deep into her neck. It was easy to take the magick from her; he craved it, savored each luscious pull as it filled him, sending him over the edge of ecstasy. Pavan moaned, not stopping until her pulse was slow. His breathing slowed and the rush of blood cooled. His chest ached and his stomach was uneasy.

Sophie slumped in his arms, cradling her head. She was pale, cold.

"Sophie," he breathed, his hand on her neck.

She made no response. Pavan stepped back, horrified, watching her slump back upon the table as her lips went blue. He leaned over her to touch her softly, tears desperate as he shook her.

"Sophie!"

Thad awoke with a start; there was a pounding on his door, it was heavy-handed. He stood abruptly, his thoughts flicking to Pavan, whom he had left asleep in the room down the hall. At once, he yanked open the door.

Dread drained the color from his face as he stared at a red-eyed Pavan. He was carrying a young elf; it was the pie maker, Sophie. She was pale and unmoving and his heart dropped.

"Pavan..." Thad breathed, quickly stepping aside to let him in. Silently, Pavan carried the young elf into his chambers, placing her upon his sofa. He took care, but the arm at the sofa's edge dropped with heaviness that made Thad uneasy.

At once he knelt down, feeling her neck. There was barely a flutter; she was not dead, but she was not well.

"I...I have killed her." Pavan's voice was a broken sob.

Rounding on him, Thad tried to calm his own racing heart, looking at the man who was wretched and horrified before him. Pavan also looked unwell, he looked grave and distraught.

"She is not dead. Pavan, what happened?" Thad asked, stepping towards him.

Pavan panicked, stepping back in great haste to keep a distance between them. Thad was helpless to watch him from a distance.

"Forgive me...God, forgive me," he cried as fresh tears streamed down his face. He grasped his own hair, leaning against the stone wall behind him. He was unable to look at anything but Sophie, her body laying quite still.

Thad hesitated, wanting to rush to her aide, but with Pavan in the room, it made it impossible to move away from him in his distress. "Please, Pavan...she is not dead. Can you hear me?"

Pavan shook his head as more tears fell. Thad watched him crouch, hunched on the floor.

Thad decided what to do. He turned to Sophie, kneeling down to listen closely to her slow, shallow breaths. He placed a hand upon her neck, then her chest. Odd. Thad felt nothing. He reached up and shifted her eyelid back, her pink hued eyes vacant of color. She was alive, but she was soulless.

He stood slowly, looking down at the young elf, his mouth gone dry. It was hard to admit it to himself, to understand the truth. Now, he slowly turned to where Pavan crouched. He lurched, reflexes in action as he threw himself forward, grasping the hand that held a dagger. Pavan growled as he yanked away from Thad hard. The cold dagger clattered to the floor.

"Stop!" Thad shouted, but Pavan resisted, thrashing away from Thad's grasp as he reached for the dagger that was out of his reach.

"Get off me," Pavan growled, his voice dark and dangerous. Kicking Thad off with force, he snatched the dagger up. Thad gripped him, holding Pavan's hand that held the dagger out, struggling against the man's strength.

"Stop this, Pavan...you must listen," he gasped harshly, now leaning over Pavan and pressing his knee into his lower back.

Pavan growled, a half wail, with tears streaming from his eyes. It was agonizing, feeling the emotion deep in his chest. Thad winced, struggling to take the blade from Pavan's grasp.

Freeing it, Thad tossed it across the room, sighing heavily. In the moment of hesitation, Pavan shifted, flipping Thad over, straddling his thighs. His hand was at Thad's throat, tightening his grip.

"Pavan." Thad grasped his fingers, already feeling his breathing stifled. "Sophie is not dead."

Pavan grimaced. "I took her magick...it's in me, Thad. I can feel it in my blood."

Thad gripped at Pavan's hand, but he was strong in this heightened state. Magick seeped out, making it difficult to breathe. He thrust up with his knee, forcing Pavan to topple over. The hand upon his neck lessened, but gripped his tunic as he fell to the stone floor. Thad was pulled along, landing over Pavan's broad chest.

He was yanked up, his tunic gripped with force by Pavan's strong hand. Thad drew back, his tunic ripping down the center. He stretched out his hands to Pavan.

"You must stop." He was soft, easing his words.

Pavan slackened, his body shifting as the force of his faie voice calmed the severity of Pavan's outburst. He brought himself to sit, his hands trembling. He attempted to hide behind his hands as the tears began to fall fresh, weeping openly. Thad's chest ached, his own chin was trembling.

Slowly, Thad shifted, first touching Pavan's knee. Comforted as the man did not pull away, Thad touched his arm, sitting close until he could wrap his arms around Pavan's shoulders.

Embracing him as he wept.

Pavan awoke in the confines of his own bedchamber, blinking against the light that streamed in through the window, basking his bed in a sunny glow. Pavan felt miserable and cold. Forcing himself to sit, Pavan swallowed back the bite of nausea. A heaviness came over him as he looked at each of his hands—chains made of magick runes and unbreakable light shimmered along his wrists.

Pavan tested them. He yanked at them, but they were immoveable.

Hearing the door, Pavan started, scrambling off the bed. He moved as far away from the door as he could, his hands uncomfortably twisted up where the chains were secured to the wall. He kept his body hunched behind the large bed, watching as his door opened. Thad entered, followed close after by Malcom.

"How did you sleep?" Malcom was the first to speak. He was standing at the end of the bed, watching Pavan closely.

Pavan's gaze drifted to Thad, watching the faie as he worked over the far table, pulling out vials and little packets from his canvas bag. Pavan gulped. He wanted him to speak, he wanted Thad to be the one to ask him questions. But Thad did not look his way.

Shame tightened in Pavan's chest and his eyes flooded with tears.

"Pavan." Malcom sat on the edge of the bed, drawing Pavan's attention back to him. "Do you know where you are?"

Pavan swallowed. "Ledenjour."

Malcom gave a reassuring smile. "Good. Do you remember the last time we talked?"

Pavan winced, thinking hard, but the last few days were a blur. His chest ached and his arms were tired, the strain of pulling them against the chains was painful. But Pavan did not move from where he crouched beside his bed. Slowly, his eyes lingered over the veins in his arms, the superficial scratches along his skin, the hideous jagged line of scab along his middle forearm.

Memories flooded him. Pavan squeezed his eyes shut, remembering one of the first moments he had awoken. He had been clawing at his own skin, finding the sharpened dagger at Thad's hip, in one last attempt to bleed the magick from his own blood. He felt disgusting and he felt dirty—magick that was not his flickered in his veins. Pavan soured.

"Yes," he breathed at last, his eyes looking back up at Malcom. Those kind brown eyes, his persistent friend, again caring for him as one of his many patients in hospital.

"Pavan, will you sit with me on the bed?" Malcom placed a hand on the space beside him.

Pavan pulled back, furthering himself away from his friend, and shaking his head. He was dangerous. Pavan felt dangerous, and did not want to hurt Mal. He would never forgive himself if he should harm another soul. Guilt rippled through him, as Pavan remembered the young elf with pink hued eyes. His stomach wretched, his face grimacing as tears fell freely.

"Pavan. Pavan, look at me..." But Pavan shook his head at Malcom's behest.

Behind them all, the door burst open, causing Pavan to jump. Malcom turned, standing defensively as Lilja stormed into the room.

"Enough of this foolery, we have waited long enough," she stated, the door closing behind her and ignoring Thad, who turned in her direction. She made her way to Pavan, but now it was Malcom who stood between him and the elf.

"Lilja, please, we have discussed this with Meilyr at length. This is the way we shall proceed." Malcom was firm, not letting the elf intimidate him with her hard glare.

She was not giving in so easily. "No one has seen him in weeks, it has been days since they have learned of Sophie. They are not ignorant of his power. He must be seen or they shall suspect what he has truly done."

"He has not done anything." Thad's voice cooled the room.

All eyes turned towards him.

Lilja scoffed. "Thad, even you are not this petulant."

"Pavan has done nothing, Lilja. Sophie is not dead. Perhaps you had forgotten, when Meilyr warned you against interrupting our little endeavor of treatments," Thad spoke with coldness.

Standing far away from them, he kept his orange eyes fixed upon Lilja.

"Not dead?" Lilja turned, abrasive. "She is a shell of a woman, no longer bearing a soul. Can you look me in the eyes and tell me again that he has done nothing? She breathes and eats, but she will no longer prosper in the world. Sophie will never enter the Veil. He has robbed her of her undying resting place."

Malcom's eyes flickered to Pavan, who had not moved. He remained hunched, but the words Lilja spoke deepened the wound within his chest, his grief was now a chasm.

"Lilja," Malcom warned.

She pushed beyond Malcom, the man stumbled back onto the bed, unable to prevent Lilja from crouching before Pavan. He held his breath, flinching as her violet eyes stared into his own.

"Pavan, answer me in truth, do you wish to remain as you are?" Lilja asked. Behind her, Thad made an indignant noise, but she gave him a warning look. Now taking hold of Pavan's chin, he swallowed hard.

"Lilja, you cannot coerce him to—" Malcom placed a hand on hers, but she slapped him away.

"He will answer me now. I will not wait." Her violet eyes returned to Pavan. "Will you submit to my enchantment, Pavan, so to keep these people, to keep *my people* safe?"

His throat burned, fighting back the coming tears. He was blinking back the crash of grief, but he could not look away. Her features were hard, her grip unrelenting. If he submitted to her power, they would all be safe. If he refused, would Pavan unleash his magick again?

Quickly glancing at Thad, Pavan knew his answer as he looked at the faie he had grown to admire more than he ever thought possible. Pavan thought of the many lives that lived within Ledenjour, who looked to Lilja for her protection. He knew little of the enchantment that Lilja would perform, but he knew it was his only option to keep those he loved safe.

"Do it," he breathed. The words felt foreign on his lips, but he would protect them all. If he couldn't end his own life, he would do whatever he must in order to protect them all from the magick he held.

"No, Pavan, please." Thad's voice was soft. Pavan looked away, unable to look into those heartbroken eyes.

"He has agreed, you must unchain him."

Pavan pulled himself up, the magick chains slithering cold upon his wrists. He finally looked up to meet Thad's eyes. They were full of a reluctance to oblige him, to commit to what he must. Pavan outstretched his hands as far as they would go and pleaded with Thad in earnest.

"It will be alright. Please."

Finally, he nodded. Lilja shifted away from Pavan to give Thad some space to work. Thad approached Pavan, taking hold of each hand. Hearing him mumble under his breath, Pavan sighed as the enchanted chains fell away, lifting a weight from Pavan he did not realize had restrained him before. Now standing to full height, he looked up to meet those orange eyes.

"This is what's right," Pavan whispered. "To protect them."

Thad turned, facing Lilja. Pavan watched the faie leave, his warm hands slipping out of Pavan's grasp, walking with Malcom out of the chamber. At last, he was alone with Lilja.

"You have chosen the right thing." Lilja smiled, reassuring.

Pavan sat, glaring up at her. "Just get it over with."

Waiting in silence he watched her stride across the room, placing a blade from her belt into the flickering flame of the largest candle that burned on the nightstand. It was quiet, as she stood there, watching the blade go red hot. His skin prickled, heightening the sensation of panic that settled in the base of his throat. He swallowed the thickening of bile.

"Do you understand what it is to be bonded, Pavan?" Her voice was soft, like a whisper. She turned to him with the hot blade in her hand.

Pavan swallowed hard, shaking his head.

"It is an old magick, founded before the elders of my people. It was first used to bind the souls of the strongest, to withstand the magick of the Ehlfern, who were sent from the Veil, to walk among us and give the ultimate gift…"

"I have no gift for you," Pavan growled.

"But I shall guide you, to help ease your burden. It needn't be more than the tip of the blade as we speak the vow, then our bodies must become one." Lilja was so close, sitting beside him on the bed. "I know you were branded, I have seen the mark left by that horrible man. I shall be gentle, when you are ready."

"You must fuck me, to complete the blood magick."

Tears scorched unwanted pain down Pavan's cheeks, as he glared at the hot knife held in Lilja's skilled hands. She took his hand in hers with her free hand. He trembled.

"It is natural to be frightened, Pavan. I am also afraid. Our bond shall change me forever, but I am willing to have you."

Pavan sighed. "I cannot hurt another, like I hurt Sophie."

"With our bond, they shall be protected." Her hand shifted around the handle of the blade. "Do you trust me to care for you?"

"I trust you more than I can trust myself."

"As blood of magick, takes oaths cannot be undone." Her words sparked, giving Pavan chills. He watched her place the tip of the blade against her pale smooth wrist, leaving a charred little mark, a nearly perfect triangle. Her eyes welled with tears.

"As blood of magick…" Pavan's voice shook. Watching her move the blade towards his inner wrist. "Takes oaths cannot be undone."

Pain ripped through his body at the touch of the blade. His insides coiled as the magick began to flutter, agitated by the attack. But it soon became a new heat, one that grew hotter. Opening his eyes to look into hers, he saw such vibrancy in those violet irises.

Tilting his chin up, brushing back a lock of his dark hair that had fallen over his eye, Lilja searched his face, before her gaze quickly settled on his lips. She drove forward to kiss him deeply, her magick hit him hard and he gasped for breath. Her fingers touched his cheek, sending waves of delight through him. He leaned into her touch, her soft magick soothing.

"Can you hear me, Pavan?" Her voice sounded like a dream, a lulling sound that sent shivers rushing through Pavan.

He nodded, reaching up to touch the delicate hair that felt like silk in his hands. Delirium shadowed his eyes. Her smell was intoxicating, unlike anything Pavan had ever smelled. It was warmer than vanilla, sweeter than honey. Leaning close to the curve of Lilja's neck he inhaled, grasping the curve of her body to bring her closer.

"I must take you, to complete the bond."

He nodded slowly and his mind was overrun with magick. Drunk on her scent, he was overwhelmed by the heat of her body pressed to his as she straddled him. Her white hair cascaded around them like a canopy. Her strong legs bare beneath his hands, Pavan touched the soft inner thigh, remembering the pie maker.

Pavan turned his face away, tears spilling from his eyes. Sophie was soft, and had smelled of honey. Her magick lingered within him, he could still feel the gentle magick swaying under his skin. Repulsed by taking it, Pavan shut his eyes, trying to push the memory away but Lilja's gasps of pleasure ignited the flame within him, fueling the memories that plagued him.

It was over. He felt numb against the bed as sleep clouded his eyes, he wanted the darkness to find him. Lilja kissed his forehead.

"Sleep," she whispered.

CHAPTER 23

L ilja sat in the chair beside Pavan.

He had begun to shout in his sleep, sweating and thrashing about, but she was there to calm him. Her magick cut through his nightmare. She sat in the silence of the chamber while the candles cast flickering shadows over the stone walls. She looked down at her fingertips, feeling the smooth skin on each tip with another. Tingling in the magick that remained. This night was different; when she placed her hands on his cheeks, speaking the words she knew by heart, an image came to her, a flash of images from Pavan's mind escaped him.

He was reaching out, his mind was seeking. When she felt them connect, the magick within him calmed, stepping back, but she saw a glimpse of his mind. Lilja saw a Pavan that made her head swim and her heart begin to hammer in her chest.

Lilja breathed in with a gasp, her eyes shooting up to look at the sleeping frame of Pavan. He looked as he did then, so serene and beautiful. Just a child.

Shaking herself and feeling foolish, Lilja banished the thought. Pavan was no longer that child. He was no longer the boy that smiled at her when she imitated the hunters. No longer the same boy that gave her the intricately woven crown of metal flowers, woven together by little scraps he collected from the blacksmiths.

Pavan was grown, now dangerous. Lilja could feel the magick that her elders only whispered about. It pulsed through her like a fast current, overpowering her body and even her mind. Just a taste of it left Lilja desperate for more.

Leaning down, she caressed the curve of his cheek. His skin was soft to the touch, and she let her fingers delve into the length of freshly grown hair, marveling at the effect the Vohlgrum magick had on his body. Thick dark curls reached below his ears; the muscles beneath his skin thickened without lifting a battle axe or weighted sandbag. Lilja grazed her hand further down, along the contour of his chest. She stopped at the scars that remained as remembrance of the Vohlgrum that had wounded him.

Desire pooled in her as she cast her eyes along the full length of his body. He slept so easily, under her magick; she could let him remain in deep slumber for days, weeks, and he would be unchanged.

Pavan stirred, shifting in his sleep, in search of her touch.

A smile played on her lips, smoothing the curve of his chin. She leaned down, but she stopped, unable to press her lips to his. Pavan did not love her, he did not want her as she desired him. He would wake and seek the affection of the faie. Lilja knew how they looked at each other, she knew from the whispers of the other hunters.

She stood, quietly dashing from the room, and locking it behind her.

Her steps were quick and silent as she ran through the cold stone great house. Her way was clear as she followed the feeling and memory through the steps and corridors until she pushed open the oak door, it groaned with the effort.

It was dark inside, but her keen elf eyes guided her as she walked the room to the farthest wall, taking hold of the tapestry covering the large window. Pulling it down, dust scattered. She turned in a hurry to see the rooms left for years in the absence of the family of Maison. All the belongings remained, the books and bedding left untouched were now covered in years of dust and webs of spiders.

She went to the bookshelf, opening the small box that was hand-carved. Lilja smiled, but tears sprung from her eyes as she pulled the small pouch from within. It was heavy, as she remembered. Her fingers gently pried open the lip of the pouch, her breath stilled as she slid the round object from within onto the flat of her palm. Taking it with her, she left the cold room, walking out into the evening air. A breeze shifted through her white blonde hair.

A promise she made to Pavan's mother, all those years ago, after the hunters returned from the forest with the pendant. Lilja had promised she would keep the pendant safe, until the time was needed. Lilja believed Eleanore was touched with a bit of the madness, after losing a child, but she had promised the grieving woman.

Keeping the pendant sealed away in her old room, forgotten.

She stepped back to regain herself, stumbling as a familiar dark-haired man crossed her path.

"Lilja, are you alright?" Meilyr asked.

She turned, clutching the pendant tight in her closed fist, hiding it from sight. "I am tired."

"Come, you are chilled to the bone." They returned side by side to the great house, into Meilyr's private chamber, where a fire roared and food lay out on a low table.

Lilja sat on a pile of furs and pillows near the fire, warming a cold frame she didn't realize she had had before then. Once Meilyr sat across from her, pouring a mead into a goblet for her, he let her compile her thoughts.

After a moment she finally spoke. "Can you tell me anything more about the Tomes of T'hall?"

Meilyr sighed. "Would this have anything to do with trying to convince Thad that your choice was right...to prove a point?"

"It was not a mistake. Already he has improved." Lilja couldn't get the images out of her mind, seeing the great Vohlgrum crumple before them, then seeing Sophie laying near lifeless, then again walking about aimlessly in the gardens. The girl had been vacant, confused.

"He has remained asleep for three days since your enchantment, Lilja," Meilyr said. He kept his voice calm, neutral, but she knew he was concerned.

"He will be right again. It will take time."

"Time, we may not have."

Lilja frowned, looking at the concern in Meilyr's face. Until at last the man leant forward, extending a letter to her. She grasped it, unfolding the parchment to read the contents.

Her eyebrows furrowed, reading the contents of the letter hungrily. "Bandits? Pillagers? They have never come this far inland. Have we really lost four villages?"

Reading again the names of the villages in the letter, hearing in great depth the harrowing tales and nightmares of these nameless men who come in the dead of night, raping, pillaging, and burning everything. Fear rippled through her.

Meilyr was uncertain. "If these accounts continue, we will have greater concern for our people than respite."

This gave Lilja a chill.

"Pavan." She nodded. "You believe he could help us?"

"If this threat comes further inland, if they reach us here..."

A moment of silence passed between them before Lilja ventured to ask. "Our numbers have dwindled in strength. We have many elders, many children. Have you sent a letter to Lahrs? Would he be able to inquire to the duke for assistance?"

Meilyr sighed heavily. "He is in Jorn, at a distance that I cannot send word until he is to return to Corad. But he shall be here before the winter months to continue his affairs with Tauf. They expect him, so shall we expect him here."

"Will he be...pleased...when he learns of our newest arrival?" Lilja knew Meilyr, these things could not be shared too readily in correspondence.

Meilyr puffed smoke from his lips, from the pipe he had recently filled. His dark eyes watched her closely.

"Lahrs will be of good confidence on this matter."

There was a long silence.

"You do not approve of my choice?" Lilja asked after a long moment, growing impatient with the man and his silence. She grew impatient of those watchful eyes and thoughtful condition that made him aware of everything and everyone around him.

"What's done, is done; there can be no room for regretting that we should not have been too hasty. All we have is to look forward to the next big step." Meilyr eyed her.

She sat straighter. "What will you have me do, Meilyr?"

There was a low chuckle. "See Thad is prepared to train him. I want Pavan to be ready for defensive maneuvers, and he needs to know the layout of the village's weak points."

Lilja colored.

"I do not think it is wise—"

Meilyr raised a hand. "You will do this, Lilja. With your aid, Pavan shall be able to contain the majority of his magick, but I still rely on Thad's expertise on battlement and training."

Lilja stood in the training yard, hating herself, watching the faie who swung his great sword with precise skill against the quick movements of one of the three top hunters. It had been days since she even glanced at the man. Now, her intent was to talk to the one person who despised her.

"Lilja, what a surprise!" Svein smiled broadly, extending his arms out towards her. Lilja forced a smile, but it did not quite reach her heart. "Come to challenge me?"

She waved him off. "Maybe later. I have come to speak with Thad." Now the training yard fell silent. Thad looked over at her, his expression blank.

"I see. Well, don't let your muscles get too slack. You know where to find me." Svein looked from Thad to Lilja before taking himself away.

She approached Thad, who was speaking quietly to one of the hunters. As she drew nearer, Thad gave a smile, one of those that was given to the others when decency and niceness was sought after, but Thad did not have the heart to give them a harsh word.

"Lilja," he encouraged, sheathing his great sword before motioning Lilja to walk with him. Graciously, the others turned away, allowing them space to walk away from the group.

"The weather is fine today, for training," Lilja said, as they both took the long turn around the outer edge of the training yard, where none of the others used it.

Thad sniffed. "It is not like you for pleasantries, Lilja. You need something. I do not have time to be wasted."

Lilja stopped, looking into those orange eyes. Bitterness curved at the edge of the faie's lips. They stopped near the large stone gates, leading out of the training yard to the orchards.

"I have been informed...that is to say, Meilyr has advised me to cooperate with our advances on Pavan's training." Her words were not received well, she saw the resentment in his eyes, the faltering of his composure.

"You expect me to listen to you?" he said coldly.

Lilja anticipated no less. "I expect you to listen to Meilyr."

Thad made a noise of frustration and indignance. Lilja knew Thad would do anything for Meilyr, because there was a strong sense of obligation he believed was due to the old wise elf. Meilyr treated Thad as a second son, next to the elusive elf Lahrs.

Neither of them were his by birth, but Meilyr helped raise them both in his own way. Lahrs had been an obvious successor, but the elf was of no consequence in Ledenjour, as he spent his days with the royal family in Corad. Thad would be Meilyr's second, this alone did not set right with Lilja. Thad's past was not unknown to her, she knew of the place he had been rescued, and she also knew the length of time Meilyr had spent with Thad in his absence to Denorn, before bringing the faie to them all those years ago.

They would neither admit to any transgressions, but Lilja was certain in the fact that Thad was a known deviant. No words of paternal affection could convince her otherwise.

Thad sneered at her.

"Shall I inform Meilyr of your defiance?" Lilja taunted, playing their little back and forth.

"Don't waste your time, of course I shall do as he commands." He looked at her pointedly. "Now, I really must get back to work..."

She grabbed his arm and his muscles tensed.

"It is important, for the good of our people."

Thad yanked his arm away.

"Do not patronize me with your whispers of what is best for our people," he hissed. He kept his tone low, but his venomous bite was lethal in Lilja's ears.

"We cannot ignore what is coming."

Thad scoffed. "He is not a weapon. He cannot be used as a shield to protect this place forever."

"You would have us fall?" Lilja felt hot all over, knowing their disagreement was drawing attention of many within the training yard, even if they pretended to not hear them.

"I would have us fight to protect what is our own, but I will not subject Pavan to be used as a mule." Thad was speaking low, his voice even, though the curve of his lips pulled back.

"This would be different," she pleaded as her voice softened.

He scoffed again, the flecks of his eyes growing brighter. "You cannot promise me it is not the same. Do not pretend you were not there when Aron rebuked the high ones when they wished to enslave me for the profit of their mines."

She flushed. It was true, everything he claimed.

"He will want to help..." she began, stepping closer to Thad, seeing the many faces of their hunters watching them, watching their captain be questioned by her.

"Pavan would lay over burning coals to let every last man, woman, and child tread to safety without so much as a scratch. He would do it, gladly. But now..." Thad's tone deepened, his eyes darkening as he spoke. "He is under your control, Lilja. Pavan is not in his right of mind. Would you ask him to sacrifice himself, knowing it is in obedience to you? You are his mistress now."

Taking hold of her arm, he showed the skin of her inner wrist, glaring at the healed mark, barely a triangle. Lilja yanked her arm back.

"I won't be the one to ask him."

Malcom was looking at him.

Pavan sighed but continued to lace up his jacket as he watched his friend in the mirror. Malcom had been in his room every hour since Lilja had bewitched him with her magick. Pavan had not seen her since then, and now a terrible longing sat heavy within him.

"If I don't leave this room, Mal, I will go mad," Pavan stated. Turning now to sit upon the wooden bench, he reached for the boots waiting for him there.

Malcom sighed. "Yes. I do believe you are right, but that is not why I am here."

Looking up, Pavan forced his foot in his boot. Catching the wary glance his friend exhibited, he sighed, slipping into his other boot.

"How are you feeling, after all of what has happened?"

Pavan stood, glancing to Malcom, but thinking now to his feelings. It was an odd kind of hollowness, each nerve in his body felt numb. He gulped, suddenly aware of how great he felt, even when he thought of what had happened, and what he had done. Pavan was unnaturally fine.

"I'm fine," he breathed, catching Malcom's gaze as his friend stood. He was suddenly nervous as Malcom approached to get a close look into Pavan's eyes, reaching to his wrist to check his heart rate.

"Her magick must act as a stimulant, Pavan. I have seen you like this before," Malcom's voice was cautious. Pavan recognized the tone, the words he used. "Please, you must be careful. This will be temporary, in this world, we do not know what this will do should your former habits arise..."

"I'm fine," Pavan repeated, forcing a smile.

Malcom gripped his tunic firm, bringing him close to eye level. His face was hard, determined.

"Don't bullshit with me, Pav. I know you better than anyone here, I know what you are capable of. Do not think for one moment that I will allow this to continue should I see it becoming a means of hurting yourself."

"I promise." Pavan gulped, his heartrate now increased. His stomach was uneasy as he pulled himself free of his friend's grasp. "You will stop me...as you said. Right?"

Malcom released him, nodding firmly.

"Very well." He nodded. "Now come, I believe you are requiring a good amount of fresh air. Is there anywhere you would like to go first?"

Pavan thought for a long moment. "The tree, I should like to give my own prayers to the tree."

This surprised Malcom, but did not deny the request. They walked from the main house, taking in the crisp air, walking the length of the yard to the north of the village where a large tree stood tall. It was a tree he had never thought of before today.

They stood before the tree, with long branches that hung down. Much like a weeping willow, the trunk was a deep charcoal with leaves the color of shimmering glass.

"Favor find you." An older woman approached Pavan, smiling at Malcom. Pavan slowly smiled, bowing slightly.

"Favor find you," Pavan replied. His eyes looked up, catching glimpses of little flutters of canvas, stained in different colors. Each was painted with a symbol, tied to the low hanging branches.

The woman offered a scrap of canvas, bare and blank. Pavan took it, looking to Malcom. He bowed slightly to the woman before she maneuvered herself to leave the area, giving Malcom and Pavan the space alone beneath the tree.

"She is one of the elders. They say she was the one who planted this tree upon the death of her son in a great battle, her tears nourished it to life. Now it is a place others come to give up their prayers to the ones they have lost."

Pavan felt the smooth canvas in his fingers, examining the blank and bare surface, letting the ribbon fall between his fingers as he held it up. It did not look as the others did, but perhaps that was the magic. Pavan glanced at Malcom briefly, before moving closer to the trunk of the tree. Reaching up to secure it in the branch, he paused, catching sight of the ribbon he wore upon his own wrist. It was dirtied and frayed at the edges, but otherwise it remained as it ever was, unmoving from the wrist where the girl had placed it.

Pavan's chest tightened, blinking back the tears. His breath caught the wind as he whispered the prayer under his breath. Letting his eyes drift closed, reaching up at last to secure the canvas to a low hanging branch. When he opened his eyes again, he smiled. Of course, it was magick. Now the canvas fluttered in a hue of green that mimicked the ribbon he wore upon his wrist, but there were two sides of the fluttering thing, each bearing a different symbol.

"It never ceases to amaze me," Malcom said as he admired the tree. They shared the silence for a long moment, as a gentle breeze whipped around their feet. It was swirling into the tree, swaying the colorful canvas, and making a magnificent sound, like quivering wings.

Color danced, each flick of the wind shivering against the sun's rays that caught between the shifting branches. The magick was brightening their moods, uplifting their spirits.

Pavan smiled. "Beautiful."

Entering the great hall, liveliness had overrun the darkened corners, every hearth in the large stone hall was ablaze, every chandelier lit with flickering candles. Music brought the hall alive, and the smell of cooked meats and breads overpowered the stench of human bodies crowded in from the long days work.

This was the scene as Pavan entered, at the behest of Meilyr, to join the celebrations of a large feast. He had spent the day with Malcom as they walked the village, which became quite apparent to Pavan as they were stopped by many villagers who wished him honor and bestowed gifts upon him; a newly sharpened sword, with etched markings in the blade from the blacksmith, well-tanned boots from the cobbler, made of a fine hide, slicked with fats and dyes. Pavan was even honored with the choice of the finest mare from the stables and a barrel of mead from the brewer.

All of this, Pavan soon learned, was in honor of his kill of the Vohlgrum. At once, Pavan became mortified after learning the meaning of such honor. But Malcom advised him against returning the gifts, as it would be more of an impertinence. Pavan accepted, but as the day went on, he became even more grave. Now, he stood at the threshold of a party meant for his honor.

Pavan stopped at the door.

"I don't think I can do this," he whispered, seeing all the villagers gathered into one place. It was laughter, boisterous conversation, and everything he abhorred.

Malcom smiled, placing a hand on Pavan's lower back and preventing him from backing away.

"You promised Meilyr you would be here, so you will not leave until the last of the celebrations," Malcom chuckled, pushing Pavan hard.

Pavan groaned. "Yes, but I did not expect...does there have to be so many people?"

Again there was a chuckle. Malcom was now guiding them towards the right, maneuvering around the large tables laden with food, men and women who sang and joked loudly. Keeping themselves to the outer ridge of the room, they made their way towards the large platform, where Meilyr sat at table.

Pavan felt his stomach tumble and his mouth going dry. There he was, seated next to Meilyr, freshly washed and wearing nice silks, with a silver circlet over the top of his forehead. Thad. The faie was beautiful, ethereal in the blaze of light. Speaking with Meilyr in a hushed tone, his gaze had not yet seeing them approach. Pavan could admire his profile, could watch the faie smile openly, drinking from a gilded cup.

"Pavan."

His blood seized, every inch of him growing hot at the sound of her voice. Pavan looked to his left to see the elf approach.

He blinked in disbelief, seeing Lilja had forgone her usual leather trousers and bulkish tunics and bracers for a more elegant, sleek gown that fell along her curves. Her long silvery white hair was unbraided, falling about her elbows. She too wore a silver circlet about her forehead, similar to the one Thad wore.

"Lilja." He bowed his head, letting his hand rest upon her hip, as she hooked her arm around his waist. She was so near to him now, he would smell the clove oil in her hair. He could practically taste the magick on her skin.

"How do you like your feast?" She smiled. It was unlike her, to show so much delight. Pavan saw the flush of her cheeks, felt the flutter of her heartbeat and he knew she was heavy in drink.

He frowned. "I hate it."

She laughed, which was unheard of from her, it carried around them over the commotion of fanfare, catching the eye of many of the hunters who eyed them, leaning together in whispers. Lilja smiled, leaning closer to whisper in Pavan's ear.

"They have all been talking of you...do you want to know what they say?" she asked, her violet eyes flicking from his own to his mouth. Pavan gulped, wanting to pull back, wanting to run out of the great hall and take off his ridiculous silken clothes.

"I haven't a clue." He shook his head, trying to keep himself afloat.

"You are Pavan the Vhear, because none but you have defeated such a creature in battle. They shout your name in the Old Tongue. Your name is even whispered among the streets of Tauf."

Pavan stiffened, drawing his arm away from her, but Lilja clutched it, bringing it close to her warm breast. She leaned against him as they continued to walk towards the platform, her scent brought on the memories of their bond as his stomach tumbled.

When they approached the table, Meilyr and Thad stood. Thad was quiet, keeping his gaze down at the floor, while Meilyr spoke loud and attentively, welcoming them to the table.

Pavan was maneuvered to Meilyr's other side, sitting to his right, Malcom took his seat beside Thad, while Lilja took a seat next to Pavan. She no longer leaned upon his arm, but she held his hand. Her violet eyes danced and magick pulsed in Pavan's veins. At once, he pulled his hands away, placing them dutifully in his lap.

"Welcome, favor find you." Meilyr began a long speech, one that spoke of honor and duty, giving Pavan his well-deserved honor as a member of the village.

Meilyr even went on to speak of how much he perceived Pavan as his own kin. It is a long moment of silence, as they all raise their glasses to toast to Pavan, when Svein shouts from the crowd a familiar word meaning great hero, beast slayer—Vhear. Another man from the crowd, whom Pavan cannot see, shouts the same, until it is a great chant that shakes the room.

Raising his hand to quiet the roar, they all drink. Pavan raises his cup to his lips, taking a great mouthful of ale. His eyes flickered to his left, where Malcom sits, a knowing smile upon his friend's face. Pavan smirked, but caught Thad's eye. Thad raised his glass another time to drink again, smirking behind his cup.

"Here it comes..." Lilja's excitement roused Pavan from looking anywhere but at her, reluctantly turning his gaze to the elf, but she held his hand again, beaming.

All around them the chant began afresh. '*Vhear*!' was shouted again and again. Pavan's chest beat with the pounding of his heart and the thrill of the voices. He watched in rapture as the crowd began to cheer as one, parting aside at the entrance of the hunters. Two held aloft the large black head of a thick, black beast that shimmered as an oil slick against the glow of the chandeliers and the hearths. Three more men followed clutching the great behemoth of pelt, now made into a cloak. Pavan's mouth went dry.

"An honor bestowed upon the mighty hunter that claims this conquest!" Meilyr spoke loudly enough for the large room to hear. Whoops and grunts of approval responded. "We of Ledenjour bestow upon you, Pavan Vhear, the object due of this conquest."

Vhear! Vhear!

Pavan smiled, but it felt forced. Raising his glass he drank three full gulps, stumbling to his feet as Lilja yanked on his arm, forcing Pavan to stand, to approach the men who held the pelt of the Vohlgrum. Pavan approached, uneasily.

It felt wrong, allowing the hunters to drape the heavy pelt over Pavan's shoulders, latching it in place with a clasp made of shimmering stone. It was one of the precious metals they mined in the mountains—a metal that was made into the circlets Thad and Lilja wore, and the heavy circlet upon Meilyr's brow.

He touched it with his fingers, the metal was cold, glinting in the warm light that engulfed them all. Pavan looked up, seeing Lilja approach him. Her smile was dazzling and it took him by surprise when her lips pressed to his. It was a momentary kiss that ended quickly, as the music began to quiet the cheers, drowning out the pounding of Pavan's chest. His fingers were laced with hers, as she led him to the empty space now alive with dancers.

He watched, as she danced around him, his smile forming as the other dancers stepped in time. Taking in the quick paced steps, Pavan was soon beginning to dance. Quick on his feet, he picked up the dance, shifting to follow as the other men did. He took Lilja's hand in the circle, following her in the parade around the room.

Pavan was content. Magick bubbling through him where the mead had little effect. He felt alive and drunk in the heat of the room, on the magick touch in Lilja's fingers. Where her lips kissed him tingled with remnants of it. He was unable to contain the smile as he brought her close, smelling the oils in her hair and loving the pleasure of her touch.

After the dance had ended, Pavan began to feel faint. Pulling free of Lilja's insistent grasp, he hurried from the dance floor. Returning to the sanctuary of his chair, he upended his goblet, drinking the last of his mead. Seeing a handmaid nearby, he requested it be filled. It was, and the drink was again emptied.

Taking one more glass, Pavan began to calm his nerves. He looked up to see Lilja enjoying the dance even further, now with another hunter with dark skin and reddish blonde hair pulled back away from his face. Pavan saw her dance with a feeling of unease. He didn't care if she danced with anyone else, but there was a certain burn within his chest that detested the thought of her touching another man.

Pavan looked away. In doing so, he saw Thad, who was in rapt concentration writing in the little book where he scribbled away his ideas and notes. Pavan unlatched his pelt from his shoulders to ease the sweltering heat that engulfed him. Pavan shifted himself from one seat to the other, so he leant close to Thad.

"Dance with me, Thad," he breathed, his hand resting close to the faie's arm.

"I do not dance...or had you forgotten?" Thad responded. His pen had not stopped writing. Pavan glanced over the shoulder, admiring the clear scrawl of the faie's hand, all in elvish. There were some runes and another few crossed out lines.

"Do not...or will not..." Pavan mused, his fingers now touching the fabric of Thad's tunic. It was silken, and cool to the touch.

"Is there a difference?" Thad inquired. His hand had stopped writing as his orange eyes shifted over to glance at Pavan, the smirk returned to those beautiful lips.

Pavan smiled, his fingers resting now over Thad's wrist.

"You do not dance, because you will not dance with anyone but me..." He saw the flicker of mischief in Thad's eyes, his grin widening, as the chuckle danced between them.

"So presumptuous...*Vhear.*" Thad lowered his tone, causing the deepest part of Pavan to ignite with fire.

Pavan was quick, snatching the little book from beneath Thad's unguarded watch. At once the faie gasped, reaching out with a quick hand to seize it back, but Pavan was quicker, the little book safely behind his back.

"Pavan—" Thad lowered his tone in a warning.

"You shall have it. After a dance." Pavan tucked it into the back of his tunic, it fit snug against his skin. Standing to his feet, he extended a hand to Thad.

In a huff, Thad stood, grasping Pavan's hand tightly.

"One dance, you black hearted thief." There was an edge to Thad's voice, but Pavan did not detect any truth.

Guiding the faie round the table by a harsh grip, he practically dragged him to the large group of dancers, pulling Thad in. Closing the distance between them, he began the dance. A hint of a smile softened the edge of Thad's frown, the look in his eye glinting with mirth with each step.

Pavan was smiling now, but he laughed at the change of step. Feeling the little book slide from the confines of his tunic, he looked over as Thad made his way around the other women who danced, smirking at Pavan with the conquest of the little journal.

He chuckled, stepping down the line as he followed Thad at a faster pace. He caught the faie in time to snatch the little book from his fingers, tucking it now into the front fold of his doublet to prevent any further thieving. Thad feigned annoyance as Pavan took the faie's hand, turning him under his arm. They continued the dance as others followed in line. Pavan stepped up, smirking. He touched Thad's waiting hand before he turned away to stand at a distance, following the remainder of the dance, until the music slowed.

Pavan let his hand fall from Thad's, feeling the loss. Stepping around many of the villagers who began to hurry about them in succession of the next dance, Pavan nudged his head, motioning Thad to follow him. Reaching into his tunic, he took out the small book. Now he led them towards the farthest corner of the room where the great doors lead out into the corridor, and to the stairs.

The cooled breeze sent a shiver up Pavan's spine, leaning against the stone wall. Thad came to stand beside him, looking up with brightened eyes and flushed cheeks.

"You dance remarkably well." Pavan smiled.

Thad smirked. "You are a dangerous thief."

Relenting, Pavan extended out the book, feeling Thad's hand over his to receive it. Warmth spread over Pavan and desire coiled in his gut as he leaned in towards the faie.

"Afraid I shall steal something more precious to you?" Pavan asked, dangerously close to him.

Thad gulped, searching Pavan's expression.

"There is nothing precious, Pavan. There is nothing else you could steal."

Pavan tsked, tilting the faie's chin with a soft hand, grazing his smooth skin that shimmered beneath his touch, eyes flickering to the warmth of his lips.

"Mmmm, perhaps not, but I wish to capture it anyway."

Thad chuckled, amused. "Capture what?"

"Your heart." His words sent a shiver through him and Pavan's magick coiled in his chest. Trailing his fingers to cup the strong jaw, he leaned in to claim the kiss.

Thad sighed, leaning in to accept him.

"Pavan."

He stopped at the sound of Meilyr's voice, glancing over Thad's head at the man who stood watching them from a distance. He did not know how long Meilyr had stood there, but heat crept onto his cheeks. Reluctantly drawing back from Thad, he let his hand fall heavily at his side, and followed Meilyr into the room.

"Proceed with caution, Pavan," the man spoke under his breath, as they walked the length of the hall to where the seats on the platform waited. He could see many of the elders waiting at the front, all holding a box. More gifts.

Pavan sighed. "More gifts, that should not be a problem."

But Meilyr shot him a look. "Not this, Pavan, you are smarter than that."

Heat flushed over Pavan's face as he maneuvered around to stand beside Meilyr, together, they sat upon the waiting chairs. Looking around them, there were those who drank, talking loudly, and there were some who danced to the low shift of music, their body language languid and seductive. Pavan quickly glanced away.

"Is it forbidden to desire him?" Pavan asked, under his breath.

Meilyr smiled, motioning for the first of the elders to approach. "It is not forbidden, but in your current arrangement...it could begin a great difficulty."

Pavan clenched his jaw. Seeing Lilja in the crowd, she spoke freely with some of the hunters he could not remember the names of, her white hair shimmering. He felt the returning of the desire that spread in his belly, the longing to hold her, to smell her. Magick flickered beneath the surface of his skin and he sneered.

"You made your choice when you agreed to her, dear boy. You cannot deny the connection between you both now." Meilyr then turned to the elder, reciting dutiful words of thanks, accepting the gift she provided. He returned his glance to Pavan.

Nausea began to build in his chest as he caught sight of the faie in the crowd as he weaved his way through, stopping to speak with Svein. Together he and the half giant departed, leaving the party, leaving Pavan alone with all of these well-wishers and happy, charming villagers.

Pavan wanted to run.

"It is unbreakable?" Pavan asked, looking directly at Meilyr, ignoring the elders who brought gifts.

Meilyr smiled politely. "Blood magick is unyielding. Only Lilja has access to its con-clusion, she may close the door upon this chapter."

He couldn't listen, his attention found the silver haired elf. Pavan watched her move from one end of the hall to the other, her dress shimmering in the golden glow. Lilja was beautiful, no one would deny that fact. But to Pavan she was an otherworldly thing, with strength and charm. His heart beat madly, allowing his eyes to drink her in from the safety of distance.

"Will you be ready to train?" Meilyr was now speaking again, drawing his attention back.

Pavan blinked, shaking back the lightheadedness. Warmth fluctuated with the racing of his heart. Need was scratching under the surface.

"Train...I believe it is time, Meilyr." He nodded, earning a satisfied sound from the man seated beside him. The elders were now gone, leaving them to sit in silence.

"Thad will begin promptly; he is an excellent fighter, and I believe he could withstand your strength." Meilyr spoke, but Pavan's concentration was elsewhere, his mouth was running dry, as he sat wiping sweat off his palms.

"Yes, that shall be fine," Pavan spoke non-committally, letting his gaze linger again to the elf, an odd sensation filling him. Magick coiled, clawing its way to the surface again. Wanting to be free.

"Pavan." Meilyr placed a hand on Pavan's arm.

He flinched, pulling away.

Pavan searched her out. She was like a beacon, he heard Lilja laugh openly with the man who stood so near. Her willowy arm was outstretched, her fingers grazing the man's arm and a fire ignited within his chest, flaring wildly to see her with him. He stood abruptly, excusing himself from Meilyr.

His eyes locked on Lilja.

"Oh Pavan, we are discussing such a delightful account of when poor Trisk was thrown from his horse last summer..." Her smile faltered, eyeing him suddenly.

"I wish to speak with you." His eyes flickered to the men who watched them. "Privately." Pavan's chest tightened, sneering at the others and looking at Lilja sharply.

Lilja smiled, taking his arm, bidding her quick farewells to the others before they walked off together. They left the noisy hall to exit into the cool, quiet corridor.

"You look unwell," was her first remark.

Pavan scowled as they continued to walk. He could breathe easier away from the heat of the great hall, but the pounding of his chest commenced, deepening. His blood began to flush his cheeks.

"I'm fine," he lied.

She shook her head, giving a great sigh, grasping his arm more firmly where she held his arm as they walked. Her press gave Pavan satisfaction, cooling his sudden extreme temperament. This reprieve agitated him causing Pavan to pull back.

"I feel your magick, shall I…" She reached for him, but he shook his head. "It will be worse for you, should you deny these spells of magick."

His eyes slithered to the stairs, leading up to the upper rooms, where he guessed Thad would be. Or perhaps he was in his little storage room that he converted to a workshop. Whichever it was, Pavan longed to see him. His longing and desire made the tightness in his chest deepen, the pull of his magick sharper.

"You shall dampen my magick," Pavan stated, looking back at the elf who watched him closely.

At once he walked on, trudging up the steps. He needed sleep, his head was hurting and he wanted to be free of her. Her charms and delights now deepened his agitation.

"You wished to speak with me," Lilja protested, following close at his heels.

"Now I wish I hadn't bothered. Go, you may talk with whom you wish. I cannot prevent you from flirting with them all," he spoke bitterly, his words escaping before he had a chance to stop them. At once, he regretted his words.

Lilja scoffed. "Me? I speak only to my duty, of the men I fight alongside. I honor them with friendship, loyalty…"

Pavan swallowed thickly, saying nothing. He trudged up the steps at a quicker step, ignoring the sure footfalls behind him. It was on the landing where his own rooms were housed, that Lilja caught his arm.

Her violet eyes flared.

"You are jealous." She kept her voice calm.

Pavan scoffed. "Jealous, of those fools pining for your attention? Don't be ridiculous…"

He felt uncomfortable as she pressed towards him, wrapping her arm languidly about the curve of his shoulder. Their bodies were close, and her heartbeat thumped against his chest. Resonating with the pull of her magick, he shivered.

"You snub them, because you are jealous," she stated, a smile playing on her lips.

Pavan growled deep in his chest, pushing her away. Reaching his room in a few more feet, he hastened to shut the door, but a hand blocked him as Lilja pushed her way inside.

"These are my rooms, please leave," he hissed through his teeth.

Lilja tsked, looking about the space with admiration and scrutiny, before turning to face him. "Not until I know your magick is quelled."

Pavan clenched his jaw, slamming the door shut. "I am fine."

She chuckled slightly. "You are a great liar. Perhaps I shall fetch Thad, he should be in his rooms. Perhaps you could express your perfect solicitude of your magick with him…"

Pavan shifted, blocking the door as she approached.

A knowing smile crossed her wicked lips. He scowled.

Lilja chuckled. "Come now, Pavan. We must put aside these childish games. Can you not sense it, your magick flexing beneath your skin?" She attempted to get closer, her fingertips grazing his arm, sending shivers through him.

Pavan's chest heaved, magick thickening, jumping, and coiling where she touched. The want was excruciating; his mouth was salivating to taste her skin.

"There," she cooed. "I can feel it. Unlike your faie, I can take your magick. I can give you what you need."

Pavan sneered. "Have a care how you speak of him."

"You do not know, do you? In all the years I have known Thad, he has only ever desired one thing." Her voice softened, her magick temptingly close, as she reached up on tiptoe to take his lips.

Pavan frowned. "Enough of your badgering. I know what you're doing. You enjoy inflicting torments on me, to taste the angered magick."

She smiled, coyly. "Your anger, so full of passion, tastes divine."

He clenched his fists, unwilling to give in. He glared at her while she began to touch his cheek, her fingers dancing like velvet over his skin. Pavan wanted to pull away, but every instinct drew him closer, leaning nearer to her touch.

"I will not yield," he whispered.

"Won't you?" She brushed back the fall of his dark hair, her body pressed to his, molded against his. Pavan wrapped his arm about her waist, drawing her in.

"I cannot. Not again." It was his last attempt to stop it, but she was intoxicating, each breath deepened the connection. Absorbing her scent, his hands grasped her sides desperately.

At last, those velvet lips pressed eagerly to Pavan's mouth, claiming him. It was deeper than the others, and bolder. A purpose of pleasure, rather than necessity. Pavan tasted the longing, her need spurring him on. He held her closer.

"Pavan," Lilja breathed, her hands clawed at his shoulder, raking up the contour of his neck to grip tightly into his hair.

He groaned, the want burning through him.

Lilja watched him with those lust filled eyes, her mouth red and full from kissing. Every inch of Pavan's body felt on fire. His desire for her was growing by the second, he felt his cock hard, eager to have her.

"You need this." She was breathless, running her thumb along the bottom line of his lip. "I need this. I need *you*."

He sighed heavily, maneuvering her long hair over her shoulder to caress the line of her warm, pale skin. Pavan felt her pulse thump against his fingertips, each thrum of her heart was laced heavily with magick and with need.

"That's it." She nods, tilting her head back to expose the line of her throat. "Have your fill."

Pavan's mouth waters, eyeing the splendid skin bare before him. He let his fingers fall upon the smooth skin, tracing a line down the dip of her throat, grasping the swell of her breast through the material of her gown. This earned him a sharp gasp, her hands now held firm over his shoulders. Trailing his lips over raised goose flesh, Pavan kissed the tender skin just below Lilja's ear. Now his hands sought the curve of her hips, grasping at the curve, pressing himself closer to her.

Lilja felt with her hands finding the front of his tunic. He reeled back suddenly as the material ripped beneath her tightened grasp. Quickly discarding the scrap material upon the floor, forgotten, she gripped his waist with long warm fingers, bringing their lips together in another passionate kiss.

"I liked that shirt," he huffed, groaning as her hands found his hair again, shifting on her toes until she maneuvered around him.

Lilja chuckled. "You shall have plenty of tunics."

Pavan watched her, his heart hammering in his chest. He chuckled at Lilja's eagerness, her slender hands hooked on the front of his trousers, yanking him across the room to stand beside the large bed. Turning then, at once, Lilja brought their mouths together, clawing down the length of his chest, unlacing the front of his trousers.

"You shall have shirts made of silks, and doublets embroidered with gold." She smiled, reaching her hand down to clasp her prize.

Pavan moaned, but gripped her wrist, turning her in one swift move, gripping her tightly to his chest. Guiding a hand across her belly, his hot mouth trailed over the curve of her neck. Lilja chuckled, hooking her arm back around his neck and extending her body against his. She flexed her fingers through his hair, arching her back.

"I will not be dressed in such finery," he hissed, nipping at her ear. His hands palmed down the shimmering fabric that separated himself from that of her milky skin. His fingertips slipped over the material, cool against his touch.

Beneath his touch, Lilja sighed, moving languidly with each grasp and curve of her body. Her body was alive with need, Lilja's magick tasted of thick honey, it was pliant and giving under Pavan's greedy hands. He frowned, frustrated to seek a way through, but there was not a clasp.

"Your gown, however, you shall never wear again in my company," he commanded, rucking up the miles of skirt. Lilja chuckled, leaning back against his chest, her hand grasping at his hair. Pavan's mouth placed hot kisses at the curve of Lilja's neck, while his hands fought with fabric.

"Defeated by mere silk. For shame Pavan..." she gasped, unable to finish her sentence.

Pavan's efforts finally proved fruitful. He delved beneath the layers of skirt, scooping her against him while two of his fingers moved deep inside her warm, wet center.

"Finally, without words?" Pavan breathed triumphantly, biting playfully at her ear, as he thrust his fingers deep into that warm, inviting heat. "If I knew this was what could silence you, I would have begun sooner."

Pavan thrilled in each breathy moan, each shift in Lilja's magick as his fingers roamed deeper, his other hand grasping a breast to squeeze. Pulling her back against him with each inward thrust of his fingers, he was grinding hard against her backside—pleasuring her was a vision, Pavan was lost to it, each second drawing her magick closer and closer to his grasp, their bond wound tightly.

"Yes," Lilja coaxed, her voice shimmering in the air. Pavan breathed hard, hooking his fingers in deep, drawing out from her lips a breathy gasp. Doing it again, and again, until Lilja's walls clamped around him, moaning loudly as she grasped his arm for support.

He pulled from her, taking hold of her hips, shifting his throbbing cock, still restricted by the cloth of his trousers, into the curve of her rear. Magick tightened its hold in his chest, the magick made it difficult to breathe.

Lilja turned suddenly, kissing his mouth with fervent passion.

"You must take me," she told him, stepping back to pull the yards of fabric over her head. She smiled at him as his eyes raked over the curves of her flushed skin.

"Clever," he growled, scooping her close to his chest as he kissed her deeply, feeling every new expanse of skin. His hands grabbed greedily at the firmness of her rear as he groaned against her mouth. "But I have taken you."

She smirked against his mouth, reaching again for the front of his trousers, seeking out her prize. Pavan bit his lip, inhaling sharply at the sudden feel of her long fingers around his aching member.

"Not until this glorious cock is buried deep inside me."

Pavan chuckled. "Such a mouth. I thought I quieted those words of yours."

He watched her with hungry eyes, as she sat herself back upon his bed, hair falling partly over her shoulder to cover her bare breasts, the fair hair between her thighs the same color. Pavan sighed, longing to kiss every inch of her, but in the moment, he would do whatever she asked. Pavan at once discarded his trousers, standing before her bare.

Lilja looked on approvingly, violet eyes soaking him in as he neared the bed to crouch above her. She giggled when he pushed her back, her white blonde hair splayed out around her.

"I grow impatient, sir." Lilja squirmed, grasping his biceps, reaching to touch the curve of his cheek.

"My lady grows impatient." Pavan smirks playfully, leaning down to kiss the tender skin between the mounds of her breasts. Lilja sighed approvingly. "But I have not devoted my time to her completely." He leaned down to take a nipple in his mouth, earning a satisfied moan. Pavan was pleased, giving attention to the other, until Lilja sighed beneath him.

"There," he sighed, drawing closer, pulling one of Lilja's knees about his waist. His cock slotted against her inner thigh, and he watched her earnestly. Her violet eyes met his. "Are you certain?"

Lilja smiled, caressing his cheek. Magick danced against his skin, making him shiver.

"More than certain, Pavan."

Malcom knocked on the large oaken door to Pavan's chambers. It was early, and they usually dined together in the morning before they trained. Perhaps there had been too much drink at the celebrations the night previous as no one answered.

He knocked again, more firmly.

At last, the door opened, but Malcom frowned. He was greeted not by his friend, but instead by Lilja, with Pavan's Vohlgrum pelt wrapped about her willowy frame. Her milky white shoulders were bare and her long white blonde hair was mused behind her.

She smiled demurely. "Good morrow, Malcom."

"Lilja...you're...good morning." Malcom gulped, eyeing the room behind her, but he could not see any movement. Lilja chuckled.

"Pavan is not here. He awoke brightened and went immediately to the training yard. I, on the other hand, like my sleep."

Malcom eyed her closely, examining the flush of the elf's cheek and the brightness of her eyes. There was an unsettling amount of regard and warmth emanating from her.

"You spent the night here, with him."

She chuckled. "Of course, though I cannot say for certain how much sleep one gets with a man like him. He is very passionate."

Malcom grimaced, not caring in that moment that she saw it. He was displeased, and did not wish to hide it. He locked eyes with the violet ones.

"You use your magick, with these couplings?" Keeping his tone calm, he directed his examination of her person with a professional glance, watching the pupils of her eyes, the rise and fall of her chest. She exhibited signs of drunkenness, but he said nothing on that score.

Lilja waved a hand, rolling her eyes as she stepped back into the room. Malcom now had no choice but to follow.

"I know that look," she told him, her voice soft and elegant. She reached a side table to pour herself a glass from a carafe no doubt brought up from an attending maid. Evidence of the roaring fire within the hearth approved with this idea.

Malcom stood closer to the door, slowly crossing his arms.

Lilja chuckled, her frame stirring indolently as she moved to face him, her drink in hand sipping from it slowly.

"You are worried for your friend..." she began. Finally, she took a seat in the chair facing the fire, directly in front of where Malcom stood.

He was suddenly uncomfortable, as her bare legs became exposed from the long, thick pelt that she held together at her waist—Lilja was not clothed. She was decorous, too familiar, acting as a lover to his friend. Malcom knew Pavan did not fancy this woman, and since their arrival, she has been nothing but a source of discomfort to Pavan's mental health.

"Yes, he is my friend. I have known him since we were ten years old. I cannot account for what his time here has been, but with me, I know him better than anyone. You are not good for his progression of stability."

Lilja scoffed, her facial expression changed so drastically Malcom did not recall her ever smiling at him.

"Stability? My, you have been working far too closely with Thad, haven't you?" She was jilted, her voice hardened as she drank from her cup.

Malcom sighed heavily. "Thad has nothing to do with my observations as Pavan's friend, nor as his healer. You are not ignorant of his past, nor of his habits..."

"I know of your friend, Penelope. She must have meant a great deal to him," she said, and Malcom felt anger bubbling up with his blood pressure.

"Meant a great deal to him? To Pavan?"

Lilja eyed him, slowly downing her drink. Malcom took a long deep breath.

"She was Pavan's wife."

Malcom watched the violet eyes glance away as Lilja shifted in her chair, but her expression remained impassive and unaffected.

"From what was once such a burden, it hardly seems to affect his heart now. When I bed him, there was no melancholy in his heart; his magick was heightened, he was...let us just surmise that Pavan was not grieving his once lost love."

Malcom's jaw clenched until his teeth began to ache.

"You have doped him with drugs, Lilja, your magick is nothing more than an aphrodisiac that dampens his brain," he said, agitated as he sat, glaring at the elf who sat so unaffected by what she had said, or did.

"You speak words of your own tongue, Malcom. I do not understand your healer's language. But if my magick is the balm to his pains, the means of anointing his once broken heart, then perhaps you are right. We are bound by blood. From where I sit, Malcom, I see no wrong in it."

Malcom scowled. "His past is clouded with demons, Lilja. Some you have witnessed in him yourself. Where we came from, Pavan used similar drugs to dull his mind. He used it as an escape from reality, and used it so often, it nearly killed him."

Now, there was a shift in the elf, her face became pale, no smirk nor a frown.

"I have control..."

Malcom scoffed. "Can you look me in the eyes and tell me truthfully that this magick will not change him? That it has not already changed him? You claim he is active, passionate, but shall I ask you the difficult questions, Lilja?" Malcom became invigorated by his anger, his frustration igniting his fiery tone. "How long has he slept? When was the last time you witnessed him eat a full meal?"

A shadow came over her violet eyes and she was not able to look him in the eye directly.

"As I thought," Malcom decided. He turned away and reached the door in a few heavy steps.

Fuming in anger, Malcom wanted to walk to calm his thoughts. Needing fresh air, Malcom hurried from the main house, ducking away from many of the servants within the house. Finally, he reached the gardens, feet stomping along the small winding trails through the little flower hedges.

It was a quarter of an hour later when Malcom found himself walking along the low wall of the training yard. He made it to the gate, and beyond, with no real thought but seeing Pavan, he stopped. His friend stood at the farthest end of the ring, lifting a large hammer above his head to slam the thing down onto a waiting slab of stone, an awful sound echoed in the empty training yard.

Malcom saw the exertion in Pavan; through the thin linen tunic he wore, he was now drenched in sweat, his feet bare, and his messy dark curls dripped along his neck. Still, the man raised his arms again, the heft of the hammer evenly balanced in his hands, before Pavan struck hard at the stone again.

"Pavan!" Malcom called. There was no response.

He walked closer, maneuvering to approach him from the front, seeing the sweat that dripped along Pavan's face, the reddened cheeks, the darkening under his eyes. Malcom felt uneasy. He was approaching with haste, but keeping his temperament calm, unchallenging.

"Can you set aside the hammer, Pavan?" Malcom asked, now standing a good three feet from Pavan.

His friend paused but did not look up, the sweat was beading along the line of his nose. As the heft of the hammer began to slacken, Malcom reached out tentatively, stepping the distance between them to take the hammer from his friend. The weight of it pulled hard at Malcom's arm as he set the handle of the great thing against the cracked and weathered stone. Returning to Pavan's side, he checked the pulse at his wrist, then again at his neck.

Pavan was remarkably cool. His pulse was quickened but not more than it should for his exertions. He looked again to his friend's face and upon closer inspection, it was not sweat that Malcom saw slithering down the length of his nose, but tears.

"Pavan." Malcom's voice was softer.

"I wanted it out of me. I couldn't stand to have the magick in my blood..." His voice was broken, rasping harshly in his throat. He raised a trembling hand to rake back the mop of damp hair, letting Malcom see the entirety of his face—it was splotched red, sweaty, and with red eyes evident of crying.

"Come, you should eat something." Malcom held Pavan's arm, guiding his friend away from the training yard. They only managed to get a few paces into a long walk through the tall wooded path, sunlight was glinting through the leaves that shook against the breeze, when Pavan stopped suddenly.

His chest heaved. He raised his hands to cover his mouth as fresh tears formed, Malcom felt his own chin quiver. Bringing his arms tightly around his friend's shoulder, he embraced him. Pavan clung to Malcom, silently weeping into the bend of his neck, hidden in the grove. He would stand there with him for hours if this was what he needed. But now, Malcom knew what Pavan needed.

Reluctantly, he pulled back. "Pavan, can we get you some food?"

Pavan nodded slowly, wiping at his face with the driest part of his tunic and taking the first steps towards the great hall. They walked the remainder of the little grove.

"Is she still there, in my room?" Pavan's voice was low.

Malcom hesitated. "Yes. I saw her, before I came to find you."

Silence fell again between them. They entered the large stone building through a side entrance, their eyes shifting in the sudden change of light. They made their way through the side corridors until they reached the great hall through the library. It was a little lively, with men who hunkered over to nurse their hangovers, where women sat idly, applying themselves to their books, or to sewing.

Malcom and Pavan took a table to the side, beneath one of the great windows. Light poured in through the stained glass. At the far end of the hall, through the doors that led into the kitchens, Malcom could see many come and go, carrying small barrels to replenish the place near the wall where many could come to drink as they felt inclined.

Malcom stood. "I will get us a drink."

Pavan made no reply, his gaze was adrift outside of the window, Malcom sighed heavily, doing as he said and walking towards the kitchens. It was between meals, but he dutifully inquired if there were cheeses and breads to give. Malcom earned a heavy sigh from the cook but the cook took pity upon him, giving a plate of boiled egg, cheese, leftover bread from breakfast, and some cold boiled ham.

Malcom gave his thanks before returning to Pavan with the plate, two cups, and a pitcher of water. He poured a cup for his friend, shifting the plate before him. Pavan sat as he had been, gazing off through the window.

"You need to eat," Malcom encouraged.

Pavan glanced his way, shaking his head, and swallowing hard. Malcom saw him struggle to compose himself, to keep his emotions sedated.

Finally, Pavan spoke. "It's like London all over again...I can't—"

Malcom sat forward. He kept his words low, but his urgency was resolute. Reaching across the table to take Pavan's hand, he tightly grasped it until he saw Pavan wince.

"You are not your addictions, Pavan. You are not her magick...whatever she believes she could solve, it was wrong. I was wrong. Pavan..." Malcom fell silent, unsure how to continue. Answers failed him, he did not understand the depths of this world, he knew nothing of magick.

"But if I break our bond..." Pavan said after a long moment. "If I separate myself from her magick...the things I am capable of...you do not know Mal, what I could do."

Bitterly, Malcom shook his head. "I can't see you go through it again. I can't do this with you. I will not support you harming yourself on purpose, after all that you've done to pull yourself out again..." He shook his head, lost in his heartache. Letting Pavan's hand slip away, he slumped back into the chair.

"Is there another way?"

Malcom shut his eyes, hot tears slipping onto his cheeks. "I don't know. Thad had said with time, you could harmonize with your magick, but…"

Pavan tsked dramatically. "Time. We have not time when it comes to my magick. I wish to control it; for a moment I believe I can, then it slips away."

Malcom looked up, quizzingly.

"When do you feel these moments?"

"When I do not let my mind wander. When I am employed in menial tasks, like chopping wood, working in the mines to carry their heaviest stone or juggling for those inquisitive children in the square."

Malcom blinked, looking Pavan over. "Do you feel in control when you are fighting, shooting an arrow, when you are reading?"

Pavan opens his mouth to speak, but closes it again. Thinking.

"I feel it then, too, but not so much as when I am in company with…" Suddenly, Pavan glanced down, his mouth a deep frown.

"Pavan, what is it?" Malcom watched Pavan play idly with the ribbon around his wrist, he had never taken it off since Denorn.

"I feel in control when I am with Thad."

"You believe that to be wrong?" Malcom asked, sensing Pavan's displeasure.

"I…I feel right. I feel at peace when I am near him. It is difficult to explain." Pavan shook his head, closing his eyes for the briefest of moments.

Malcom sat in thought for a long moment, reflecting while they ate in silence. After a considerable time, he said, "You should spend more time with him."

Pavan looked up from his food. "You think I should? You don't think it…wrong?"

Malcom smiled, knowing his friends' hesitations upon this particular subject. "This is not London, Pavan. Besides, when was the last time you cared what the neighbors think?"

It was good to see him smile.

"I suppose you are right…as usual."

Malcom approved of Pavan's ease, watching him now take more fervent bites of food set before him. But Pavan's gaze returned to the window, looking out over the lawn just beyond, taking in the hustle and life of the village.

Pavan's feet stood cold in the mud, watching the blending of the line of trees just at the edge of the forest. It was now evening; he had sufficiently avoided Lilja. Now, he was in Thad's company. They went out together at Thad's request, to practice shooting a bow and arrow, he was hesitant, walking so near to the forest again.

Thad had reassured him so here he stood, the slender bow unfamiliar in his hand, looking to a forest that looked to him as one singular entity. Pavan sighed heavily.

"You won't shoot anything sulking."

Pavan rolled his eyes, looking over at Thad who was kneeling on one leg, his bow poised over it as he tightened the string, pulling at the limb as the sinew string flexed against Thad's grip. Pavan admired the skills the faie seemed to exhibit; he was a skilled fighter, proficient in the sword, throwing an ax, and was a near perfect shot. Svein had informed Pavan that it was the faie in Thad, with the sight many of magick did not possess.

"I am not sulking." Pavan inclined his head, keeping his eyes on the thin hands of the faie, they were thin, dexterous, but strong.

"Pavan."

He looked up, catching Thad's curious gaze.

Pavan rolled his eyes, resuming the position of stance, lifting the bow up to notch his arrow. Pavan was reminded of school, he had taken archery on a whim, needing an excuse to be near Penelope.

Bitterness flowed in a harsh tang through Pavan, making his magick shiver. Uneasy in his aim, Pavan looked upon the makeshift target hung upon one of the trees yards away. The arrow was released, and Pavan swore, watching the fleck of the metal arrowhead shoot long, disappearing into the forest beyond.

Thad chuckled. "What were you thinking of, Pavan?"

Pavan did not answer. He clenched his jaw, taking another arrow from his quiver, and returned to his beginning position to notch his arrow. Thad came to stand beside him, pressing his arm to lower the bow, Pavan unwillingly relaxed his form, glaring down into orange eyes.

"I did not think of anything."

Thad was not convinced. "Your magick is strong, Pavan. You wear it so openly, it is impossible not to feel it. You thought of something, a moment before you shot. What came to you just then?"

Pavan sighed.

"I learned archery in school, where I lived before. It was boring, pointless." He glanced back up to see the amusement in the faie's eyes.

"You learned this skill to be close to someone?"

Pavan could not keep the vexed chuckle from passing his lips. He was unable to retreat from this confrontation.

"Penelope…"

Thad's smile fell, and Pavan felt the shift in the air, magick flickered in him—his own apprehension, and the sorrow from the faie.

"Again…"

Irritation flooded through Pavan, but Thad shook his head, maneuvering to stand close to Pavan now. His own bow was forgotten.

Pavan shook his head. "That's not…"

But Thad looked stern, retrieving a second arrow from the quiver and handing it to Pavan. "I said again…and this time, I am going to show you how to do it properly."

Taking the arrow, Pavan notched it in the bowstring. He stood as he had before, but this time Thad kicked at Pavan's inner feet.

"Feet farther apart." Thad came around Pavan, kicking his back foot again so it was further back. The shift made Pavan's hips lock forward. "There. Now, lift up your bow, but do not draw back."

Pavan did as he was told, raising his arms as he had done before, but Thad was quick to correct his wrist, giving his hand a firmer placement and tilting his back elbow up.

"Your center is unfocused," Thad informed him.

Pavan slid his eyes over, Thad stood so near, looking up to Pavan's height and his hand tightened on the bow.

"My center?"

Those orange eyes flickered with gold, pressing the palm of his other hand close to the middle of Pavan's chest. Not over his heart, but pressed against the base of his sternum. A shattering breath extended in Pavan's lungs as magick stabbed sharp and his eyes stung with tears.

Thad leaned in, his lips a breath away from Pavan's ear. "Your pain will always be with you, Pavan. It is here. I can feel it, but you must center yourself or it will consume you."

His breathing became ragged. Tears welled, and his chest ached where the hand pressed against his chest was unrelenting.

"You magick must flow, Pavan. From your body to your arm, from your arm to your heart, from your heart to your head. But you must find your center." Thad's voice was smooth, sending shivers through Pavan.

He gulped. "I don't know my center."

"Look out there," Thad spoke softly, and Pavan turned his head to follow, the forest stretched out beyond them. It was vast, a large blur of shifting branches and fluttering leaves on the breeze.

"I see trees."

Thad smiled. Pavan caught a glimpse of it in the corner of his eye, making his chest tighten.

"Yes, the trees. Your aim is there, but in the world, you see there is much you do not. The flutter of a bird's wing, the honey bees that swarm a hive, the fox that has emerged from his burrow in search of his next meal...your center is somewhere between the world you see, and the world you do not. Only you can discover it for yourself." Thad pressed his hand, one last shift of magick, but then he felt Thad stepping back.

Panic made Pavan shake, the tear fell unbidden along his cheek, as he was gritting his teeth against the pain.

"I can't..." He began to feel the crawling bitterness.

Thad still remained close but did not return to his side.

"You have it in you, Pavan. Believe in yourself, believe in your own power...no one can stop it but you."

Pavan blinked hard, breathing to dampen the crawl of anger up his spine, the harsh tang of magick in his mouth that wanted to break free. Shutting his eyes, he willed it away.

"Draw back, Pavan..." He heard Thad's voice, his senses were heightened and there was a ringing in Pavan's ears.

Pulling back, Pavan kept his frame firm, the position of his stance strengthened. But his magick strained, pulling hard to resist him. At last, opening his eyes, Pavan looked beyond at the forest, to the shift of the trees, trying to shift his focus to see more. Pavan began to hurt, unable to find his center.

"Let go."

A breeze fluttered, warm against Pavan's cheek, drawing his eyes to the flap of ribbon that shifted against his wrist. Tattered and stained, the green cloth drew him to it. He could smell the ocean, hear the crash of waves on the beach, and seeing the flutter of dark hair on the breeze. He sighed, a shiver running up his arm. Magick trembled, but quieted. Focusing beyond the bow, Pavan saw the marker.

Thunk! Pavan had not realized he had released the arrow, but the whiz and snap of the string beside his ear, and the satisfying jolt of seeing the arrow make its mark made Pavan's mind alive with satisfaction. He dropped his bow, stepping over it to where Thad stood, smiling, and embraced the faie in a hard, bone crushing hug.

"Thank you," Pavan whispered.

CHAPTER
24

Pavan was welcomed into the warmth of Meilyr's private offices. A large warm fire brightened the small room, and furs lined the chairs and floor, blocking out the cold that had begun to descend upon them as winter fast approached the village.

The leader of this village was seated at his large desk, looking over the large books and ledgers that lay open upon the large mahogany wood. His quill in hand, ink splotches covering his fingers. When the door clicked shut, Meilyr looked up.

Meilyr smiled.

"Ah, Pavan, come sit, my dear boy..." He stood, his work forgotten, walking about his office to uncover a teapot from the far corner. Pavan smirked to himself, sitting as Meilyr had told him to, watching him.

Meilyr's long hair was braided, matted into long locs. Small metal rings decorated the strands, making him jingle when he moved. His usual garments were covered with a long coat lined with fur.

"You have done well for yourself, these last weeks of recovery." Meilyr returned to the table, carrying two cups full of steaming drinks. Pavan took one, sipping gratefully.

It was not tea as he knew it, but it was warm and tasted sweet.

"Thank you. I feel better, Thad has really helped me to control my magick."

"A blessing indeed."

A long moment passed as Pavan sipped his tea before a thought that ate at him could not be contained any longer.

"What happened to Sophie? Her shop is closed, I have not seen her in Ledenjour."

Meilyr sat back, again taking his pipe to his lips. "It was arranged for her to live in Divna, a southern province of Corad where those devoted to Ehnarea take the vow of silence."

Emotion was thick in Pavan's throat, making it difficult to swallow.

"I have ruined her, haven't I, Meilyr? Not just taking her purity, but by taking her soul. I know what I have done is unforgivable."

Meilyr sat in rapt contemplation for a long silent draw from his pipe, letting the smoke curl from his lips like a dragon.

"Sophie shall live out the remainder of her years in the comfort of the sisterhood, Pavan. She will be content there in the security of Divna."

"She won't live long."

Meilyr became pensive. "We all must die in our time, Pavan."

"But, without a soul...this world, your people...they believe in the Veil, that they shall walk again with Ehnarea in the great forests beyond that shroud of death. Sophie believed it...she believed in your goddess, but I have taken away her right to it..." Tears again, Pavan was sick of crying. His head ached from it, his chest hurt.

"What is done, is done, Pavan. You cannot change what you have taken from Sophie, just as much as I cannot change what is done in my past. We do not hold the hands of time in our power."

The tear finally rolled down Pavan's cheek.

"Regrets have carved into my heart. I don't believe there is anything left." Pavan looked down at his hand, touching the skin of the finger where a ring once sat. Now, his eyes were drawn further down where a small triangle scar flared red.

"When I was a younger man," Meilyr began, with a story much like all the others he had told in the past. "I lived with my mother by the sea. Every day there were new visitors, for she ran a comfortable inn where sailors could have a hot meal and a bed to sleep, and they would tell us stories of their adventures across the treacherous seas. It was then that I heard the first tales of Entheas.

"It was Entheas that I longed for, to seek the adventures I had heard so many men talk of in the company of my mother. But she was wary to let me venture so far from her reach. There were dangers that I would face leaving the home by the seaside."

"But here you are."

Meilyr smiled, smoke curling along the curve of his mustache. "Here I am, Pavan. Because I took the great ships across the treacherous sea, I made the choice to leave my mother behind in a realm where danger pursued us."

"You were from the realm beyond the great shroud?" Pavan asked, knowing the stories of those shipwrecked in the treacherous seas. "Did you take one of the great ships?"

"I bought passage on the largest of them all, captained by a man known to my mother. He was to sail his last, never to return."

"A great sacrifice." Pavan was thoughtful, trying to understand the story, because Meilyr always gave advice in the narrative.

Meilyr nodded. "He was a devoted man, loyal to my mother's service. She knew she could trust him to take her son across the sea on a great errand."

Pavan furrowed his brow. "Errand?"

"Kiret was an elf of the great tribes, given to the King of Nyr and she bore to him a son. But her son was to be sacrificed to the Old Ones, to appease the sins of the king for lying with his brother's wife. She was desperate to save the boy, and begged my mother to help."

"You loved Kiret?"

"I loved Kiret with the very beat of my heart. When at first our eyes met, I knew that she was meant for me. For her, I would sail the ends of Veilore to keep her from harm."

"You regret loving her?" Pavan saw the man frown, feeling the flicker of magick shiver throughout the room.

"I regret that I could not save her forever. She flourished in Entheas by my side, but she was a healer and gifted by Ehnarea with the hands that could heal any ailment. She taught me, as she had taught her son. But even our skill could not draw out the death that took her—a fast disease that whittled away her body."

Pavan gulped, his heart hammering hard in his chest.

"Lahrs is Kiret's son. The elf they all talk about." Pavan understood Meilyr's tenderness, the sentimental heart that was desperate to keep those closest to him who needed him the most.

Meilyr set aside his pipe. "If I had gone with Kiret, had I been with her, she would not have suffered. I could have saved her with Lahrs' help, but she kept me in the dark of her illness. She kept it from us to not take me away from my duties in Ledenjour."

He felt hot all over, as emotion flushed his skin. Looking at his hands, Pavan saw the skin rubbed raw upon his finger. He absently scraped against it as Meilyr told his story. Pavan's throat was tight.

"Regrets do not define us, Pavan, but they should guide us for the choices that we make," Meilyr said.

"Did my father have that choice?" Pavan's breath came short.

"Charles was troubled. It was my heartfelt wish that I could have changed his mind, but it was not my choice to give. It was beyond my power when he began to seek the answers to those dark twisted questions."

"He killed the King of Jorn."

Meilyr sighed heavily. "It is beyond my power to know if it was him..."

Pavan gulped. "When I was a child, the men that chased me wanted to take me to my father. It was by his orders that my mother was to be brought forward."

"They sought justice for the king..."

Pavan frowned, knowing better. "He has influence in Jorn, Meilyr. He is using his magick to gain superiority there. Why else would there be such a dwindling of faie?"

Meilyr looked pale. "Your father is dead."

"My father is a narcissistic, murdering blackheart who talked only about the glory and birthright that was snatched away from his family. He is Ehlfern, with the same power that flows through my blood. He can siphon magick. He has been here for nearly fifteen years at his own command."

"Be calm, Pavan," Meilyr instructed.

Sitting back, Pavan saw the ice that began to crawl over the desk between them. At once the chill receded, Pavan had not noticed the change until Meilyr had mentioned it. Pavan calmed himself, clearing his throat.

"Come, I wish to show you something." Meilyr stood.

Pavan followed, walking with Meilyr to the chamber that was joined to his offices, a long wall lay bare. He watched in amazement as Meilyr pressed the stone, watching it push away, the stone shifted easily back to expose a large darkness beyond.

They descended down steps, entering into a chamber below. Meilyr now cast a light above them, flickering the heavy lanterns to blaze anew in a golden glow. Pavan cast his eyes about the little furnished room.

"This is my private collection of treasure," Meilyr remarked, walking beyond the shelves of precious stone mined from their own mountains. Gilded daggers and stone statues line the little shelves, along with leather books inscribed with runes upon the spines. Scrolls sealed with wax were stacked neatly in little piles.

Pavan saw the armor that hung neatly upon a body rack, made to not crease the leather. It was hefty, glittering in a sheen of gold. It was real gold, and every link and rivet shimmered.

"This way." Meilyr walked deeper, Pavan following his path, passing the three large trunks to the farthest wall. A tapestry hung down, covering a large painting.

Meilyr drew the hefty fabric aside, bringing a light closer to inspect the large framed work of art. Pavan gasped. Stepping closer, he drew his eyes to the lady in the picture.

It was his mother, painted in likeness, and dressed in a richly ornamented gown. But his eye flicked to the man who stood beside her, wearing a dark royal blue jacket, painted in likeness to the man he remembered.

"This was a gift from your mother, a year after she left us."

Pavan stepped closer to inspect the faces of each. The man was tall, but in a portrait like this, it was hard to depict a true height. But his mother, Pavan felt a pang in his chest, she looked beautiful.

"Was she happy?"

"She loved him, as he loved her dearly. She was content with him." Meilyr turned from the painting, taking with it the light. Pavan had no choice but to turn away, following Meilyr as the man then maneuvered to the wall that held a large trunk.

Waving a hand over the top, Pavan watched in wonder as Meilyr unlocked the large trunk with magick, hearing the click and grind of gears as the mechanism inside slid into place. At last Meilyr opened it. He leaned down to take from the belly of it garments made entirely of leather. They were dark and shimmering in the light. Pavan gulped, stepping back. He could feel the slither of magick coiling tightly in his belly. It disturbed him.

"I do not think of myself as proficient at many talents, but in this I am content in conveying a certain pride in its making. These shall fit you well, I think."

Pavan recoiled when Meilyr extended the bundle to him.

"Thank you," Pavan began, trying to keep his voice from conveying hard emotion. "But I cannot accept such a gift...I cannot wear..."

Eying the bundle of garments so desired and well made, Pavan trembled. The magick within his own blood began to shiver in anticipation. He wished to touch the smooth buckles, feel the excellent craftsmanship of Meilyr that he had seen in many of the garments fashioned for the hunters, but this Pavan could not do.

There was no alarm in Meilyr, who smiled as he did, returning the garments safely within the trunk, and closing the trunk to secure it away where Pavan could no longer feel its pull. At once he was lightened, and able to breathe more freely.

"Perhaps in time, Pavan. It shall always be here for you."

They retreated, no more business attended them in the locked chamber. Emerging again in the lightness of the chamber above, Pavan blinked hard. Suddenly, he grew tired after so much exertion of his own powers.

Pavan excused himself. There were chores he needed attending before the fall of the sun and Meilyr would not detain him. Pavan walked, as he usually did when his mind was prone to darkness, until he came to the blacksmith's, but he found the wood had already been chopped. Walking on, he inquired to the baker, but she told him the deliveries had all been made. When he asked who by, she could not answer, for they had arrived without a disturbance of who could have left them.

He was unsettled. Pavan walked for nearly an hour, meandering the roads that he knew so well. Nodding to the smiles and hellos and good morrows from the villagers who happened upon him on their daily walks. With nothing to occupy him, Pavan became disjointed, unable to quiet the rattling of his mind, nor calm the nervous stagnancy of reserve.

He needed to be doing something, but his former employment was all accomplished before he had the duty of seeing to them, this vexed him. Pavan was irritated, stomping into the stables, eager to find some suitable work.

"Vhear, what an honor."

He was greeted by the kindly old stable master. Pavan hated that many of the villagers now called him Vhear, but they would not call him anything else. Pavan forced his smile, trying to calm his nervous attitude.

"Good morrow, sir," he began ardently. "I have come to ask if I could do anything for you?"

The man looked puzzled. "Do anything for me, Vhear?"

Pavan heard the hesitation in the man's voice, the uncomfortable demeanor as the man stood taking in Pavan, who was now the hero of Ledenjour. Pavan grimaced, but tried to hide it.

"Yes, I should like to be of service to you, sir. I could bring fresh hay to the stalls, feed your wonderful mares..." Pavan faltered, seeing the distress begin to form in the man's kind face.

"Oh, no, Vhear. You have done us all a kindly service already. You must not put yourself in our hardships."

Pavan clenched, but quickly checked his emotions. He was already feeling the emerge of magick fluttering in his belly.

"I insist. Please, give me something to do."

Here, the older man relented, giving a pitiable expression Pavan did not appreciate in the least, but he was resigned to be grateful as long as the man just thought of a job.

"There is something you can do." He walked around Pavan, desperately scrambling in the little office where he kept his books. Finally, he emerged with a thickly bound leather book—it was small but thick with orange pages. He extended it out to Pavan.

"A book?"

The stablemaster smiled, all teeth, politely nodding. "Please return this to Meilyr's library. I borrowed it last week, but have forgotten to return it."

Pavan sighed, taking the book in hand.

"Of course." He was happy to oblige the stable master, already feeling the awkward tension of the man not really wanting to inconvenience the Vhear from actual hard labor.

Pavan went away, book in hand.

Further down the lane, Pavan examined the little book, opening it to browse the title. He stopped, flipping the pages again and again, exhilaration overpowered him. Sitting on the nearest bench, he read line after line of English. Not Common, not Elvish, nor any of the other dialects that peppered the pamphlets and books that were kept readily at hand in Ledenjour from all over the realms.

It was old English-type. Set in such familiar terms, Pavan began at once to read aloud from the page that he held open.

"This thou perceivest, which makes thy love more strong,
To love that well which thou must leave ere long..."

Shakespeare. Pavan had so many questions; the origins of this book to these lands, how it has been kept in such pristine condition. It was old, but the binding was blank, nor were the inlaid pages stamped with a printer's mark. But whatever the origin, or manner in which it arrived, Pavan was thankful. He closed the book. Sighing heavily, at last, he opened it again. He began at the beginning.

CHAPTER
25

S ir Lahrs shall return soon, princess."

Brendolyn sighed heavily, looking back at the lady who sat nearby the large table. It had been nearly an hour since her studies with Lahrs were scheduled to take place, when the lady from Jorn had come to attend to her at Sir Lahrs' request. She was an elf, with long golden hair curled beneath a veil.

"He is not usually kept away so long." Brendolyn returned her eyes to the window where she sat upon the cushioned seat. From this place, Brendolyn could see the lawn and the lower end of the training yard, her eyes caught glimpses of glinting steel and bronze.

"Shall I read to you, Princess Brendolyn?" came the soft voice of the lady.

"My head aches, perhaps I shall go to my rooms."

As the day had gradually progressed, her body had grown tired after being in company with the court. Being around so many with tiring emotions had made the usual quiet she experienced with Lahrs' company in the tranquility of the garden desperately wanted. She wished for the solitude of her rooms.

"It is past midday, Princess. Not yet time to dress for the evening."

Brendolyn rolled her eyes at the window, listening to the lady explain to her the way it was done in Jorn, hearing again the etiquette that a princess should obey. She was growing impatient from the rules that tortured her. Brendolyn wished to return to Corad, to return to her home where the wishes of those superior to her did not order her about.

"Then perhaps a walk in the gardens?"

"I believe that could be a change we shall both benefit from."

Cautioning her steps, Brendolyn took her time as she walked beside the lady out of the great library, greeting those of the court who stopped to address her. Brendolyn felt the anticipation building within her chest, as excitement flourished into hope. She quickened her steps after descending the steps.

"Calm your steps, princess."

Brendolyn nodded, walking slower, but her feet were alive with movement. Her chest fluttered as they neared the archway leading out onto a side vestibule. She blinked into the light as fresh air embraced Brendolyn with a warm caress.

Walking gladly with the lady, they took the narrow gravel path leading into the edge of the vast gardens that wrapped around the castle, weaving around hedges, stepping up stone steps, and winding into the well-landscaped flower beds.

A breeze came, bringing with it the smell of roses, geraniums, coreopsis, and mint. Brendolyn brightened at the warmth of color that surrounded her, closing her eyes to the swell of delight that raised her spirits.

"We must keep to the path, princess." The lady was walking along the gravel path, the one that led closer into the more structured lanes with straight hedges leading closer to the fountains.

"This is the path I take with Lahrs." Brendolyn stopped, looking from the vibrant path laden with uneven stones and the overgrown hedges of roses.

"Your gown shall get dirty, princess. It rained during the night."

Brendolyn took a step away from the lady, feeling the heightened flicker of the woman's irritation. She was trying to keep Brendolyn closest to the castle, to keep her to the path less likely to cause her trouble. No doubt she knew Brendolyn's inclination to adventure.

"Princess."

It was unmistakable, hearing the tone, authority slithering within the pretty voice that masked the lady's irritation. Brendolyn slipped her feet from the slippers that barely clung to her feet, watching the eyes of the lady grow wide with horror.

"Come, princess. We shall return to the library."

With practiced speed, Brendolyn tore her stockings from her feet.

"Never!" Throwing them onto the cobbled path beneath her, she left behind with the gilded slippers. Gripping up her skirts, she ran as fast as she could away from the lady, away from the confinement of her cage. She was fast and quicker than many of those that had tried to chase after her.

Ignoring the shouts of the lady, Brendolyn ran deeper and deeper into the gardens, feeling the wet soil and sharp stones beneath her feet. Exhilaration brought a smile to her lips, her hair dancing behind her.

She stopped short of a tall stone wall. Nearly ten feet high it was marking the end of the path. It curved to the right, back towards the castle. Brendolyn wouldn't go back, not until she was over that wall. Fitting her fingers into the notches, she began the climb. Her fingers hurt, she was digging her toes deeper into the sharp stone, until she reached the top of the wall, and heaved herself up.

Brendolyn smiled, looking down into the back pasture of the stables. Before her, over a thirty yard distance, was the well-kept building. It was a long single-story structure with twelve large windows.

She turned, preparing herself for the descent. As she began, her eyes caught a glimpse of a familiar knight standing beyond the roses watching her. Brendolyn frowned as Sir Varick smiled. She had no patience for him, or to decide what he would do now that he saw her. Brendolyn gripped for the stone, her gown catching on a thick bramble that grew along the inner wall of the pasture, it snagged in her hair as she lowered herself.

Slipping on the next stone, Brendolyn scrambled for purchase on the wet stone. But finding none, she was sent sprawling back, falling through the brambles.

It took her breath away as she hit the hard soil. Lying on the pasture while her head spun, the ache grew tighter in her mind, she was suddenly spinning as nausea churned in the pit of her stomach.

Her vision awakened to the vivid dream that visited her in her slumber.

She was standing upon the shores of the great seas, looking onto the beach of Signe. She knew it to be so by the sweetness in the air, and the familiar call of the gulls that flocked the beaches. Brendolyn stood upon the white sands, her feet dug deep into the warmth, basking in the sun high above her.

She felt his presence, turning her eyes to the waters.

Brendolyn saw him there, the man with the green eyes, standing as he did so often in her dreams. Always watching the water, always at a great distance from her. She called him, but her voice was without sound, though she was screaming over the crashing waves and the call of the gulls that shrilled in her ears.

Panic settled desperately in her chest, as she ran down the beach. Each step pulled her deeper into the grips of the sand, drawing her further and further away from him. Shouting, her tears sprang to her eyes.

Gasping for breath, Brendolyn sat up, embraced by large arms.

"You're alright," Sir Eero whispered.

Brendolyn clung to him, her tears streaming down her cheeks as she gasped for breath. He smelled of mint and fresh hay. His mind was quieted and did not intrude upon her as she fought to regain control.

"He can't hear me," she whimpered, grasping at the thick tunic of the knight.

"I can hear you, princess," Sir Eero told her. Kneeling in the mud beside her, he held her in his arms. "I can hear you."

"He's gone...they have killed him, and he can't hear me."

Sir Eero pressed a kiss to her temple, resting his fingers against the curve of her jaw. Brendolyn knew he used magick. She could feel the warms of it calm through her, resonating like a hum that soothed the violent tremors of her mind.

"I can hear you, Brendolyn." His voice was like the ocean, crashing against the shore as the tide came.

"Did I die?" she breathed, lessening her grip on the knight.

Sir Eero chuckled, smoothing back the curls that hung about her face.

"You fell, Brendolyn. I saw it from the stables where I had happened to look up at what I believed to be the largest songbird land upon the outer wall." He sat her up slowly, leaning her against his arm. "I believe there is nothing broken."

"My gown is ruined." Brendolyn saw the tatter of silk at the hem of her skirts, groaning at the mud that stained the fine fabric.

"It can be mended. Your body, perhaps not so easily." Sir Eero took her hands in his, looking deep into her eyes.

Brendolyn stared at the remarkably stormy gray eyes, with flecks of golden hue nearest the center. His features brightened with magick.

"Don't tell my father," she begged.

He gave a sad smile and Brendolyn felt his hesitation. He was leaning back now that he was reassured that Brendolyn was unharmed.

"I shall not say anything to him, princess, if you do not wish him to know." Sir Eero nodded. "But I shall inform Lahrs."

Brendolyn lowered her gaze.

"He is your guardian. It is for the best that he should be aware of your adventures over that wall. Only he shall be the best to decide what course of action to take." Sir Eero got to his feet, offering his hand to Brendolyn.

She took it, but her heart was saddened.

"I understand." She nodded. "It was wrong of me to climb the wall."

Tucking her hand under his arm, Sir Eero guided her towards the outer gates. Brendolyn stepped forward, sore but able to manage with ease. They were a few yards from the gate when Sir Eero spoke.

"May I offer advice, princess?"

She glimpsed the side look, his full mouth pulled down into a frown, his short cropped hair caught the light in a silver glow. Brendolyn knew him to be elven, but his features were so human, that it caught her off guard after sensing his magick.

"You may."

Sir Eero slowed his steps. "For your best interest, while Sir Lahrs takes his meetings with the kings and their advisors, you would be wise to not venture far from the garden walls."

"You wish me to remain a caged songbird?"

"I wish you to be safe, Brendolyn. This realm is not kind to faie. Should you go beyond the reach of those that would protect you, there are many who would not hesitate to do you harm, princess or not." His grey eyes were honest.

"Like the merchants of Denorn who sell slaves?" Brendolyn was frightened.

"Who told you about that?" Sir Eero looked aghast.

Brendolyn blushed. "I saw them after our arrival. Lahrs and I stayed behind on the ship while the rest of my family was driven to the Hedgerig Estate. I grew bored and curious, that's when I saw the cages."

It was the first time Brendolyn had ever seen any man other than Lahrs look pale with fear. Sir Eero was too stunned to speak for a long breath, his jaw clenched, as the vein upon his temple bulged. His voice remained soft, but she could feel the bite.

"Foolish girl."

"Do you know why the king is so blinded? That he can allow the faie to be caged and sold as they are in Jorn?" Curiosity had been pressing on Brendolyn's mind, she could not help but ask the knight.

"King Beaumont is not like your father, who relies only upon his advisors and his own rule; there are many in the court of Jorn who hold a certain power. In Denorn, just as in the other great cities throughout the realm, rules are governed by the reigning seat of power." Walking together along the secluded path behind the pasture, Sir Eero kept Brendolyn's arm secured in his.

"But he has the power to stop it, doesn't he?"

"He does," Sir Eero replied.

Brendolyn frowned, keeping her eyes upon the path. Her mind was alive with so many questions, her feelings sprouting so much discontent. Brendolyn respected King Beaumont, who was so kind and attentive to her. Wherever she went there were many who spoke well of his abilities.

"This displeases you."

"He must be a very poor king." She blushed suddenly. "Forgive me, that is cruel to speak of your king in such a way."

Sir Eero did not pull away, or scold her.

"Beaumont is kind, with a strong aptitude for hunting and reading great volumes of books. He seeks pleasure in the many paintings that hang in the gallery, traveling to all of Veilore in search of beauty." Here, Sir Eero frowned. "He was raised for the war, but not for peace."

"King Broderick was cruel to him?"

"His cruelty, as you would describe it, was not out of malice, but out of the duty to the crown. King Broderick, in his time, was a strong man who ruled with an iron fist. He never approved of Beaumont's choices," Sir Eero explained.

"He married a common lady from Entheas before the alliance was completed." She remembered her lessons with Lahrs, who knew Queen Eleanore before she became Queen of Jorn.

"Yes," Sir Eero chuckled. "That was a very great part of King Broderick's disappointment before his death. Beaumont went against his wishes and married a common lady, from a land King Broderick wished to conquer."

"Do you believe the treaty to be wrong? That Beaumont is being guided falsely by his court to join the houses of our realms?" Her mind became alive with questions. "It could give them the power to expand their reach to Corad; we have many faie who live freely without need of registering their magick."

"I cannot answer for the court, princess." He stepped closer to her, so he could whisper without raising his voice. "War is a cruel beast that breaks even the kindest of men. We must pray to Ehnarea that this treaty shall be swift and shall endure."

Sir Eero pressed her hand, bringing it to his lips to kiss the curve of her knuckles. They were standing side by side in a seclusion of trees, near the steps leading into the side courtyard. It was cooler in the shade, and in the distance they could hear the voices echoing from the gardens as courtiers took their daily turns about the gravel paths.

Brendolyn smiled. "I pray every day in the chapel."

"Good," Sir Eero beamed. "Stay out of trouble, Brendolyn."

"No promises."

"Forgive me, your majesty, but this is a matter of great importance."

King Beaumont looked over the large table displaying the map of the Veilore, painted by his best cartographer from Aavin. He glared at the man with soft matted grey hair set in neat curls about his wrinkled face. With puffy bags under cold grown eyes, there was little animation of the face of Lord Parcival, one of the many lords that were seated around him now.

Beaumont sat a little straighter, his back already beginning to hurt from the carved chair he had sat in for the last five hours. It was much the same, as the days progressed to weeks. No closer were they to an end of the rolls of parchment, agreeing to one article, then disagreeing to the next. On and on it continued. It plagued Beaumont with great headaches that made him cross.

"I received a letter from the Duke of Tauf regarding his absence. It had been resolved after his letter arrived this morning." Beaumont shrugged.

Nearly twenty lords seated around the large table began to speak at once, the sound grating on Beaumont's nerves. He did not care to be listening to the discontent of another day's delay, but the delay would not come about.

"How can it be settled by letter, Your Majesty?" Lord Parcival spoke louder than the others, his voice carrying to quiet the crowd.

"His heir just happens to already be in Jorn, within this very castle. I have invited him to take a meeting with us and he shall arrive within the hour." Beaumont smirked, watching the southern king's lips twitch with amusement at the council's uproar.

Sabian was seated at the farthest end of the table with his men of council. They were a quiet few, with dark curled hair and patient faces. They observed the spectacle with cool indifference. But it was to Sabian that Beaumont drew his eye the most, speaking as he would to make the man laugh, to give the hint of amusement in the eye of his particular old friend.

"There is no heir of Tauf, for the duke has no sons. Does he send his daughter to befoul our council?" Lord Parcival balked, disturbed by the thought.

Beaumont frowned. "Duchess Kristjana is a well-known leader in Entheas; her people love her, and honor her with unashamed loyalties."

"There is no one here discrediting her merit, Your Majesty, but simply to make a point that a war room is no place for a woman."

Beaumont's gaze slithered sharply to Lord Simeon Bannon, who sat unmoving and silent from his place amongst the others. His grey eyes were like stone slabs, cold and void of anything. It gave him the chills.

"We are not at war, Lord Bannon."

A smile festered on the thin lips. "Of course not, my king. It is after all, the reason we are all here, setting aside the difference between these two great realms to nullify the slaughter that befell under your father..." Lord Bannon's eyes looked down the table towards Sabian. "And *your* father."

"Then let this heir be brought forward. If it is not the duke's daughter, then what man should he distinguish over the birth of his own kin?" Lord Parcival demanded.

Opening his mouth to speak, Beaumont was interrupted by the click of the great doors leading into the map room. Entering was a servant who announced Sir Lahrs of

Corad and the room fell silent, watching the knight enter, wearing a neatly embroidered tunic, one that represented the home of his people in Entheas, while maintaining the style of Corad.

"Is this a jest, Your Majesty?" Lord Parcival turned up his nose.

"Welcome, Sir Lahrs. Please join us at the table." Beaumont ignored the lord, motioning to the servants in attendance to bring forward a chair.

In haste it was done, and a place was made near Sabian's end of the table, placing the elf between the realms. Sir Lahrs smiled politely, taking a seat.

"You are kin to the Duke of Tauf?"

Sir Lahrs shook his head. "No. I am engaged to be married to Duchess Kristjana."

"You are a Knight of Corad."

It was Sabian who spoke first. "He is born of Entheas, Lord Parcival. His duties to me in Corad began with the honor his mother held in being the royal healer. Lady Kiret was beyond the skill of those that study in the best institutions of healing."

Lord Parcival frowned. "Magick that had been unchecked. She was not registered in the Healer's Tomes of Aavin. Her sanction in this realm was unlawful."

Beaumont felt heat rising within his chest, as anger began to build.

"Speak carefully of what is unlawful, Lord Parcival."

"I only speak what is the truth, and what no one else in this room will not." He was emboldened by his words, his face growing flush with the greed of his new power. "We have let those with unregistered magick into our realm. If we allow them to continue, then we shall be overrun. Our trades shall be forfeit to those that can break stone with a touch of their finger, or heal a wound with one word."

"There is no magick in the realms that can accomplish either of those things," Sir Lahrs spoke. All eyes at the table turned towards him. "We use potions and alchemy to heal the injured, just as those without magick. To break stone with just one touch would be remarkable, beyond what any gift Ehnarea has given."

Lord Parcival was red in the face. "You cannot refute the knowledge of the beasts that let Augusta fall to ruin!"

Sir Lahrs was complacent, unchanged. "They were faie, Lord Parcival, not beasts. And it was not the faie that slaughtered thousands in rooms of smoke."

Beaumont could hear the tension in the elf as he held his composure. He could feel the chill in the room as his words sent a ripple of apprehension throughout the room, stunning them all into silence.

"They set ablaze the fields of T'hourns!" Lord Parcival looked nearly purple with rage, sitting forward in his chair, his hand tightly clenching to the arm rest.

"A field of lavender in R'hun," Sir Lahrs stated. "Scorching the battlefield and those that lay waiting for Ehnarea's embrace. Scorching corpses with Dragon Fire."

Lord Parcival stood abruptly, his temper unchecked.

But Beaumont was quick, towering at the head of the table. Slamming his hand down hard against the map, making the goblets placed before each lord quake, glaring across the table at the lord, who held the hilt of his dagger in hand, directing it towards the Knight of Corad.

"Raise a hand of vengeance against those in my kingdom upon good faith again, upon my honor as king, it shall be the last moment you have a hand." Beaumont straightened, to his full height, towering over the table.

Lord Parcival sat, quieted and small in his chair.

"Forgive me, Your Majesty, if I have spoken out of turn," Sir Lahrs apologized.

"It is done." Beaumont shook it off, returning to his seat. "Let us commence with the next articles." Taking up a stack of parchment, Beaumont blinked hard to focus upon the fine scrawl of text.

Beside him, his scribe took up the parchment he was given, reading off the written words that detailed the entail of the treaty—it was in regards to the marriage contract. Beaumont took the letter from the man's hand.

"Not that one..." Beaumont flipped through the pile, extracting another letter and giving it to the scribe. "We shall begin with this one."

"Article of negotiation to reopen trade routes between the port of Signe and De-norn..." They all listened intently as the scribe read the article, detailing the benefits of reopening the trade route, listing off the letters given to them by the tradesman of Denorn, in what they desired to accommodate with the expansion of their goods to include the purchase of textiles, perfumes, exotic birds, and food goods that would otherwise be unobtainable in Jorn.

"Your tradesman makes requests of goods that would boost the economy of Jorn tenfold," Sir Lahrs spoke first. It was surprising to Beaumont to hear the usually quiet knight so open and surefooted.

Lord Parcival sniffed. "An adequate assumption, Sir Lahrs."

"Yet your articles do not include the compensation required for the purchase of textiles handwoven in Mvors, perfumes perfectly crafted by the women of Divna, nor the exotic birds bred in Nihtar. Perhaps your merchants and tradesmen have not taken into account the century-old practices of these objects that are bestowed as gifts, made to last the wearer their lifetime." Addressing the room, Lahrs did not speak only to Lord Parcival, but to the other lords in attendance.

"Gold should be sufficient in satisfying the cost, Sir Lahrs," came a reply from a large bulky man that sat amongst the lords of Jorn.

"Gold?" Lahrs raised his eyebrow. "Lord Hoban, you mistake the humble people of Corad for the merchants of Denorn, and the tradesmen of Dern. Perhaps you have mistaken the necessity of your gold, when Corad forges their breastplates, forges their spearheads and their streets with *gold*. What need have we of Jorn's gold in exchange for the labor of that which is most precious to us, to be bartered away to those here that shall squander our treasures?"

"You let this man speak for you, King Sabian?" Lord Hoban demanded, looking hautly at the southern king.

Sabian leant back in his chair, a hand resting over his mouth, pushing down the sides of his great mustache. But Beaumont knew that look, the way he was hiding his smile behind his hand.

"Sir Lahrs is well educated, Lord Hoban. He shall one day be seated at the high table of Tauf, to reside over Entheas." Sabian shrugged, looking stolidly at the lord. "It would be unwise of the duke to admit a man who could not take up his seat with fortitude. No?"

Lord Hoban flushed.

"What would Corad exchange for the purchase of that which is most precious?" Lord Bannon's voice shivered through the air.

"Should our realms become one, Lord Bannon, and my daughter is seated on the throne of your kings to govern the province of goods that she knows to be sacred, then shall Corad be willing to open trades between our realms," Sabian stated.

"Let us settle this contract, my king, and be done with this business."

Beaumont listened painfully to the eager ears that wagged their tongues in delight at the prospect of such a contract. It was sought after by most of the lords. If Prince Barrow married Princess Lisetta, then her dowry would bring more wealth and power to the hands of the court. Beaumont frowned. His eyes lingering across the table at Lord Bannon, the man as eager as the rest of them to hold the dowry of a princess in his hands.

"Queen Natalia is with child."

They all looked again to Sir Lahrs, hushed into a stupor of deep thought.

"Whisperings of another girl, Sir Lahrs. Your queen's midwives are all superstitious. No doubt stemming from their Felourian birth." Lord Bannon smiled gleefully.

"If it is a boy, and if he shall live, then Princess Lisetta's birthright, her *dowry*, shall be nothing to Jorn but a title. All the rule she once held would be given up to her brother, the heir to the Coradian Throne."

"Enough of this idle chatter." Beaumont felt the pangs of a headache. Pressing the pads of his fingers into the soft spot at his temple, it was weighty, the pain that settled behind his eyes. "I grow weary and hungry."

Lord Bannon stood, at once, bowing to the king of Corad, then to Beaumont.

"It shall be done, Your Highness." The man nodded, ushering them all out of the map room, following the lords of Jorn towards the great hall.

King Sabian stood, addressing his advisors in hushed tones. He whispered in his native tongue to Lahrs, and then they were all walking out. Beaumont sighed, a sigh of heavy relief. But there was a stirring in the air. Hearing the shift of clothes and the clatter of goblets, followed closely by the gentle burble of pouring drink.

"Wine." A tanned hand placed the half-filled goblet before him.

Beaumont felt his cheeks flush hot, his eyes following the hand to the wrist, just visible beneath the length of sleeve. Sabian wore a deep maroon jacket embroidered with little beaded flowers. He stood near the table watching Beaumont closely.

"Thank you." Taking the goblet, their hands touched.

Sabian sips his drink. "I had begun to lose hope in us ever meeting again, not since our fathers..."

Beaumont's long fingers wrapped around his wrist, shooting to his feet, letting the chair scrape against the stone floor. Heat was radiating so hot from their bodies, each breath making it more and more difficult. Beaumont could smell the perfume, mixing with the shaving powder.

"Do not speak of our fathers," Beaumont hissed.

Beaumont moved to press against Sabian, pinning him to the large table where they all had once sat. It was quieter now, letting Beaumont's headache begin to lessen. Now, trailing his hand up from Sabian's wrist to the curve of his neck, looking deep into the dark, unwavering eyes. He kissed him fervently, drinking every mouthful of hope.

"We shouldn't..." Sabian pulled back, breathless.

Beaumont kissed Sabian's neck, and nibbled the man's jaw. "We two are kings, there is nothing to stop us," Beaumont whispered into Sabian's ear, bringing them closer together.

"Not here," Sabian stated, managing to pull the larger man from him.

"Always so cautious."

Sabian smirks. "I am sensible. What would you do if one of those lords stepped foot in this room and saw us like this; they would have us both dismantled."

Beaumont smirked, coyly. "Not before I had you properly...dismantled."

"Monty!" Sabian gasps, laughing heartily, clapping a hand over his own mouth to stifle the noise. "Your words are as sharp as ever."

Beaumont smiled, twirling a lock of Sabian's hair around his large finger. "Will you away to my chambers tonight, when everyone has gone to bed?"

Sabian touches the smoothness of Beaumont's shaven cheeks in his grasp.

"I will."

Brendolyn tried to remain still in the uncomfortable chair, seated at the little table in her queen mother's apartments, while they took tea. Lisetta sat to her right, demurely pouring herself another cup. Queen Natalia rubbed the swell of her belly, humming to herself an old Ferlourian lullaby.

Reaching for her cup, Brendolyn winced. Her shoulder ached, she could feel the bruise that sprouted along her back. Brendolyn had seen it when she rushed to change, frantically hiding her ruined gown at the back of her wardrobe, scrubbing her face in the basin of water to rid the evidence of falling off the wall.

"Brendolyn!"

Turning her head, she realized Lisetta had been speaking to her, or rather *at* her. She was holding out the plate of tea cakes, but Brendolyn flushed.

"I am not hungry." In truth, she could not raise her arm high enough to take the plate. Brendolyn desperately wished to return to Lahrs, to ask him to heal her arm.

"You have barely touched your tea, *amore*," Queen Natalia cooed, her voice tender.

Brendoyn gulped. "I am only tired, I have not rested this afternoon."

"Not rested, but you should have been after your lessons."

"Tell her what you were doing, Brendolyn," Lisetta stated suddenly.

Brendolyn glared at her sister; it was none of her business. "I was in the library with Lady—"

"She was climbing the outer wall."

"Why were you climbing the wall?" Queen Natalia was curious.

"I was not climbing the outer wall, Lisetta." Brendolyn felt the lie slip from her tongue. She glared at Lisetta, who flushed angrily at her.

"Sir Varick saw you climbing the outer wall leading to the pastures."

"I was not!"

Lisetta scoffed. "You cannot deny that you have done it, not when Varick saw you, Brendolyn. You have been sneaking around when Lahrs is called away. You do not keep to your lessons. In Denorn, you hacked the orchards of Lady Ehlain. Now, you lie about sneaking off, it is an embarrassment to our seat. Plus, to have you riding the countryside with the prince...It is improper."

"He asked me to accompany him for a ride and he took me to the stables. There is nothing improper when Lahrs approved, he was even there!"

"Lahrs is very thoughtful of all these things. I remember being taken to the pastures when I was your age, Lisetta, your father and Monty jumped fences and showed off for me and Hana." Queen Natalia seemed lost in memories, her smile apparent as she touched the curl of her hair.

Lisetta groaned in agitation. "You were meant to marry the crowned prince, Mother; she is not his betrothed."

Natalia came to herself. "Who told you of this promise?"

"You think this secret would have been kept for long, Mother? Varick told me that the arrangement between me and Prince Barrow had been planned since infancy."

Natalia held her round belly. "It is merely a negotiation."

"A negotiation of my future? I have been raised to be Queen of Corad, Mother. *Our realm* and the realm of our people, not the realm of hard headed...cold...uncultured...horse breeders."

"You have been well educated on the court of Jorn as well, *mi amore*. Do not doubt yourself of your future here, if that should be your path." Natalia smiled, offering her hand to her daughter.

There was a long pause between them. Lisetta did not move.

"If you loathe him, why can I not enjoy his company?" Brendolyn asked.

"*You*? You cannot enjoy his company. You are to do only as you are told. It is your duty to look pretty upon their arms, not to enjoy them. But it is not your place, you have no right to go on horseback with a prince, or stand up with the king. You are the offspring of a whore, Brendolyn. Your mother did not deserve her place in bed with my father...and you most certainly do not have the right to take my place.

"I may loathe the cold and the ugly visage the Realm of Jorn possesses, but it will be my duty alone to change it for the better when I become queen of it. You who have nothing, who will rule nothing, have nothing to offer. He is a prince, Bren, who will one day be king. You are a half-breed, mixed with the blood of faie..."

Natalia stood, a hand slapping hard at Lisetta's cheek.

Lisetta gasped, holding her cheek. As tears streamed down her reddened skin, she stood, hastening from the rooms in a flourish of rustling silk and weeping.

Brendolyn sat stunned, willing herself not to cry.

Seeing her mother huff, breathing out slowly as she rubbed the swell of her belly, Brendolyn quickly flew from her chair to stand at her mother's elbow, guiding her across the room to lay down upon the bed.

"You will be more comfortable if you lay down," Brendolyn said.

Lifting Queen Natalia's legs, she covered her mother with a soft blanket. A warm hand pressed to hers and she raised her eyes as Queen Natalia touched Brendolyn's cheek.

"Do not believe for a moment your worth is less because of your mother. She was beloved to us all. I shall tell you something about your mother, something that even Lisetta does not know."

"But she knows everything."

Natalia chuckled, her hands now grasping Brendolyn's, bringing them close to her chest. "You are old enough to know that your mother was one of my dearest friends."

Brendolyn was shocked. "Friends?"

"Yes." Natalia nodded. "She was by my side since I was just a little older than you are now. We did everything together, and when I married your father, she was there. Sabian is a man of great love, Bren, he loved people and always made them laugh. Hana made me laugh, too." Natalia dozed, as she fell into her memories.

She was only roused by a squeeze of Brendolyn's hand. "Mother."

"Oh dear, where was I…yes-yes, your mother was there with me…when I lost my child that I carried. It was too soon for many to have known, I don't think I ever told your father, but Hana knew. She held my hand and cried with me…" There was a long silence. "It was too soon, the advisers of Corad were urgent in an heir, but it was too soon. So Hana, your dear mother, did as I asked and went to the king's bed.

"You are old enough for these talks of bed-making, Brendolyn, they will happen upon you soon enough. But the king was distraught, he could not put his seed in Hana. He protested." Natalia smiled, her hands squeezing tighter to Brendolyn's.

"Did my mother use her faie voice?" Brendolyn's throat was dry, looking up at the queen, her dreamy look coming to look at Brendolyn again.

"Yes. She sang for Sabian, calming his angry fit. He had many of them as a young man, but they stopped when Hana sang. His fit stopped, and he was righted again. But he still would not, not until I came to him, and insisted, telling him of what I had lost. He is a kind king. Knowing my love of children, he put his seed in Hana and then she gave me you." Natalia again touched Brendolyn's cheek.

"No one told me how my mother died."

Brendolyn saw the shift in the queen's eyes, they darkened and her skin grew swallow.

"It was a sad day when Hana died. She held you in her arms for only a day. She was heartbroken to not give Sabian an heir, but she loved you and named you. I watched helplessly as she bled out, and by the time a healer came she was gone."

Brendolyn's chin quivered.

Natalia tucked the long dark curls behind Brendolyn's ear, exposing the point of her faie ears, which she kept hidden by her hair.

"You look so much like her," Natalia breathed, looking tired. Pity flashed in the queen's eyes, holding Brendolyn's chin. "Do not cry, my child. I have loved you dearly these fourteen years, held you to my bosom, cherished every smile and misadventure. You are so headstrong, like your father, and so kind, like your mother."

Natalia's eyelids were growing heavy as she spoke, her eyes growing tired.

"Rest now, Mother. Favor find you..." Brendolyn whispered, leaning up to kiss her queen mother's forehead.

Quietly walking from the room, the steps she took faltered.

Brendolyn's eyes were blurry as she hurried through the halls, tying her gown closed as she walked and walked, her tears spilling hot trails down her cheeks as she searched for her rooms but became lost.

Turning down corridor after corridor only to be farther and farther from any recognition. Finally, she pushed into a small door, which led to a small stairway leading down. A rush of cold air came over her as she descended. Walking back, she could see a full wall of glass and light streaming in from the sun through blue painted glass.

It was an indoor garden, roses planted in raised beds as rivers of cold water flowed through small ravines in the floor. Blinking through her tears, she was able to calm herself in the cool place. As she smelled the flowers, she could hear footsteps approaching.

Brendolyn crouched down, quickly.

"Princess Brendolyn, what are you doing down here?"

Brendolyn jumped up. "Sir Eero! I...got lost trying to find my room."

"Staying out of trouble?" He smiled, a glint in his eyes making Brendolyn laugh.

"Yes."

He stepped closer. "You have been crying. Are you alright?"

She quickly wiped away her tears. "I'm perfectly alright, Sir Eero. Just a quarrel with my sister..."

Sir Eero extended his arm out, offering it to her dutifully. Taking it without hesitation, she smiled weakly up at him, letting herself be guided from the room.

"What was that place?" she asked as they walked.

"It is a rare breed of rose that grows in the northern realm, beyond the sea."

Brendolyn looked over her shoulder. "It has survived this long?"

Sir Eero smiled down at her. "It was a prized possession of the late Queen Aletta; she grew them in her gardens, but the blooms died when she did. We were lucky enough to find a surviving branch. It was nursed back to health and bred over the years to extend its life. Now, the king enjoys them in solitude."

They walk in silence for a while.

"Do you quarrel with your sister often, Brendolyn?"

"Not usually, but then again we usually do not speak. Today was unusual on account of us taking tea together with Queen Natalia." Brendolyn trembled.

Eero nodded, his hand patting hers tenderly.

They emerged into a side drawing room, then they walked in silence again. They made their way through the halls and corridors until they arrived at a familiar staircase. Sir Eero stopped.

"Here is where I must leave you, princess."

Brendolyn curtsied. "Thank you, Sir Eero. I shall always be grateful for your kindness."

Chapter

26

Lahrs pounded on the hard wood to the King of Jorn's chambers, his tunic hanging open and hair laying wild about his shoulders, eagerly waiting for the answer on the other side.

Finally, the door opened, revealing the tall king beyond, who stood disheveled from sleep, with a dressing gown thrown over his large frame.

"Apologies, Your Majesty, but I must see Sabian, at once."

King Beaumont was stunned, but he stood aside. Walking towards them was a nearly dressed Sabian, equally alarmed at the sudden appearance of the knight.

"Lahrs, what is the meaning of this?" he asked as he tucked his tunic into his trousers.

"A maid roused me when you were not in your rooms. Natalia is having fits; her temperature is hot, and she is not herself. I beg you to come at once."

Sabian pushed past him, rushing down the hall.

King Beaumont made to follow, but Lahrs held a hand to the king's chest.

"It is best you arrive when a guard comes to call, Your Majesty. No one saw me coming, there will be a man to come up when I shall return."

The northern king nodded, still reeling with emotion.

As Lahrs turned to leave, the king stopped him briefly. "Thank you, Lahrs...for your discreet manner. I am truly grateful."

Lahrs nodded to him, before turning and running after his king.

He was moments after Sabian to the room, where maids hurried about and a nurse stood beside the bedside of the queen, who lay in a feverish display upon the bed. Her eyes caught sight of Sabian and she called for him.

"Natalia, my love." Sabian took her hand, sitting beside the Queen of Corad.

"Please do not fret, I am all at ease." She smiled, her eyes glossy, and her pupils so large her eyes were dark.

"Where are the queen's attendants?" Lahrs asked the nurse directly.

The young woman, who flitted about, came to a stop before the elf. Her face paled, she was nearly hysterical.

"My lord." She bowed. "Her attendants have all gone, I have looked for them, but they have all gone."

"Gone? They have never left her side since our ships made port in Signe."

She flushed, tears streaming hard on her face. Lahrs recognized the young face of the assistant to the queen's ladies. She was just beginning her training, still just a child.

Lahrs reached out to take hold of the young maids arms, he could feel her anxiety and her distress. Lahrs smiled, extending his calm towards her, his magick was a balm against her anxieties.

"Please," Lahrs began. "Tell me what happened."

"Her Majesty was uneasy, in discomfort from being with child. She called for me to help with a simple salve then she called for tea to be brought. I was gone for a moment to collect fresh linens and came back to her in a fit. You arrived when her fits stopped, she was calling for the king." The nurse clutched the linens tightly to her chest.

Lahrs thanked her and then went to the maid who brought the tea; she still clutched the tray.

"Was the queen asleep when the tea arrived?" he asked her calmly but the maid shook her head.

She was clearly shaken. "It was there on the table. I didn't...There was nothing to do."

Lahrs knelt down, retrieving the cup from the floor. All of the contents had spilled, but a cast of substance remained in the cup that did not look like tea.

"Who brought the tea, Poppy?" Lahrs asked, his voice lowered, looking down at the young nurse.

She was pale, and her eyes were wide. She shook her head vigorously.

"I do not know." Her hand was clasped to her mouth, and she was weeping freely.

"Sabian." Lahrs moved around her, beckoning the king to come.

At once Sabian stood, going to Lahrs' side, where the knight showed the cup to the king. As the king smelled the cup, Lahrs turned his back to the room, leaning in close.

"It is an elixir. Given in small drops at a time, it can alleviate restlessness, but in large doses...This is not a potion given to a woman ready to give birth."

"Poison?" Sabian spat under his breath.

"Someone sent her attendants away, we must find them for questioning, but right now...right now it is best to help Natalia." Lahrs tried not to allow his emotions to reach his voice, but he could not suppress the wave of regret and sadness that washed over him.

"Is there nothing to be done?" Sabian clutched the cup firmly, shaking in anger.

Lahrs sighed. "I will not lie to you, Sabian. Its properties are deadly."

Sabian braced himself on the knight's arm.

Lahrs looked up, looking back to the nurse. "Is there not a surgeon in Jorn City?"

She colored pink, ringing out the rag in the washbasin. "There is a surgeon in Denorn. He is a large man who is skilled at taking limbs, sir...nothing as delicate as this."

There was heat that rose in Lahrs chest. "Who is the healer in Jorn City?"

Again, the woman colored.

"The healers are apothecaries who give basic potions...nothing more. We do not have the facilities, nor the skill for better healers. None so skilled as Corad, nor Entheas, sir."

Beaumont was pale as he walked up to the elf, having just arrived within the room to stand near where they stood.

"Who is given charge of women when they give birth?" Lahrs' eyes flashed in anger, looking at the nurse again.

"There is a small handful who help in birth. When I inquired for the list of necessary items, they were not willing to accommodate me from their own supplies."

"There is not time, Lahrs. You are the only one to do it. Your mother was the best healer known to the Three Realms. Please, help her friend. Now." Beaumont looked with worry at the queen, who lay pale and feverish upon the bed. His hand found purchase on Sabian's shoulder, who grasped it desperately.

"Have you checked the queen's progression?" Lahrs asked the nurse. Poppy blushed.

"She is not close to her delivery, sir. I had not thought..."

Lahrs was annoyed as he stormed over. Leaning over the queen, he placed his ear upon the queen's belly, listening hard. His concern turned over on his face. He looked into the queen's eyes as she was looking up at him. He smoothed moist hair from her face.

Natalia smiled. "Oh Lahrs, for a moment I believed I saw my dear Kiret again. I believe I am ready to hold my baby. Will your mother be here soon? I very much wish to see her again."

Her words sparked heartache within Lahrs, looking again at the two kings who stood watching, they could not hear the queen's words. He calmed, letting his magick spread over the queen, and returning the queen to rest before standing at the bowl, rinsing his hands.

"She is delirious and confused. The overflow of toxins has reached her blood flow. You must speak with her now, Sabian, and I will prepare myself to do what I must to save the child."

Sabian stood to his feet, coming terribly close to the elf.

Sabian asked, "The baby is full of life?"

Lahrs nodded. "I felt a kick and could hear movement within. I was able to cast a charm on the child to protect it, but it will not keep the poison that courses through her veins away for long. We must not delay. What I must do, Sabian, will not be easy. I must make a cut at the lower abdomen to extract the child..."

Beaumont covered his mouth going green, his thick brows creasing together in agitation.

"There is no elven spell to reverse the elixir, no counter potion to be fetched?" Sabian's voice shook, holding tightly on Lahrs' arm.

"There are many spells and enchantments, Sabian, but none that would work in time."

Sabian nodded, overburdened with the grips of sadness that overwhelmed him. Lahrs turned to the nurse, giving her the list of everything he needed.

Sabian gave Beaumont a squeeze of the hand before turning to his wife. He sat beside her, holding her hand.

"My darling." He smiled.

Natalia kissed Sabian's hand. "You must not fret, my love. Our young prince will be here soon." She laughed, hysteria breaking through her feverish features. "His nursery! We have not prepared the nursery. Shall I fetch nanny tomorrow to have his nursery fitted? He will like gold, I think; little princes should have gold."

She was rambling, and as she spoke Sabian began to cry.

His tears were falling hard from his eyes as he brought Natalia's hand to his lips, kissing her fingers.

"His room will be fitted." Sabian nodded. He was unable to hide his sorrow. "I am so sorry," he whispered, unable to contain himself from the oncoming grief. He looked down at Natalia, her smiling face now pale and serious.

"Sabian," she said, her voice clear.

The king looked down, and her eyes returned to lively brown. Sabian leaned in, kissing her.

"Natalia."

She became worried. "I fear there is something wrong. I believe I am dying," she whispered, a sense of clarity overcoming her as tears filled her eyes. "My legs won't move; my hands grow cold. Sabian..." She saw the dread and agony in her husband's face.

"Forgive me," Sabian whispered with a rasping voice.

Natalia shook her head. "I know your love overflows, Sabian. You have not to apologize for your heart, not to me. Not for loving him who loves you so fully even after a world breaks you apart." She kissed his hands as a stab of pain ran across her features.

"Save our prince...you must save him." Natalia reached for him.

"I love you," Sabian whispered, leaning in to kiss her lips. She held him there for a brief moment.

Her face scrunched, pain beginning to envelope her as she writhed beneath him.

Sabian turned, calling for Lahrs, who came to their side at once.

He felt her hands, then felt her legs, they were like ice. Her eyes rolled back in her head as her body shook. Lahrs placed a leather trap within her mouth, calling for the maids to hold the queen's head. Lahrs helped the king to his feet, leading him away from the bed as the man stumbled. They came next to Beaumont, who was ghostly white and trembling.

"It is the moment you must remove from the room, both of you. I must start," he told King Sabian, who remained pale and quiet. "Do you permit me to remove the child from her?"

Sabian looked at Natalia, who remained convulsing upon the bed.

"We are certain there is nothing else that can be done for her, Lahrs?" Beaumont begged, tormented by the past reanimated in the events now unfolding.

"I can remove as much of the pain as I can, but it will not change the outcome. If I do not act now, they will both be lost."

Sabian stood taller, squaring his shoulders. Resolve tightened in the king's face as he gave Lahrs a confident nod.

Lahrs nodded in response. Going to stand beside the queen, he held a hand above her heart, his other hand he held upon her forehead, whispering under his breath.

"I must work quickly. Please...I advise you to step out, while it happens."

There was hesitation within the two kings who stood side by side, a maid came beside them, leading them from the room before gently closing the door.

Lahrs turned to the bed, looking down at the woman now in his care. His chin shook, tears filling his eyes. He gently touched the curve of the queen's cheek, her wild brown eyes looking up at him through the pain. She bit down upon the leather strap held in place by the maids. Her body was unmoving, but those eyes watched him, pleading.

Help me. Help my child. Her voice was sharp in Lahrs' mind.

"Forgive me," he begged.

He raised the sheets, where the nurse had prepared the queen's belly, swollen from the pregnancy and now moving on its own as the baby within began to recoil, sensing the change. Lahrs placed his hand upon the belly, and the movements slowed, relaxing.

Lahrs took a deep breath.

He was handed a small instrument from the nurse, a thin metal knife. He paused, saying a prayer, before his hand lowered to the flesh of the queen that grew grey as the blood left Natalia's flesh. Starting from one pubic bone, he made a thin cut along all the way to the other side. Where blood would have spilled, the flesh barely dribbled a gray seeping liquid. Lahrs worked quickly, working one swift stroke at a time until the last layer came into view.

Now, using his fingers to pry at the muscle, he worked quickly to find the sac. It broke easily with the swipe of his fingers. Fluid spilled forth as Lahrs dove his hands deep inside, emerging with the slippery purple baby, handing the small thing to the nurse who stood waiting with fresh linens draped over her arms.

Lahrs cut the cord connecting mother and baby.

He stood with blood-slicked hands while the nurse rubbed the baby until they heard the piercing cry of the lungs clearing. It was a blessed sound to them both.

The nurse gasped. "A boy, Lahrs...it is a boy!"

"Call to the village, find a wet nurse, at once."

Swaddling the baby up, the nurse rocked the small prince in her arms as she rounded the bed, making for the door as Lahrs stood over the queen, covering her freshly made wounds as he placed a dried bloody hand upon her chest. Her breathing had stopped, her heart was no longer beating. Agony wrenched through Lahrs, unable to compose himself, tears spilled from his eyes as he wept against the back of his hand.

The tragedy of it all tormented the hope within him.

Lahrs straightened, breathing deep, he placed a hand over the stillness of his queen's breast, whispering the words of the prayer.

CHAPTER

27

Two days had passed since the loss of the Queen of Corad and the castle was silent in mourning. Brendolyn sat in the gardens, her heart heavy, her eyes were puffy from the tears. Her eyes were now dry, but the pain was like daggers in her heart. She sat in solitude, where the birds chirped, the wind blowing through the trees whispering against her face.

Approaching feet turned her eyes to the entrance of the gardens where Prince Barrow approached. He sat quietly beside her on a marble bench. She looked down as the prince reached over, taking her hand in his, bringing it to his lips to press a kiss to her fingers.

Brendolyn lowered her gaze, her throat tightening. She took a deep breath. "Does the pain stop?" She looked up at the prince, who shared in her tears.

"Over time, your heart shall heal, but there will always be a scar."

Brendolyn wiped her tears, gritting her teeth. "If this is what losing someone you love is, then I don't want it. I never want love."

Her tears stained the satin of her gown where her hands gripped relentlessly.

"No, Bren, do not abandon hope of love. Your mother loved you very much. As my mother loved me. Death will come to everyone, at their time, but love reminds us to cherish each moment we have. It is the absence of pain when there is no love." He took both her hands in his, expressing himself so fully it took Brendolyn aback.

This was the first moment she saw him clearly, without the facade of pleasantries. His eyes were crystal blue, his yellow hair fell about his face in a gentle curve. He gently wiped away a tear from her cheek, never shifting closer than where he sat. His eyes watched her closely as she straightened with a deep breath.

Brendolyn stood and Barrow was immediately at her side.

"Shall I walk you to the castle?"

She smiled faintly. "Not yet. I wish to walk the gardens some more."

He nodded, offering his arm. They walked from the small garden area they were in to the lavish and well-endowed garden surrounding them. It was pleasant.

"Your father left early this morning?" Barrow began, his tone calm and gentle.

"Yes. He went himself to ride to Rhun along with his guards. They shall appeal to the Duke of Rhun to let us pass through. Lahrs tells me it is a safer way to take back through the high roads. At least when they return to Corad with..." She faltered, drawing in breath.

A new wave of tears flooded her.

"We do not need to talk of this. Come, the Devaulian trees should be in full bloom today." Barrow led them through the high hedges, mapping his way between the statues until they reached the desired destination.

As Brendolyn walked around the trees, looking up at the brilliant purple blooms, she could see the prince watching her. He blushed to see her catching him, but he did not excuse himself. They stared at the blooms together, embracing the silence.

Reaching up to a branch, Barrow plucked off a bloom and returned to her side.

"These trees were planted for my grandmother. She saw the trees on her tour of Corad, and the lord of Devaul gifted her two saplings. When she returned, she watered them herself. Every year the trees grew, until the night my father was born. That very day the tree bloomed for the first time." He placed the bloom in her hands. "Now, they bloom again, this year for the birth of a new prince."

Brendolyn smelled the bloom, the soft petals tickling her nose. They smelled sweet, with similar notes of apple blossoms. It made her happy.

"Devaul is a city known for this flower. They have perfected many uses for it; dried to be added to teas for calming proprieties, ground into a fine powder for dyes...and even the oils of the bloom are collected for the sweetest perfumes." She looked up at the prince, a smile on her lips.

Barrow smiled down at her.

She took his hand in hers. "It is also a token of prosperity. Your grandmother was given the token of the Devaulian's sacred trees. It is an honor to have my brother born on the day of their bloom."

A voice called out from a distance and Brendolyn could recognize Sir Lahrs at once. He was calling her to him.

Before Barrow could say a word, Brendolyn stood on her tiptoes, bracing herself on his arm, she kissed the smooth flesh of his cheek.

"Thank you." She hurried off.

King Beaumont stole a chance into the nursery, as the nanny curtsied and walked by. He was surprised as he entered the room to see the young princess holding the small bundle in her arms.

She was singing softly, the voice uncanny but peaceful. As he stepped farther within the room, Brendolyn looked up at him, her voice became a soft hum. She gently placed the little prince in the crib, looking up at him, her smile caught him. She placed a thin finger to her lips, silently shushing him. Beaumont remained silent, watching the princess settle the baby to sleep. Curtsying briefly before picking up a thin book from a side table, she walked past the king without a word.

He followed, now feeling slightly foolish for entering the small rooms. He was glad to see the princess waiting for him in the corridor, her smile sweet and yellow eyes bright.

"Apologies." He smiled. "I was told the nanny was cleaning the nursery."

Brendolyn nodded. "She was, but the prince has grown quite restless. There is no nursemaid in the city, so a man has been sent to Denorn."

The king looked shocked. "No nursemaid...so then..." He briefly looked back towards the door of the nursery, but Brendolyn touched his arm.

"Do not fret. There are ways of feeding a child without."

Beaumont chuckled, looking down at the young princess. "Yes, I believe you are right. It has been many years since a baby has slept in these halls."

He looked around the familiar corridor of the small wing designated for the babies of the court.

"You speak of Princess Fiona?"

"You know your royalty well. She is a sweet darling girl, a little younger than you, nearly eleven." Beaumont followed Brendolyn as she walked, taking his steps slowly to keep in time with her pace.

"Her mother was your second wife."

Beaumont nodded. "Lady Eleanore. A beauty beyond what words could describe."

Brendolyn smiled, looking up at him with a gleam in her yellow eyes. She handled her book gently.

"There is no portrait of her in the gallery."

A sting. "She was very beloved, but I am afraid looking upon her portrait is painful. But it remains in the upper gallery, where the older portraits remain in storage. She would have liked you. Eleanore was a lover of music."

"I am fond of music." Her expression lowered. "Do not tell my father. I'm not supposed to sing, but the baby was so restless."

She gazed up to Beaumont, her eyes glossy with tears.

Beaumont nodded, understanding. "Your father is worried others will misread your faie voice. There are many in Jorn who are afraid. Do not be afraid of me, you are perfectly safe in my presence."

They walked, in silence but he could sense she was uncomfortable.

"We have many rooms and see so many guests within the castle, I can hardly imagine what it's like to ever be alone. But sometimes even kings need solitude and respite from duties that encompass their daily lives." He spoke without really expecting a response but she listened intently.

"There are many hidden passages that lead throughout the castle, some have crumbled away and are unusable, but there remain enough that lead to the unused sections of the castle." He caught her wild expression of excitement and he winked at her.

She smiled sheepishly.

Beaumont went on. "On one of my delightful days of exploring the old towers of the castle, I came upon a room so full of dust I could hardly breathe. But after intense cleaning, it has become a refuge. There I can read as I please, lounge as a good king shouldn't, and write letters I would always wish to send but never could."

Shoulders sagging, somehow some of his tension vanished.

"Barrow shares in your wish of solitude and the wish to escape from his duties as prince."

Beaumont laughed at her words.

She continued, "He visits the queen's garden, the ones that have been overgrown. He happened upon me one day, I had intruded on his secret place. But he welcomed me to his world, showing me everything he loved about it." This sentiment made Beaumont's chest fill with pride.

He smiled. "He is so much like his mother, Lady Aletta. Not just his looks but his vast love of the world around him. She was a lover of nature, so too has Barrow become, in his time."

"I wish my father spoke of me the way you do about Barrow." Her comment made Beaumont pause, blinking hard to grasp her words.

"Your father cares so much for you..." Beaumont trailed off. He was pained, seeing the disbelief in the princess's eyes.

"He talks of fortitude and honor and duty; he told me once that I looked very pretty, but is that all I am to ever be, pretty and compliant?" She shook as tears threatened in her eyes.

There was a shift in the clouds outside of the windows behind them as rain began to fall.

She continued, saying, "He is kind, as anyone would expect, but he places his heart so readily in what is good for our people, so much so that he has forgotten his kin. For fourteen years, I have been brushed aside for the good of our people. Never talk, for no one would listen. Never look up, for you may see what is beyond your understanding." The princess stopped as her eyelids drop, tears trailing down the line of her cheeks.

Beaumont listened and his throat tightened, never expecting this expression to earnestly from the child before him. Before he could respond, the small voice of the princess spoke again.

"Every day I hear whispers. I know the people of court speak of me, and my mother, my real mother. She bled out to bring me into the world, I was told the truth about her death, it was the last thing the queen said to me. The queen, she convinced my mother to use her faie voice to calm my father's anger when confronted with the idea to lay with him but he did. He gave in to her will. I was a gift to my queen mother, but became a mark upon my father's arm.

"They speak of only his compassion, but look upon me with contempt. They believe me a simple child but, in my silence, I have watched. I have listened. I cannot hide who I am, I cannot shrink away from my ears or my voice. This is who I am and in every waking moment there was only one who loved me for me...and now she is gone."

Beaumont dropped to one knee before her, taking hold of her hands with his, tears brimming in his stormy blue eyes. His heart ached to hear these words.

"Sweet, innocent child...I hear you," he whispered, his voice nearly failing him. Reaching up, he wipes away her fallen tears. "No words can come from me to ease your heart, for words have done you wrong, but know that I hear you. Not as a king, but as a father."

Her face wrenched anew, Brendolyn flung her arms about the tall king's neck. Startled, but not unwilling, Beaumont wrapped his arms around her, embracing her as tears finally fell from his eyes and he held her as she wept into his neck.

When she was ready, Brendolyn pulled back, drying her eyes on her sleeves, she began to smile, her golden eyes looking into the King's with renewed warmth.

It pleased him. "There you are..." He caressed her hair gently. Then, he stood to his full height, looking down at her with admiration, offering his arm. She took it, and they walked in long silence to one of the long-windowed halls. Standing together, they watched the rain fall upon the gardens, admiring the storm.

Lahrs stood with Brendolyn in the hot house out along the far wall of the Jorn castle, they were there to cut flowers for a banquet table that would be laid out in honor of the Queen of Corad while they remained. He cut a stem, removing any thorns before handing the thing to Bren, who in turn placed it in her basket.

He paused a moment, before exhaling. "I must travel soon."

"You return to Corad?" Bren was shocked, but her tone remained gentle.

Lahrs looked at his ward.

"No. Entheas." He paused to snip another stem. "King Beaumont has asked if I will deliver the account of the treaty arrangements to the Duke of Tauf. He does not trust such a venture to a messenger, it has reached his ear of rumors of marauders that lurk near the roads." Brendolyn took the flower that the elf offered, stunned.

"Oh..." she managed.

He shook his head. "I will be gone no longer than three weeks. In my stead, King Beaumont has offered the highest guard from his personal escort."

Brendolyn bit her lip before replying. "May I choose a man for my guard? It will make you rest easier knowing I am in good hands in your absence."

Lahrs snips another stem. "I believe it could be arranged. After your incident in the gardens, you wish Sir Eero to escort you?"

"I know his duty is to Prince Barrow, but while you are away...that is, he is very kind and is not too forward..."

"Sir Eero is not like Varick." Lahrs knew the trepidation in the princess. "He does not leave Lisetta's little circle, and she has been kept in her rooms."

Lahrs sensed her change in countenance.

"Will it change everything, now that Corad has an heir?"

Lahrs forced a smile, taking Brendolyn's free hand. "The council has agreed that it would be best to maintain amity and not proceed until the child has passed through the dangerous years reaching an accountable age. When he does, there will be held another accord between the realms to decide our futures. All other matters of the treaty will be thoroughly examined before a tangible decision can be presented."

"Will we return to Corad before the winter comes? It grows colder here, the sea shall freeze over."

Lahrs chose his words carefully. "King Sabian will take the high roads through Rhun with the cortège. When I have returned from Entheas, you will be taken to the house of Garren in Alnwick."

Brendolyn paled. "Not to Corad City?"

Lahrs regretfully shook his head.

"I shall not return home, not even for the ceremony for my queen mother?" She could barely ask it, her voice just over a whisper.

"Sabian thought it best."

Brendolyn steeled herself. "I see." Her breathing hitched as she picked up her basket of fresh flowers. "I am tired. Can we return to my apartments? I wish to rest before tonight's banquet."

Lahrs nodded, escorting Brendolyn out of the hot house. They walked in silence; nothing else needed to be said.

CHAPTER 28

Ledenjour, Realm of Entheas.

There was rain, heavy and cold.

Pavan stood at the door of the greenhouse, looking out onto the muddy scene. He had been walking from the training yard to the main square, by way of the long walk around the outer roads when the sky had darkened dramatically. Before he could make it more than a few feet, the sky opened up and rain poured down on him.

He was drenched, his fingers flexing against the bitter cold as the wind swept through, chilling him to the bone.

Thick globs of rain pelted the green house, making a charming sound, he watched in fascination as the water drizzled along the glass overhead, admiring the dance each droplet made as another was added to it. Pavan was so lost in thought, he hadn't noticed the approaching man who was hurrying up the slope towards the green house, until the man collided with Pavan. Clearly not looking up, he was shielding his head from the sudden pelts of hardened ice.

Pavan stumbled, the man swore, and Pavan looked down into bright orange eyes.

"Pavan!" Thad exclaimed, his face had gone pale and water was dripping down his face from his dark copper hair.

He smiled. "What wonderful weather we are having."

Thad scowled, glancing up at the rain, now heavily pelting along the walk. It was rapidly flooding the ground in puddles.

"*Wonderful*...not exactly the words I would use to describe it..."

Pavan chuckled, shifting his frame to allow Thad more space to shake out his hair, to check the state of his tall boots, and finally, to despair that the edge of his fine coat was three inches seeped in mud.

"What are you doing out here, anyway?" Thad stopped fussing over his damp clothes to examine Pavan carefully.

"Walking. This path is one I take after a short time in the training yard. It takes longer, but there is less of a chance that I should meet with anyone in the great house. Returning later while everyone is within the great hall, I can be in my rooms without detection."

Thad tsked, but there was playfulness in his golden-flecked orange eyes.

"Now, the truth is known. But do not be afraid, your secret shall be safe with me." Thad smiled, giving Pavan a wink.

It was good to see the faie in such high spirits, but there was such a change to him. He was no longer somber, no longer grave, making Pavan glance at him curiously.

"Are you alright, Thad?"

There was a smile. "Perfectly content."

"You are a great liar."

Thad chuckled, a charming sound. Temptation drew Pavan closer, eyeing those playful eyes, that smirk upon such supple lips. Quietness, save for the pattering of rain above them on the enclosed glass, embraced them. It was closing them in to shut out the unwelcomed chaos of the world around them.

"Tell me," Pavan entreated, drawing ever closer to Thad. "I wish to know your secrets..."

Smiling, Thad shook his head. "I have no secrets."

Pavan could smell the familiar tang, acidic potions, sandalwood, ash. He would have been brewing, in his little hut made just for him. Pavan took Thad's hand, examining the faie's fingers; they were stained with ink from writing. Coming from such a distance out of the way from where they stood now, Pavan wondered.

"Did you follow me, Thad?"

"You are illusive when disappearing, someone has to keep you out of trouble."

Pavan smirked, chuckling. "You do not deny it. How remarkable. To be so well guarded..." Pavan did not release Thad's hand, but kept it in his own.

"It has stopped raining."

"I hardly noticed." Pavan sighed, leaning close to press against Thad's shoulder, bringing the hand up against his chest.

Thad watched him with widening eyes, glancing up quickly.

"Keep me out of trouble, Thad. No one else is best for the job, for with you I would follow endlessly," Pavan whispered. A long stillness hushed around them.

Thad drew his hand hastily away, frowning.

"You do not know what you speak of, Pavan."

Pavan leant back. "I am very sound of mind, Thad. Do you think me unfeeling?"

"I can feel her magick lingers upon you. It is not right that I interfere with your bond. You know of my heritage, and the particular magick my of bloodline threatens your awareness."

Pavan stepped back, stagnant in feeling, glaring at the faie who watched him closely. Those wondrous orange eyes were so tempting, but Pavan resisted, recoiling back.

"Your magick does not threaten me, Thad." Irritation made Pavan's skin burn, a growing headache sprouting behind his eyes. "It is her magick that I cannot stand. I do not wish her company."

"I know of the blood magick that binds you to her. I know how your skin must crawl to be apart from her. How it burns you..." Thad stepped closer, wrapping his arm around Pavan's waist. "The very touch of anyone other than the one you're bonded with, a touch of their lips, can drive your mind into frenzy."

Pavan felt his whole being ignited with a feeling that made his skin crawl. Feeling Thad's mouth so close to his skin, desire mixing with the taste of revulsion. His wrist burned, sending a shocking wave of pain through his body.

"Please, stop."

"It's torture, to see you bonded to her," Thad hissed, stepping back.

"She is not the same as the bastard who kept you as his slave." Magick pulsed hot beneath his skin, fading away the residual revulsion that linked him with Lilja's magick when he touched another.

"There is no difference, Pavan. Not when your heart's not in it..."

"My heart." Pavan stepped closer. Crowding Thad back, he pressed the faie against the curved frame of the wall. "It does not belong to her. It will *never* belong to *her*."

"It will cause you pain."

Pavan smirked, touching Thad's cheek. Running his fingertips across the delicate curve of his jaw, he was near enough now to smell the citric tang. Desire furled through him, tempting him with the beautiful face before him. Thad stood motionless, breathing rapidly. Their eyes connected, and Pavan looked into the dark eyes of the faie. His pupils were so large that the orange was a sliver of color.

Anticipating the pain, Pavan leaned down to kiss the warmth of Thad's cheek.

It was electric, sending a jolt through his chest. Pavan sighed, daring to lean closer, curving his hand to caress Thad's neck. He lowered his lips, waiting for Thad to rebuke him, to push him away.

Thad raised his chin.

Their mouths touched in a gentle kiss. Soft warm lips melded into his own, as the heat began to build into hot searing pain. Pavan gasped, wincing, but pressed on, eager for more. He wrapped his hand around the curve of Thad's middle, bringing them closer. It was at that instant that Pavan's body reacted, overflowing through him in such ferocity that he growled, as the ache ripped into his gut.

"Pavan, enough."

Stepping back, Pavan felt drowsy with the lingering pain. His mind sought for the milky skin, desperate to dive his fingers into the white hair...

He fled from the sheltered quiet to trudge through the wet, muddy roads.

He needed to be free of his own resentment. He hated the revolving door of entrapment with the aching need he felt. Lilja was always on his thoughts, always second on his mind, but he had begun to resent her. He hated how she made him want, his desperation being pushed back. Now, it was scraping to get out, clawing its way to be free.

Pavan wanted to devour her, but it was only her magick he wished to possess.

He stopped in front of a door, his feet had carried him there, to her rooms. Setting his jaw, Pavan knew he needed to end this. He had had enough. Pavan knocked.

"Come in." Her enchanting tone sent a chill through him.

Pavan opened the door.

Lilja was seated at her fire, the outer layers of her garments hung over an iron grate to dry. She sat unbraiding the length of her long white blonde hair. When he entered, her violet eyes looked up, smiling.

"Caught out in the rain, I see," she remarked, her eyes drifting over the length of him. "Remove your boots, I detest mud upon my floors."

Pavan rolled his eyes, but did as she asked, yanking his boots from his feet and leaving them outside her door. When he returned to stand before her Lilja was now standing, combing her fingers through her long hair.

"Is there something you need?"

He fought to keep his composure. "I wish you to break our bond."

Lilja remained quiet, busying herself with walking the length of her chamber in her linen undergarments. Retrieving a comb from the shelf, she began to untangle the mess of long blonde hair. Pavan watched her, waiting, but there was no end to the elf's silence. He scoffed.

"Lilja, please. I beg you."

She looked up. "Beg? Pavan Vhear does not beg."

Pavan scowled. "I am not your Vhear."

Lilja smiled coolly, turning to face him, her willowy frame graceful. As she walked about the room, Pavan could not stop his gaze from following her every movement, seeing her body through the thin material.

"You wish me to remove our bond...why?" She replaced her comb upon the shelf. Her violet eyes were demure as she looked him over.

Pavan felt his face go hot.

"I do not need your magick. I have control."

She chuckled half-heartedly. "Yes, Meilyr has enriched me with tales of your vast improvement."

A long silence unsettled the room. Pavan began to grow impatient.

"You will not release me?"

Lilja was before him, touching his cheek. "You are so dear to me, Pavan. Can you not feel it?" she asked, her voice like honey. Her touch warmed Pavan through.

Resistance was pointless, Pavan could smell the sweetness of her magick, feel the pull of her desire. He sighed, leaning into her touch, blinking heavily as magick slipped towards him.

"You are distracting me," he sighed.

Lilja's lips pressed to his, gently, savoring a heated kiss. "Good." She smiled, her hand reaching up to delve deep into Pavan's hair.

Pavan sighed, reaching out to grab hold of her slender waist. Her body pressed to his. "You are still resisting me."

Pavan winced, trying to pull back, her hand in his hair tightened. Her warm lips pressed to the curve of his jaw. A sigh fell heavy from his lips.

"I wish to be free of this. You must end it."

Lilja deepened her hold, her teeth scraping over the flesh of his jaw. He stuttered a breath, grasping her hard, jolts of pleasure mingled with magick.

"I have grown attached to you, Pavan. Must you wish to be free of me forever?" Lilja asked, peppering kisses.

Pavan shook his head. "It's not real. This feeling does not last. You do not love me, Lilja, you love only the magick I hold, my power that I give you in exchange for yours..."

He gasped as her hand palmed the front of his trousers.

Her violet eyes glanced up. "You talk too much. Come, you wish to end it, but we must do it properly."

Lilja turned from him, unlacing her undergarments, they fell to the floor in a heap. His eyes roamed the length of her milky skin, her white blonde hair reaching to graze the base of her bottom. Pavan averted his eyes.

"It's not right. I cannot sleep with you again, Lilja."

She sighed, returning to stand before him. She took hold of his jacket, prying the damp garment from his shoulders.

"I cannot separate us, Pavan...I cannot undo the enchantment I have set without drawing from that forbidden well. Do you trust me?" Lilja pulled at Pavan's tunic, removing the thin material.

He felt exposed, unwilling, but finally he nodded.

Pavan removed himself from Lilja's chambers, feeling despair. Not only did his body ache, but his mind, and his magick was strained. He felt weighted again, heavier in the existence of the magick that burdened his soul. Pavan took his muddied boots, walking along the corridor, and taking the stairs up toward his own rooms.

Evening settled over them, the world beyond the wall of the great house was slowed, the cold shifting the water to ice. Snowflakes fell as Pavan watched from the window of his own room, the fire was unlit and darkness shrouded him.

Fire caught his eye.

Pressing himself closer to the window, Pavan squinted to see; fire illuminated the night sky within the village square. Panic fluttered in his chest. Yanking on his boots, Pavan dashed from his room, bounding down the steps he so recently ascended. He threw open the door of the grand hall to emerge into the bitter cold of the night.

As the village slept, a fire burned.

Making his way to the village square, his blood ran cold. He could see the entire stores of their warehouse set ablaze, burning through and billowing smoke. Pavan glanced around, his eyes scanning the village, he saw villagers begin to step out into the cold.

Pavan was afraid. Unsettled.

"Go to the great house, do not remain in the streets," Pavan said at once, his voice carrying about them.

It grew colder, making him shiver.

Farren emerged, bundled in a great fur blanket. Pavan approached her.

"What has done this, Pavan?" she asked, her face fearful, her bright eyes taking in the large burning goods.

"I don't know, but you must help escort these villagers, and anyone you can. They must get to the great house; it is protected." Pavan grasped her arm, earning a quick nod.

Not remaining, Pavan heard Farren call to her people, getting them away from the fire. Pavan walked about the large pier burning, scanning the dark, emptied roads.

"Vhear, what is it?" a man asked but Pavan shook his head.

"Something's wrong," Pavan stated. Quickly, he glanced towards the forest, but all was quiet. His skin shivered, and his magick was heightened enough to make Pavan warry.

"What shall we do, Vhear?" the man asked.

Pavan heard it, a sharp whistling. Then, high above them the sky sparked with orange light, like stars in the darkness making Pavan's stomach drop.

"Get down!" he shouted.

In a flash, his hands were raised, instinct flashing through him at the onslaught of falling fire. Arrows pierced the night, but stopped amongst the sky. Magick was sharp, prickling his skin as he pushed them back.

All of the arrows fizzled above them into burning ash.

Pavan turned, looking at the villagers that remained near him, they all huddled, crouched low but they were unharmed. Relief flooded him, urgency moved him.

"At once, go to the great house. Do not delay." Pavan rushed back, but the man kept at his heels. "Sir, you go, tell Meilyr what is happening."

The man was wide-eyed. "What is happening, Vhear?"

"We are being raided."

Pavan did not wait for the man to respond, he needed to alert the others. Coming to the first house, he banged on the door, hearing a commotion from within.

"Attack, we are under attack! Get to the great house!" he shouted.

Again, and again, he went from door to door, thankful as a few men remained with him to knock on more doors. Until suddenly there was a loud clamor from the road. Finally, hunters emerged from the main road, coming towards him. Svein was spotted first, approaching Pavan with great haste.

"They are coming from the west road. There must be some here already, for they have emptied our storage, it burns in the square," Pavan told him, hurrying with him as they went for the training yard.

"Aye, we shall make a perimeter, leave it to us."

Stopping, Pavan looked at the hunters who readied weapons, harnessing great swords. Pavan glanced up at Svein.

"Where is Thad?"

Svein looked about, then grumbled, "He must be in his workshop."

"I shall find him, you know what to do." Pavan turned away, bounding up the icy path. Ignoring the bitter cold in his bones, he headed towards the little shack he knew so well.

Approaching it with caution, he saw that the door was broken ajar. Pavan stepped through, looking into the depths, a figure lay sprawled upon the floor. Pavan knelt, turning him over, to his relief it was not Thad, but a man in a hooded cloak, face scaled with putrid acidic poison.

A noise caught his ear. Pavan turned.

Thad was slumped in the corner, coughing. Pavan rushed to the faie's side.

"No...Pavan...it's toxic..." Thad coughed between words, but Pavan ignored him, scooping Thad under his arms, and guiding them both to the fresh air. Pavan had not realized before how putrid the smell was, it burned his nostrils.

Thad gasped, clutching at his chest, he collapsed to the dirt as Pavan blinked away the sting in his eyes. He knelt beside the faie, who was choking, desperate to breathe.

"Thad, what can I do?"

Pavan leant down, pressing his mouth to Thad's. Taking in a deep breath, sharp, stinging poison was bitter in his mouth. He could feel his magick burn it away with a fiery burn. Coughing hard, he winced, but covered his mouth with Thad's once more, breathing in deeply again, and again, until Thad pushed Pavan back, gasping in air.

"Pavan, you fucking idiot!" Thad coughed, glaring up at Pavan.

"Your voice is grateful enough. Thad, I would do it again without hesitation." Pavan smiled, holding Thad's cheek warmly.

Thad rolled his eyes, pushing himself to his feet.

"I chased that man to my workshop, he set the blaze in the square." Thad looked around, focusing as he slowed his breathing.

"There are more, approaching from the west, they will need help. Can you stand with us?" Pavan asked, looking Thad over. Worry still overwhelmed him, Thad remained paled, his breathing shallow.

Thad shook his head. "I shall be fine."

They hurried from there, drawing closer to the shouts of villagers. As they neared the road that leads towards the mines, villagers rushed past them.

"The mines; they have trapped them in the mines!" one of the women wailed.

Both Thad and Pavan moved quicker, running along the path, taking the way quickly over ice, now approaching the entrance of the cave. It was a vast opening, nearly twenty feet high, and nearly as wide. Carts sat vacant near the mouth, stalls where horses would have been were emptied. It was quiet, as Pavan stepped through slowly.

He descended the slight slope that led into the first chamber, a chasm that was long since devoid of precious stone, but was now used as a storage shelter for supplies, axes, and lanterns.

Thad gripped Pavan's arm.

"They are in the lower cavern," he whispered harshly, his orange eyes flickering.

"You can hear them?" Pavan questioned as they shifted stealthily down the slope that led deeper and deeper into the mine.

"It is faint, but there is a shift of magick below us. They carry unchecked rage, we must proceed with caution, Pavan. There are men down there we cannot risk endangering."

So, they went on, descending into the darkness. It was much colder in the antechambers, where the shift of air through the mouth brought with it a bitter chill. Pavan's fingers ached from the cold, his breath was visible in the dim light that flickered from the low hung lamps.

They stopped just before the third chamber, the largest of the rooms. They could hear the hushed tones of three men, talking in a strange dialect Pavan did not understand.

"They are of Jorn..." Thad hissed, his voice low in Pavan's ear. He felt the warmth from the faie, where he knelt so near to him. They both listened.

Pavan peaked around the corner, the three men were dressed as the others in Thad's workshop. All in black, their faces obscured by the black hoods they wore.

He also saw the villagers, standing in line at the far wall. Their hands were bound, and their mouths were gagged. There were five villagers, two older than fifty and the other three in their teens, all of whom Pavan recognized. One of the older gentlemen glanced his way. Pavan jolted back as the man gave a shout behind his gag.

He was struck a blow by one of the hooded men, to silence him.

Pavan clenched his jaw, his hands forming into fists, hearing the struggle of the man, who whimpered behind the muffled gag. Thad gripped Pavan's wrist.

"Breathe, control," he whispered, shifting his frame to stand, he pulled out the dagger that was concealed within his boot.

Before Pavan could stop him, Thad stepped lightly around him maneuvering on silent feet, hiding behind a large wagon that was holding great sacks of stone. He stealthily glanced about, calculating and strategizing. Pavan shifted his head to watch the faie warily.

One man shouted; it was the same man as before, crying out now in a garbled agony. Pavan heard it, his chest tightening. He was unable to see exactly what the hooded figure was doing, but he saw enough of the man's features to recognize his desperation.

Pavan stood. He did not try to use the same stealth Thad used; he shifted around the corner, staying in plain sight. Now all the villagers saw Pavan. They grew wide-eyed, making a noise behind the silence of their gags. Pavan kept his sights on the three men in hooded cloaks.

They shouted, Pavan ignored them. Reaching the first man who came at him, he shifted on his feet, muscle memory dancing through his limbs as he dodged, ducked, then struck hard, following through with his punch with magick. He watched the man be sent back, crying out in agony.

"Pavan, not that one, he's..."

Pavan shifted, his fist raising to direct at the second man, but he hesitated, hearing Thad's warning. But the man was quick, sweeping his leg to knock Pavan onto his back. Magick was sharp on his tongue as he glanced up at the slender features of a hard-faced elf. Gray eyes bore into him, the hood had fallen back to expose the shaved head of the elf, his head riddled with scars and burns. He was strong. Pavan felt it in the force of magick that ached through his limbs.

Behind Pavan, in a flash, Thad jumped out of hiding, using his short stature to hunker down and shift into the space of the third man, who went for a sword. Thad stomped hard upon the man's wrist, striking an upward blow. An agonized scream echoed throughout the chamber as the hooded man crumbled, gripping his wrist and reeling back.

A glint of steel brought Pavan's eyes to the elf, his expression was deadly and his teeth were bared. Pavan scrambled to his feet, charging at the elf, shouldering the man as a footballer would, shifting them back on loose gravel. Above him, the elf shouted curses, driving his elbow hard into the side of Pavan's head.

Pavan stumbled back.

The elf flashed the steel of a curved blade to Pavan, a smirk upon his haggard face. Pavan spat blood on the ground, ignoring the pain that sprang behind his eyes.

Invigorated, his magick coiled hard and his fist clenched. He caught a momentary glance at Thad, who wrestled with the third man; even with a broken wrist the hooded man was fierce and determined. Pavan had had enough of this.

The elf took his chance, slicing through the air and catching Pavan's arm. But Pavan ignored the blood that slithered along his upper arm. Locking eyes upon the man, hatred clawed tight up his throat. Gripping the man hard by the throat, he lifted him off the ground.

It would be easy. Pavan already felt the magick begin to pool; the markings shivered along his skin, coming to life as the man struggled in his tightening grasp. The man's throat was supple, easily crushed. It would be quick. It would be easy to snap the man's neck.

Pavan grimaced. At once, his blood began to cool.

He let the man down to stand upon his two feet. Pavan would not suffer himself to claim this man, he did not wish to take another's soul. Instead, Pavan hardened, frowning at the elf who was turning blue.

"Sleep," he commanded, thrusting him back. The man fell hard.

Lethargic, Pavan blinked. Breathing in, and out, glancing about him to see the villagers being released. Thad was alive and unwounded. Pavan saw the three hooded men, all laying unmoving upon the ground.

Around them, the ground began to shake making them all freeze.

"The mines..." the older man spoke, his accent thick, as he rubbed at his sore wrist. "They laden the deeper veins with explosives, Vhear..."

Pavan felt the ground shift again; this time, it was more potent.

They all ran. Emerging from the inner chambers, they followed the path leading out into the cold brisk air outside. Another grumble shook them, hard. They all fell to the ground, Pavan huddling over the nearest of the villagers, protecting them as debris and stone flew through the air, falling in thuds about them.

At last, the rumbling stopped. Pavan looked up, coughing. He blinked against the sting of dust, smoke, and ash, as he helped the man beside him to stand.

"Pavan. Pavan!"

He coughed, stumbling forward with the villager close beside him. He guided them along the path away from the collapsed mine behind them.

"Here, Thad!" Pavan called out, as they finally made it out of the smoke to clearer air.

"Ehnarea help us," the man beside Pavan gasped, despairing at the sight. Ledenjour was on fire.

They returned to the main square, seeing hooded men upon horseback and hunters wielding shields and swords. Bowmen were taking shots. Pavan watched many hooded men go down in bloodied heaps, but still more came, barreling in through the darkness now nearly overrun with smoke. Thatched roofs burned and trees had been set ablaze; everywhere Pavan looked, he saw despair and horrors.

Stumbling through the muddy ground, magick swam, mixing with the smell of blood, the smell of death and fear. It was too much. Pavan blinked, hardly knowing which way to look, but then, his eyes fell on the great house. It was standing tall, still pristine.

Pavan saw Meilyr casting a barrier of magick before the doors leading to the great house closed. Lungs burning, Pavan dug his heels in, running towards the house.

As he raced nearer to the man who stood alone, he kicked back a hooded figure who loomed nearby. Meilyr shouted, but Pavan could not hear him over the ringing in his ears. Fighting back the few hooded men who brandished swords and axes, Pavan retrieved a fallen sword. Thrusting and blocking, he knocked them back. He looked over as two large men surrounded Meilyr. His blade pierced one, but the second drew back, ready to swipe.

Pavan shouted, stepping between the blade and where Meilyr stood.

Searing pain struck through him as the sharp edge of the blade slid the length of his body, hip to shoulder, slicing through the layers of his tunic. Staggering back, Pavan groped the length of his chest as blood spilled over his hands, thick and dark.

Before his eyes was the hooded man, now beheaded by the blade Meilyr grasped.

Pavan grew cold.

His strength was leaving him as he stumbled back. Slipping on the blood beneath his feet, he crashed to the mud. Meilyr was beside him in an instant.

"Foolish boy," Meilyr sighed, his hand grasping at the wound, the blood spilling over Meilyr's hand.

"Thad!" Meilyr's voice rang out. "Hold on..." he whispered to Pavan.

"Thad!"

Meilyr's voice became muffled and Pavan's breath grew shallow as he soon became lightheaded. Meilyr whispered under his breath, his hand grasping the wound. But Pavan was heavy, feeling consciousness fading from him.

His body seethed in pain as he swam in and out of consciousness. He remembered Thad above him, his hands pressed to his chest as he muttered the incantations. Pavan felt the agony as his skin was pulled together crudely, the magick burning his flesh as it closed the wound enough to stop the bleeding.

"He will need a better healer. Can we send for one?" Thad's voice could be heard. Pavan wanted to call to him, wanted to be comforted by those warm hands.

"There is one who could close the wound completely, but he may not be here for days." Lilja's voice.

Pavan groaned in agony at the sound of her voice. Trying to pull away from it; it was unwelcome in his current state. Soft hands came upon his cheeks, his hair, and his neck, soothing him with her magick. He knew what her magick felt like—it was a warmth of honey and summer breeze, sending him drifting away into a painless slumber.

Delirium followed Pavan like an old friend as he tried to awaken, but the pain he felt deep in his chest was excruciating. Flashbacks of the night before came to him in panicked dreams, he would sometimes awaken with a cry, only to be guided back into sleep by soft familiar hands.

Pavan called for Malcom.

"He is safe." a familiar voice sounded far off.

Pavan tried to answer, but his words were trapped in his throat.

Again, he called for Malcom. He was unable to rest until he knew for certain, until Pavan knew he was safe.

Now, he heard his friend's voice echoing in his mind as a strong hand held onto his. Pavan squeezed back, trying to get a grip on his wakeful eye, but he fast succumbed to sleep once more.

A dull throb was there in his chest as Pavan blinked, opening his eyes. The light was harsh against the darkness he had known. As he groaned, coming to, he opened his eyes to see someone beside him. Blinking back the spots of light, Pavan looked at the familiar blonde-haired elf.

An elf he remembered.

"You?" Pavan's voice was barely a whisper.

The elf turned to Pavan, his face endearing. "You are one very lucky man," he stated in a slight accent, his hands working calmly over Pavan's chest.

Trying to sit up, Pavan was pressed down by a firm hand.

"I would not move just yet."

Pavan looked up at him, still adjusting to the light.

"I know you." There was a memory knocking at Pavan's head.

The elf looked amused. "I get that often, my mother was a healer in this realm for many years."

But Pavan shook his head, his mind reeling as he sought after the memory. "No...it's something else..."

Pavan was gritting his teeth. Now, rolling to his side, he began to sit up. The elf did not stop him but leaned over to retrieve a bucket, he handed it to Pavan in time for the vomit.

Pavan growled, his stomach empty and complaining.

He leaned back on the small bed. He could see the same blonde hair of the elf, and that his clothes were made of fine linens.

"I hate doing that." Pavan balked, the sour taste in his mouth returning. The elf gave Pavan a cup, to which he drank, thankful that it calmed his stomach. "Thank you." Pavan rested his head back, finally meeting eyes with the elf.

"I am Lahrs," he stated, nodding to Pavan, a hand placed over his heart as he bowed his head.

"You are the one they speak of...Meilyr's first son."

Laughing, the elf nodded. "I have been called many things, and yes, Meilyr's son is among them."

"I am sure you know me."

Lahrs smiled, showing a full set of white teeth. "Yes, you are Pavan. I have heard much about you as well. Do not worry about the vomiting, it is very common when first learning magicks. Your power is greater than your body can withstand, and the vibrations it causes gives you a very bad stomach ache."

"Oh, is that all?" He winced, his head throbbing.

"It will pass as your powers grow stronger," Lahrs stated, taking the cup and now examining the bandage placed over Pavan's chest.

Pavan winced as the cold cloth sticky with a slimy substance was pulled away. In astonishment, Pavan looked down at the purple scar that looked months old but was still tender to the touch.

"You have a fine collection of scars. Perhaps this one shall be a fine story to tell." Lahrs wiped at the sticky substance.

"I should have died."

Pavan breathed in, looking at the long scar that ran from the collar bone, near his armpit down the side of his left chest to the upward curve of his hip bone. It was raw and angry, but healed.

"It is hard to kill an Ehlfern. Especially one with the power to heal oneself."

"I'm not a healer."

Lahrs looked Pavan in the eye. "There are a number of things that separate an Ehlfern and every other magick caster, Pavan. But the main difference is their ability to use from within all the realms of magick. When I spent years learning to heal and protect, and Meilyr to cast off and guard, you have the ability to utilize every aspect of magick you encounter. You can learn any spell or enchantment, any number of things that take years of servitude to master."

Pavan was blinking hard as the elf spoke.

"But with every magick there is a cost. There is always a danger."

Pavan listened, but his mind opened as the elf spoke. His words brought a memory to his mind, a memory which opened him up to a flood of new emotions. Pavan grasped his wrist, eager to know if the ribbon remained secured. Luckily, it remained, stained but otherwise intact. Pavan looked into the eyes of the elf, who looked at the ribbon Pavan now held close to his chest.

Lahrs blinked, examining it closer.

"Where did you get this?" he asked, suddenly serious.

"It was a gift..." Pavan breathed, bleary-eyed as a mist came over his vision. "A girl gave this to me, while I was enslaved in Denorn. She was so kind. I didn't understand her; she spoke a dialect I didn't know, but when every other person walked by, without so much as a glance...she was there."

Lahrs stood above him. Silent.

"Perhaps I imagined her." Pavan rubbed the ribbon into his skin.

Finally, Lahrs spoke, his voice calm and gentle. "Perhaps destiny will bring your paths to cross again."

Pavan laughed, wiping his eyes. "Destiny. I hear that very frequently when people are talking to me. I have no destiny here. I am just a shadow passing beneath the sun."

Lahrs touched Pavan's forehead, bringing the blankets over his chest. "You should rest, you still have much healing to do."

Pavan rolled his eyes. "I am not tired."

"Do not quarrel with me. I can easily render you unconscious."

Their eyes locked and Pavan gave in, laying down with a huff and a groan as his body eased into submission. Pavan watched as the elf walked away, hearing the footsteps disperse as he began to drift back into sleep.

Lahrs barged into the private office of Meilyr.

He was interrupting a meeting between Meilyr and Lilja, their faces looked up at his entrance. Lahrs crossed the room, his footsteps muffled by the layers of furs upon the floor. Pouring himself a glass of wine from the cabinet at the war wall, he drank it back in thick gulps, his mind racing with so many thoughts.

"Is everything alright?" Lilja asked.

Lahrs looked past her to Meilyr. "Who is he, Meilyr?"

"Isaac Maison."

"*That* is Isaac Maison? You did not think to write—"

"This matter was not something that could be spoken of by letter. Not to the castle in which you have been currently. Should I have written, and your letters been sifted through..."

Lahrs waved a hand, downing the remainder of his wine. He crossed the room, and shifted to pace the other way. He glanced up to Meilyr, then to Lilja. Agitation knotted in his stomach, as Lahrs sat quietly upon a chair placed closer to the fire.

"He is supposed to be dead. He was..." His memories flashed before his eyes, seeing Brendolyn in Denorn crouched at the cage where she looked in at the man there. Lahrs shook it away. "He was in Jorn."

"That is where Thad bought him from Sir Adrian, as well as Malcom, our other healer." Meilyr nodded, reaching into the top drawer of his desk and offering the folded parchment he had kept there.

Lahrs stood to take them, unfolding the parchment to see the insignia. His blood ran cold.

"Sir Eske is still running a business in Hilvaer? His titles had been revoked when Orin Gaur was put on trial and executed. Those in dealings with Lord Gaur had been disbanded." Lahrs felt the revulsion thick in his throat.

"Orin Gaur was held accountable, his name was spoken on the very lips of those that were once his partners." Meilyr nodded, deep in thought. "I believe they were bought for their cooperation."

"Orin the merchant, who traded in silks with Entheas?" Lilja asked, her knowledge of the matter very little.

"Orin Gaur traded in silks, but he kept another business within his own estate." Lahrs returned the parchment to the desk. "He kept personal slaves that attended to those that he could influence, bribing them with sexual exploits in exchange for loyalty."

Lilja looked appalled.

"Be careful there, Lahrs," Meilyr warned, his tone had a touch of anger, his dark eyes settled on Lahrs with a pointed stare.

"What do you mean, Meilyr? Those girls were freed, after Orin Gaur's execution?" Lahrs felt the air ignite with tension.

Lilja stared at them both, her anger growing. "What happened to the girls?"

"Orin kept no girls, Lilja," Lahrs stated. "He bonded himself to his slaves, for complete submission. He bonded himself to boys, so they could not be free until he released them...or his death severed their connection."

There were tears in her eyes as she pressed a hand to her stomach.

"Did they all..." Lilja's voice was a trembling whisper.

Meilyr spoke. "Orin had only one remaining faie in his service. The others had all been disbanded for some years. There was only one he valued above the others, one who took part in many of Orin's business endeavors as well as utilizing his...personal talents."

Lilja frowned at them both, her glittering eyes wide with realization.

"You can't mean...that isn't possible."

"Thaddeus was taken from his home, at fourteen, and sold to Sir Eske who transferred his bond to Orin Gaur after breaking Thaddeus with torture, with rape. He was just a child sold into slavery, Lilja. Brought up by a man of faie birth that used him cruelly." Meilyr sat straighter, his voice hardened as he addressed Lilja with a ferocity that Lahrs had not seen in nearly twenty years. "I know your prejudice against him, the hypocrisy you believe me to have felt for him when I first brought him here. But it was at that crucial moment, before Orin was apprehended, that I took him from Denorn. His bond was not yet severed."

"Thad went back, every spring, at your request," Lilja stated flatly. "You sent him back to them, to that place where he was sold."

"It was his choice to make, Lilja. He endeavored to be certain no other would have the same fate, that no one would have to endure what he had endured..."

Removing her hand from the flat of her stomach, Lilja straightened, hardening her emotions to remain in control. "I see."

"It is important that Thad must travel to Tauf, he must remain where they cannot find him. He knows secrets that make him a target to the one that put it into the minds of the lords to turn Orin over."

"You believe I can convince him?" Lilja laughed.

"I believe you can make him see reason," Lahrs stated but there was a shift in Lilja, her countenance faltered and he saw the hesitation. She was no longer the same as she had been before.

"Thaddeus is displeased with me, Lahrs. I have done something that he shall never forgive, something I had not realized was so significant," she whispered.

Lahrs stepped closer to her, taking hold of her hand, he felt the quickened pulse and looked into her violet eyes to see the shimmer.

"How long have you been with child?"

Lilja pulled her hands away, her cheeks crimson. "That is none of your concern."

Kneeling before her, Lahrs turned her wrist, touching the flat of his thumb to the small raised mark upon her inner wrist. It was similar to the mark that he had seen upon Pavan when examining his wounds. Lahrs was saddened, seeing the faded little triangle that was once a bond she shared with the Ehlfern.

"You took your oath as a Daughter of the Brotherhood," he whispered as he held her hand tenderly to place a kiss upon her fingers.

"It was necessary to help him, Lahrs. He was so broken when he first came to us, I thought it would save us." Her tears fell freely down her pale cheeks.

Lahrs spoke softly. "You need not be afraid Lilja."

"I am not afraid to have his child." Quickly as the tears had come, she wiped them away. "But it is done. There is nothing more I can do for him, he wished for me to end our bond, and so I have. We shall go to Tauf."

"Pavan will not travel with us," Meilyr said suddenly.

"He must come to Tauf." Lilja sounded desperate, she made ready to stand, but Lahrs pressed her back down. "If he does not, then they shall find him!"

"Be at ease." Lahrs attempted to calm her.

Lilja pushed his hand away, storming out of his grasp, glaring at them both.

"He cannot leave me like this!"

"Pavan must never know you carry his child, Lilja." Meilyr stood, silencing them both. "You will go with us to Tauf, you will convince Thad likewise that it is best for him to follow us. Pavan shall never be free to walk the streets of Tauf, not while his father remains alive."

A chill passed through Lahrs.

"His father is dead," Lilja hissed. "Charles Maison was imprisoned for killing King Broderick. He died there, years ago."

"He is very much alive."

Meilyr reached again into the drawer of his desk, pulling out a long slender box carved of deep red wood. It was a wood made of the trees that came from across the great, treacherous seas. Lahrs knew it came from Rehael, Meilyr's mother, and he knew it was important to be kept in such a box to prevent the magick from seeping out.

Unlatching the box, Meilyr opened the lid to reveal a dagger, with a shimmering blade nearly transparent like glass, but it reflected the light of colors, making it move. It was dragon glass, pure and untouched, a blade that when honed with strong magick could pierce the heart of an Ehlfern.

Lahrs sighed. "We do not have the magick to hone a blade of dragon glass."

"There is one such stone. It was a gift for the king of old, locked away in a hidden secret place." Meilyr did not touch the dagger. "Eleanore knew of its location."

"You believe Pavan should return to Jorn?" Lahrs asked, unbelieving.

Meilyr closed the lid of the wooden box, shutting away the dagger again. "He must seek out Sanna so he can set upon the path to retrieve it. He must have power enough to use it..."

"She knows where Charles Maison is hiding?" Lahrs asked thoughtfully.

"Sanna has had visions. She waits for Pavan in R'hun."

Thad sat in the ruin of his workshop; there was nothing left.

He sat, going over the horrors of the attack. Wretchedness plagued his heart. He was trying to keep at bay the panic that arose within him, thinking of the blood beneath his fingers. He had been quick to Meilyr's side while the battle dwindled behind him, to kneel by Pavan as he bled freely. Thad gulped back the sour taste, blinking away the tears as he remembered the thick blood that seeped from the deep wound slashed over Pavan's chest.

He wiped away the tears that angrily slithered along his cheeks.

"Good morrow."

Striding over broken stone, and the crumbling building that was once set ablaze, Lahrs emerged to approach Thad in his little workshop.

"Lahrs. I did not hear you approach," Thad spoke quickly.

"It is not often I can sneak up on you, Thad. Meilyr had told me you have kept away from the great house. You have given up your rooms to the families that lost their homes." There was a softness to Lahrs, as he watched Thad with an approving gaze.

"I do not need it. I sleep in the kitchens."

"Come, embrace me, brother." Lahrs outstretched his arms.

Thad eagerly moved forward and embraced the elf, welcoming the warmth of the affection. Thad was unable to contain the wrenching of his heart, he sobbed into the shoulder of the elf, Lahrs' strong arms holding him upright.

"You have been so good, Thad," Lahrs whispered.

"I have missed you, Lahrs."

When they finally did separate, Lahrs kept Thad at arm's length, looking him over with a satisfactory expression. "Look at you, I believe you have improved in looks since I met with you last..." Lahrs smiled.

Rolling his eyes, Thad smirked. "Three months is hardly enough time to change my looks. We met on the shores of Jorn, if you recall."

"I did not forget." Lahrs looked serious. "You have drawn closer to Malcom, I believe? I have understood from Farren that Malcom has been of great help with your duties as healer."

"I could not have done it all without him."

"And Pavan?" There was hesitation, as Lahrs brought up the other.

Thad felt his face grow hot. "That's...I have trained him, he is a quick learner. I saw his skill put to the test that night, when we were attacked. Pavan behaved admirably."

"Yes, they have told me of the great Vhear. Come, I wish to walk with you a while." Lahrs took a look at the destruction of the building where they stood. Together, they walked free of that place, walking now amongst the remainder of trees untouched by the fires that burned most of the village.

After a long moment, Lahrs broke the silence.

"Meilyr is unsettled by the attack upon the village, as he rightly should be. But from what has been gathered, the men who came that night were of unaffiliated allegiance. They carried no banner, nor wore any insignia upon their arm."

Thad glanced away. "They broke through all of Meilyr's spells, without warning. I managed to kill the one who broke into the storehouse, but there were others in the mines. They were from Jorn."

Lahrs paused, glancing at Thad with astonishment.

"They spoke to you?" he asked, his features severe and attuned to caution.

"No...not directly to me, but we overheard their voices. They spoke to each other; they spoke of their duty to the cause. Pavan did not understand them, but I could hear them clearly."

Lahrs thought for a long moment. "That is interesting. And are they the same ones that have raided the other villages, the ones nearest the coast?"

Thad gulped. "I don't know, but they were looking for someone, Lahrs. I believe they were searching for Pavan."

Lahrs was quiet for a long moment.

"You come from Jorn, what are the realms like?"

Lahrs sighed heavily. "There is unease." Suddenly the elf turned, looking at Thad with a stern expression, a serious look Lahrs only got when he was worried.

"Did something happen?"

"It has been decided that the remainder of Ledenjour shall return with me to Tauf. I have sent a messenger to the duke, they shall be ready. It will be difficult, shifting to city life again, but in time you will grow accustomed to it..."

"Leave? I cannot leave." Thad felt his chest tighten.

Lahrs shook his head. "Thad, it is best, but you will remain in the castle. I believe that with my recommendation, you shall be welcomed into the alchemist order. They teach healing, potions, and enchantments."

But Thad felt his face grow hot.

"That is generous, Lahrs, but I do not wish for notoriety, not in a place as that. Perhaps the stable yard, or the smithy. I am strong, I shall do well there."

"No, Thad."

He clenched his jaw. "I shall not return to that great city, or any city..."

Lahrs gripped hard on Thad's arm. It was not enough to hurt, but enough to make an impression from the elf who always remained so calm.

"Don't be a child."

Thad yanked back. "You forget that I am older, Lahrs. Meilyr may have raised you by his side since your youth, but I am more than your years."

"Then act with thought, Thad, do not think with your impulsive nature. There is more at risk here than returning to a city built on peace."

Irritated, Thad rolled his eyes. "Shall Pavan be a member of the duke's court? I should think they would want him close at hand."

Lahrs remained silent.

"They won't want him there at all?" Thad discerned Lahrs' hesitant look.

"It is not simple, Thad. You know it isn't my choice…"

Thad scoffed. "Change your duke's mind, or the mind of your duchess. Kristjana cannot be so afraid of Pavan that she would not wish to dissect his mind…"

"*Sanna* refuses to hear of him entering that great city."

"That witch. She is in her hovel, hidden away in Rhun. What business is it of hers if Pavan enters Tauf?" Thad hissed.

"A great number of things, Thad. She has had visions."

"About Pavan?"

Lahrs held a firm gaze. "Charles Maison is alive."

Thad felt the color drain from his face.

"While he lives, Pavan cannot enter our city," Lahrs said flatly. "It shall be painful, to be separated from him, but with time you shall regain your heart again."

Thad glared. "You expect me to sit in Tauf, while Charles Maison hunts for Pavan?"

"He will be escorted to Rhun, I have commissioned Svein to travel with him in the spring. They shall make port in Signe where I have secured travel papers that will allow them to enter the middle realm. Sanna is waiting for him."

"Has he agreed with your plan?" Thad hissed. "Does he know he is being shipped off to be your lure?"

"I am doing my duty. Pavan has expressed to Meilyr that he does not want to burden Tauf, he is choosing to stay. You must let him go, Thad."

"And you command me also?" Thad shouted, tears stinging his eyes. "I am to obey the wishes of that witch? I am to obey you and leave Pavan to the mercy of his father?"

"Charles Maison was not looking for Pavan."

Silence crashed through Thad, knocking into his chest.

"You have not been quiet in your dealings in Jorn, Thad. Your last encounter with Sir Adrian has drawn the attentions of those you have known. It was you that they were searching for…it would not take long for Charles to discover you, should Sir Eske seek him out." Lahrs grasped Thad's shoulder, speaking softer. "Please, come to Tauf, Thad. You are my brother and I cannot see you harmed."

Thad felt the lump, thick in his throat. A tear fell from Thad's eye. "But I love him."

CHAPTER 29

Jorn City, Realm Jorn.

At the banquet, Brendolyn walked around, every courtier jovial and dancing while robust music played. When she passed the crowd of lords and ladies who crowded King Beaumont, she witnessed him as she walked by, noticing that his countenance had changed since they spoke. He was no longer all reserve, his shoulders stood upright instead of hunched down. He was tall and broad, and vibrant in his words as he addressed his courtiers.

They caught eyes and he smiled, Brendolyn smiled back, curtsying briefly before walking on. She was enjoying her freedom to just walk around the banquet hall without the expectation of needing to be present before the crowd.

There was distinct laughter. It was from Lisetta, Brendolyn realized, who was chatting with a group of young lords who collectively gathered around her.

Brendolyn ignored her sister, walking to the farthest end of the hall, where the music was less and hardly any courtiers walked. The candles in their holders had been neglected and light spilled in from the open window of the evening beyond. She watched the sun graze over the garden scene. How she longed to bathe in the glow of the sun, but she remained, as she promised to Lahrs, within the castle walls until his return.

She only ventured out to the gardens in company of her guard, Sir Eero. Who, at this moment, Brendolyn knew was walking not far from the banquet tables, she had last left him talking to a lord about the care of his horses.

"I knew I would find you here." That voice, one that Bren knew, prickled the skin on her neck, raising the hairs, and making her jaw clench.

Finally, she turned to face the guard of her sister, Sir Varick, who was dressed in his embroidered silk tunic for fancy occasions. His brown hair was combed away from his face, which presented a thin smile and weathered skin that creased around his mouth.

"Where else could I be, Sir Varick, if not at the banquet to honor my late mother?" she stated coldly.

Varick frowned. "I am sorry for the loss of the queen, she was loved by many."

His words meant nothing to Brendolyn, she did not wish for his good will.

"Thank you." She did not even stop to curtsy as she went to walk past him, but he stepped in her way, a hand gripping her upper arm. He now stood so close that Bren could smell the shaving powder he used, and his hair wax.

"Why does a man of Jorn protect a flower of Corad? There is nothing he can do, when there are others more equipped for the job."

Brendolyn yanked her arm away.

"You are unwelcome in my company, Sir Varick." She walked away, her fist clenched at her sides. Behind her the knight followed, annoyingly, he caught up to walk in stride.

"A horse-master is only useful in the stable yard, not for the protection of a princess," Varick hissed, his voice vile in Brendolyn's ear.

She rounded on him. "I did not ask for your good opinion on the matter, nor is it your business, Varick. Sir Eero is an honorable knight, just as you, only he holds true honor."

This struck a chord with the knight's patience, his jaw clenched and his eyes had gone feral, he made to grab her again, but another hand took hold of his wrist. Sir Varick froze, stammering, he looked up at the stone face of Prince Barrow.

"You are needed at Princess Lisetta's side, Sir Varick. She wishes to return to her apartments." Barrow's voice was cold. This tone had never passed his lips in the presence of Brendolyn, who blinked up at him.

At once Varick bowed, his cheeks flamed, as he hurried off.

Once he was gone from them, Barrow finally turned from Brendolyn. A few lords had begun to stare, but did not quite hear what had happened. Barrow bowed to Brendolyn.

He took her by the hand, another at her waist, and quickly whisked her away to the center of the hall where courtiers danced.

He brought her to face him. Looking at him now, Brendolyn could see anger flashing on the prince's face.

"Thank you," Brendolyn whispered, trying to keep her footing with the steps of the dance.

Barrow seethed. "That man is vile."

She could say nothing.

A moment passed and the prince relaxed his features, sighing heavily. "Forgive me, I should have asked if you wished to dance."

"Don't be," Brendolyn encouraged, giving him a smile. "You saved me from unwelcome company."

Barrow turned her on cue, returning her to his side in a moment.

"He had no right to grab you as he did...I saw his advance and I could see your discomfort."

Brendolyn's cheeks heated.

"Does he do that often?" Barrow suddenly asked, his tone urgent.

Brendolyn averted her gaze, unable to bring herself to look at him. "More than he has before. Now that Lahrs is away, he believes it his duty to be my guardian."

The music changed to another dance, but Barrow stopped at the very center of the floor. While the others danced, they stood still.

"I need some air." Barrow offered her his arm, his face still distorted in anger.

Brendolyn took it and was led from the dancing courtiers, out of the hall onto the large balcony. The air was cool as the sun had set, and a gray cast set over them as night fast approached. Barrow stood away from her then, breathing in deep as he walked to the ledge of the balcony. Brendolyn went to stand beside him. She could see now that his features had softened and his shoulders were relaxed, breathing in the late evening air as the silence fed his thoughts.

"Seeing him grab you the way he did," Barrow began, choosing his words carefully. "Is it wrong to want to end his life?"

He looked tormented, saddened by his own words.

Brendolyn placed her hand over his, the one that gripped the balcony railing with such force his knuckles had turned white.

"Death is not a realm of ruling, nor is killing for the sake of another man's gain. I understand your wish to protect my honor, Barrow, but do not discredit your own actions to step between him and I because there is more honor found in facing what is difficult." She placed her hand on the smooth of his cheek, pulling him to face her.

He was wrought with sadness, tears pooling at the corners of his eyes.

"You are stronger than you believe," she whispered.

He leaned down, ready to kiss her, but a sudden cough stopped him. They both looked over to see Sir Eero standing at the entrance leading indoors from the balcony. He gave them a knowing smile.

Brendolyn blushed and Barrow stepped back.

"I believe it is time for Princess Brendolyn to return to her apartments," Sir Eero said, his tone kind.

Brendolyn gave Barrow a smile, touching his arm briefly before walking after Sir Eero.

In the dimly lit library adjacent to his apartments, King Beaumont sat flipping vacantly through the pages of a text he held no interest in, across from him stood a man in dark robes. Lord Bannon spoke of matters of state, reading from his books, but Beaumont could hardly think, his mind wandering thinking of the elf he had sent away to Entheas, and the road that would take him to Tauf. He hoped there would be no altercations, for the sake of the young princess. He hated taking away the girl's friend and guardian in this hard time, but in the moment, there seemed no one better than the elf to accomplish this task.

Lahrs had been more than willing to do as the king wished.

His head began to pound. Beaumont stood, causing Lord Bannon to pause.

"I grow tired, excuse me." He bowed to his lord before beginning to walk away, but he stopped, taking the two scrolls from the lord. "I shall read over these like you wished."

He smiled, taking them from the man who now bowed, appeased by this gesture. With the scrolls in hand he slumped his way into his apartments, latching the door and turning to his roaring fire. The silence in his rooms was deafening.

Beaumont tossed the scrolls onto the table, pouring himself a drink from the decanter of wine placed on its tray. His ears prickled at a shift of sound within his rooms. Alert and prepared, Beaumont placed his glass down gently, moving around to a slat of shelves; there a sword was hidden. He gripped it, turning in an instant to the intruder.

There, to the king's surprise, was a familiar frame, whose face was concerned and hair disheveled. King Sabian.

Beaumont let the sword fall in a clank as it hit the stone floor beneath his feet.

"I could have killed you," Beaumont said dryly.

Sabian smiled, flashing his teeth. His beard had grown in his travels. Beaumont went to put the sword in its rightful place.

"Had I announced my arrival it wouldn't have been as thrilling to surprise you." Sabian was elated, watching Beaumont walk away from him.

"I could have decapitated you, Sabian. It would have started another war."

There was nothing jovial in Beaumont's tone as he turned to look again at the king, who had followed him and was now placing his palms on his hips, grasping him through his layers of clothes.

"I can't think of war now, not when you are so near."

Beaumont recoiled from his lover's touch, he could smell the alcohol rolling off of him—this game no longer thrilled him.

Sabian stopped, his glossy eyes scanning Beaumont with confusion.

"Come, tell me what is the meaning of this? Why do you spurn my touch?" Sabian asked as Beaumont took a step back, looking down at the southern king.

"You are grieving Sabian, there is no need of this now." He felt the distance between them begin to grow wider as he looked at the wounded look in Sabian's eyes.

"You know as well as any that this is exactly what I need. I need you, I need your touch to make the emptiness go away."

Beaumont shook his head at the other kings' words, his mind reeling and heart hurting. "I cannot comfort you, not like this. Maybe this is what is best."

Sabian's face creased as anger began to roll over him.

"You wanted me. You asked me to your chambers, Monty." Sabian was angry, his eyes full of tears as he spoke.

Beaumont hated himself, just as much as he hated the truth of the other king's words. There was a brief pause.

"Yes. I took you from your wife's bed. It was wrong, Sabian. "

Sabian walked the length of the room, turning around and pacing again the other way, stopping again to face Beaumont.

"You spurn me now, when I need you more than ever? I returned here to be close to you. Please, I need to feel love again."

The southern king touched the front of Beaumont's tunic, feeling his chest. He wanted to. Beaumont wanted to give in to his lover's demands, hating to hear the depravity and agony in Sabian's voice, but he knew if they went down this road it would not be well for either of them.

Beaumont closed his eyes, breathing heavily.

"There is more love in the world than what could be found in the confines of a bed."

Sabian threw his arms up, storming away, again. "Oh, behold him now, the virtuous King Beaumont! He takes what he can whenever it pleases him. A true king at his core, who cares little of any other."

This proclamation made Beaumont prickle.

"I did not run into the arms of a secret lover before my wife was buried in her grave." His words were dark on his lips, his chest growing burdened as he felt the anger edge its way in.

Sabian rounded on him. "What then, virtuous one, would you have me do? My wife is gone and there is nothing left!"

Beaumont could hardly believe his ears.

"Nothing? You believe your children to be nothing?" His voice could barely be heard.

Sabian collapsed onto the nearby chair, hands pressed at his eyes.

"You have an heir, Sabian. You have two daughters...you have people who look up to you. This is your legacy. You cannot abandon them, not now that they need it the most and need you to keep going." Beaumont felt for the southern king now more than he ever had, he knew the heartache of losing a wife, he knew the road that Sabian would travel down.

Sabian looked up from his hands, weeping.

"Your children love you, Sabian." Beaumont knelt before the other. "Do not abandon them now. I, who understands this future you face, need to tell you that in the darkest of times the thing that matters most are the ones you love and they who love you."

Tears fell down Sabian's cheeks as he looked up at Beaumont.

"Do you love me still, Monty...after all this time and when I am at my worst?" He was broken, searching for something to grasp onto in his darkest moments.

Beaumont pulled the other king into his arms, holding him. "It would take death for me to stop loving you, Sabian," he whispered, kissing the dark hair of the king who cried into his chest.

Brendolyn walked one last time in the gardens, taking the last quiet walk along the gravel path. Coming upon the spot where she had once diverted from her path to climb the wall leading to the pastures, she realized it felt like a lifetime away, when she foolishly dashed from those that tried to keep her safe.

Keeping her walk within the boundaries of the gravel path led her to the trees that fluttered in bloom with purple flowers. Even on the cold breeze, they blossomed. She took in every delicate flower, never knowing when she would see it again.

She turned her head slightly at the approach of feet.

She was expecting Lahrs to be there to tell her their carriages were prepared, but it was not the elf recently returned from the king's errand—it was Prince Barrow. He was somber, wearing his dark colored cloak, and approaching with the sweep of his blonde hair fluttering in the light breeze. Brendolyn's heart swelled and fluttered at his princely beauty.

"Sir Eero told me you were out here."

She nodded. "I wanted to have one last look, I shall never see them again."

"Do not say that."

Tears blossomed anew in her eyes. She was unable to look up at him as he approached, she could not bear to see his hopeful eyes, or the beauty that she would miss when she was gone.

"It is impossible." She swallowed thickly. "I go to Alnwick, I go to my family's summer home, where I shall be forgotten."

He touched her chin, tilting her head back, she had no choice but to look at him. His eyes were blue, so blue she saw the flecks of green hidden there.

"I could never forget you, Brendolyn," he whispered. "Write to me and I shall be your companion. You should not be alone, not when your heart is so wounded."

Brendolyn touched the hand that held her chin.

"It would not be right, Barrow." She shivered, her heart breaking at the thought of losing him. To lose the kindness of the prince, to no longer have his friendship was more than she could endure.

"Write to me, Brendolyn." He was firmer, leaning down.

He would have kissed her, but she turned away. It felt wrong to kiss him when she felt so miserable. She sighed, the breeze shifting through her hair, a chill running along her spine. Suddenly, she heard a voice on the wind, faint and electric. Brendolyn thought she heard her name.

Turning her eyes up, she watched the blossoms upon the tree flutter against the shift of the wind, the purple blooms fluttering wildly, until one snapped free. She watched it flutter down and down, reaching up a hand as it gently curled into her waiting palm.

Beside her Barrow chuckled, his hand coming to rest upon her side.

"It is a sign," Barrow smiled, his voice gentle.

Brendolyn watched the purple blossom open within her palm, the petals furling open to reveal the tiny spores of the inside, releasing their scent. It was lavender, an odd smell that met Brendolyn's nose and made her gasp.

"What does it mean?" she asked, more to herself than to the prince who stood at her side. She watched the petals fall apart from the stem, fluttering away in the wind.

Again, the voice whispered her name, sending chills through her and calming her aching heart. She smiled, if only slightly, looking up at the tree that danced upon the wind. It was a whisper that hushed the roar of despair in her heart.

"Brendolyn." Barrow pressed his lips to her forehead.

His words took her away from her thoughts, returning her gaze to his warm eyes, his welcoming mouth. She was leaning up to bring her lips to his, a brief kiss, to seal her thoughts, and calm her nervous apprehensions of being apart from him.

"I will write you, every day," she promised, touching his golden hair and smoothing her fingers along the line of his jaw.

Slamming the knight hard to the wall, Simeon glared at the frightened man, whose brown eyes widened. A yelp escaped his lips when he yanked the knight into the darkened alcove, using his free hand to cover the man's mouth, silencing him.

"Fool," Simeon seethed.

Sir Varick cringed, the fear oozing from his pores.

"I did as you commanded," the knight hissed, when his mouth was finally freed. Simeon did not let up his strength, pressing the knight deeper into the wall and making him wince in pain.

"You failed. With the queen dead...there is suspicion."

Varick's eyes widened. His fear tasted of fine aged wine as Simeon closed in the distance, letting the man question his fate, that rested in his hands.

"I-I didn't mean for her to die...the king. Sabian did not have his evening tea, he was with someone else."

Curiosity flickered through him, but Simeon cooled his features, appearing unaffected before the simpering man.

"Who was he with?"

Varick looked conflicted. Simeon began to lose patience, shaking the man hard by the throat until he whimpered.

"Monty...Monty. It was your king." The words stumbled through Varick's teeth.

Simeon stopped, glaring at the knight.

"You claim Sabian was with Beaumont. They were not in a meeting that night," Simeon hissed.

Varick licked his lips, his face sweating. "They were in Beaumont's bedchamber. I overheard Beaumont's scullery maid, she was turned away from starting the fires. She overheard the kings' talking...I pressed her for answers."

Simeon lessened his grip on the knight, allowing him the liberty to speak. Varick went on cautiously.

"She stayed too long, she was afraid she would be killed if she told what she heard."

Simeon scowled. "She heard their secret plot?"

Varick shook his head, whimpering.

Simeon's lip curled back with disgust. "She heard their lovemaking, then. Perhaps I shall inquire to this scullery maid, to find the truths in your neglect..."

Fear returned to the knight.

"I didn't want Natalia to die." Varick was soft, weak in his sniveling over the dead queen. "She was kind to me...she doted on me."

Simeon gripped the man's throat, it was thin under his hand, supple and easily broken. But Simeon paused.

"I wish to kill you," he whispered, leaning closer to the knight, tasting the fear, sour on his tongue. Magick coiled beneath his touch. Want flared to life in Simeon, he wanted to devour this man's arrogance, his stupidity.

"Please, my lord," Varick begged.

"In recompense, you shall do something for me." Simeon pressed his thumb into the soft place on Varick's throat, his nail was digging dangerously close to his artery. He could smell the hint of blood, the scent of desperation growing in the knight's body.

"Anything," Varick pleaded, all too ready to save his own life.

Smiling, Simeon leaned closer, letting his magick fester beneath the surface. He locked eyes with the knight until those brown eyes were vacant, transfixed.

"You will report to me, on the happenings in Corad. Every move, every decision the king makes. Even the smallest whisper shall reach my ear," he hissed, keeping his tone even.

Varick's cheeks flushed.

"I shall do as you say." He nodded. "Shall I have my reward?"

Simeon frowned, drawing close to the knight's face.

"You may not touch the faie cunt," he hissed venomously. "Do not breath her name, nor touch her flesh, not until I have procured what is rightfully mine. If you do not heed my warning, if you do not do as I wish...then I shall deliver her dead body to your doorstep and have you strung up for murder."

Varick gulped, eyes widened.

"If you do not do as I wish, her body will be mutilated, there will be nothing left when my man is done with her. He is thorough; he enjoys it. When he has had his fill of her, then shall you be delivered to her father for justice. Do not cross me, Varick."

Chapter 30

Ledenjour, Realm of Entheas.

Pavan was exhausted.

He examined himself in the full length mirror, the thick, purplish scar that ran from the line of his collar bone down across his body to the edge of his opposite hip. He ran his finger along the raised skin, a scar that would never fade, but showed a miraculous survival—Pavan should have died. He furrowed his brow, deep in contemplation as the memories of that night flashed in his mind.

He winced at the memory of each man that fell. Pavan was spiraling into himself, into the horror that consumed him.

"Pavan."

He opened his eyes. Malcom stood in the reflection beside him. Pavan shifted, turning to see his friend so near him, eagerly bringing him into a warm embrace.

"I thought I would never see you again." Pavan did not want to let go, but let go he must. Bringing his friend to arm's length, he paused to get a good look at the man who was alive and well.

Malcom smiled. "I remained in the great hall, with Farren. She brought me the injured, and I attended to their wounds. But when Thad carried you in...I feared the worst, Pavan. You were so pale...there was so much blood."

Pavan felt a pang in his chest, not knowing how many were dead. Darkness clawed at the edges, dragging him under.

"Do not think of what we lost, Pavan. I know your mind. There are so many who live because of you. These people have seen it. Meilyr has seen it, too," Malcom spoke hastily, following Pavan as he pulled away to retrieve the tunic cast over the back of a chair. He yanked it on over his broad chest.

Pavan could not face the shame of his despair, his wretchedness.

"Please, Mal, do not conceal it from me..."

"Thirteen. More than twenty injured. Burns, broken limbs, wary spirits. Meilyr tells me these men are Scalanis pirates, a murderous crew that leave none alive. There are other villages, near the coast. Those villages they had raped, murdering everyone in their beds, and burned the food supply for any that managed to escape."

"I see." Pavan nodded, anger replacing the deepening anguish in his chest.

"We are to go to Tauf. Lahrs has welcomed the people into the city, there it will be safe. They are great in magick; they use enchantments and protection. There is a feast prepared. An envoy arrived this morning with food to sustain the people as we travel north. Lahrs advises we leave before the week is out, before the frosts set in..."

"As they should. Once Meilyr leaves, the magick shall fade and the damage to the great hall shall begin to crumble." Pavan felt gutted, he did not wish to be subject to people who praised him. "I know what the people say about me. I cannot go there."

"You belong with us, Pavan. After all that has happened these last few months, these people adore you."

Pavan shook his head. "I do not want adoration, Mal. Not this. I admire praise upon the stage, acting a part written by craftsmen, by poets. This is not praise I can accept."

"You believe it is unearned?"

"It is undeserved, Mal. They praise me for keeping them safe from a beast that I killed with my own hand with magick that can easily slaughter them all. I have deceived them, I am a wolf in sheep's clothing. I have betrayed a trust, I live a fictitious honor. You cannot ask me to pretend to be a hero, when I am the furthest thing from it." Pavan clenched his jaw as anger rattled his bones.

"Don't do that." Malcom gripped Pavan hard by the arm.

"There is nothing I can do to reconcile what I have done. No matter how many times I save them, how can I be anything but a killer?"

"You are not a killer, Pavan."

Emotion swelled in his throat as he swallowed the pain back. "Danger will follow me there...if I go to Tauf, those searching for the great magicks shall follow me there."

Pushing himself away, Pavan returned to dressing. His stiffened muscles made it slow, but he pulled the padded doublet over his shoulders and latching the buckles, hiding the remnants of his scar beneath. Pavan sat, beginning to place his wool stockinged feet into his boots. But he felt heavy, Pavan's magick was weighty within his chest.

"Pavan." Malcom sat beside him.

"I am only tired." He shook the feeling away.

"Do you want to rest, Pavan?"

"I do not wish to be confined here any longer. I must walk about, even if it is painful." Pavan stood, wincing at a sudden sharp pain in his tender skin over his breastbone, ebbing away to a dull burn.

"You have not taken any of the potions Lahrs has left for you, they will help with the pain. Your skin is still healing." Malcom followed after Pavan as he lumbered towards the door where his pelt hung.

Malcom quietly, but efficiently, helped secure the pelt in place over Pavan's shoulders. The warmth eased the tightness in Pavan's bones, he relaxed slightly, grasping the latch of the door. Malcom pushed it shut again, locking their eyes together.

"I won't go to Tauf, Mal."

Malcom shook his head. "You won't be alone, I will..."

"You cannot stay with me. Not this time." Pavan saw the hurt, the betrayal written in his friend's face. "There is something I must do."

Pavan unlatched the door, but Malcom slammed the door shut again.

"Don't be daft, I'm staying with you."

Pavan locked eyes with Malcom. "You have chosen me, Mal. Since we were kids, you have been by my side, you have always chosen my happiness over your own. Don't allow me to burden you. You belong with Farren."

"You have never been a burden."

Touching his cheek, Pavan smiled sadly. "I wish I was strong enough to take us home. To take you away from the danger that is here, but at least while you remain in Tauf you shall be away from the darkness that haunts me."

"Let me help you," Malcom whispered. "We can fight whatever it is together."

Pavan shook his head. "This time, I must do this on my own. I know what needs to be done, but I cannot face it knowing that you won't be safe. Please go to Tauf."

"Pavan, I…"

"Don't argue. I would be forever cross with you if you chose me over a pretty girl."

"Git."

"Prat."

Malcom chuckled, a deep rolling sound that resonated between them. Pavan smiled, embracing his friend one more time, a deepening embrace.

"No more of this," Pavan stated. "I wish to eat, I am starved."

Malcom said no more, and together they walked from Pavan's chamber. Walking along the corridor, Pavan tried to be quick, but as he neared the stairs, Pavan sighed. Every inch of his muscles became tight with every step, pain radiated through him as they descended lower and lower, drawing even closer to the sounds of laughter, of boisterous voices. They began to smell cooked meats, and Pavan's stomach grumbled.

As they entered the great hall, the music quieted and voices hushed.

Pavan prickled, as hundreds of eyes crowded into the large room, making it seem smaller than it really was, took him in. His cheeks flushed, and he gripped Malcom's arm suddenly.

Malcom guided him through the throng of villagers. The people watched him in reverence, murmuring Vhear under their breath, many stepped aside to make a path for Pavan to reach the large table at the top of the room. Meilyr was there. Sitting beside him was Lahrs, the elf, and to the other side of Meilyr was Thad.

Pavan's heart swelled, unable to take his eyes from the faie as they drew nearer. He could ignore the murmurs, the touch of villagers' hands as they touched his shoulders and his arms as he walked by. Pavan kept his eyes on Thad, as the faie blushed.

Slumped, Pavan sat in the chair beside the faie, happy for the relief on his body as his muscles and bones screamed in agony. Pavan ignored it, his eyes remaining on Thad, who glanced away.

Meilyr began to speak. "Let us begin."

Voices commenced as music began softly, filling the room again with constant chatter. Food was brought forward, and drink was poured into silver cups happily. As the evening progressed, they began to talk loudly amongst themselves. Eventually Meilyr and Lahrs stood to have conversation with those that remained in the great hall.

Pavan reached out, taking the hand of Thad's that rested upon the table. Those orange eyes quickly glanced his way. Thad smiled, such a smile that made Pavan's pulse quicken.

The hand slipped away and Pavan frowned.

"Do not draw your hand away," Pavan whispered, leaning closer to where Thad sat stoic and grave, as he had remained for the entirety of the dinner.

"I am glad to see you well."

Pavan heard the formality in Thad, the reserve was unlike him. This was enough to make Pavan draw back slightly, glancing about the busy room. No one watched them, they were busy with their meal, deep in conversations of their own.

"Thad, why so reserved?" Pavan inquired.

Thad's smile was slight, half-hearted. "I am quite alright."

Pavan scoffed. "You are a magnificent liar."

Orange eyes blazed, looking up at him with a heat of mischief. It was a flicker of the faie Pavan remembered, setting his heart a flutter. Pavan smiled now, leaning nearer.

"You are incorrigible," Thad muttered, those eyes looking down. Pavan had slid his hand over the smooth skin of Thad's wrist.

"I am not going to Tauf. There is something I must do. Svein is to escort me to Signe, but I cannot go there, I cannot go where they wish, I must go to Jorn."

Thad said nothing.

"Come with me, Thad." It was a plea, desperate, warm. He grasped Thad's hand.

Thad looked away, lost in thought.

Pavan leaned closer, his chest now pressed to the curve of the faie's shoulder, trailing his other hand up along Thad's spine to settle upon the base of his neck where his dark copper hair rested.

"Do you wish me to beg, Thad?" he whispered, casting a look around for watchful eyes but they remained in solitude.

"Meilyr desires me to go with them to Tauf."

Pavan scraped his nails along the base of Thad's skull, leaning closer to him until his lips touched the lobe of his ear.

"What do you desire, Thad?"

Magick trembled, a shiver of heat pulsing between them. Pavan could sense the desire that coiled in the faie. Those orange eyes glanced across the room where Meilyr talked with interest to Lahrs.

"Thad," Pavan whispered, drawing the attention of the faie again. "I know you believe me enchanted by your heritage. That your faie birth influences me in my regard for you, but you must feel the difference. You must understand that there is so much more to my regard than..."

"I must go with Lahrs to Tauf. He is my brother, and he knows that I will be in danger should I go to Jorn."

Pavan sighed. "Then will you teach me magick, in the time we have left?"

"We have only a fortnight, Pavan."

"I am a fast learner." Pavan smiled, his words slipping into the elven dialect with ease. *"You have taught me so much already."*

A smirk pulled at the edges of Thad's mouth. *"My knowledge is not that which is commonly done. Books that were collected for decades upon my master's shelf have educated me with deeper magick. Forbidden magick."*

Slipping his hand beneath the table, Pavan found the leg that pressed to his. Soft silken trousers slipped beneath his touch. He moved his hand further up, but Thad placed his hand over it, looking intently into Pavan's eyes. His pupils were dilated, smiling.

"Not tonight, Pavan. You must heal."

"I have had enough of being told to heal, to sleep." Pavan squeezed the thigh beneath his hand. A familiar pull rippled through him, wanting desperately to take hold of the magick that fluttered within the faie. It was not yearning as Sophie's, nor yielding as Lilja's. Thad's magick beat faster with anticipation.

"You are not ready to learn the magick that I can show you, Pavan."

They were interrupted by the sudden approach of a youthful face. He was not as vibrant as he once was, but Trisk stepped up to the table where they sat in earnest hesitation. Pavan removed his hand from Thad's thigh, looking up at the young elf with a look of irritation.

"My lord Vhear." Trisk bowed, looking timidly between them. "Lilja requests to speak with you, in her private chambers."

"I decline her invitation, Trisk. There is nothing she could have to say to me that she cannot say here. If she has need of me, she knows where to look." Pavan tried to keep the irritation out of his voice.

"She...Please, Vhear, it is most important."

Pavan growled beneath his breath, taking a sharp swig of his drink before standing, glaring at Thad who frowned into his own cup. Pavan stormed away from the table towards the stairs, taking them two at a time with impatient steps.

Reaching her door, he pounded with brutal force.

"Come in." Her voice was invitation enough.

Pavan opened the latch, glaring hard at the elf who stood in the warmth of her great chambers wearing a beautiful gown. It was made of many layers of wool and silks, intricately embroidered with leaves along the sleeves. Her hair had been brushed and neatly braided. She looked nearly angelic in the golden light of the fire, casting a halo of gold upon her head. Pavan sneered.

She tried to smile. "I wanted to say goodbye."

"If that is all, then I will take my leave." Pavan turned on his heel. He reached the door, but he stopped at the plea behind him. Her voice, her magick still weakened him.

"Please, wait," she called from behind him. Lilja was desperate.

Pavan looked over his shoulder, watching her as she smoothed the front of her gown. He was not used to seeing her nervous. Her cheeks were flushed, her looks so altered since the attack that Pavan could hardly recognize her as the same elf.

Reaching from around her neck, Lilja unclasped a chain that hung there, hidden within the front of her bodice. She closed the distance between them to bestow the gift upon him. Pavan frowned.

"I cannot take your gifts."

She sighed. "It is yours. It belonged to your mother."

Taking his hand, she placed the necklace into his waiting palm. His eyes grew wide as the glint of metal flickered, recognition for the pendant filled his heart with such strong emotion. It was the same pendant his mother had given him the fateful night he ran into the woods. He ran his thumb over the warm metal.

"I believed this to be lost forever."

Lilja nodded. "We searched the forest for weeks. This was all that was left."

Pavan's eyes filled with tears, unable to look up at the elf who stood too near to him. Her warmth was suffocating.

"Your mother told me to hold on to it, in case you were to ever return," she whispered. "I believed she was lost in grief, to believe you would ever return from death. I had long believed you were taken to the Veil. But perhaps she knew the magick that I did not, she knew the magick that would return you to us again."

Daring to reach up and touch him, Lilja caressed Pavan's cheek. For a moment, he longed for it, her scent overwhelming his senses again. He was leaning into her touch, clinging to the pendant of his past.

It ended quickly.

"Your generosity in returning the pendant is favored." He drew back. "Thank you, Lilja."

"Please, Pavan, you must come with us to Tauf. You must be there when…" Lilja's lips quivered as tears spilled from her eyes, drawing back away from him. "You must not be quick to abandon those that admire you…who look up to you."

"I am not their *Vhear*. I do not belong to them." His voice lowered. "I do not belong to you, Lilja."

"I see. Then it is really goodbye."

Pavan nodded. "Farewell, Lilja. Favor find you."

Pavan returned to the great hall, but he did not see Thad at the table. Finding Malcom, who sat with Farren in deep conversation, he asked, "Have you seen Thad?"

Farren smiled sweetly. "I believe he retired for the night. His chambers are taken, but I believe he has settled in the upper levels. Above the kitchens, though it is no more than storage now."

"Thank you."

Retreating to where the kitchens now remained empty, Pavan found the narrow staircase leading up to the rooms above. Each room along the narrow corridor was filled with storage bins, packaged goods and empty crates. At the end of the long corridor was a shut door, with a faint illumination of light. Pavan approached it, knocking lightly.

It opened slowly.

Thad stood watching him with wide orange eyes. He was no longer dressed in his silken garments, but in the white under linens, his dark copper hair was disheveled.

"I have come for my first lesson."

Thad smirks. *"Did I not advise you to rest?"*

"You are my teacher, and I have not learnt all that I can from you." Pavan pressed into the room, slowly shutting the door behind them. A hush fell over them, closing out the world beyond the storage room that Thad had made into his room.

Empty crates had been moved to the farthest wall, stacked in a way to be made into shelves. On the shelves were placed the remnants of Thad's tinctures and books that had not been ruined with the attack. Pavan glanced around to see the bed on the longest wall, furs covering the down pillowtop, and patchwork quilts draped over top to make a comfortable bed beneath a backdrop of drapes made of an old tapestry.

Beside the bed was a crate with a lantern. At the farther end of the room, upon the table, was a basin for water. Pavan felt the room abuzz with gentle magick, keeping the room at a temperate warmth, staving off the cold. He felt warm beneath the great fur pelt.

Pavan smiled, unclasping the buckle and, tossing the pelt aside.

"Then I shall teach you." Thad walked to the shelf. *"First to make potions..."* He took down a book of herbs. Then, he scanned the other books, his finger touching the worn down spines, and he hesitated over a dark leather at the end.

Pavan was intrigued, leaning in to examine the many leather bound texts that lined the crate shelves. They stood shoulder to shoulder as his attention gravitated to the dark leather, he reached out, but Thad grabbed his wrist.

"Not that one," Thad stated.

"Your personal journal?" Pavan smiled, noting the blush that tinted the faint freckled cheeks. As he grasped the spine, he could feel that it tingled with magick.

"It is a more difficult magick. One that you are not ready for." Thad allowed him to take it down, but he lingered closer, nervously hovering as Pavan flipped through the hand-written print and sketches.

"I am not a novice." Pavan smiled.

His eyes grew wide at the contents, written in elven scrawl. Not like Thad's hand, which Pavan had read from the little black notebook the faie carried everywhere, but a slanted, more looping scrawl that described magick that seemed impossible. Each page was filled with more descriptions of tantalizing rhythmic movement combined with magick that heightens the sensual zones throughout the body. Pavan's eyes flicked up to Thad, who looked frozen in terror.

Pavan flipped the page to an illustration of two bodies sitting facing each other, without touching but to grasp the other's wrists. Each figure held their eyes closed, and the script of elven scrawled upon the page was a description of connection between two people without a marrier.

"*Roinnt aigne...*I have never heard of this in the elven tongue," Pavan whispered, his eyes roaming the document.

"It is forbidden magick. My master had particular delights in procuring these from those that travelled to Veilore. His distant clientele had a particular delight in the more carnal of magicks..." Thad turned the pages, giving Pavan a view of a figure being held by enchanted chains that hung from hooks. He flipped it again, showing page after page of more intense lewd scenes involving one individual or multiple.

Pavan looked at Thad. "He made you participate in these?"

"That was a long time ago." Thad shrugged. "I have no shame in keeping what belonged to him, nor that many of these books were written by his hand. But the magick he knew of was extensive. In the time I spent with him, I read these books daily to learn whatever I could."

"But you do not wish me to see these?"

Thad's face was still pleasantly flushed, and a smirk played at the corner of his mouth. He was standing so close to Pavan that he could feel the warmth through the layers of his tunic.

"Forbidden magick is not common in the realms. Nor is it sought after by those of more gentle upbringing." He tried to keep his voice serious.

"I am not a novice." Pavan looked to the faie's mouth. "*You wish to teach me your forbidden magick?*"

"That is impossible, Pavan." Thad shut the book in Pavan's hands, returning it to the shelf at the end. He picked up the book that held the herbs.

"*Roinnt aigne.*" His words made the faie stop. "The description is very clear; there is not physical touch, Thad. I can touch you there." Pavan dared to place his hand upon Thad's back, the material a thin wisp of linen. He could feel the warmth of the faie's skin hot against his fingertips.

"It is dangerous," Thad sighed.

Pavan stepped closer, pressing himself behind the faie, smiling. "I do not hear a word against it, Thad. If you did not want to show me, you would have told me no."

"There is a great amount of trust between the pair that share one mind," Thad breathed. "To enter another's mind willingly takes a great amount of strength."

"I trust you completely."

Pavan desperately wanted him, wrapping his arm around the faie to bring them close and pressing the flat of his palm to Thad's flat stomach. Feeling the muscles beneath the thin layer of linen and brushing his lips over the curve of the faie's ear, trailing down to kiss the soft skin of his neck. His body flushed with want, pressing the evidence of this into Thad. A sigh escaped the faie.

"You have teased me endlessly, Thad. I am desperate," Pavan breathed, dragging his hand upwards, caressing Thad's throat. "I have been wanting to take you, to have you beneath me...*my longing for you sets my soul on fire.*"

Thad turned, kissing Pavan feverishly. His mouth was hot, his desperate hands were roaming through Pavan's dark hair, not hesitating to yank apart the jacket where the ties held the garment secure, exposing Pavan's loose fitted tunic that lay open to the scar beneath.

Pavan felt the magick tighten, groaning at the force.

"Apologies," Thad gasped, as he stepped back to rake a hand through his dark copper hair. Licking his reddened lips, he examined Pavan thoughtfully. "I should not have tested the longevity of your control."

"Begin your lesson, Thad, or my control will shorten further."

"Sit on the bed," Thad instructed.

Pavan yanked off his outer jacket, remaining in his loose tunic. Lowering himself to sit at the edge of the bed, he watched Thad with darkened eyes. He was a vision in the low light, his skin flushed. He was angelic in the white linen undergarments and Pavan felt the strain of desire in the tightening of his trousers.

Thad knelt before him.

"Quiet your mind," Thad whispered. "Focus on your breathing."

The faie knelt so close to Pavan without touching him that it was difficult to resist reaching out to touch the glowing skin of the faie's flushed cheeks. Seeing the glistening of sweat begin to dampen Thad's hairline, the dip of his throat, Pavan watched the trail of sweat trickle down into the depths of the linen tunic.

"Clear your mind," Thad repeated, raising his slender hand upwards, gently touching the contours of Pavan's brow. "I cannot enter your mind if you are not at ease, if you resist then it shall be painful. You must allow me in, Pavan."

His body relaxed, breathing in and out slowly, his senses were alive as Thad touched his cheek, the fingertips trailing down to his lips.

"That's it, Pavan...relax." Thad nodded. He held his hands out with his palms facing up. "Take my wrists."

His arms felt heavy, weighted like bricks as he raised them to do just as Thad asked, placing his hands on the exposed wrists of the faie. Magick danced beneath his touch, slithering between them. Pavan lurched as the sensation sent jolts up his spine.

"Relax." Thad's voice was muffled.

Pavan blinked, trying to bring him into focus, but the room began to spin. A heat in his palms was replaced by a cooling tingle that began to crawl up to his elbows, snaking its way through his veins up to his elbows. His breathing was coming in sharp. He was being drawn into a state of awareness between the sleeping world and being awake.

"Thad."

"I'm here, Pavan," Thad replied, his voice an echo. "Follow my voice, I will guide you to the threshold."

He followed, reaching out in the growing darkness for the drifting voice, coming to stop at the face of a door made of dark wood that was carved with intricate designs. His magick being drawn to the door, Pavan reached for the handle, but it opened before he could, swinging back to let in a stream of light.

Pavan stepped through, emerging into a long corridor. Doors stood on either side, each with a different detailed design. The corridor stretched out further as he looked and a shiver ran up his spine.

"This way," Thad's voice danced. Pavan's eyes were drawn to a door with shimmering lights beneath the footing, calling to him like a pulse.

Pavan opened the door, stepping through. His breath caught as the heat greeted him as the room fell into view. It was similar to the room where they sat, but there was a dance of color that changed as he moved, like sun shimmering through the water.

"Pavan..." Thad's voice was otherworldly.

Pavan turned towards the bed where Thad waited. Sitting up from laying back, his copper hair was like a flame, draping over his shoulders and his eyes were a glow of embers as he watched Pavan step forward. His movements were languid. Approaching the great bed, Pavan sat beside Thad, astonished by the ethereal being before his eyes.

"Is this your mind?" Pavan asked, his voice dancing between them.

"It is...this is the shared space, where our minds meet." Thad dragged his hand over the bedding, his hand drifting up to touch Pavan's jaw and caressing his neck.

This sensation was new, unlike being touched in the wakeful world.

Pavan groaned. "Can I touch you?"

"Yes." Thad nodded, leaning into Pavan.

He was slow, at first, taking his time. First, running his fingers through Thad's hair, the soft texture felt like silk. Then he moved to his face, tracing his fingertips over his eyebrow, over his freckled cheeks, and the pouty curve of his lips. Each delicate sensation sparked further delight, igniting a desire within his belly. Pavan lowered his hands to graze the line of the faie's neck, following the skin to the collar bone, stopping where the tunic fell open. Pavan gently passed over the garments, traveling down until he reached the hem.

Looking up, he met Thad's watchful gaze.

Grasping the fabric in his own hands, Thad tore the garment from his body, exposing the bare chest beneath. Pavan marveled at the new skin exposed for his feasting eyes. At once, Pavan touched the curve of Thad's navel, where his skin was folded from sitting, tracing the lines of his muscle up and up over his chest, and raising the hairs of Thad's freckled chest and shoulders.

"You're beautiful." Pavan's thoughts danced around them.

Thad chuckled, letting his head fall back. He leaned back on his hands as Pavan touched the curve of his collar, moving towards the center of his throat.

"It's always disorienting when you first enter the mind space...you are doing well," Thad said with approval, his smile showing a glint of teeth as he watched Pavan from beneath hooded eyes.

"I told you I am a fast learner." Pavan leaned in, moving his hand to push his fingers into the nape of Thad's hair.

Thad chuckled. Quick and nimble, he took hold of Pavan's hand, flipping them so Thad straddled Pavan's thighs. Pavan's head fell back against the bedding, gazing wide-eyed up at the faie, who was laughing.

"Your reflexes are dwindled." Thad leaned forward, kissing Pavan's jaw, drawing from his lips an undignified moan. "Your pleasures are mixed with mine."

Pavan grasped at the faie's hips, each roll sending a shockwave of euphoria through his body, electrifying his senses tenfold. Pavan pushed his head back, rocking his hips with Thad's slow movements. It was strange to be so disconnected from his magick, yet so alive within it as they shared in each other's touch.

"Focus Pavan, do not lose yourself to it," Thad moaned, breathless, raking his nails along the center of Pavan's chest to draw him out of his thoughts. "You cannot let your mind drift or you shall lose the connection."

Passion made his blood hot as Thad swayed his hips with rhythm, a well-practiced dance that excited a duality of pleasures, his own combined with the joint pleasures of their minds. Pavan gripped Thad's thighs, seeking the pressure that joined their bodies together. But Thad took his hands away, returning them to his hips.

"I want to feel you," Pavan begged.

"Not yet." Thad shook, his head dipping back. "It would be too much for you at once. For now, just feel this...feel this pressure."

Pavan focused on the feeling of Thad's hips through their clothed bodies, the friction that sent shockwaves of pleasure up his spine. He wanted more. There was a nagging pull in the back of his mind, but Pavan pushed that away, bringing the pleasure he felt in the moment to the forefront of his mind. He was caught up in the wave of movement, a dance of their hips as he followed the sway, closing inwards as the end began to coil tighter.

"Not yet," he gasped, pushing himself up onto his elbows, and wrapping an arm around Thad to keep their bodies close. Sitting up in a way so that Pavan was near enough to bring their mouths together in a fierce kiss.

Thad kissed him back, shifting his knees further apart as he drew them together again into a slow climbing dance. Heat built up, pressure danced in his spine as the pleasure spiked, swallowing their cries as they both tumbled over the edge.

Pavan fell, crashing back into his body with a cold ferocious gasp.

"I'm here, Pavan. Just breathe...I've got you." Thad's voice was a beacon, as Pavan blinked through the groggy haze into consciousness.

Clinging to the warmth of the blankets, Pavan shivered, looking around the room as it finally came into focus—he was returning to the little room above the kitchens. Thad leaned over him, pushing his damp hair out of his eyes.

Pavan gripped tighter to the blanket.

"Our minds bled together, while we were joined. A little of your memories are my own, just as some of yours have become mine," Thad spoke, bringing Pavan closer to himself, bringing him further out of the haze of magick.

Turning slightly, Pavan blinked up at the great canopy above him, focusing on one singular point within the patchwork of tapestry that hung high above his head. Slowly, he drifted his gaze towards the faie, who sat at the edge of the little bed, a silk shirt hung loosely over his shoulders.

"Welcome back," Thad cooed, continually brushing his fingertips over Pavan's hair, leaning in to kiss the curve of his temple.

Pavan gulped, unable to trust his mouth just yet, the words a jumbled mess on his lips. Instead he breathed slower, focusing on the shift back into his own mind. Exhaustion sagged in his muscles, but he was no longer wound tightly. Pavan was pleasantly sated, having exhausted his magick and quieted the longing within him.

"You did really well. Shall you like to sleep...."

Panic rose in Pavan as Thad pulled back. He reached out to grasp the faie's wrist, his mouth trembled. "Don't leave."

"I am not going anywhere."

Reluctantly, he let the faie slip out of his grasp. Thad walked across the room to retrieve the Vohlgrum pelt from where it hung, returning to Pavan's side. Without ceremony, the faie climbed onto the bed next to Pavan and draped the pelt over the top of them both. He settled in close to his body for warmth.

Sleep was dangerously close to Pavan.

"Who is she?" Thad whispered. "The girl upon the beach?"

He shook it away, unable to concentrate completely on what Thad was asking him, or how he knew what he dreamed about. Instinctively the smell of the sea drifted up, along with the crashing of waves as the voice began to sing the lullaby.

"Just a dream," Pavan sighed.

CHAPTER

31

Pavan was alone when he awoke the next morning in Thad's little room.

Pushing off the thick Vohlgrum pelt and taking up his discarded garments, Pavan made his way down the little staircase into the kitchen where the smells of the cook's food made his stomach growl indignantly.

"Vhear!" Exclaimed the cook, nearly dropping the platter of hot buns she had made to use up the remainder of her storage of wheat.

"Forgive me." He nodded, his cheeks turning hot as she glanced from Pavan to the staircase where he descended. He awkwardly left the woman in a state of shock as he ventured through the narrow corridor towards the staircase.

"Good morrow, Pavan."

His foot stopped on the first step. He frowned as he looked up. Lilja stood before him, dressed in her training clothes of warm leather and padded wool. She descended towards him, her violet eyes taking him in, in full. A smile was forced upon her lips.

"Did you sleep well?"

Pavan felt the flicker of jealousy ignite within her.

"Exceedingly well." He gulped, turning towards the front door but Lilja was quick on her feet to follow after him.

"You were missed at the feast. Meilyr made a toast in your honor."

Annoyance grated in Pavan. "I was in no mood for receiving a toast."

"Does he warm your bed well?"

Pavan stopped short, rounding on Lilja. As he glared hard at her, she shrunk back slightly, but kept her firm ground.

"Enough of this, Lilja. Stop your petty remarks," he hissed. "Jealousy does not flatter you."

She chuckled, pushing past him as she tightened the bracers upon her arms.

"I have no intention of stopping my remarks, jealous or otherwise." She smirked. "He shall soon forget you, Pavan. There are many in Tauf that will take his mind away from you. That is his way of things, I'm afraid. He can't help it…"

Pavan clenched his jaw, holding in his anger. "You don't know him."

"*You* don't know him," Lilja repeated, her words strong and fierce. "You have not seen him like I have, Pavan. He makes you believe that what you feel is love, then when he has what he wants from you, he finds the next fresh cock to wet."

In an instant, Pavan forced her back against the wall, coming face to face with her terrified violet eyes. Anger flared beneath his skin as his magick ignited. As quick as it begun, it stopped. Lowering his hand that had found the curve of her throat, he breathed through the shock of his anger.

"Cut him, as you please, but know I shall never speak to you again, Lilja. You have shown yourself in a true light. Cruel. Spiteful." His voice trembled.

"At least you can see me for what I truly am, and are not blinded by fallacy."

Meilyr sat upon his horse, feeling the cold early morning bite settle into his gloved hands. He looked over the misty morning, as the dew settled in frost over the grassy plains set far out before them.

"The road is clear ahead, the wagons shall make it through the pass." Thad approached on horseback from ahead, his fair skin reddened from the cold.

"Good." Meilyr nodded, approvingly.

"We shall arrive in Tauf before the next quarter moon." The faie looked to the stars, and the sliver of moon high above them in the dusk blue of the early morning before the sun would emerge over the mountain peaks.

Thad glanced back, towards the few miles between them and Ledenjour. Meilyr knew the look of forlorn sadness. There was a change that had come over Thad in the last week. Not only the losses, and the attack, but Meilyr had sensed a great change since the final feast, before Lahrs had left them.

Meilyr was not ignorant of the feelings that Thad had cultivated for Pavan over the months after their arrival. He could see the struggle in his dearest son to see Pavan in pain, to see him bonded to Lilja. Now, to see them separated, drove a dagger in Meilyr's heart.

"Thad," Meilyr began, but the faie did not stay to listen.

Galloping after him, Meilyr blocked the road with his own horse, glaring at Thad in the low morning light. There was a glint of tears in the faie's eyes as well as a sheen on his cheeks, Thad quickly swiped them away.

"We are gone, Meilyr. There is nothing more to do..."

Meilyr sighed. "You did not say goodbye."

"It is just another village, Meilyr. In Tauf we shall begin anew." Thad scoffed, in the way he did when he was being evasive.

Meilyr drew the horse up alongside Thad.

"You chose duty in following as Lahrs asked of you to come with us to Tauf," Meilyr stated. "For your safety, because we love you dearly, Thaddeus."

Tears spilled from the faie's eyes, he angrily swiped them away.

"Safety...I am not a child."

Meilyr smiled, nodding. "No, you have not been a child for many years, Thaddeus. Forgive me for treating you as one, instead of trusting your own strength."

Thad glared but said nothing.

"I was wrong in my fears, to keep you so guarded as I have done. When we first met, you were so fragile, broken. I was caring for the injured child that I took from Orin Gaur." He took a deep breath. "You are no longer that boy, but a man free to make his own choices."

Thad hesitated.

"Make your choice, Thaddeus."

"Goodbye." Malcom embraced Pavan with a bone-crushing hug.

Standing on the hill outside the gate, there was no fanfare as the villagers pushed their carts, or pulled their wagons behind the men of Tauf who had come down from the great elven city to escort the remaining villagers of Ledenjour to safety. Malcom remained in the last group to leave, standing with Pavan and Svein as they waved goodbye.

"Write to me, that you have arrived in safety," Pavan told him.

Malcom chuckled. "I shall request the same of you. After the winters have passed and you reach Corad, please, Pavan, send me word of your safe journey."

"I will, Mal. I promise."

Sadness washed over Pavan as he watched the long line of villagers backs as they descended the hill. Thad was the earliest to wake, leaving before the break of the sun to take the first ride ahead to be sure that the roads were clear.

"He didn't say goodbye," Pavan whispered, unashamed to let his friend see the hurt that stung so fresh in his heart.

"Pavan..."

"It's done now. He made his choice to go with them. I can't stop him."

Malcom nodded, frowning.

As the last of the villagers disappeared out of sight down the hill, Farren approached with her own horse to hand the reins to Malcom. She gave the half giant a warm hug then approached Pavan.

"Take care of him," Pavan whispered, extending a hand out to her.

"It is you we worry for, Vhear." Farren smiled with her kind dark eyes, clasping Pavan's arm with a fierce hold. "Keep yourself out of trouble."

"There's a rider approaching," Svein spoke up.

They all looked up, and Pavan felt his heart skip a beat, watching Thad's grey mare trot up the hill towards them. Fair cheeks flushed from the wind, he dismounted with incredible speed. Pavan barely had a chance to think before Thad's arms were wrapped about his neck, hot lips crashing into his.

Breaking off the kiss, Pavan clung to Thad, smiling as he embraced the faie.

"Forgive me, Pavan, I wasn't thinking."

Pavan chuckled. *"You're here now, mo ghrá..."*

CHAPTER

32

Alnwick, Realm of Corad.

The end of autumn sings upon the hills of Alnwick.

It is a vast estate, set upon acres and acres of lush greenland. Trees line the road leading up to the large house made of white stone, a beacon against the colorful flowers and lush green of landscape. There are archways as tall as two men in height. Rust colored shingles line the roof and colorful tiles line every floor.

Sighing, Brendolyn stepped through the doorway into the place that was to be her home, as a pang in her heart left her empty. She watched as the servants took her trunks and boxes up the large spiral stair to her rooms.

It felt like a whole lifetime since she had stepped into these halls. She walked them, in silence, tracing her fingertips upon the textured walls of bare stone. She smiled at the familiar statues, the uncovered paintings, and the furniture freshly undraped.

This would be her home. This would be her prison for the rest of her days.

"Brendolyn." Lahrs' voice brought her attention to the elf who stood at the doorway, watching her through the open archway of the balcony.

"I am alright," she reassured him with a warry smile.

"There is a fresh bath, whenever you are ready. A tray shall be brought up for you within the hour. But perhaps you should like to take a walk within the gardens before you retire?"

"Not yet. I am tired." Brendolyn swallowed the pain.

"It was a long journey." Lahrs nodded. "A rest shall revive you."

She joined him, walking beside him down the tiled hallway towards the great staircase, a calm silence stretched between them.

"I must leave you upon the morrow, Bren, but it shall not be long."

Brendolyn frowned, she did not like that he left her so often.

"You do not speak, Bren." Lahrs kept talking as they stepped onto the first few stairs. "You do not badger me with questions of my journeys, and you have given me no requests for little trinkets to fill your room with hidden treasures."

"Will you be gone for a long time?"

He sighed. "Only about a week, I go to Signe."

She nodded absently, lost as the sounds of the sea drifted towards her, unusual to her where Alnwick was set so far inland. Brendolyn stopped to look back, scanning the great windows that faced the south. A breeze had fluttered the glass that hung from the vaulted ceiling, shards of colored glass that danced with color when the sun hit it just right. Now, the sound reminded her of the sea.

"My hope is to bring you a companion."

Brendolyn turned her eyes to Lahrs. "You are my companion."

"I am nothing more than an old tiresome tutor. My days are numbered in your esteem." His smirk was playful, but his remark made Brendolyn weary.

"You shall always be in my esteem, Lahrs. You are the only true friend I have ever known. Have you displeased my father? Is that why you must go away?" Her emotions began to build as the thought of his being sent away made the lump form thick in her throat, her eyes filled with unwanted tears.

Lahrs quickly embraced her.

"Nothing like that, Brendolyn. I shall never leave you." He kissed her hair, drawing her closer to his chest. "I go to find you a womanly companion. Someone that can help dress you, and sit with you. Someone you can tell your secrets and speak of things you cannot with me. A proper lady-in-waiting. You are of age now, Bren."

Brendolyn clung to his doublet. "I do not wish to grow up."

He rested his head upon hers, they stood upon the steps at different steps, nearly matching their heights. It was comforting to be held in his arms, to feel the warmth of his hug, the presence of his light.

"We must all grow up," he whispered.

"She will be cross, she shall hate me, she shall make me change my hair and make me cruel." Brendolyn pressed her face into Lahrs' chest.

He chuckled, drawing her back to swipe away the tears.

"She will love you, Brendolyn, just as I have. Who else could choose a better companion for your wild spirit? I, who has seen you in your cradle, who taught you to walk, to read, to nurture the world around you...Brendolyn, I would never let anyone nearest to you who would cause you harm." His voice trembled and Brendolyn could see the sparks of gold within his grey eyes.

"Must you leave me?"

Lahrs sighed, touching her chin gently. "After Signe, I shall not leave you again for a full twelve-month."

Brendolyn raised a little finger between them. "By Ehnarea's promise?"

"By Ehnarea's promise." Lahrs hooked his little finger with hers. "Now, you should rest. I shall come for you for dinner."

Brendolyn smiled, content as she lifted her skirts to ascend the steps, following the familiar corridors towards her chambers. She entered into the airy bedchamber that overlooked the gardens, the tepid climate of Alnwick had influenced the construction of the palace with large iron hinged doors that could be opened to let in the warmth of the air or the cool of the evening. Draping curtains remained as a barrier to keep out the bugs and to shade the warmest of days. Even in the winter months, most of Corad remained in warmer climate to that of the northern realms.

Stepping out onto the balustrade, Brendolyn gazed out onto the gardens below. Leaning against the outer pillars to hold up the structure from above, Brendolyn looked out at the calm and serenity before her. Here in Alnwick, there were no courtiers to whisper in the corners, to feel their emotions that plagued her.

In Alnwick, it was quiet.

A breeze from the east brushed across her cheek. Brendolyn raised her hand to touch the tear that trickled along her skin, she had not realized she had begun to cry. Her thoughts carried her eyes towards the far east, looking out onto the horizon, in the direction of the great channel. She believed she could see the great spires of Corad City glinting in the sunlight.

Brendolyn knew it was the trick of the light.

Perhaps she would never return home. Her father did not wish to see her again, did not wish to keep her in his sights, not even for the ceremony of her queen mothers death. Nor for the blessing of her prince brother. Her head began to hurt, she forced herself to swallow the tears that threatened. In the sanctity of her bed, she cried.

She let her sorrow drown her, until she fell asleep.

It was dark when Brendolyn opened her eyes. Rubbing the dried tears from her cheeks, she turned to the door, as a second knock came. The first had been the knock that awakened her.

She stood.

Brendolyn knew it was Lahrs, even before he stepped into the room. She smiled faintly at him, seeing the elf dressed in a silver tunic embroidered with birds.

Her heart felt heavy; it was the Felourian Dove.

"Come." He extended a hand to her.

Slowly she took it. His palm warm in hers, she walked beside him in silence. The halls and corridors were darkened and quiet as they walked the length of the house, descending the steps into the belly of the house, emerging at last into the courtyard.

Brendolyn stopped. Her eyes misted with tears to see every servant, from cook to scullery maid, to horse master, standing in the courtyard, as they would in the royal house, two lines facing each other. It was a ceremony, each servant holding a flickering lantern made of folded paper, each inscribed with a name written in the elven dialect.

She looked up at Lahrs, who still held her hand.

He looked down at her then, his own eyes misted with tears. He smiled, barely curving the edge of his lips.

Turning to the servants who stood waiting, Lahrs breathed out as they stepped forward, walking between the lines of illuminated paper lanterns, his voice sounding like a hymn.

Lahrs sang a song in the Old Tongue, a dialect she herself knew very little. But the song she knew by heart as a traditional song of the elves in Entheas. It was a reception, a song to welcome a loved one into the arms of Ehnarea.

They stood now at the center of the servants who stood around them, Lahrs lifting Brendolyn's hands in his open palms as his voice carried around them. She felt warm as light emerged before them. A whirl of golden dust danced, shaping into the frame of a paper lantern, the words of Lahrs' hymn embraced them. Her fingertips tickled against the paper lantern between them.

Brendolyn watched in amazement as the magick filled her.

The song finished, Lahrs closed his eyes. Then one after the other, each of the golden lanterns lifted into the air.

AFTER

Signe, Realm of Corad.

D o you know why I am here, Lady Elsa?"

Lahrs lifted the delicate teacup to his lips, sipping it, eyes never leaving Elsa as she poured her own cup and carried the pot back to the service tray. Her long hair cascaded in waves of auburn over her shoulder, worn freely as a young girl of Corad usually did. It reminded Lahrs how young the lady was before him. His thoughts went to the letter in his pocket, addressed from her eldest brother Eugene.

Elsa stiffened, setting the teapot down with purposeful movements.

"You are looking for suitable companions for Princess Brendolyn, now that she is of courting age."

"Yes."

Elsa turned back to face Sir Lahrs, leaning against the sideboard. "And my brother wrote to you to ask if I might be one of them."

"A breach in protocol and most unusual, as your father is a duke and you should have no trouble attracting a suitable husband without joining the king's court, but I am willing to overlook such things if I find you to be suitable." Lahrs smiled kindly. "Do you believe you are? Suited to the task, I mean."

"No." Elsa's throat was tight and the blood had drained from her face.

Lahrs quirked an eyebrow. "Do you say that because you do not wish to leave Signe or because of the mark on your side?"

She unconsciously pressed a palm to the bodice of her gown. "How..."

"Your brother wrote to me of that as well." He set aside his tea, voice taking on a serious tone. "Tell me, Lady Elsa, the man who bound you to him, has he taken to your bed... as a husband might?"

Tears sprang to Elsa's eyes. "I..."

"It is all right, Lady Elsa, you may speak freely. I shall not utter a word of what is spoken here to anyone, but I must know. Did he merely mark you or did he claim you as a possession? Did you give him your virtue?"

A sob clawed at Elsa's throat. "I did not want to."

Lahrs waited for her to find the words.

"He said he loved me but then he...he was so much stronger than me. I couldn't fight him." She wrapped her arms around herself. "I cannot be the princess's companion. I'm damaged. If anyone ever found out..."

The tea cup in Lahrs' hands clattered, he set it down so hard.

"You must never say that again."

Lahrs rose from his seat, striding over to her and gripping her shoulder kindly before guiding her over to a chair and telling her to sit. He added sugar and cream to her cooling cup of tea and placed it in her hands before taking his own seat again.

Elsa twisted the teacup in her hands.

Lahrs went on. "You are not damaged or worth less than anyone else because one selfish man did not give you a choice. But he did bind you to him, which complicates matters. The way I see it, Lady Elsa, you have a choice to make. You can go to the silent sisters in Divna and join their order, where he may find you, they do not have the resources to keep him from taking you if that is his wish. Or you can come to Alnwick and take up service as Princess Brendolyn's companion, where I will protect you."

"And if I do not want to leave Signe?"

"That is also a choice you can make, but if you stay, there is nothing anyone can do to protect you from this man. By Signe's laws you are his wife and he can claim you as such. Your father has no power to stop him from claiming you and your dowry for his own."

"But you do?" Somehow she found that difficult to believe.

"The king does." Lahrs took another long sip of his tea. "Is that your wish? To stay here and marry this man?"

"No." She grit her teeth. "I have no desire to marry."

"Then what shall you do?"

FAMILY OF MAISON

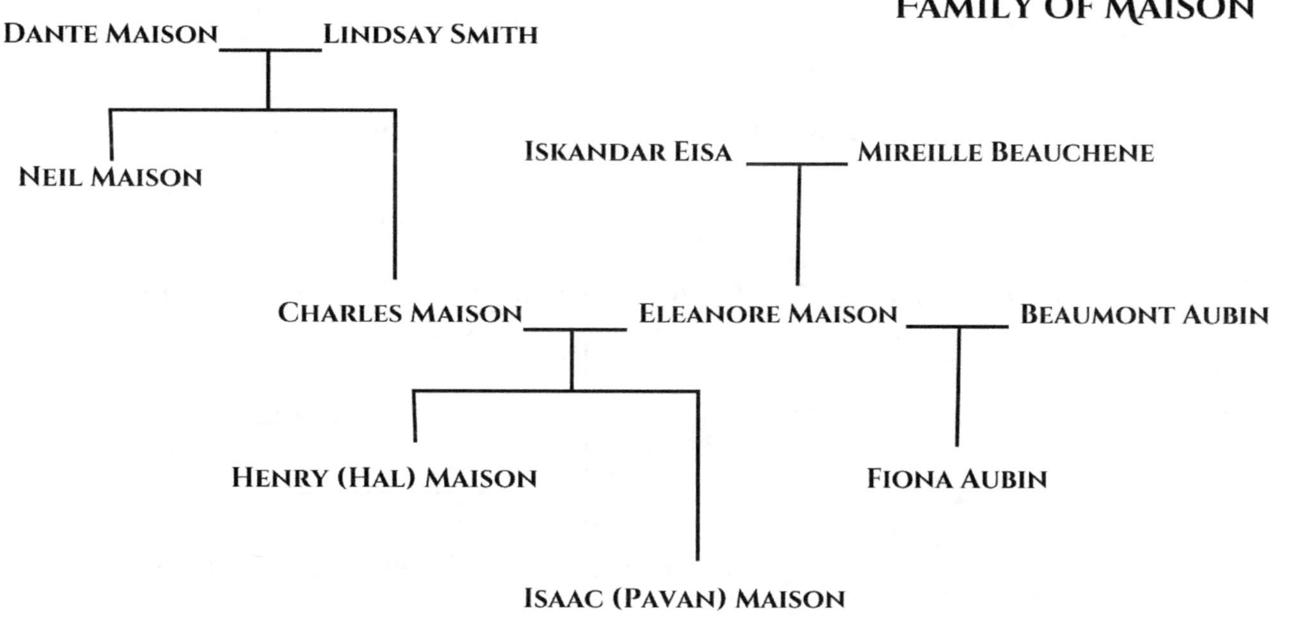

FAMILY OF AUBIN

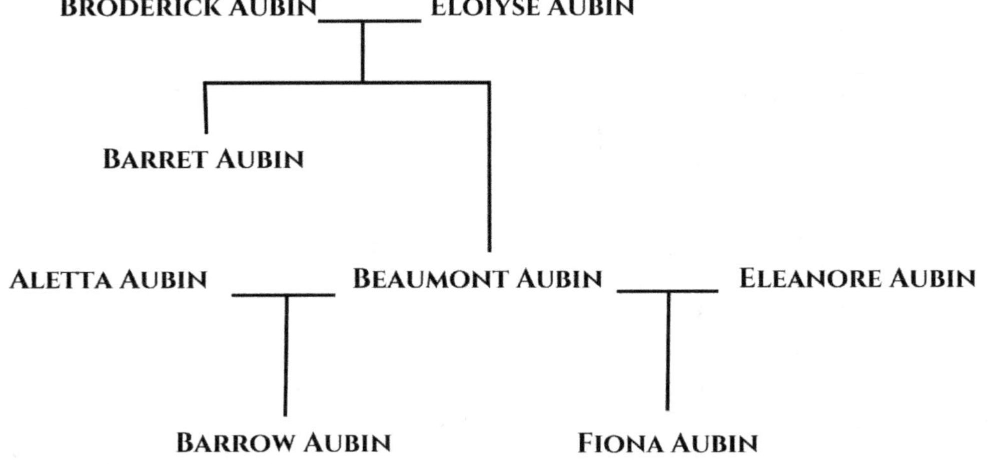

FAMILY OF MOREAU

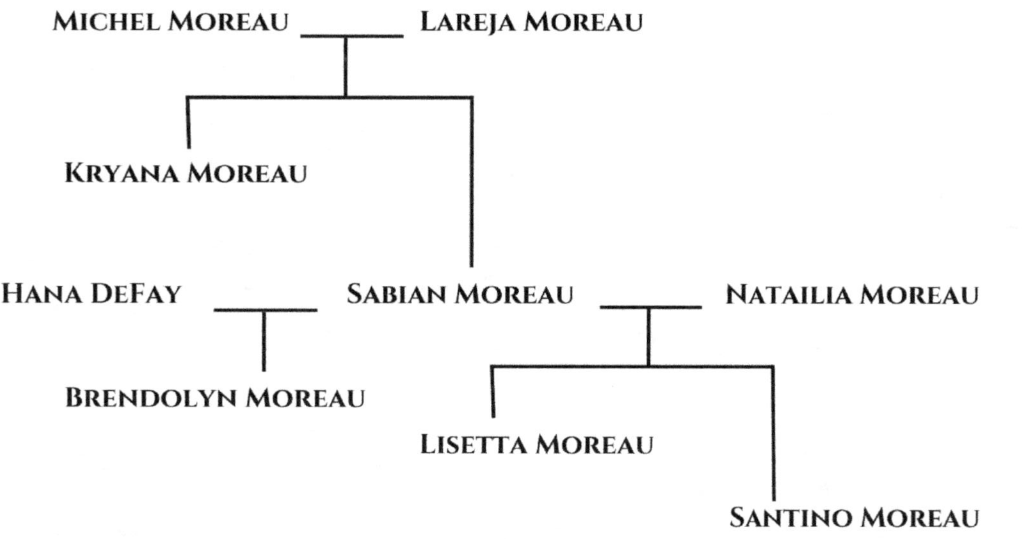

Fate of Kings

Signe, Realm of Corad.

'Then what shall you do?'

Elsa thought over again the words of the elf from Entheas. Sir Lahrs had stayed for a fortnight in the great city of Signe, waiting for her answer, but her head ached with the possibilities that would emerge from going to be a companion to the princess. She would be alone in her companionship, Sir Lahrs had made it clear that there was no need for another to attend the youngest daughter of King Sabian.

Her head lowered at the remembrance of Queen Natalia, to which the realm grieved the death of the beloved queen. Elsa had never met her in court, she had not been presented there to be eligible for courtship. Now, she would never go there, unless it was as the companion of Princess Brendolyn.

"I have not seen you look so serious in months. What has captured your thoughts, dearest little sister? Not the nearing departure of your odious tutors."

Elsa turned from the window, where she had been standing as she watched the carriage take away the elf that could change the path of her life. Sir Lahrs was long gone, and Elsa now stood looking out over the empty cobbled courtyard. Behind her, stood her eldest brother, Eugene, with his thick arms crossed over his broad chest. A glint in his stoney eyes. His dark hair swooped back away from his face.

Eugene waited patiently for her answer.

"It is not that...Eugene, I am not sure I can leave."

There was a serious look that crossed Eugene's chiseled features, his jaw set in a hard line. Crossing the small space of the sitting room to stand beside his sister at the window. Elsa felt her chest tighten, gulping back a wave of emotion that threatened to take over.

"You have not decided then if you shall go with Sir Lahrs when he returns after my wedding in the spring? He assured me it would be a promising situation." Eugene softened, keeping his tone even.

"It would be an honor to be a companion to the princess, it is just that..."

Eugene's stoney eyes flicked to the door as if someone would barge right in at that moment. But there was no one coming today. The knights had all gone to train in Nihtar for the quarter moon. It was calm and quiet in Signe without the ruckus of men in the training yard. Eugene returned his eyes to Elsa, she felt his concern like needle pricks in her fingertips.

"He is not here, Elsa. He cannot claim you."

There was power in his words, but the flicker of doubt had already begun to settle into Elsa's heart. Eugene was the closest to Elsa, practically the one who raised her, to teach her how to fight, to use magick. It pained Elsa to keep a part of her truth from her dearest brother. Eugene knew about the brand, but he only knew in part the truth of how deeply the magick bonded her to the knight. She dared not even speak his name in fear of him.

"Does father know?" Elsa asked in a hushed voice. "About the brand?"

Eugene sighed, "No. He does not know, or we would not be having this conversation, Elsa. You know the laws of our people. That our father would be forced to uphold the old magick and give you over to Alaric."

Elsa trembled.

"So there is no choice but to accept Sir Lahrs' offer." A lump was firmly lodged in Elsa's throat, her chin trembling as tears welled in her eyes.

"There is always a choice. You can go to Divna, and take the Silent Oath, you already have been taught the languages of the three realms. He cannot touch you there under the laws of the sisterhood."

Elsa wiped her running nose on the sleeve of her tunic.

"Elsa." Eugene took hold of each of Elsa's arms, looking into her eyes. "Please take to heart the guidance of your closest and dearest brother. I would wish for you to remain here and take charge of fathers household when I am gone. Or find a great ship to sail away on and discover beyond the great seas, but that path was taken from you by someone you were meant to trust. Your path is destined to do greater than what Signe can give you."

Embracing his middle, Elsa clung to her brother desperately, gritting her teeth against the burst of sharp intense pain that erupted within her through the brand upon her ribs. It was agony. Elsa wept into her brothers' tunic. A mixture of a broken heart and the pain of the magick that burned through her.

"You will write to me, won't you, when I am in Alnwick?"

Eugene chuckled, touching the top of her head to smooth the wild hairs that had fallen from her braid. "Every day, if you'd like."

Elsa pulled away, becoming more serious. "You shall have a new wife, and you shall live in Entheas. You cannot write every day."

"I shall write every day until you are perfectly settled in Alnwick. How else shall I discover what princesses get up to when they are not dancing with courtiers at parties and balls?" He was jesting, making Elsa laugh.

"Sir Lahrs told me Princess Brendolyn is not like that, but perhaps it is because she is faie." Elsa frowned. "Perhaps she is very lonely."

"An honest consideration. Who else would be perfect to keep a lonely girl company than my fiery sister who can teach her more than needlepoint and silks?"

Elsa smiled, taking a glance out through the window. Beyond the courtyard, over the wall of the estate, she saw the sun beginning to set. The night was drawing closer. Creeping up Elsa's spine, unsettling her. Her smile fell.

"Nightmares again?"

She quickly glanced at Eugene, a blush heating her cheeks.

"This one was a vision, I am certain of it, Eugene." Elsa wrung her fingers together nervously. "I was standing in a field of lavender, nothing but lavender...then I could hear it calling to me, like a whisper."

Eugene furrowed his brow, crossing his arms as he listened, ready to decipher the visions that so often plagued her. He held the gift, as only a few of the elven lineage possessed. Eugene was good at deciphering the visions he had, he was the one who taught Elsa her magick.

"It was my destiny...my freedom. Like I was meant to be somewhere else...meant to be with someone else." She felt foolish. "The magick has become stronger these last few months. Perhaps it is silly to believe them when they are not so clear."

"There is always truth in the sight." Eugene nodded. "What else did you see?"

She took a deep breath, "I saw my future in a pair of eyes that glistened like emeralds. He will lead me to my destiny."

ACKNOWLEDGEMENTS

I would like to express my deepest gratitude to my husband, who has patiently stood by me throughout the last decade as I wrestled with character development, plot twists, and the intricate worldbuilding of Veilore. Thank you for enduring countless out-of-context plot points and for your unwavering support over these last few years. Without you, the dream of becoming a published author might have remained just that—a dream.

Next, my heartfelt thanks go to Kat. There's so much I could say, but none of it would be news to you. From the inception of this book and every one that followed, to every stage of its creation, you've been the backbone of this journey. Your passion for my characters and your constant encouragement have been truly inspiring. I couldn't have made it this far without you.

A huge thank you to Stacey for your invaluable help in polishing this book, ensuring it was ready to face the world.

And finally, my endless appreciation to J.R.R. Tolkien, whose *The Hobbit* was the first fantasy book I read as a child, sparking my love and enduring respect for the imaginary and fantastical.

Author Bio

Ireland Lydon is a native of Utah. Having spent the better part of a decade navigating the world of Veilore, she is ready to open those doors and let others inside. When she is not writing, Ireland is going on hikes all across Utah with her husband and three kids, bookbinding, or rewatching Pride and Prejudice for the hundredth time. Fate of Ruin is her debut novel, with seven more on the way.